SURVIVING HIM

Rescue Me
Book 2

KENZIE YOUNG

Published by Blushing Books
An Imprint of
ABCD Graphics and Design, Inc.
A Virginia Corporation
977 Seminole Trail #233
Charlottesville, VA 22901

Surviving Him
Kenzie Young

eBook ISBN: 978-1-63954-441-7
Print ISBN: 978-1-63954-442-4

To my readers... thank you for your support and loving my characters as much as I do.

To the people who said I couldn't write... obviously you were mistaken.

Prologue

NIRVANA — *14 years old*

I can't breathe, I can't breathe. Those thoughts are rushing through my head as I hide under my bed. I swallow down the anxiety rushing through me and press my forehead against the wooden floor. The cold wood calms me slightly. I should've left when I had the chance. When I first heard their conversation. But did I? No. Now, here I am, stuck under the bed waiting for time to pass.

I knew better, I even talked to Delaney about it. She offered to take me to Ophelia's or Layla's but what good would that do? They would find me. They always found me. Maybe if I told her what would happen to me, that it didn't end at just a slap in the face. Delaney knew what it was like, to be slapped and hit for no reason, but they had a reason this time. I did something that went against everything in life, I disrespected the one thing I was taught.

I went against the Bible, I knew better. I knew but I still did it anyway. A sob catches in my throat. I hated this, I hated feeling trapped and ashamed of who I was. But my dad instilled it in me from birth. I was never, *never* supposed to go against the scripture. If I did it would be eternal Hell for me. So why did I do it? My thoughts are interrupted by the loud thud of boots.

Thump, thump, thump. It was overly loud in our small house, making me tense with each step.

"Where's Nirvana?" My father's deep baritone voice echoed off the four walls of the hallway. I tensed, my heart stopping before pounding wildly. I didn't hear the response, but the twisting of my doorknob meant the question was answered. The blood rushing to my ears made it impossible to hear anything. I folded into myself as best as I could. I forced myself to calm down as boots came into view from under the bed.

But it was worthless, no matter what I did he'd find me. It was like time stood still as he bent down, his hand curling under the bed rail to lift it up. I couldn't hold it in anymore, I screamed. A big meaty fist came and wrapped in my hair, pulling me out from under the bed. I kicked and screamed, fighting the hold he had on me.

"No!" I shout, tears burning down my cheeks. I glance up and see my father in the hall, his blue eyes devoid of any emotion as he looks at me. "No! You can't let them take me! I'm sorry! I won't do it again I promise!" I'm fighting more and more now, the need to be free a breathing entity inside of me.

But did my father care? No. He just looked on, blocking my little sister's view of me. But I knew she was there, I could hear her quiet sobs as I was dragged out into the stormy weather, and pulled towards the black van. The back door opened, and I saw more church officials all watching me with emotionless and cold eyes.

I cried harder as I was shoved inside, falling against the hard floorboards.

"This is to save your soul, child," a deep voice said. I brace my arms over my head and cry. Cry out the anger, the shame, the life I once knew. No one touched me, no one stopped me. In fact, the sound of prayer sounded behind me. They were praying for my sins, but I knew better. I always knew better. It didn't matter how much they prayed my soul was gone. Being replaced by something I was scared to look too closely at. But it was there, and it would become the only thing that saves me.

Nirvana — 15 years old

I lean my head back against the wall, watching through narrowed eyes as the preacher, Father Brent walks into the room. He's with another man, someone younger than him but older than me. He is holding a Bible against his chest.

"Nirvana," Father Brent says, the way he says my name makes my skin crawl and my stomach turn. "This is Cannon. He is in the same boat as you. We must take away his sins."

My gaze goes to the boy, Cannon. He is tall, almost taller than the preacher with haunted dark eyes and even darker hair. Father Brent walks deeper into the room and places the Bible on the small table in front of me. He stares expectantly, when neither of us moves, he sighs. "We are here to help you. To rid the demons from your bodies, the demons that turned you into promiscuous children. For that to work I need you to do your part."

I lean my head back, staring ahead at the peeling wallpaper on the opposite walls suddenly too tired. "I'm tired. I want to sleep. Me and my 'demons' had a long day," I whisper, sarcasm dripping from my tone.

Father Brent slammed his palm on the table, shaking the already fragile foundation. "You will listen to your elders, Nirvana."

I sigh and slide out of bed, grabbing the book from the table. I sank to my knees, kneeling on the concrete floor and began reading the scripture already marked for me. Cannon kneels beside me and does the same, our tones matched almost in perfect harmony as we spoke the prayers. Father Brent nodded his head and headed out of the room leaving us alone, standing outside the now closed door.

I stop reading and turn my head to Cannon. "Do you know what we have to do now?" I ask.

He swallows hard and nods, "Yes. But I-I can't."

I nod and sit down on the floor, crossing my legs. "What was your sin?" I ask.

He stares down at the ground. "I came out to a friend. I guess I picked the wrong friend. What about you?"

I shrug. "I got caught kissing a girl. By my dad who is the preacher of our local church." Cannon winces in sympathy.

"I'm sorry."

I shrug, what was done was done. There was no going back, and I knew that. "How long are you here for?" I ask.

"The rest of the summer."

"Whatever you do, don't get on anyone's bad side. It won't be pretty."

Cannon tilts his head to look at me. "What happens if you do?"

I shiver, remembering what happened the first time I was here, the first moment when I didn't do what they wanted me to do. The pain. The pain was awful, I still get blinding headaches from it. I was told that was the sins building up, wanting to be exorcised from me. Sins I would soon commit at the first chance I got. And they were probably right. At the first chance I would do it. Not because my "demon" told me to, no, I'd do them out of spite, out of hatred.

"It'll hurt," I say when I notice Cannon is waiting for my response.

He flinches. "Have you been hurt a lot here?" I nod. Cannon shakes his head, lowering his voice, "That can't be legal. This isn't normal."

I shrug. "Doesn't matter. If we are sent here, it's going to happen. No one cares. They want us to be better, so we need to follow their orders, at least until we're out."

Cannon sighs sadly. "We should stick together, at least until we leave." I glance at him wondering why this stranger would care if I'm fine or not. Especially when my own father sent me here. I glance away, nodding. There's a sharp pounding on the door and I tense, wanting to be anywhere else. But it wasn't so bad now, not when I have an ally inside.

Nirvana — 15 years old in school: After Summer

I walk inside the school, my body tensing when I see the girl in front of me. She glances my way, her eyes trailing down my body seeing too much. I haven't spoken to her in months, not since that day.

She said something to the person she was talking to and made her way to me. My heart skipped a beat and I turned away and moved as far from her as possible.

"Nirvana!" she called, but I kept moving until I felt a hand on my arm, pulling me to a stop. I close my eyes and turn to look up at her. Her black hair hung in waves down her back and her brown eyes were staring at me intently.

"Marcy." I cleared my throat, "Hey."

"Hey?" she repeats. "All I get is a hey? After everything that's happened and all I get is a hey?" she snaps.

I shrug, unsure of how to respond. Panic was slowly setting in. Marcy scoffs, glaring at me. "You ruined my life, Nirvana. I got my phone taken away from me, and now I get it checked every day after school. I have no privacy now and it's all your fault!"

I rear back, stunned by her words. "My fault? How is it my fault?" I lower my voice, "You kissed me, I didn't kiss you."

Marcy sneered at me. "Yes. Brodey dared me to. And then your weird ass dad caught us and told my parents! Now they think I like girls when I don't!"

I shake my head, tears burning behind my eyes. "Don't lie to me, Marcy. You practically begged me to kiss you."

Marcy stepped closer, raising her hand. Before I could do anything or react, she slapped me, her palm connecting with my cheek. My head snapped to the left and I tasted blood in my mouth. "Don't you ever come near me again!" she shouts. I don't say anything. I just stand there, my face throbbing from the slap.

"Nirvana?" a soft voice says behind me.

I tense and turn, to see Delaney standing there, holding her books against her chest, watching as Marcy storms away. I don't say anything, just walk away. It's still early in the day and my house isn't far from the school, I can just walk home without worry. I know my dad won't be home and I just can't go back to school. Not right now.

My heart is racing as I run down the sidewalk towards the small house I shared with my dad, stepmother, and sister. It's blissfully empty when I get there and I run to my room, the one I now share with my little sister and throw myself on the bed, tears running down my face. I bury my head in my arms and sob, something I couldn't do if my dad was home.

The sound of my door opening has me shooting out of bed and tensing.

"It's just me." I turn and look at Delaney as she comes into my room and sits on the edge of my bed. I scoot away from her, not wanting her to see me like this.

"Are you okay?" she asks gently. Her multi-colored eyes burned into me as she spoke, her tone soft and caring. I couldn't answer. Delaney already dealt with too much at home, she didn't need my issues too. "Vana?"

"Don't you hate me, too?" I ask, my voice harsher than I intended. I don't look at her, just play with the rip in my jeans. Her hand covers mine, stopping me from moving nervously. I glanced up at her.

"Nirvana, do you remember how we met?" she asks softly, her eyes still holding my gaze.

I swallow back tears, nodding slowly. "Yeah. Someone was picking on Ophelia's hair, and you stood up for her. I thought you were the bravest kid on the playground." I still did. Delaney was the only one who stood up for her, even if it caused her to become the target. She still stood up for her. I felt ashamed that I didn't say anything at the time, and a part of me envied Delaney for having such courage.

Delaney shook her head, smiling at me. "Yes, but it's what you did for her. You stayed all recess and helped her take the twigs out of her hair. It took all recess and even when the teacher called us in, you stayed with her."

I scoff, using the sleeve of my shirt to wipe my eyes. "So?"

"So, this doesn't change who you are. Who you'll always be."

I sigh and turn my head. "I try to be normal, Lane," I whispered, my voice broken. "I try so hard. I didn't know she'd kiss me. I liked her for the longest time and just didn't move."

7

"You're normal, Nirvana. They aren't. There's nothing wrong with you." Delaney's tone is fierce when she cups my cheeks. "And Marcy is a bitch for what she did to you at school."

I swallow hard. "I don't just like girls, Delaney. I like boys too. I shouldn't be like this." Tears are forming in my eyes again and there's a tightness in my chest.

Delaney shakes her head. "Stop it. You're the way you are and you're perfectly fine. It doesn't matter what you like as long as you're happy in your true self. It shouldn't matter who you fall for as long as they make you happy and treat you right. What's between their legs doesn't matter."

A sob lodges in my throat. "But what will people think of me?" I'm crying a lot now.

Delaney shrugs, her thumbs moving over my cheeks to wipe away my tears. "Fuck what people think. As long as you're your most authentic self, who cares what people think?"

I give a shaky laugh." You should be a therapist. You'd be good at it."

Delaney gives a small smile. "Maybe I will. I want to make a difference in the world. One broken person at a time." She drops her hands, sadness creeping into her. "Starting with us. We deserve to be happy, Vana."

I nod, she's right, I know she is and I want that. For all of us. But what will that happiness cost us?

I glance at the wall tangling my fingers with hers. "We do deserve it. Starting now we need to find our own happiness no matter what."

"No matter what," she repeats. If only we knew what that would entail.

Chapter 1

NIRVANA - PRESENT *Day*

Ravi drives slowly towards the hospital leaving me to look out the window, watching as the rain slopes down the window. His words ricochet in my head. He wants me. Even after everything. He hasn't asked me questions, but I didn't really expect him to. He is usually the type of man who waits until you can no longer hold it in any longer.

And maybe I'll eventually tell him. When I no longer carry shame from it. But it wasn't going to be any time soon and I knew that. The drive to the hospital feels longer than usual, but I don't mind. It gives me time to prepare what I want to say to Aero, or to prepare for whatever it is I'm going to see. He pulls up to the hospital and parks, turning to me.

"Would you like me to come in or stay here?"

Glancing at the entrance, I sigh. "I don't know," I say honestly.

"We can sit here for a minute if you'd like," he offers.

I nod in thanks, gazing out into the distance. "I wish there were books on how to deal with watching your person die," I mutter.

"Even if there were, I doubt it'll be accurate."

I smile softly to myself. "Why's that?"

He shrugs. "People grieve differently."

My eyes go to him. "How do you grieve?"

"I sign contracts for the military or become a firefighter," he said with a serious expression on his face.

For some reason that shocks a laugh out of me. "Delaney would call that proactive though."

His laughter joins mine. "I guess she would."

When we stopped laughing, I grab the handle of the car door and turn to him, "Thank you for making me laugh. I'll be back in a few minutes, okay?"

"Take your time. I'm not going anywhere." I believed him too. He wore such a sincere expression that I knew he'd be here when I left her room. I lean forward and press a kiss to his stubbled cheek. "Thank you," I repeat and climb out of the car, uncaring that it was raining. I walk into the hospital, go to the front, and get my visitors badge.

I make my way down the hall, shaking out my hands struggling to calm the nerves sliding through me. This feeling is becoming too familiar to me. Almost like a routine I've fallen into. And I guess in a way I did. Swallowing the nerves, I walk into Aero's room where I see her lying there alone. The room is dark, and the sound of machines is loud, drowning out the sound of the rain. Or maybe it's just overly loud to me, like a timer that consists of constant beeping. Counting down the dreaded day when she takes her last breath. And it's soon. I can feel it. I can see it.

Her face is nearly gray, and her body is so much smaller than is healthy. Her hair is dry and brittle, and her lips chapped and pale. Moving closer, I pull a chair next to her bed, sitting next to her and pulling her cold hand into mine.

When someone is dying, they never tell you how it would feel, how it would look or even smell. It was a sick feeling, almost as if you were stuck between life and death. The room was colder and had a sweet scent followed by the stench of disinfectant that somehow surrounded the room even when Isola brought flowers.

I don't say anything, I just hold her hand. Rubbing my finger over the top of her hand. "You're stronger than you give yourself credit for," whispered a soft, hoarse voice.

Pressing Aero's hand to my face I stare at her. "If I am so strong, why can't I let you go?" I ask.

She smiles slightly. "Because I'm the best, duh."

"Yeah. Yeah, you are," I whisper, holding her to me until she falls asleep again. When her breathing evens out I stand and press a kiss to her warm head. "I'll be back soon," I promise. And I keep it, showing up every day.

Sighing softly, I run the sponge up Aero's arm, washing away as much grime as possible before dipping it into the basin again and going over it a second time. It's been two weeks since her wedding and over a month and a half since her diagnosis and she is declining more and more. I know the doctor had said only a few months, but I couldn't have imagined it being this fast. I hated seeing her in pain. I hated seeing her mind slowly lose itself.

I've been here every single day after I visited her that night of her wedding. Even then she was declining, but I didn't think it would progress at this speed. She's either forgotten where she was, who I was, or she was angry, lashing out at anything and everyone. She's been vomiting and seizing a lot and I fear that I can expect her to be gone any day now. I've spoken to Isola, and she's confirmed that she and Aero planned the funeral after finding out and everything is set up. That knowledge weighed heavily on me, knowing my sister had to plan her own funeral broke a little piece of me.

Sighing again, I move to the other side of the bed and lift up her arm and begin washing it using soothing circles. Today she was being moved into hospice to make it easier for her, to decrease the pain, the torment it will likely be for her, so she can hopefully pass in peace. My vision blurs as I dip the sponge in water again. I force myself to take a shaky breath and start on her legs. It pains me that Isola isn't here with her, but I understand. I get not wanting to see the love of your life suffering, to watch as they forget you as if she were never in her life.

The signs were there, they probably always have been. At least this last year. Aero got more headaches and was told it was from stress and not eating enough. I guess we should've pressed more instead of taking it at face value. But there's no use in wondering about the what if's. Everything is done and there's no going back. I finish her bath and dry her before putting on some fuzzy socks to keep her warm. I dump the water and put it on the cart the nurse left before walking back into the room. Her breathing has been labored and choppy for the last few days and I can feel the life draining from her. Even with the oxygen moving through her with the help of the machine I knew it wouldn't be enough.

I step beside her and rub a hand over her head.

"I'm not ready for you to go. Not yet. It shouldn't be like this." I press a kiss to her hair, swallowing hard. "Do you remember that one Christmas, the one with just me and you? I was nineteen and you were fourteen. You were so excited because you had saved up money to go shopping and we went to our very first Black Friday sale."

"You… tripped… into that… old lady," Aero slurred out, coughing with each word. It's the first semi-coherent sentence I've gotten out of her.

I sob softly. "Yeah, you wanted that new Game Boy. We almost got kicked out of the mall fighting with her."

Aero's dry lips lift up at the corner but she doesn't open her eyes. "Best… Christmas… ever."

I nod, pressing my head against hers. "Yeah, it was. I have never seen you so happy." And it's sad that one gift made her so happy. The only gift I was able to afford after spending nights working in a small diner by my dental school. But just seeing her smile made all those long nights worth it. "I'm so sorry, Aero."

"Love you," she whispered. It sounded like goodbye. There was a finality in her tone that sent my heart dropping before speeding up. I pressed another kiss to her head and stepped back, looking at her one last time before I left the room. I just needed to get out of the room to breathe. The smell of death hung so heavily in the air that it was slowly choking the life out of me. I leave the room, closing the door behind me, and lean against it. Taking a deep, shaky breath.

"Hey," a voice says beside me. I glance to the side and see Marcy standing there, twisting her fingers together.

"Why are you here?" I ask, my tone sounds more tired than I would've liked but it is what it is.

Marcy swallows, places a hand on her throat then says, "Can we talk?"

"We are talking."

"I mean, in private."

I shake my head. "No. If you want to talk you can do so out here."

Marcy sighs then looks at me, her dark eyes trailing over me. "I wanted to apologize. For what happened back then."

I scoff. "What? You mean when you kissed me on a dare, had me sent away to absolve me from my sins at a camp, then proceeded to shout at me when I got back for your phone being taken away for the summer and having no privacy? Oh, and then you slapped me. That's what you're apologizing for?"

Marcy rolls her eyes. "It was a camp, Nirvana. A stupid Bible camp. We've both been to them."

I step closer to her, anger filling me, blinding me with a burning rage that was slowly boiling over. "It wasn't a Bible camp, Marcy. It was a fucking conversion camp. Where we were put through therapy that was traumatizing. I still get headaches from the fucking shock therapy. I still remember the time I was forced to watch a heterosexual couple have sex in my first ever porno. It wasn't even good porn. It was weird 80s porn with the pizza guys and bad acting. It sure as fuck wasn't Christian fucking Gray."

She pales. "What? I was told you were sent to a Bible camp." Her eyes widened, but I didn't care. I sure as fuck didn't want her pity. It was her fault. I was good at pretend-ing, I could fake being straight, I liked dick as much as the next person. But if I could've pretended for the next few years I could have explored when I was a legal adult. I could have come out when I was good and ready. But no, it was stolen from me, like everything else. My life wasn't my own for years, my mind, my body. No, that belonged to a camp that was supposed to fix me "for my own good". But the fact that Marcy stood here in front of me, thinking it was like some lame Bible camp that we were forced to attend for a week every goddamn summer was laughable.

I scoff sarcastically, "Who told you that? My father? When was that? When you were on your knees for him or when he stood behind you?" I shudder dramatically, just the image made my stomach turn and bile form in the back of my throat.

Marcy flinched. "Don't be so vulgar. He's your father."

I roll my eyes. "Oh sweetheart, I wasn't vulgar when you had your tongue down my throat. Don't apologize to me. You and I both know it's only to help you feel better and to help you get over your guilt. Just because you give a half-assed apology doesn't mean I have to give you half-assed forgiveness."

Marcy stepped closer placing her hand on my chest. "Nirvana, please. We used to be so close."

I grip her hand and push it away. "*Used to* being the operative words. Touch me again, and I will defend myself."

"I'm pregnant. You wouldn't harm a pregnant woman."

"You may be pregnant, but your face isn't. And we both know how much you enjoy slapping people," I say, stepping back. Not that I'd actually touch her, but I'll be damned if she comes at me trying to touch me. Not after what she did to me. Not after everything, especially not in front of my dying sister's hospital room.

Marcy throws her hands up, tears filling her eyes. "Nirvana, I'm trying here."

I turn away, taking a breath. I needed to get this out of my head. I look at Aero's room and press my hand to the door, forcing myself to speak. "Why are you married to him? He's old enough to be your grandfather," I finally turn to her and ask.

She doesn't answer, just looks at her feet. "Is it even his baby?" I ask when she doesn't say anything for a prolonged amount of time.

Marcy shakes her head. "No. No, it's not."

I burst into hysterical laughter, "Oh my god! This is too good! The preacher's new precious wife is an adultering whore. Well, good luck there mommy dearest. You're going to need it."

"Have you always been such a bitch?" she snaps, all pretense of making amends gone. Not that I believe she had good intentions to begin with. I was used to her fake ordeals, used to being told that I should forgive and forget. But she could bite me.

I shrug and reply, "I'm what you all made me."

Chapter 2

NIRVANA 28 — *Two Weeks Earlier*

Gasping I leaned my head back against the damp brick wall as fingers were thrust into me. Lips trail down my neck to my breasts, pushing my corset top down and pulling one of my nipples into their mouth, sucking hard. My hand went to their soft hair pulling slightly. It was just what I needed, that release from the long week. One hand clutches in their hair as the other one curls around the neck of a bottle of vodka. I pull the bottle to my mouth and take a long drink, letting it burn down my throat as those fingers thrust again. My hips jerk and I pull back moaning softly.

Muffled music sounded through the club making my body hum as I got closer to coming. A door opened and a voice rang out, "What's going on back there?" Looking down at the couple at my feet I put a finger to my lips and tilted my head to the left.

"Go, before he calls the cops," I say, handing them the

bottle I held. The woman, I think her name was Veronica, pouted but took the bottle.

"If you ever want to finish playing, give me a call." She kisses my cheek, close to my mouth, before walking away pulling her man with her. They are a couple I met a few hours ago while dancing. They wanted a threesome and I was more than happy to oblige as long as they didn't cross my boundary of a bed and kissing. I've only had one kiss in my life and it ended in heartache. I'll be damned if I ever did it again. Shaking those thoughts out of my head, I pull my jeans back up my legs and fix my corset. Making sure I was decent, I walked from behind the wall where Cannon's bouncer stood, arching a bright pink brow at me.

Sighing, he opens the door ushering me inside. "One of these days Cannon is going to kick your ass."

I laugh and make my way through the throng of people to the bar where Cannon was laughing with some patrons. He sees me and shakes his head with a smirk on his face as I sit down, staring around me.

Music blasted from the speakers of Club Anarchy. Loud country music to be exact. As I sat at the bar Cannon slid me over a drink. Taking a tentative sip I taste the distinct taste of peach in a Sex on the Beach. I give him a thumbs up and turn in my seat so I can watch as people are tossed from the mechanical bull over and over again. I laugh to myself. I didn't think Cannon would actually take my suggestion to heart but here we were. Laughing as people stood in line to ride.

"Are you going to get on?" Cannon shouts to me, sliding another drink towards me. I glance up at the man, and quirk an eyebrow at what he was wearing. A black cowboy hat sat atop his bald head and his dark eyes glittered with mischief as he dramatically stroked his beard. Cannon and I became friends in unfortunate circumstances, both forced into "therapy" to fix us. But here we were, drinking on a Thursday night watching as people fought to stay on that damn bull we both knew Cannon was controlling from behind the bar. Making it exceedingly difficult so people would get on it again and again to prove they could hold on longer than two seconds.

I take another long drink. "Hell, yeah, I'm getting on. But go easy on me, baby, because I can't bruise my money maker." I shimmy my non-existent ass at him which just makes him laugh harder. I lean up and grab the hat off his head and place it on my own. Cannon laughs as he hands me a shot. I salute him with it and tilt it back, letting the liquor burn its way down my throat.

I don't know what he gave me, nor do I care. I'm not here for a long time. I'm here for a good time. Or whatever it is those guys say on Tinder while holding a fish. I tilt the hat to him and make my way towards the bull. People make way as the MC calls my name and I bask in the attention. I love it. A large man standing by the side of the bull tilts his hat at me and I smile, letting him help me up onto it. I have no idea what I'm doing, but fuck it.

I wrap one jean clad leg over the side of it and heft myself with the help of the man. The bull is warm from so many people riding it. I settle into the seat, squirming slightly to get comfortable, and I grab the top of the saddle, flexing my fingers ever so slightly against it. Anticipation ran through me causing my heart to beat faster and the blood to rush to my ears.

I glance across the floor and see Cannon. He glanced up at me and I nodded once. He smirks at me and the start of *"Pony"* by Ginuwine starts playing. Laughing to myself I flip him off and he starts the ride.

It starts off slow and everyone begins to cheer, loudly. And it makes my blood soar. I whoop loudly and move with the bull, moving back and forth left and right. It was smooth at first until it got faster. My thighs squeezed the sides holding on as best as I could but even I had my limits. So after one rather hard turn I let go. There was something euphoric about it, letting myself freefall onto that inflatable bed at the bottom.

"That's a new record ladies and gentleman!" the MC shouted, cheering loudly. I let out a gasping laugh as I stared up at the ceiling, at the strobe lights bouncing from the walls. "Fifteen seconds! You did good!" the man who helped me said, standing over me. I smile and take the hand he's holding out to me. He hefted me up and bent low to retrieve Cannon's hat and set it back on my head, staring down at me with a bright dimpled smile and dark brown eyes.

"Thank you," I say, fixing my low cut corset, noticing how his eyes tracked the movement. I arched a brow at him, drawing his attention.

He cleared his throat, his face turning slightly red, "I'm sorry. I'm Blake."

"Nirvana," I say. Looking behind me to where Cannon was making drinks for the growing crowd. After all the excitement, the bull riding people were bound to get thirsty, or drunk enough to get the courage to even climb on. I glance at Blake, seeing his gaze is still steady on me. I shift on my feet and point to the bar. "I should be going. It was nice to meet you, Blake."

He nods, disappointment in his dark eyes. "Right. It was nice meeting you too, Nirvana." I nod once and make my way from him aware that he was watching me. For some reason it felt weird, almost threatening. Or maybe I was just fucking weird and over thinking it. I glance behind me and see him still watching. A shiver slides through me and I rush away towards the bar. My night has already been eventful enough, hooking up with that couple behind the bar, not to mention I was already feeling the effects of the alcohol and should probably head home. As I did have a root canal scheduled in the morning and I had to pay my sister a visit. I head to the bar and take Cannon's hat off.

"Done already?" he calls over the loud music.

"I've got work tomorrow," I say and mock pout. He smiles at me and takes the hat from me.

"Are you good to get home?" he asks, watching me. Always the concerned teddy bear. It was a wonder he was even remotely kind after everything he's been through, but I'm glad he held that part of himself still.

Nodding, I pull my phone from my bra and hold it out. "I'm going out to call an Uber. I'll text when I get home!" I lean over the bar and press a kiss to his cheek smiling when my black lipstick came off on his cheek.

Glaring, he rubs at it. "Now Mark will have questions."

Shrugging, I jumped down. "Tell him your first love gave it to you."

"You're a menace!" I wave him away with a laugh and make my way towards the front of the club to step out into the humid dry air of Texas heat at the end of May. The door shut behind me muffling the loud music and laughter. It gave me a chance to breathe. To breathe away the sweat and stale perfume was needed, the cloying smell of it was almost nausea inducing. I lean against the brick wall, shrouded in the shadows as I pull up the Uber app on my phone.

The door of the club opened and a large man stepped out. I barely spare him a glance as I order my ride.

"It's so loud in there," a deep voice said, drawing my attention. I gaze up and see Blake staring down at me.

I force a smile. "Yeah. It's a bit wild. It's the first time Cannon has had something like that in the club."

Blake laughs, getting a little too close for comfort. I inch away and he follows. "You looked good on the bull though. Had every man panting."

I hum under my breath. "Nothing sexual about it though. Just a bit of fun." Well, that was a lie. The song made it sexual. But nothing that would suggest him coming out here.

"Would you like a ride?" he asks, his breathing a little heavier than it was seconds ago. He steps into my space, bracing a hand on the brick above my head, sort of caging me in. I try not to panic, to feel the way he presses his body into me. He was taller than me by at least a foot and had well over a hundred pounds on me. Not to mention the smell of beer was potent on his breath.

"I'm good, thanks. In fact—" I look at the black Honda pulling into the parking lot. I glance at the license plate and the plate on the photo to make sure they match before trying to move away from him. "My ride's here actually."

He doesn't move however, making me irritated and more than a little nervous.

"What's the hurry? Don't you want to have a little more fun?" He pushes a strand of hair behind my ear gripping the nape of my neck roughly and pulling me flush against him.

"No. I've had my fun for the night. Now if you can let me go, please," I say, clutching my phone tightly in my hand. He doesn't though, if anything he tightens his hold and smashes his thin lips to my mouth. Goddamn it. Here goes another kiss that was pushed on me without my permission. It pisses me off more than him trying to fuck me when I said no. Squirming, I push at his chest wanting to get him off of me, which just eggs him on and he bites down on my bottom lip splitting the skin. Gasping in pain, I finally manage to push him off of me. Anger rushed through me. Overriding the fear and panic I felt moments ago. He fucking kissed me.

"What the hell?" he snaps. Looking offended.

I wiped at my lip, glaring up at him. "Don't touch me."

He scoffs, his large hand snapping out and wrapping around my throat, squeezing too hard, and says, "You go in there and tease me. Putting your tits on display and you come out here to be a cock tease? Or are you just a whore who likes it rough?" Gasping, I raise my knee and push upwards connecting with his groin. He howls in pain and drops me to the ground. I put a hand to my throat and gasp in a breath.

It takes a minute to contain my coughs and gasps before I pull myself up, my hand gripping at the brick on the wall. Blake is holding his balls and cursing at me, his eyes full of anger. Fuck that. I have reason to be angry, my neck was almost crushed and my lip is split open and he has the audacity to look angry?

No, no fucking way. I lift my hand, the one clutching my phone and slam it against his cheek. "I said, no! No! No means no in several fucking languages, so if you don't understand here it is in Spanish, no. In English, no, in fucking German *nein*. How about Russian? *Nyet!*" He falls to the ground with a loud *thud*. But I wasn't finished. I was pissed and shaking. I slam my booted foot against his side, hitting his ribs with as much force as I could muster. "I wasn't teasing you. It's called being polite. Something you clearly lack. If I wanted you I'd be upfront about it. No teasing, no playing around." He's groaning now, lying on the ground and holding himself as steady as he could. Especially his bruised balls. And me, being me, I don't care. I press my boot against his hand and press down.

"And I like pussy more than I like dick, sweetheart." With one last push I step over him. Well, I walk over him, earning a scream from him. I walked towards the car, glad they were still there and didn't leave. I open the back door and climb in, wiping at my bloodied mouth.

"Holy shit, holy shit," a young man in the front said, eyes wide behind his coke bottle glasses.

"Sorry for the wait," I mutter, fluffing my hair trying to stop the shaking in my hands.

"Do you need me to call the police? Are you all right?" he asks, staring at me.

I shake my head. "No. I'm fine. Just need to get home." I lick my lips and grimace at the metallic taste of my blood. "Do you have a napkin or tissue?"

He nods, sending red curls bouncing around his face. "Where to?" He leans forward and opens his glove compartment and pulls out some wrinkled fast food napkins and hands them to me.

I rattle off my address and sink back in the worn seats, dabbing at the blood on my lip. I was going back to the house I never wanted to go back to. The drive is silent and for that I was grateful. When he finally pulled up outside the depleted shack of a house I once called home, I quickly paid him and left a tip before climbing out. He pulled away and I stood there, staring at the house.

Why Aero wanted this house, I'd never know. That girl was an enigma and had a sentimental heart that no one else shared with her. But she asked me to help fix it up, so here I was. Sighing, I step up to the porch, wincing when the bottom step creaked against my weight. Ignoring it, I walked to the door and pushed inside. The house was almost like a time capsule, stuck in the time when we lived here as a "family". Snorting to myself I forced the front door closed.

When it didn't shut all the way I pushed my back against it, forcing it closed. The house was just as I remembered, a ripped red sofa sat in front of a box TV in the living room with an old tattered rug and a crooked coffee table covered with dust. The kitchen wasn't much better. The kitchen table was a circle with chips of wood peeling off of it, surrounded by four chairs, all in various stages of decay set around it.

It was odd, seeing the house I once grew up in. It was cold then, and even colder now. Leaving nothing to the imagination other than the "perfect" family. We were far from perfect though. Shaking my head I made my way to the bedroom I once shared with my sister. It was just like we left it all those years ago. It hadn't even changed once the two of us were gone.

There were the two twin beds, covered in a fine blanket of dust, an end table between the two with a Bible sitting on it. And one single dresser. Nothing more nothing less. Just the basics.

Crossing over to the night stand I grab the Bible and shove it in the drawer before dropping on my bed. I didn't even change out of my clothes, I just fell back and closed my eyes, willing sleep to take me.

Chapter 3

Nirvana

Gasping for breath I pushed the man away from me. "No!" I shout. Father Brent sighs and motions the man out. I scootch away and press my back against the wall, breathing in deeply.

"You're not participating in therapy. This is what we are supposed to do," Father Brent said, trying to sound soothing but failing with the grim look on his face. He was young, around thirty, younger than my father and he was decent looking. But by being around him I found him nothing but hideous. The way his thin mouth would thin even more when one of us displeased him, or we didn't listen.

I hardly ever listened. There was nothing wrong with me. And this wasn't normal. I knew that much. Father Brent stepped closer and before I could move away he grabbed my arm, pulling me roughly from the cot I slept on. "You will listen, Nirvana." He pulled me towards the door. I fought. Trying to press my weight down so he couldn't pull me.

I dug my heels into the concrete, wincing as he pulled, forcing me to drag my feet. It was rough, almost like a pumice stone that was hitting the same spot, over and over again. It hurt. It hurt a lot. Tears burned in *my eyes and I grabbed the side of the door with my free hand, fighting his hold.*

"No! No!" I scream. I knew where he was taking me. I wasn't going back there. I didn't want to go there. Not again. It was dark and cold. I could never tell what day it was when I was there.

"Nurse!" Father Brent shouts. I claw and kick, I thrash. But it was no use. Especially when I saw that sharp needle heading towards my neck.

I gasp for breath when I wake up. I'm on my stomach and nausea fills me forcing me to turn to my back. I glance up at the ceiling, my heart pounding rapidly in my chest. I haven't had nightmares in a while. Well, that's not true, I have nightmares a lot, but not like this one. And this one was bad. I slowly sit up pushing a hand through my hair. My fingers snag on a knot and I wince when I pull it free, taking a few strands of hair with it.

Shaking my head to rid myself of the memories, I stand and make my way to the bathroom. I move to the tub and turn on the shower, watching with a grimace as the water turns from brown to clearish. I pull up the stopper and watch as the water sprays from the showerhead, not in a hurry to climb inside. I should, I smell of booze and sweat but I didn't care. Turning away, I go to the medicine cabinet and pull down one of the bottles Aero had placed inside.

Palming the bottle I stare at the label, Trazodone. I contemplate if I want to go back to sleep or not. To fall into oblivion where I can't seem to escape the past. My eyes go to the dirty mirror and I see the hand print against my throat, and the fact that my mouth is swollen and bruised. Before I can think nausea burns in my throat and I am hunching over the toilet and throwing up what little contents I have in my stomach.

The bottle clatters out of my hand and falls to the floor as I grip the edge of the sink. I dry heave into the toilet and sweat dots my skin. When I'm sure there's nothing left to throw up I lean back, wiping my sore mouth with the back of my hand. I flush the toilet and pick up the bottle from the floor, groaning when I hear the shrill sound of my phone ringing.

God, couldn't I just catch a break? I slam the bottle on the counter and leave the bathroom searching for my phone which is settled under my bed. Cursing, I reach under it and grab it.

I stare down at the caller ID and see Isola's name flashing on the screen. My brows furrow. Why is my sister's girlfriend calling me at three in the morning? With my mind racing I answer.

"Hello?"

"Nirvana? Thank God you answered! I need you to go to the hospital right now! Aero collapsed during her shift and I can't get to her. You're closer. Please I need you to go check on her," Isola's words are muffled by the blood rushing to my ears. She's speaking too fast for me to follow. But I did catch the gist of it. Aero collapsed. She's in the hospital. I hang up and rush to the kitchen to grab my purse and run outside to my Jeep. Everything else is forgotten.

Climbing into the white Jeep I push the key into the ignition and drive away from the house and get on the highway. Making my way to the hospital. I haven't been to the hospital in nearly a year, not since Delaney's attack. My hands clench on the steering wheel as memories push into my head. Memories that are better off forgotten.

My mind is in shambles from the phone call from Layla. Delaney was hurt. I run into the hospital. I don't know what's going on. The ambulance is there when I run up to the entrance and I see her. Delaney. Being wheeled in on a gurney, a small man is straddling her and doing compressions on her chest.

"Delaney," I breathe. "Delaney!" I shout, running forward. A strong hand grabs me but I shake them off still running after her. Uncaring about anyone else. Delaney was family, one of my only family. She had to be okay. She had to be. "Delaney!" I scream again. Strong arms surround me, finally pulling me to a stop. A masculine scent surrounded me, almost smoky and spicy, with a hint of mint. I stop struggling, breathing in deeply.

"Settle," he hissed in my ear. His voice is deep and rich. I swallow hard, watching as Delaney is wheeled behind thick metal doors. I settle a little more until I'm finally calm. The man moves away from me, allowing me to turn around.

He is taller than me, with light brown hair and earthy green eyes. He's covered in blood and wearing a Houston Fire Department shirt. I step back, wanting to be with Delaney wondering where the others were. Panic set in, being alone with a random man touching me. I glanced up at him and swallowed hard.

"What happened?"

He looks at me for a moment then turns to another man who walks up to him. I glance away, worry sliding through me. Where were the others? I see red hair and my heart nearly stops until I notice it's Layla. I move away from the man and rush forward.

"What's happening?" she asks, her voice shaking.

"I don't know. It's Delaney, she was hurt."

I shake off those thoughts, that was nearly a year ago. Delaney is fine. Aero will be fine. She's fine. I repeat this in my head as I park in the visitors parking lot. I climb out of the car and rush inside, muttering to myself that Aero is fine. I don't get very far into the hospital before I hear my name.

"Nirvana." I turn and see Caden sitting in the waiting room, his dark eyes full of exhaustion.

I stop and look around him, confusion setting in. "Caden. What are you doing here?"

He runs a hand through his black hair sighing softly. "I was on the scene. I wanted to wait until someone came for her," he explains.

I nod, licking my lip nervously. "Oh. Is she——" I swallow hard nerves setting in. "Is she okay?"

He sighs again, his dark eyes holding mine. "She's stable. I don't know her full status right now. Only what happened when we got there." Caden stands, staring at me more intently, "What happened to your mouth?"

I stare at him with wide eyes. "Um, bull riding. Dangerous stuff." His eyes narrow and he looks as if he wants to say more, but I'm already turning so he doesn't get a chance to see my neck. "Thanks for staying. I appreciate it. You should head home or whatever it is you need to do. It must've been a long day."

I hear him sigh behind me. "Call if you need anything."

Nodding quickly I head to the front desk. "Hi, I'm here for my sister. Aero Bridges." The nurse looks up from her computer, a bored expression on her face.

Her thin eyebrows go to her hairline as she glances at my neck and lip. I smirk trying to convey sarcasm as I say, "It was a rough ride if you get what I mean." I wagged my brows when in reality I was panicked.

"She's in room 203. Last on the left," she says, and hands me a clipboard to sign in on before sliding me a visitors badge. I sign my name, my hand shaking as I wrote. I slide her back the clipboard, grab the badge and put it on my corset, uncaring that I look like a college student on a binge.

I wipe my hands on my jeans and make my way down the hall.

It was so early there was hardly anyone here. It was eerily silent and cold. Goosebumps rose on my arms and I rubbed my hands over them, trying to spread warmth. I should've changed before I went to sleep. But it was pointless to think about now. I had to focus on Aero. I stop outside the door and breathe deeply.

"Aero will be fine," I whisper and push open the door. The room was cold and sterile as I walked in, the sounds of the machines beeping overly loud in my ears. I glance at the bed first where Aero is lying. Wires are connected to her head and chest and she looks so small.

My gaze goes to the nurse in the room. A nurse I know well. Well as well as he'd allow. "Drew?"

Drew turns towards me, his ice green eyes devoid of any emotion. I shiver involuntarily as he stares at me. "Nirvana. What are you doing here?"

I gesture to Aero, "She's my sister." I walk deeper into the room. "Do you work with everyone you know?"

He sighs, "I don't know her. And I work in the emergency room. This was deemed an emergency." He steps closer to me and grips my chin tightly and lifts my face to the light, staring at my bruised neck. "What happened?"

"Fell off a pool table," I lied, pulling away from him and staring at my sister.

"I didn't realize pool tables had fingers. Or teeth," Drew said, his tone icy.

I don't respond. I grab Aero's hand. "What happened?"

Drew is silent behind me, as if he were contemplating answering or pushing for answers. Sighing, he said, "No one told you."

I shake my head. "Your sister had a seizure. Hit her head when she fell. I'm waiting for neuro to come and check her over better. We did a CT scan but it was inconclusive," he said and pauses. "Are seizures common for her? Does she take any medication?"

Swallowing hard I shake my head. "No. She's never had a seizure nor does she take any medication. At least none that I know of. She's healthy as a horse. Always active, does those weird cleanses." I squeeze Aero's hand. "Why isn't she awake?"

"I gave her some pain medication for her head and to help her relax. She complained of a headache once emergency personnel stopped her seizure." Sitting next to her I rub her hand between mine, trying to warm her up. I can feel Drew's penetrating stare on me but I don't look away from my sister.

We sit in silence before he speaks up, "Are you okay? Do you need anyone to check you out?"

"No. I'm fine, just tired." Which is true. I was exhausted and needed a few more hours of sleep. Sleep that I knew wouldn't come. I see Drew nod from my peripheral before he leaves the room, leaving me alone with Aero. The silence is deafening, and when the door closes with a soft *click* a sense of finality hits me. Making my heart thud in my chest. I swallow hard, running my thumb over the hand without an IV in it.

"If you don't wake up soon I'll never buy you another Christmas present again," I whisper.

Aero snorts, turning her head towards me, her eyes are glazed over from the pain medication and a goofy smile tilts her mouth. "You'd never do that. Giving gifts is your love language."

I scoff, tears burning in the backs of my eyes. "You were faking this whole time weren't you? If you need a break from work use a sick day like a normal person," I tease, my voice catching slightly.

Aero rolls her blue eyes, much like my own, "You know I need to do things with flare." She studies me intensely, "What happened?"

Her hand raises to my bruised neck. I shrug it off, forcing a smile, "A guy got too handsy and didn't understand the word 'no'."

Her brow raises. "Did you kick his ass?"

The tension I didn't realize was holding me up straight slowly eased from my shoulders. "Of course. I couldn't let him think it was okay."

"Good." She looks around the room, frowning, "Where's Is—"

I sigh. "She couldn't get off right away so you're stuck with me for now."

Aero smirks before squeezing my hand. "If I die you need to wear an outfit with all rainbow to my funeral."

I roll my eyes. "You're not going to die, Aero." Although when she said that, panic seeped inside of me. I couldn't lose my sister. I tighten my fingers around hers, hoping she wouldn't feel me shaking.

A knock sounds on the door and I jump. Clearing my throat I call, "Come in." The door opens and an older man comes into the room. He smiles at us, his brown eyes crinkling at the sides.

"Good evening, well morning I should say," he laughs at his own joke, pushing a hand through his balding gray hair. "I'm Dr. Coleman. What seems to be the problem?"

Aero sighs, closing her eyes, "I have a headache. When I was at work I kind of got dizzy and a little nauseous and then I woke up here."

Dr. Coleman hums under his breath. "You don't remember anything else?"

Aero shakes her head, making her dark blonde hair whip against her face. "No."

The doctor moves towards us, pulling a silver pen from his pocket and holding a light in her eyes. "Can you follow the light, please?" He moves the light and Aero slowly follows it. He hums again. "I think I'd like to do a few tests. Keep you overnight for observation." I gaze at Aero and she shrugs, sending me a sweet reassuring smile.

Dr. Coleman claps his hands. "Great. It'll be a few minutes and I'll send a nurse in to get you." Another knock sounds on the door as he gets ready to leave. When he opens it Isola rushes in, her normally tan face pale and damp with sweat as if she ran here.

"Aero! Oh thank gosh! Are you okay? What happened?" she asks, pushing her brown hair out of her face. I stand up and move away so Isola can take my spot. She pushes past me and grabs Aero's hands. I stand back watching as my sister answers her questions. My heart is heavy as I watch the two hug and kiss. I feel as if I am intruding on an intimate moment between the two and I'm unsure how to act. I glance away taking a deep breath.

I go to leave but Isola stops me, "Thank you for coming!" she says, turning to me.

Nodding, I turn away. "I'll always be here for my sister. Whatever she needs."

Aero glances at me. "Why don't you go home and get some sleep? You look like you haven't slept in a while. Maybe get your mouth checked out."

I shake my head. "No. It's fine. I don't mind." I haven't slept much and after tonight's nightmare I doubt I'd get back to sleep. Even if I was exhausted I would rather stay with my sister. But it didn't matter. Aero narrowed her eyes.

"You look dead on your feet. Go home. I'll call you when we get home tomorrow. I start to argue but Aero shakes her head firmly.

Giving up, I nod.

Isola squeezes my hand. "We'll call you. I promise."

Without much else to say, I turn to Aero and press a kiss to her head. "The moment you're home."

"I'll call you," Aero promises. Somewhat satisfied, I turn and leave the room. I go to close the door and watch as Isola climbs into the bed with Aero, holding her close.

"Nirvana," a voice says, surprising a yelp out of me. I turn and glare at Drew.

"Drew. Hey," I say, watching him cautiously. I didn't hear him walking up to me. How could such a large man walk without making any noise?

He motions for me to follow him and I do. He leads me to a small room and closes the door. Panic sets in and I start breathing heavily.

"Calm down. I'm not going to hurt you," he says, holding his hands up.

"Then why the hell did you trap me in some closet?" I snap, backing up defensively.

He glares at me. "Because I know damn well you won't get treated on your own. Now sit down and let me make sure your lip doesn't get infected."

I still, confused at his demand. He sighs and points to a little stool in front of him. Watching him closely I ease myself onto the stool. He sanitizes his hands and puts on some gloves before lifting my face and grabbing a bottle of peroxide and a gauze pad. He pours some onto the pad and dabs at the marks on my lip. I wince but hold still.

"Are you going to tell me what really happened?" he asks, tossing the stuff into the trash beside him.

"Does it matter?"

He gazes at me. "It does in case I need to give you medication."

I look away. "Some guy at the club didn't take no for an answer."

He sighs under his breath and puts a little butterfly stitch on the split. He pulls out a pill bottle and hands it to me. "Antibiotics. Take one twice a day with food and water."

I gaze up at him. "Can't you get in trouble for this?"

He shrugs. "Probably, but I don't really give a fuck. I'm not having Delaney chewing my ass out."

Rolling my eyes, I stand. "She's not scary."

"Anyone who can drive with a knife stuck in them and park, is scary. Plus she kills with kindness. I'd rather not be on her shit list anytime soon." Laughing, I thank him and leave the closet. My sister was in good hands. I leave the hospital quickly. Even with the distraction of Drew fixing my lip my thoughts were all over the place. When I got home I sat back in the driver's seat, my hands seemingly stuck to the wheel. I couldn't move. It was like every muscle in my body was frozen to the damn seat.

"She's all right," I whisper to myself, trying to calm that small part of my mind that always thinks the worst. There isn't much I can do until I find out more, so I push those thoughts out of my head and climb out of the car walking into the house. The first thing I hear as I walk inside is the sound of running water. I pause in the doorway, tilting my head to the side to listen better. The noise is coming from the bathroom. The color drains from my face.

"Fuck, fuck, fuck." I left the shower on! I run through the house towards my bathroom. "No, no, no." As I run down the hall I slip on the floor, falling in a puddle of water. I stare up at the ceiling, letting the water coat my hair and body as I wonder if this could get any worse. I lie there debating if I should call someone or let this damn shower somehow drown me.

Chapter 4

RAVI

The muscles in my arms and back burned as I pulled myself up. I hung on the pullup bar, testing my strength, only to stop when my phone started ringing. I grunt as I drop from the bar, grab the towel I had on the floor to wipe the sweat from my brow, before scooping up my phone. I glance down and see Caden's name flashing on the screen.

Swiping the green arrow I answer. "What's up? It's nearly four-thirty," I say, running the towel over my face.

"I know how to tell time, Ravi," was the sarcastic response.

I snort, nodding at Zander as I pass by him in the locker room. "Then why the fuck are you calling me? Are you all right?"

"I'm fine. I need a favor though."

"What is it?" I ask, suddenly wary of whatever he was going to say.

"Can you head over to Nirvana's house? Apparently she called Delaney and Delaney called me, but I'm covering a shift for Lou so I can't go. She said Nirvana was panicked," Caden explains.

"I don't know, Cade," I start, tossing the towel on the bench in front of the showers. "The girl is a little—" I pause, I wanted to say unhinged but that wasn't quite true. I only really had one conversation with her and she looked at me like I was the devil himself. "She hates me," I finish lamely. "I doubt she'd appreciate it if I just show up to her house randomly."

"She doesn't hate you. You just haven't interacted much, that's all."

I scoff at him. "The woman is more likely to bite my head off than have a normal conversation with me, Caden."

"She's shy."

Shaking my head I turn on the shower. "Yeah, whatever. I'll go check on her. But I'm sure she's fine."

Caden sighs. "I don't know. But thanks, man, I owe you one." Before I can ask what he meant when he said he didn't know, he hangs up. Shrugging, I drop my phone on the towel and strip out of my workout clothes and put on my shower shoes before stepping into the shower to wash off my work-out. I set it to the hottest setting I can handle and lean forward, letting the water soak my hair. Closing my eyes I let the water soothe the aching muscles in my body. After a few minutes I lean up and wash quickly before climbing out and dressing. It takes me maybe thirty minutes before I'm finished and heading out of the gym and waving at Franny at the front desk. After climbing into my car I hook my phone up to the GPS and type in the address Caden sent me.

I've never been to her house but as I'm driving I realize my house and Nirvana's is a straight shot. No more than five minutes away. When I pull up to the house I see her little white Jeep in the driveway but the house is completely dark. I climb out of my car and move towards the house. Climbing the broken steps had concern shifting through me. Surely this wasn't a safe house to live in. Shaking those thoughts off I knock on her door.

Nothing. I knocked again and called out her name, "Nirvana?" When I don't hear movement on the other side, alarm bells go off in my head. I twist the door knob and it gives way. Cursing, I shove the door open and walk inside. I push the door closed and lock it behind me, making a mental note to tell her to lock the door.

The sound of the shower is overly loud in the small house. It's also dark as fuck. I shake my head and move down the small hall grimacing when my feet step in a puddle of water. "Nirvana?" I whisper shout in the darkness.

No answer. Again. "For fuck's sake Nirvana answer me." She doesn't. I rush forward until I'm in the bathroom. The door is closed and I hear a soft groan. I don't even think as I push inside. But what I see stops me in my tracks. Nirvana's head snaps up and her blue eyes collide with mine.

"Ravi? What are you doing in my house?" I don't answer, too stunned to speak. She's currently kneeling in the tub, water pouring down on her as she tries to turn it off with a pair of pliers. Her usually white blonde hair is now darker due to it being wet and plastered against her pale face, making her freckles more pronounced. She wore a black corset that was sliding down her chest, leaving little to the imagination. She wore even tighter jeans and boots. But what stops me is the darkening bruises I see on her neck and her split lip.

"What the fuck happened?" I demand, instead of answering her question.

With a huff she leans back, motioning to the handles. "I left the shower on too long. When I tried to turn it off the handle broke." She shakes her head. "I guess I shouldn't have lain on the floor for so long after I fell," she muttered, pushing wet hair from her face.

My gaze snaps back to her. "You fell?" I demand. "And what the fuck happened to your mouth and neck?" She just nods absently, turning back to try and twist the pliers. "Did you hurt yourself more?"

She scoffs, "Nothing but my pride." Cursing, I kick off my shoes and move carefully into the bathroom, stepping into the shower behind her.

"What are you doing?" she asks.

I roll my eyes. "Calm down and give me the pliers." With another of those little huffs she hands me the tool and scoots to the side, pulling her knees to her chest. I take her place under the harsh cold spray and put the pliers on the broken handle and turn. There was a loud squeak as I turned the water off leaving the room in silence, aside from the occasional drip of the faucet. Nirvana sighs with relief leaning her head against the wall.

"Finally," she breathes out. I glance at her, taking her in. Her face is paler than normal and dark circles sit under her eyes making them appear too big for her face. My eyes move lower to her bruised neck and lip.

Her gaze meets mine and she nods. That's it. Scoffing, I step out of the shower, wringing out my hands. "You're welcome," I say sarcastically.

"I didn't ask you to come here," she said, staring up at me. I hold my hand out to her, my jaw clenched in agitation. She stares at my hand for a moment before sliding her smaller hand into mine, allowing me to pull her up. I felt a slight shock run up my arm as our skin touched. She sucks in a breath and pulls away quickly. I gaze at the floor and the mess that was left in the bathroom. "Your floor is fucked."

Nirvana looks down, then shrugs, "Oh well."

Arching a brow, I watch as she steps out of the bathroom and throws an old towel on the floor. She presses her foot into it and moves it around, spreading the water.

"You're just making it worse," I say.

Her eyes moved to me. "It's just water."

I nod. "Yes, but water causes a lot of damage. Not to mention the floors are already rotting in some spots. It can be salvaged but not by you spreading the water more."

Nirvana just shrugs again, as if she doesn't care what happens to the house. I shake my head and push her away from the towel, kneeling to clean up the water myself. "Do you have a standing heater or something?"

"Maybe. I don't know. This isn't my house."

My eyes widen. "What?"

"It's Father Bridges' house. Or was I guess. I'm staying here trying to fix it up for my sister and her girlfriend," she chuckles as if it's the funniest thing to her.

"Father Bridges?" I question under my breath.

Nirvana nods. "Yes. Her father left it for her. Or bought it. I don't know all the details."

I glance up at her and ask, "So this is your father's house?" Nirvana's face goes blank and she shakes her head.

"No. Just Aero's father. I was disowned a long time ago." She says it so casually and I stare at her. She doesn't say more, just turns and leaves the bathroom. I want to ask more questions, this is the most the two of us have actually talked since Delaney was in the hospital, but she's closed off.

Every time I thought about or saw Nirvana she was always laughing and cheerful. The woman here tonight? She was closed off, distant, and sad. I sigh and finish cleaning up most of the water as best as I can before standing and wringing out the towel in the tub before tossing it into the plastic hamper that was behind the door.

Once that is done I follow the path Nirvana took. But before I can search for her I see her leaving another room, pulling a heater behind her. I step forward and take it from her.

"Thanks," she muttered. I don't respond as I crouch low and study the outlets. They are in shitty shape but there's not much to be done with them so I pick the one I think is least likely to cause a fire and plug it in, kind of surprised when it turns on. I put it in the doorway of the bathroom and angle it so it can get most of the floor.

"Don't let this get covered and if you smell burning, turn it off," I instruct as I stand. I cross my arms over my chest and stare down at her. "Are you okay?"

She sighs. "Why does everyone keep asking me that? I'm fine."

I roll my eyes. "Whatever you say." Leaning over I grab my shoes and tug them back on.

"What's that supposed to mean?" she says, her face turning red from frustration.

I snort. "Well, your lip is about two times its normal size and as bruised as the bags under your eyes, not to mention your neck has a large handprint around it. So unless you're into choking, someone hurt you." I lean forward staring into her eyes. "Who the fuck was it?"

She rolls her eyes. "How do you know I'm not into it? Maybe I asked for it."

I roll my shoulders. "Because anyone who's into it knows how to choke enough for pleasure and not pain. Besides, it's right against your esophagus. It should be at the sides of the esophagus, not pressed directly against it. The hand place-ment isn't right and it could've done damage to your throat." It could've killed her.

Nirvana places her hand against the bruises. "And how would you know that?"

"Unlike your mystery man, I know what the fuck I'm doing. Now, answer me. What. The. Fuck. Happened. To. You?"

Nirvana shrugs, looking away, a small flush tinting her cheeks. "Some guy at Anarchy didn't know how to take no for an answer. Said I was teasing him. It hardly matters now. I busted his balls. Literally. At least I hope one of them popped. It would serve the bastard right," her eyes narrow, "not that it's any of your business. Why are you even here?"

"Delaney," I say, walking past her and opening the door. "And lock the goddamn door," I snap, slamming it behind me.

The door flies open again. "Don't slam my door again, Ravi!" she snaps.

"Drink some tea, it'll help your throat. Eat something. Then go to fucking bed." She stares at me, her eyes full of fire. She looks like she wants to argue but in the end she just nods, closing the door behind herself. I climb into my car and take a deep breath. She's different from when she is around others. Almost like a different person. Not that it's not something I'm unused to. Everyone has their masks. The ones they wear around the people they love, to the ones they wear when they are at work. However, this one seemed more chaotic. More angry and all over the place. Almost manic. Scoffing to myself I start the car.

I shouldn't have pressed for answers. Why I did, I had no idea. Just seeing her hurt and bruised made something hot and angry burn inside of me. I shake off my thoughts and head to the station. When I get there the first person I see is Caden who is sitting folding up different bundles of rope. He gazes up at me when I walk over.

"What are you doing here? Aren't you on vacation?" His eyes narrowed. "And why are you wet?"

Shrugging, I sat beside him, grabbing another rope. "Nothing else to do. Figured I'd see if there was anything that needed to be done today." It's not like I could just go home. Well, I could, but I'd just be bored and stuck in my own head. I needed something to do. I had to keep busy.

Caden snorts, drawing me out of my thoughts. "You do realize a vacation is meant to be spent away from work. Besides, I thought you were helping Nirvana."

I grit my teeth, my hands flexing in the rope. "I did. She broke her shower handles and couldn't turn off the shower."

"Is she all right?" I glance at Caden. "I mean did she seem okay?"

"Aside from the damn busted lip and bruised neck you mean?" I growl out. "She was scatterbrained. Probably preoccupied," I mutter when Caden arches a brow at me.

He nods slowly. "That's what Drew said. He's the one who cleaned her lip."

That pulls me up short. "What do you mean? When did Drew see her?" For that matter, when did Caden see her? And why did I suddenly care?

"Her sister collapsed at work tonight. Seizure. She seemed freaked out and scared earlier so I was worried about her. And like you said she was hurt," he explains.

"Did she tell you what happened?" I ask.

"She said bull riding. But I know a bullshit lie when I hear one."

I nod, wondering why Nirvana lied to him and tried to lie to me. But I ignore those questions and ask, "Is Aero okay?"

He shrugs, standing up and gathering the ropes. "I don't know. I was going to go home once Nirvana got there. I was called to cover another shift." I nod. That explains why she was so out of it. Why she was angry. It makes me wonder if the other women knew, and why they weren't with her. From my understanding they'd do anything for one another. So that means Nirvana didn't tell them. And she was probably alone at the club. Where she was hurt. It wasn't my business, I knew I should forget about it, but a part of me was worried about her and why she didn't call her friends for help. Aside from Delaney with her shower. But even that was odd.

Chapter 5

Nirvana

Sitting across from my friends, I sigh. It's Sunday and one of them had the bright idea to go to brunch. Probably Layla or Rory if I had to guess. So here I was, gazing down at a full plate of eggs and bacon and scooching it across the plate, over and over again. Gazing at it as if it were a bomb. The fork was loud against the plate making me wince every time I moved one food from one side to the other.

"You're supposed to eat it," Seraphina said beside me, drawing my attention.

"Oh. I'm not that hungry," I mutter, sipping at my mimosa. There's never a wrong time for a mimosa. Champagne with a dash of orange juice? Yes, please. I can feel my friends' eyes on me. Staring intently as if I were on the verge of a breakdown.

Ophelia clears her throat. "How's your mouth and throat?"

Without thinking I press my fingers to the dark bruises,

grimacing. That bastard. It's nearly a hundred degrees outside and I have to wear a damn turtleneck to hide the fact that fingerprints are embedded in my skin, and not from a fun night, well the start of the night was fun. Then I remember what Ravi said. He knows what to do. How would he? But then again I didn't know the man. Nor did he have the right to get angry at something that didn't pertain to him at all.

He's been stuck in my head for the last few days. If I wasn't thinking about him I was worrying about Aero. It was an endless cycle, my mind being consumed by them. It pissed me off. Not Aero, never her. But to have this man invade my space, taking a huge chunk of my mental peace? Yeah, that made me upset and I wasn't sure why. I gulp down my drink and stop the waiter to get another one. Maybe I should call Veronica, Vanessa? Whatever, they were funish. Nothing I can complain about. But they weren't exciting. If anything they were a distraction, which is what I needed right now.

Clearing my throat, I shrug, asking my own question instead of answering Ophelia, "Have you ever been choked during sex?"

Five sets of eyes stared at me. I tap my fingers on the table trying not to ask again. I was genuinely curious. After Thursday, well, after Ravi, I was curious about it. About him. How would it feel to have his fingers wrapped around my throat? Nope, not going there.

"Like to the point you can't breathe or just holding it?" Delaney asks, sipping at her water.

"I don't know. Either I guess." Was there a difference?

Delaney laughed softly. "Well, then yes. A few times."

I gaze at her shocked, I didn't take Delaney as the type to being into that. Well, that's a lie. She told us about her hookup in the club with Sorrow. I was still proud of her for that.

She shrugs, pushing her dark hair over her shoulder. "It's fun, especially when you trust your partner who is doing it. If you're interested in exploring that part of yourself make sure they know what they're doing. It can be dangerous."

Unlike your mystery man, I know what I'm doing. I can't get Ravi's words out of my head. I shake out his voice and focus on the women around me. "It's silly. I doubt it's my thing."

"Is that how you got those marks?" Layla asks, tilting her head to the side, her red hair shining in the summer sun.

I shake my head and grab the mimosa the waiter brought me, downing it in one go. "No," I say, "this asshole at Anarchy thought he could touch me. Said I was a cock tease." I've been having nightmares since that night. I wake up in my childhood room drenched in sweat and gasping for air as if I was being held under water over and over again.

There's a collective gasp and Rory reaches over the table placing her hand on mine. "Why didn't you call one of us? Did you get treated? Did you go to the police?"

I squeeze her hand gently and shake my head. "It's fine, Ro. I'm fine. I didn't tell you because I have a lot going on. Plus I almost had a threesome outside, so that probably wouldn't work in my favor anyway." They stare at me as if I had grown two heads but choose to ignore my last statement, moving to a different topic.

"How is Aero?" Layla asks.

I shrug. "She's been resting. I'm taking her to the doctor tomorrow for the results of her tests. For now she's been in bed. She's still having bad headaches so maybe they can figure out what's going on with her and fix it." They nod and change the subject to everyday life. I'm hardly listening, stuck in my own head about what's going to happen. I can only hope it's nothing bad and we can get back to normal.

Sighing, I moved my chair over to the filing cabinet to pull out more patient forms. Yesterday after leaving brunch I went to Aero's and she looked sicker than when I saw her last. Her face was pale and she hardly moved when I went into her room. The house was pitch black and any slight noise had her crying. I didn't stay long, nor did I go to the house. I drove around for hours until I had to go to work. Then I went and showered. I haven't slept and my bones felt like they weighed more than a ton.

I was almost to the point of crashing, but I didn't have that luxury. I had to get this appointment done with. Pulling my phone from my scrubs I glanced at the time. It was almost time. I blink my dry burning eyes, forcing myself to stay awake as I put the files up and grab the forms.

"Nirvana! How's it going?" I jump at the sudden voice behind me. Glancing up I grimace when I see Brad leaning against the reception desk, his overly gelled hair shining from the overhead lights. Making it look almost plastic.

I plaster a fake smile on my face. "It's going, Brad. Nothing new here. How are you?" Not that I really care. Because let's be honest, I don't give a fuck.

Brad smiles, showing overly white teeth. We work at a dental office but surely that level of brightness isn't healthy for teeth. Not that it matters, they were in his head not mine. He leans over the desk clasping his hands. "I'm good! I was just wondering if you could set me up with your friend again. I feel awful for missing our first date."

I arch a brow at him, sliding the forms on the desk. "You do realize it's been over a year right?" He grimaces and gives me a fake apologetic smile. Scoffing, I grab my bag, "No. She's engaged now. You missed your chance on that one. Besides, she's too good for you." He reels back as if I slapped him. I didn't care. I was already halfway out the door. He's standing there sputtering like a fool but that's his issue. I can hardly breathe as I climb into the Jeep and drive away from the office. My anxiety is higher than it's ever been as I drive to Aero's apartment. As soon as I pull in I see her standing outside with Isola. She smiles warmly at me and hugs Is one last time before bounding over to my car.

She's dressed in a bright yellow dress. I give her a strained smile as she straps herself in.

"You look cute," I say.

Aero laughs. "Yellow is supposed to be a positive color, Vana," she pauses, "are you ready for this?"

I pull out of her apartment complex flexing my fingers on the steering wheel. "Me? Are you ready for this?" My sister smiles weakly and shrugs. There's not much we can do if we don't have any answers yet. We fall into silence all the way to the doctor's office, neither one of us wanting to talk, afraid of the news we may get. I pull up to the brick building about to climb out of the car when Aero stops me with a firm hand on my arm.

I glance over at her. "Whatever happens, know that I love you and I'll always be here."

I swallow thickly. "I know." My throat is dry and a lead ball is forming in my stomach as nerves settle over me. But Aero seems unaffected. She just nods and climbs out of the car. I take a calming breath and follow after her, trying to think positive thoughts. We walk in and the smell of disinfectant is thick in the air. Aero moves to the reception desk and signs herself in as I sit down, looking around the room. There are pictures of brains on the wall and different magazines sitting on a dark oak coffee table. All featuring brains and their functions, and other scientific stuff that I had no interest in. Soft music plays in the distance and plants are in each corner of the waiting room making it feel more airy inside instead of stuffy.

Aero sits beside me on the leather couch and grabs my

hand. She doesn't convey her nerves but the clammy hand I'm holding tells me she's more afraid than she lets on. Not that I blame her. I squeeze her hand encouragingly. We don't speak, just wait for the moment when her name is called. It feels like hours, the sound of the clock overly loud in the silent room. *Tick, tick, tick.* Then the door opens. "Aero Bridges?" Aero trembles beside me, her body tensing as she stands slowly. I stand beside her, grabbing her hand to guide her towards the door. Towards whatever waited for us. We are led to an office which was barren aside from the large glass desk, and two chairs in front of it.

The nurse motions us inside. "Please have a seat. Dr. Coleman will be with you soon."

I thank the older woman and sit in one of the chairs, my heart racing. Sitting still has never been my strong suit. I'm fidgeting, bouncing my knee up and down, pulling at the thread on my pant leg. Anxiously waiting.

Aero glares at me. "Will you stop shaking your knee?" I press my palm down on said knee and force myself to calm. I take a deep breath and smile. Trying to show her that everything is fine. Even if I felt like everything was far from fine. It wouldn't do us any good if I panicked. I had to be here for my sister. So I stopped shaking my knee and folded my hands on my lap as we waited in an abnormally cold office. Waiting to see the scans. It's only been a few days and when we were called last night, on a Sunday evening from Dr. Coleman himself, I knew it probably wasn't going to be the news we wanted. It made me nervous.

The silence was tense by the time the doctor came into the room. Dr. Coleman wasn't smiling either, not this time. In fact he was sober and that didn't bode well for us. He placed a white folder on his desk and sat down.

"Good afternoon, ladies. I apologize for keeping you waiting." I look over at him, my heart pounding.

"What is it?" I ask, not wanting to wait longer than necessary.

He looked at the two of us and a look of sympathy passed in his brown eyes. "I'm so sorry. I truly am."

"What is it?" I demand again.

Aero placed her hand on mine, "Nirvana, calm down please," she turned to the doctor. "What's wrong with me?"

He sighed, running a hand through his graying hair. "It's glioblastoma."

I shake my head. "Wh-what's that?" I ask, my voice quivering.

"It's an aggressive form of brain cancer. In your case, Aero," he glances at my sister, "it's very advanced. We can attempt chemotherapy and radiation. It could buy you some time but I can't guarantee it." His words sounded far away. The color in Aero's face slowly leached away, sending a chill through me. My blood rushed through my ears, making everything around me sound as if it were echoing.

The whining of the small desk fan, to the sharp intake of breath from my sister. I turn away. I couldn't look at her anymore. Not when I could see the acceptance in her eyes. I swallow the lump in my throat before speaking up, "What does that mean? For Aero?" But I already knew what he meant. Aero knew what he meant. It was in the way he looked at us, the air around him. It wasn't good news. Tears burned the backs of my eyes and I had to run a tired hand down my face so none escaped.

Dr. Coleman gave me a sympathetic look, sliding over a box of tissues. "It gives her three months to two years. At most. But that's with treatment."

I grab her hand, squeezing it hard.

"If you decide to do the treatment it has to be started soon, to slow down the cancer's progression."

Clearing her throat, Aero speaks up, "If I don't do the

treatment what happens?" My head snaps in her direction. I stare at her sharply, but she doesn't look at me.

"Aero," I say, but she doesn't answer me.

Dr. Coleman leans forward clasping his hands together. "If you don't get the treatment, Aero, your cancer will spread and it will spread fast. You will lose all cognitive skills. All sense of self and you won't be the person you are right now for much longer."

"How much time?" she asks. No! She wasn't thinking clearly. I want to protest but for some reason I couldn't find my voice. I was too shocked to speak and nothing came out but a tiny squeak of denial.

"At best two, maybe three months."

Aero nods, standing up on shaky legs, she straightens out her yellow skirt. "Thank you, Dr. Coleman. I don't want to get the treatments."

"Aero," I start, finally finding my voice.

Turning her head she looks at me sadly. "It's only going to prolong the inevitable, Vana. I rather it be done with than go through months of treatment for a disease that will still kill me in the end." She smiles at the doctor. "Thank you for your time." With that she walks out of the office, leaving me gaping at her. I stand to chase after her. I'm halfway to the door when his voice stops me.

"Nirvana," Dr. Coleman says, drawing my attention to him, "if I were you I'd get ready. This is going to be a long road and she won't be the sister you know. Not anymore." I nod, my heart pounding as I leave the room. I can't breathe as I walk outside in the humid Texas heat where I see Aero standing by the Jeep. She doesn't say anything to me. Just waits until I unlock the door. I press the lock on the key fob, waiting for it to unlock and watch as she climbs in. She places her head on the window and closes her eyes.

I climb in, my heart heavy and broken. I don't speak as I

start the car. We are driving in silence and once I'm at her apartment she turns to me. "Vana."

I shake my head. "Aero, please. Please do the treatment. Please." My voice cracks on the last word but she's already shaking her head. She's already made her decision and knowing my sister there was no changing her mind, but I couldn't help wanting to try. Needing to try, to give us more time.

"I can't. I don't want to be stuck in bed for my last moments. Please understand."

I shake my head again, my fists clenching on the steering wheel. How can she ask me to understand this? "I can't lose you. I can't."

Aero grabs one of my hands, peeling it off the wheel to hold it between hers. "Let's make the most of it. Let's do everything we can until I can't anymore."

I take a shuddering breath. "Like what?"

She smiles at me, her eyes lighting up, "I want to marry Isola. I want to die as a married woman."

"That's not long to plan," I whisper.

"You can do it. We can do it. Say two weeks from now? What, that's June 18th? Does that sound good to you?" She looks so hopeful, so content with dying and it's killing me a little inside. It's shattering my heart, but I can't take this from her so I nod. Her smile widens and she kisses my cheek and climbs out of the car just as her apartment door opens and Isola comes out. I see tears in her eyes and I know Aero probably called her while I was still inside. I watch as Aero hugs her making me choke on a sob. I pull away quickly, nearly hyperventilating as I merge onto the highway. Tears blur my eyes and I'm swerving on the road. Horns honk behind me and I stop, just stop on the highway.

I press my head against the steering wheel and scream, slamming my hand down on the wheel over and over again.

Tears are falling down my face and I can hardly breathe. Horns are honking loudly and I jump when a knock jolts me out of my mind. The sound is sharp and loud. I glance up and see the round face of Officer David, glaring at me.

"Fuck," I mutter, rolling my window down. I try to wipe my eyes but the tears don't stop flowing.

"You do realize you're in the middle of the highway blocking drivers don't you?" he snaps.

I gaze around me wiping at my face again. "I'm sorry. I thought I was merged on the other side. Hazards on and all that." I'm speaking fast and incoherently.

"Please step out of the vehicle, ma'am," he says, already opening up my door. I curse in my head stepping out of the car. I'm an emotional mess and I'm still crying. He made me do that drunk walking test and say the alphabet backwards and with my emotions all over the place, I failed.

So now, here I was cuffed in the back of the cop car crying and pressing my head against the window trying and failing not to freak out even more. The ride back to the station is a quick one and it doesn't take long before I'm booked and taken to a holding cell.

"Don't I get a phone call?" I ask softly, defeat and weariness weighing down on me.

Officer David nods and slides over a desk phone to me. I dial the only number I know by heart. The phone rings and rings and I think she's not going to answer when I hear her voice on the other end, "Hello?"

I breathe deeply, pulling the phone away from my face as a sob chokes me.

"Hello?"

"Laney?" I whisper into the phone, turning sideways away from Officer David.

"Nirvana? Who's number are you calling me from?" she asks.

"Laney, I need you," I say.

She goes silent, then asks, "Where are you?"

"I was arrested."

"I'll be right there," was all she said and hung up.

Officer David pulled me up and shoved me into a holding cell, alone. I sank down onto the cold bench pulling my knees to my chest letting the tears flow freely.

Chapter 6

RAVI

Delaney's phone rang drawing my attention. We were currently at Layla's bakery helping Layla set up for the opening coming up in the next two months and the women were waiting not so patiently for Nirvana to show up. But when Delaney's phone rang she glanced at the number and her brows furrowed in confusion.

"Who is it?" Sorrow asks, standing up from where he was fixing the floor that was chipped when an extra table was brought in.

"I don't know," she says and slides the phone open and presses it to her ear. "Hello?" Whoever is on the other side doesn't speak. "Hello?" Delaney repeats.

She waits in silence and I notice the color drain from her face. "Nirvana? Who's phone are you calling me from?" She pauses again, and I see anger cover her features. "Where are you?" She's already grabbing her bag and keys before muttering, "I'll be right there," and hanging up.

"Delaney, what's going on?" Layla asks.

Sighing, she shrugs. "Nirvana was arrested. I need to go get her."

Before she can move everyone steps in and is moving as a unit. The women are talking and making calls and Max is shaking his head. "Never a dull moment," he mutters.

"Now wait, before you start freaking out. We don't know what she did," Sorrow starts, stopping Delaney before she could leave.

"She didn't sound good. I don't know. Something's wrong, Sorrow. I know it." Sorrow curses and motions her forward.

"Max, you stay here with Spencer and Sam. Ravi, you come with us. Just in case one of them decides to start more problems."

"Or blackmail a cop," Max adds.

Delaney huffs but doesn't respond as I follow them out of the bakery. I climb into the back of Sorrow's truck. "I can't believe I have to bail out two people in less than a year."

"It's been longer than a year, bright eyes. You know this," Sorrow responds, pulling away from the bakery. The drive is quicker than I thought it would be, but then again I've never been here before. But seeing as Delaney has in fact bailed out another person before, she seems to know the quickest way to get there.

"I swear if she's hurt," Delaney mutters, climbing out of the truck and slamming the door harder than needed. I meet Sorrow's gaze and he sighs, shaking his head as he follows her. I climb out and move in behind them. Delaney is a force when she walks in. "Where is she?" she demands.

"For God's sake. You again," a voice snaps. Delaney pastes a smile on her face and turns to an officer who walks from a room. He's red faced and rounded, as he glares at Delaney.

"David. Good to see you. I'm here for a friend. Small, blonde, like yay tall," she holds her hand low and Officer David curses.

"No. Not this. She is staying until she sobers up. She was stopped in the middle of the goddamn highway. No hazards on, can't form a sentence. She could've crashed, gotten herself and others killed."

I gaze at Sorrow and Delaney who both look as confused as I felt. "Let us see her at least," she says.

Officer David curses and tilts his head for us to follow him. The walk down the hallway felt longer than the ride over but we finally got to the holding cells and I saw her. Nirvana was in the corner of the cell, folded in on herself, her head pressed to her knees and her body shaking slightly.

"Nirvana," Delaney calls, drawing the woman's attention. Her eyes were swollen and red and tears trekked down her pale cheeks.

"Lane. You came?"

Delaney nodded. "Of course I came. I'll always be here. What happened?"

Nirvana's gaze went to the cop, she shook her head and said, "Make him go away."

"Ten minutes, then you leave." Officer David turns to leave shooting one more glare at Delaney before shutting the door.

"What happened?" Delaney asks. Nirvana stretches her legs out and I see she's wearing scrubs as if she just got off of work.

"I don't know. I panicked, I just couldn't drive. I didn't mean to stop in the middle of the road," she rambles, wiping her face.

"Are you drunk?" I ask before I can help myself.

Nirvana narrows her blue eyes at me. "No. I was crying. I don't know." Her words were jumbled and she was running her fingers through her hair in agitation. A trait I was starting to notice she did when she was stressed out. She notices me looking and drops her hand leaning her head back against the wall turning her gaze back to Delaney.

"What happened to make you cry?" Delaney asks soothingly.

Nirvana stands, pacing the cell as if she were on the verge of panic again. I study her again and see her fingers twitch and those bags under her eyes are more pronounced than the last time I saw her. Not to mention her cheeks were slimmer than before. "Not good. I can't do it. I can't do it, Lane."

Delaney motions Nirvana forward. Nirvana stops pacing and looks at Delaney moving slowly as if she were afraid. "Tell me why you're so afraid, Van. Let me help you like before."

My gaze is stuck on her. Watching all of her nuances. She was manic. Sort of like when we got out of that last mission, reacting like Sorrow did. Reckless, hardly sleeping. But this was different. Almost as if she couldn't help it and didn't realize she was being reckless. "Die. I don't want her to die. She won't listen to me. She said she doesn't want to," Nirvana mumbled.

"Who did?" Delaney asks.

"Aero! She won't do the treatment, she's going to die and I can't stop it! Why won't she just do it? It'll give her time! Time she needs!" Nirvana shouts, pressing the heels of her hands to her eyes.

"When's the last time you slept?" I ask, trying for a gentle tone. Not that it was working, I was never good at being gentle. But I'd try if it would get her to calm down, even for a little bit.

Nirvana gazes at me, shrugging. "I don't know. Thursday?" She shakes her head sending blonde hair everywhere. I move closer to Sorrow motioning for him to follow me. He peers at Delaney who nods. We leave the room and I can hear Nirvana sobbing and it does something to my chest. I wasn't even sure why I suddenly cared.

Ignoring it, I say, "She's not drunk. She's sleep deprived and sad."

"She could've wrecked," Sorrow said, always the voice of reason.

I nod in agreement. "Yes, but she didn't. She needs sleep, possibly food. She's lost weight."

"You saw her, Thursday. After Aero had her seizure, how was she then?"

I rub the back of my neck. "Out of it. Distracted. She didn't really care about anything. She looked tired but not like this." We make our way back to the front.

"What now?" Sorrow asks.

"Now we pay her bail and get her home so she can rest. I don't know what's going on with her sister but, right now it's safe to say it's not good."

Sorrow studies me for a minute, a smirk playing on his lips.

"What?" I demand.

He shakes his head. "I just didn't know you cared so much."

Rolling my eyes, I take the papers from the officer at the desk. "I don't. But even I can be civil enough to notice when someone needs help."

"Of course," Sorrow says, tapping his tattooed hands on the desk. "But you don't usually take charge is all. It's new."

"Go to hell," I mutter. "When is her birthday?" I ask.

Sorrow shrugs. "Fuck if I know."

"November 29th, 1982," a deep voice says behind us. We

turn and stare at the man. "Hi. I heard Nirvana was here. I was coming to sign her out. I'm Mark."

"Ravi," I say, glaring at the man in question. Who the fuck was this?

"Cannon's husband?" Sorrow asked. "You were here last time."

Mark nods, shaking Sorrow's hand. "Yes. Cannon and Nirvana go way back. He'd kick my ass if I didn't do what I could to get her out. There wasn't sufficient cause for arrest."

I tune the man out and finish signing the papers before standing straight and staring at the man. "Cops here need better training. Because she clearly wasn't drunk or in the right headspace for an arrest. Someone should've been called for her. She shouldn't be sitting alone in a cold cell." My voice is colder than I anticipated, but I didn't care. It was clear she was struggling, not drunk. I could see that when she walked towards Delaney.

"I agree. Training officers for mental health issues isn't talked about enough. I apologize for what happened. She should be out in an hour. I'm letting Delaney stay with her," Mark said.

I nod, turning away from him. "Someone should go make sure she has what she needs at the house," I tell Sorrow.

"I have Sam and Layla on it." We wait an hour until we see Delaney and Nirvana. Sorrow and I fall into step behind them and leave the station. Delaney helps her into the truck and I climb in beside her, nodding to Delaney when she arches a brow at me. She searches my face before nodding slowly and closing the door. Nirvana sits away from me sniffing slightly. No one says anything on the drive to Nirvana's house. She still silently cried against her seat. When Sorrow pulled up to her house she swallowed hard, and looked at it.

"Thanks for coming to get me," she muttered and climbed out of the truck.

"Wait," Delaney called, following after her. I climbed out, too. Why? I had no idea. But the thought of Nirvana being alone didn't feel right. Nirvana gazed over her shoulder, her eyes connecting with me briefly before she walked away, leading the way into the house. She pushed the door open and sighed.

"I don't have a lot of furniture if you're planning on socializing," she said, her voice lowering.

Delaney grabs her hand and leads her away whispering, "We don't care about that, Vana. Come on, let's get you into bed."

When the women disappear I turn to the tall blond man next to me, glaring at him. "What the hell, I thought you called Sam and Spencer to get stuff she needs?"

"Layla," Sorrow says.

"What?" I say in confusion.

"It's Sam and Layla," he elaborates, his mouth twitching up.

I curse, "I don't give a fuck who it is. It can be Santa Claus and the goddamn Easter Bunny for all I care."

He laughs then. "I never thought I'd see the day that Ravi Banks gets all flustered over a woman. Especially after one interaction."

"I'm not flustered." I move to walk away only to walk back to him poking him in the chest, "And I know your ass isn't talking Mr. I fucked my future wife in the bathroom at a club then found out she's my fucking therapist."

That wipes the smirk off of his smug face. "Hey, I didn't know she was my therapist."

"It didn't stop you from fucking her again. So you can't really cast stones. And I'm being a decent human being and helping another one who needs it." Because there wasn't anything other than the need to help this woman.

Sorrow rolls his eyes. "Oh please, when have you ever done anything for someone else without motive?"

"When I pulled your ass out of that hole. Should've left your big ass there too."

Sorrow scoffs, "Please, I would've gotten out without you."

"Really? I can drop you back there and see how long it takes you to get yourself out."

He glares at me. "Don't make me kick your ass."

I stand toe to toe with him. "I'd like to see you try. Stop being a dick," I hissed.

"I will when you stop being a little bitch about being attracted to that woman," Sorrow taunts.

A knock on the door had us pulling apart. Glaring at Sorrow, I pull open the door and see Sam and Layla standing on the porch. "Sorry we're late, Layla wanted to grab some water. And cupcakes."

The redhead smiles at Sam. "Oh hush, we don't want her to drink dirty water. Now make yourself useful and go get the case of water out of the car. Ophelia said she was bringing another one." Sam shakes his head running a dark hand over his face.

"This is the last time I let you and Spencer make lists."

Layla waits until he's gone to look up at Sorrow and me. "Well? Are you just going to stand there or let me in? Where's Nirvana and Delaney?" She pushes between us and goes in the direction of the other two women. Shaking my head, I go and help Sam as the others slowly show up. It's not long before everyone is here and I'm standing in the shadows watching over them.

I watch as Delaney and Layla come out of the room, it

took them thirty minutes to get Nirvana asleep. She quietly sobbed until she finally wore herself out enough to sleep.

"There's nothing in the fridge or cabinets," Sam said, drawing my attention away from the room she slept in.

My brows raise slightly. "Nothing?"

He shook his head. Rory moved to the kitchen and opened the doors herself, as if expecting a different outcome.

She turns towards the other women. "Sera? How long has she been staying here? Do you know?"

Sera shrugs, pushing her blue hair out of her face. "A few days. I know Aero asked her to help remodel it so she could move in." Ignoring them I walk into the kitchen and open the old fridge expecting to find at least something in there, but there was nothing. It was cleaned spotless but nothing sat in it. I opened the freezer and saw the same thing. I check the trash and again... nothing.

"No takeout either. Is she not eating?" I demand to no one in particular. A knock sounds on the door stopping all conversation. Max steps out of the shadows and opens it, showing an older woman with gray hair and big blue eyes hidden behind bottle cap glasses. She looks around at us and she narrows her eyes as if we were doing something wrong.

"I saw so many cars here I felt the need to check on Nirvana. Is she all right? She hasn't answered any of my calls these last few days nor has she been over for dinner." The older woman peered inside glancing at everyone before falling on Seraphina and Rory. "My, have you two grown up. It's been ages."

"Mrs. Murphy. I didn't know you still lived next door," Layla said walking out of the kitchen.

"Well, of course I do. I've lived in my house for nearly forty years. Why change now?" Mrs. Murphy looks inside the house, her nose wrinkling at the sight. "That old bastard could've painted over the years."

"Nirvana is sleeping, Mrs. Murphy. She's had a long few days and is exhausted," Delaney says.

Mrs. Murphy nodded. "Poor child, I don't know how she could stay here after everything. I hear her walking back and forth all hours of the night. I don't think she's been taking those pills." She shakes her head sadly. "I wish she would've stayed away from here. She seemed so happy until she came back here. I saw her sister pulling up down the road on my way here." As if on cue the sound of a car door closing sounded, almost like a gunshot. Silencing the room of any talk or noise. The sounds of footsteps echo ominously as Aero gets to the door.

"Shit, shit," Layla says, jolting into movement before she rushed towards the door and opened it as Aero came up the stairs with her girlfriend behind her. I glance at the woman and notice her eyes are red rimmed and swollen.

"Aero," Layla starts, standing awkwardly.

"Hi Layla. Is Nirvana here?"

Layla sighs and replies, "She's sleeping. We had to give her something to help her."

Aero nods. "Good. Makes it easier for me to talk to you all." Her blue gaze lands on Mrs. Murphy. "Can we talk at your house, please?"

Mrs. Murphy's gray brows rose, but she nodded. "Follow me. Don't mind my mess. I haven't had company in a while."

I glance behind me at the door where Nirvana is sleeping, my heart aching for the woman on the other side. Max slaps my shoulder. "I'll stay here in case she wakes up. Just so she doesn't freak out."

I nod in thanks before I follow the women out towards the other house. The walk is a few minutes of crossing over tall grass and small bouts of rocks before we get to another smaller house. Panting from the exertion, Aero sits on the sofa with her girlfriend beside her, holding her hand tightly glancing at Nirvana's friends intensely.

"Can I get you some water, dear?" Mrs. Murphy asks her. Aero smiles politely and nods. The older woman gets her water and comes back, handing it to her.

"Nirvana told you?" she asks after she takes a drink.

"Yes. I'm so sorry, Aero," Delaney starts softly. Aero smiles sadly. There isn't much a person can say to someone who is dying. It wasn't something that could be soothed away with a few words. It didn't change the outcome and we all knew it.

"I came over for a reason. I'd like to talk to you. I don't have a lot of time, I didn't tell Vana but I've had two seizures since the first one. I know it's not going to be very long. But as her best friends I need you to look after her when I'm gone."

"Aero, why not get the treatment? I know it's not going to be the best, but you'll have more time with Nirvana, with Isola," Rory says gently. She pushes her curly hair over her shoulder and stares at Aero intently.

Aero shakes her head. "No. I don't want to be stuck in a bed for my last moments. I want to do this on my terms and my terms only. I won't have long but I'll be able to live these last moments to the fullest without having to be restrained to a bed." When she said it like that I understood where she stood, why she'd rather not have the treatment. But after seeing Nirvana break down the way she had I couldn't help but see the selfishness in it.

"What cancer do you have?" I ask.

Isola answered for her, "Glioblastoma. It's advanced."

"So even if you don't do the treatments there's still a chance you'd end up bedridden before you're ready?" I ask.

Aero looks me up and down, tilting her head slightly to the side. "I guess so. Only it's not being prolonged."

I nod. "But it's considered an aggressive cancer isn't it?"

"Are you a doctor?" Aero asks snarkily.

I snort. "No. But I do know basic anatomy and have some practice in medicine. You do know such a cancer without any form of treatment is debilitating not only for you but those around you? What of your sister? Your partner? They'll be the ones who take care of you in your last moments."

"Nirvana understands what's going to happen," Aero says softly.

I arch a brow. "Does she?"

Aero sighs. "I know it's selfish. And I know I'm asking a lot from her and that it's not fair to her or Isola. But either way I'm going to die. There's no stopping it. I want to enjoy what little time I have left before I begin to deteriorate. I want to know her friends are going to pick up the pieces of her broken heart. That she will be in good hands when I'm gone."

Leaning forward Delaney grabs her hand and asks, "Do you have a will? A beneficiary?"

"I do." Aero stands. "And once it's out there be aware that shit will hit the fan. I don't care that I die, everyone dies. But my sister took care of me, she loved me after everything. I won't do any less for her. I have your promise, I expect you to keep it."

She moves to the door stopping beside me. "You're a gruff person. Rude and blunt. I like you, and how you stick up for my sister. Just know whatever it is you are doing with her, or thinking about doing, if you hurt her in any way, shape, or form I'll haunt your ass until you die."

Chuckling, I shake my head. "I'm a friend. Helping a friend."

She stares me up and down. "I said Isola was just a friend too." With that she walks out. The women are talking and I don't understand anything that's being said. But I know after seeing Nirvana like that, so broken, huddled into herself in that cold cell, it did something to me. It made me want to try my best to protect her from anything. But I know there's no escaping death, there's only acceptance. The only thing is, will she accept it? Or will she let it destroy her?

Chapter 7

Nirvana

Groaning, I turn over in bed. My head is pounding and my eyes feel dry and swollen. God, what the hell happened? I blink and see that I'm in my childhood bedroom. I look over at the vacant twin size bed that my sister used to sleep in then it all comes back to me. Dying. Aero is dying. I was arrested for drunk driving even though I wasn't drunk. Fuck, Ravi and Sorrow saw me like that. Embarrassment slides through me as I sit up in the bed letting the cover fall to my waist. She's really dying and she's not getting treatment. She wants to get married, in two weeks. She wants to live her life, what's left of it anyway, and we have no idea how long until the timer runs out.

I curse to myself as tears burn the backs of my eyes. I wipe at them angrily, now wasn't the time to cry. No, I need to be there for Aero and do what she wants. I will do what she wants until the bitter end. I see my phone sitting on the depleted nightstand and grab it. When the screen lights up I see a text from my sister and Isola. Unlocking the phone I open the texts seeing the messages.

Aero: *She said yes!*

Isola: *June 18th 2 pm.*

I sigh, two weeks from now on the dot. I send a thumbs up and congratulate the two before leaving the messages and calling Cannon.

"Hello?" His deep voice answered on the second ring.

I sniff. "Hey, Can. I was wondering if you had a minute?"

There was a long pause. "Vana. My God, how are you doing? I heard about what happened with your sister. Fuck, I'm so sorry. And David arresting you was a dick move. God, I fucking hate that guy. When Mark told me that, I wanted to go find the bastard."

I nod even though he can't see me. "It's okay. He was just doing his job, I stopped in the middle of the highway. It could've turned bad," I pause, pushing my hair out of my face, "I, um, I need a favor."

"Anything," he says automatically. It brings a slight smile to my face. That was Cannon, always willing to help even if he didn't have to. He was there no matter what and I loved him all the more for it.

"Your aunt and uncle still have that ranch, right? The one that's on the outskirts of San Antonio?" I ask, picking at the loose threads on the comforter.

"Yes, it's not used anymore though. Why?"

"Aero's getting married in two weeks, and I need somewhere to do it. I can pay you."

Cannon sighs. "Sweetheart, you don't need to pay me. I'll be honored to have it there. I'll even provide the booze."

I sniff again, running my arm over my face. Trying not to cry, I clear my throat, "Thanks. Send me the address and I'll start the setup tomorrow."

"Of course," he says and pauses. "Nirvana, I'm here for you. If you need me, call me. I mean it."

I smile softly to myself. After years he still looks out for me. But nothing could fix this, I just had to grin and bear it. For now at least. "Thanks, Can. I will." I hung up and stood. I had so much to do and so little time. I glance around the room and see a small picture frame sitting crookedly on the dresser. I walk towards it and lift it seeing a picture of me and Aero with our parents. My father's face was stern, while our mother smiled widely. A part of me always wondered what the woman saw in him. I study his cold blue eyes and square jaw, his thick brown hair was thinning at the top and he wore his signature vestment even though we weren't at church.

I roll my eyes, he always wore the black and white garment even when he was home. I always thought it was weird to wear a religious robe outside of the church, almost as if he was trying to be God Himself, but I never said it to his face. It wouldn't have turned out well for me if I voiced any type of critique to him. Shaking my head, I put the picture back down. I turn away from the dresser and move towards the closet and open it to see the one piece of clothing that still hung there.

My mother's wedding dress. It's the only thing she left behind when she ran away, leaving Aero and me in our father's care. I remember missing her when she left and taking this from their closet. I pull it down and set it on the bed, slowly opening the garment bag to show the plastic covered dress. The puffy sleeves seemed overly big in the bag and the small amount of lace looked a little too worn to be sewn together. But I always loved this dress, so did Aero. She always said if she got married she'd want to wear Mom's dress.

I swallow hard and peel back the plastic, pulling the dress

from the bag, and letting it unravel on the bed. The smell of dust and moth balls was heavy in the air but I didn't care. This was the one thing that held our mother to us. This piece of silk and lace. It held what little memory we had of her. I puff out the sleeves more, touching the cool silk and lace. I straighten out the neckline, running reverent fingers over the tulle and beaded strap that connects around the neck. Once I'm done straightening it out I take a quick picture and text it to Aero who reads it right away sending crying emojis.

Me: *Does this mean you want to wear it?*

Aero: *Duh. But I kind of want it black.*

Me: *I can dye it.*

Aero: *Fuck it, do it. Thanks Vana.*

Me: *Anything for you.*

I lock my phone, sparing the dress one last glance before I move towards the bathroom. The sound of my alarm going off stops me. I look and see it's time for my medication but I ignore it. There's more important things to worry about, like planning a wedding and a funeral. The thought causes my heart to clench in my chest, but I ignore it. I'd rather put those thoughts on the back burner than face them right now. So that's exactly what I do as I head to the bathroom and do my business. Once done, I head to the living room where I pull up short when I see Ravi sitting on the couch scrolling through his phone.

"What are you doing here?" I ask.

He glances up, his earthy green eyes assessing me slowly. "You're awake." He stands and motions towards the kitchen. "You need to eat."

I arch a brow waiting for him to answer my question but he doesn't, he just moves past me towards the other room. When I don't immediately follow him, he stops and stares at me. Groaning inside my head I follow him.

"Ravi," I start.

"Layla made you some cupcakes," he interrupts.

"What?" I say confused. "How long was I asleep?"

Ravi shrugs. "Twelve hours. You needed the rest." He moves towards the fridge and pulls out some tupperware and a cake box. I don't say anything as I watch him move through the tiny kitchen putting food on a plate. I don't remember the last time I ate a real meal and my stomach cramps from hunger. He puts the food in the old microwave which is surprisingly clean and I'm even more surprised that it even works, before turning to me.

"How do you feel?"

I look at him for a moment. "Fine. Slight headache but nothing I can't handle." He studies me longer than I would've liked but eventually he nods. I'm not used to being around the men. Even though they are Sorrow's friends I try not to be around them, unsure of how to react to them. Not that they give me bad vibes, but the thought of getting to know more people makes me uncomfortable, to talk to them and put on a facade makes me want to gouge my eyes out. So I try not to be around them.

But these last few days it seems like they are multiplying and I'm not sure on how to handle it. Hell, I don't even think I've had a real conversation with Sorrow, yet here I am with Ravi, in the same house as me.

Shaking off those thoughts I ask again, "Why are you here?"

The microwave dings, drawing Ravi's attention away from me. He turns and pulls the plate out. "Didn't want you to be alone."

That makes my heart pound a little bit. "I'm fine."

Ravi nods. "I know." He goes to the cabinet and pulls out a bottle of Tylenol and takes out two white pills and holds them out to me.

I gaze at them, then him.

"It's to get rid of your headache," he says.

"I'm aware of what they are."

He pins me with a pointed stare, and says, "So take them and eat."

Sighing, I grab the pills and take the bottle of water he offers.He watches as I put the pills in my mouth, swallowing with a mouthful of water. "Thanks," I mutter. He just nods. I stand there awkwardly.

"Eat."

I roll my eyes, grab the plate and head back to the den and sit picking at what looks like fish and rice. I poke it with the fork ignoring the fact that Ravi is still in the house, leaning against the wall watching me.

"You have to actually put it on the fork and eat it, Nirvana."

I glare at the plate. "You're pretty bossy for a virtual stranger."

Ravi snorts, "A stranger implies just meeting. I've been in your life for well over a year now."

I stare up at him. "Yet this is the first time we've been alone together. So that still means you're a stranger." Except when he was in my house a few days ago.

"Or I have a heavy respect for your boundaries," he counters.

I scoff, "I don't have boundaries."

"You do. You never made an effort to converse with any of us unless absolutely necessary. That was a boundary you put in place. I won't force my presence on a woman who clearly doesn't want it," he explains.

I sit back against the old couch watching him. He meets my eyes head on before he makes a move near me. "This doesn't look like you're respecting my boundaries now," I point out.

"That's because you don't need to be alone right now," he counters.

I stare at him with wide eyes, unmoving as he crouches low in front of me. "I have the girls. Besides, I'm a grown woman and can take care of myself."

Ravi shakes his head and grabs the plate, saying, "Tell that to the bruises still on your throat and lack of sleep and nourishment." I open my mouth to argue but he stops me with a stern look. "Shut up and let me help you." I don't move as he cuts up the fish and scoops up a bit of it with the rice and holds it out. I still, unsure of what to do. He gazes at me expectantly. Swallowing, I lean forward and take the proffered bite. I chew slowly savoring the unexpected flavor of the fish, lemon with a hint of spice.

"Good?" he asks. I nod and take another bite. I hum softly and take the plate back and eat in silence. He watches me as if worried I won't eat it which is strange when no one, especially a man, has cared before. Well, aside from the girls, but this felt different than them. More intimate. I study him as I eat, his hair is longer than I remembered from the first time I met him, thick and light brown with a bit of gray in it. His eyes are a dark green with a little brown in them covered by thick lashes that many women would kill for.

His jaw is strong and chiseled with a bit of a beard on it and his skin is tan as if he works outside a lot, which I guess he does as he's a firefighter. He has a muscular lean build and is tall. He's a complete package so why is he here with a random woman?

When I finish my meal I set the plate to the side. "You know you don't have to babysit me."

His mouth tilts up slightly. "I wouldn't call it babysitting. More like a concerned acquaintance."

I snort and lean back into the stiff cushions. "Don't you have work or something heroic to do?"

"Nah, I'm on vacation."

"This doesn't look like a very exciting vacation for you. I suggest the Bahamas or France. That way you're not stuck with a sad woman for the evening," I say.

Ravi stands and grabs the plate. "I've been to France, can't say I was impressed."

"Well, I kind of have things to do..." I hedge suddenly, uncertain of what to do.

Ravi puts the plate in the sink and runs water over it. "I can help."

"Why would you want to help me?"

He shrugs. "It's not like I have anything else to do."

I groan, so much for doing this by myself. "Fine. Let's go."

"You do realize it's two in the morning, right?" he asks.

I shrug. "It's the perfect time to get things done. You decided to be a babysitter so you have to go along with me or go home. It's your choice." He thinks about it for a moment before replying, "Fine, but I'm driving. Spencer and Caden got your car out of impound for you."

I tense, but don't respond. It was strange having people around me. But I know it's to help Aero and I'd do anything for her.

Chapter 8

RAVI

I didn't think this through. After we left Mrs. Murphy's house I sent them away, offering to stay until she woke up. I didn't anticipate staying so long. But when I saw her standing in the living room her eyes puffy and red rimmed from crying I couldn't leave. So I fed her and gave her her medicine after she said her head hurt. Her alarm went off and she came out of the room and I couldn't bring myself to leave her after seeing how absolutely alone she looked.

So here I was, a self designated babysitter walking down the craft section in a 24/7 Walmart looking at fabric dyes.

"Nirvana, why do you need fabric dye?" I ask as she puts a few bottles of black and purple dye into the cart. We've been in the same spot for nearly thirty minutes. We've already had two workers ask us if we needed help and I had to stand closer than probably necessary when a man got too close to Nirvana.

"Have to dye the wedding dress for Aero," she mutters,

putting in some streamers and other random decorations into the cart. She glances at the cart then wrinkles her nose. "Have you ever been to a wedding?" she asks, gazing up at me with her big wide eyes.

I shrug. "My grandmother's when I was like ten."

"Well that hardly helps," she says sarcastically, moving down the aisles putting some foam balls and fake flowers into the cart.

"So Aero is getting married," I say conversationally. I wonder briefly if Nirvana would be pissed if she finds out what I said to her sister. A part of me wants to tell her but then I don't want to put more pressure on her than she already has. So I keep quiet, standing off to the side watching her pick decorations and then putting them back.

Nirvana nods, pushing her blonde hair from her face, "In two weeks. So I have to figure out how to do it."

I whistle. "That's soon." When she turns I take what she puts back and put it in the cart. There's no use in putting it back if she may need it.

Nirvana has a rueful smirk on her face as she turns away, muttering under her breath, "For a normal person, for a dying woman it's far away."

"I guess you have a point. What can I do to help?"

Nirvana watches me silently then turns away, her jaw clenching. "I don't... I don't know what to do. Like the set up."

"We can figure something out while the dye is setting in." She nods and walks on, her back stiff.

I stop her with a gentle hand on her shoulder. "Hey, you don't have to do this alone. You know that right?"

She nods. "I know."

"So let us help." Her head bobs again and she walks forward. I take out my phone and send a quick group text to the others explaining the situation.

Me: *Need help ASAP.*

Caden: *Is this a code red or can it wait until business hours? I have a girl in my bed as we speak.*

Sam: *Why the hell would you answer the phone when you're with someone, Cade?*

Caden: *Relax Father Celibate, it's not like she's riding my dick as I type. I have some manners.*

Max: *If you answer the phone while a woman is riding you something is seriously wrong with you.*

Me: *For fuck's sake! Can you focus please?*

Spencer: *You do realize it is nearing four in the morning, yes?*

Caden: *Jesus, when did you become an old man Spence?*

Spencer: *Fuck you.*

Caden: *Sorry, not my type.*

Sorrow: *I swear to God if you dumb fucks don't go to bed I will personally shoot each of you in the dick.*

Sam: *Geez, someone is cranky.*

Sorrow: *It's been a long night. Now why the spam messages?*

Me: *Need help planning a wedding.*

Sorrow: *You texted this early for a goddamn wedding?*

Me: *It's in two weeks and for a dead woman walking. Yes, I messaged you at this time. Now, put on your big girl panties, get out of bed and come help Nirvana and me plan a wedding.*

Spencer: *You're still with Nirvana?*

The question hangs between us and I watch as several message bubbles pop up and disappear. Probably wondering why the fuck I cared so much. Shit, I was wondering the same thing. Sighing I turn from the messages and glance at Nirvana who is picking up different decorations before putting them down. I turn back to my phone sighing in frustration.

Me: *Don't ask questions, not right now. Just... come help.*

Drew: *Give me thirty minutes.*

That's all I need. Even if they tease me, or complain I

know these men will help. No matter what, no matter when they'll have my back, and that means they'll be there for Nirvana. I shove my phone in my back pocket and head over towards Nirvana, grabbing the decorations she put back and tossing them in the cart.

"Let's head back, we can make a plan," I say, grabbing the cart from her.

"Okay. I just need to get a big pot and a large spoon." I nod and follow her to the pots. It doesn't take long before we are at the check out and getting everything. Nirvana sees the stuff she put back up and arches a brow at me. I just shrug. She picked it up so she must've liked it for a reason. Even if I don't know what everything is, nor do I ask, I just pull out my wallet and pay.

"Ravi, I can pay," Nirvana says with exasperation.

"I'm aware," I say and place my card in the chip reader waiting for the payment to process before grabbing the bags. Nirvana sighs and follows after me.

"I'll pay you back," she murmurs.

"Consider it a gift," I respond, heading to the Jeep we took.

Nirvana stops beside me. "Why, because my sister is dying? I don't need charity, Ravi."

I put the bags in the backseat and turn to her. "No. Because I was doing something nice."

"Well don't," she replies, placing her hands on her hips letting the bags hit her legs.

I snorted, taking the bags from her, "Don't tell me what to do, pixie."

"What did you call me?" she demands.

I stand in front of her, gazing down at her. "I called you pixie. Do you have a problem with that?"

"Yes! It's silly and juvenile."

Humming under my breath I push her hair behind her

ear. "Yeah, maybe you're right. It's not as fitting. Maybe Tinker Bell." She opens her mouth to argue but I shake my head, "No, no that's not right either. I think Tinker hell works better. Yeah. That's the one. Tinker hell."

Her face turns red and her fists clench at her sides, giving me the chance to push her a little more. "I bought it for you so just say thank you. Sometimes people do nice things for people. There's not a catch, it's not charity, nor do I expect you to pay me back. Yes, you're in a terrible situation and I sympathize and want to help to make it easier for you, but that doesn't mean I want to give charity or expect something in return."

She looks confused. "Why?"

"Fuck if I know," I answer. And I didn't know. This is the longest I've spent with Nirvana in all the time I've known her and it's been a total of a few hours in two days. Shaking my head I motion her to get in the Jeep. She hesitates slightly but goes to the passenger side and climbs in. The drive back to the house is silent, both of us lost in thought. When I pull up to the house the others are already there.

"What's everyone doing here?" Nirvana asks.

"Told you it's okay to ask for help. Two weeks isn't long for one person to plan a wedding."

Nirvana peers at me, her blue eyes glassy. She turns away quickly, clearing her throat. "Thanks, Ravi."

"Of course," I reply softly.

Chapter 9

Nirvana

I was still reeling from Ravi as I climbed out of the Jeep and stood still looking off into the distance, my heart heavy and empty, so tired both mentally and physically. But somehow he made me feel a little better. A little less alone. Not that it took away all my feelings, not all the way because it still feels like everything is crashing around me. On such short notice, my life has been altered for all time and somehow an unlikely friendship came from it. I turn my head as Ravi grabs the bags and see Caden and Sorrow come off the porch to help him. Squaring my shoulders I climb up the steps and unlock the door and stop when I see Isola sitting in the dark. I jump back startled, nearly falling but Ravi steadies me. His touch was like electricity going through me and that scared me more than Isola's sudden appearance in the darkened living room.

"Is?" I say shocked, slowly moving away from Ravi and the way his touch made me feel.

"Hey, Vana, I um, I noticed you weren't here so I waited," she stammers, looking past me to the men. Shuffling on her feet awkwardly.

"Why didn't you let them in? It's kind of strange to be sitting in the dark," I reply, turning on the lamp by the door.

Isola laughs weakly. "I have to talk to you. About Aero." I sigh and point to the men to put the stuff on the counter. I'm suddenly too tired to do anything more, but I knew I had to get started.

"Okay so talk," I start, pulling out the big pot I got to dye the dress, turning my back on Isola.

"Aero wants your father at the wedding, and your mother." I stop, my blood chilling. Just the thought of being anywhere near that man again makes my skin crawl. It makes the acid in my stomach churn to the point I feel like I'm going to be sick over and over again. A cold sweat breaks out on my skin and my heart is pounding so fast I fear it's one beat away from jumping out of my chest.

I don't respond right away, aware of the others watching us. "Where's Delaney?" I say, instead of answering her. I needed to process Isola's words for a second.

Sorrow clears his throat behind me and says, "Getting coffee and medicine."

"Is she sick?" I ask walking to the sink to fill the pot with water. There, pretend that the woman isn't even here. Then maybe she'll leave.

"Nirvana, please, can't you put your differences to the side for your sister?" Isola begs. Damn, no such luck but then her words register in my brain.

I slap the tap off and slam the pot down in the sink.

"I love my sister, but he won't show up. Even if she is dying," I say. These weren't simple "differences", it was the way he destroyed my life. How he physically harmed me. Let other people harm me. But I wouldn't tell her that. It wasn't her business. I know she loves Aero, and I'll be eternally grateful to her for that. But I can't, I can't even think about my father.

"Why?" Isola asks.

I sigh, pinching the bridge of my nose trying to find the words. I breathe deeply before speaking, "Because I'll be there, and I'll be damned if I miss her wedding for that son-of-a-bitch." That and the fact that her father doesn't respect same sex marriage and would rather walk on hot coals than see his daughter with a woman. I'd be damned if my sister's day was ruined because of his closed minded views.

"Nirvana, please."

"My answer is no," I snap. Her dark eyes widen and I swallow hard before adding, "Father Bridges isn't like your parents. He won't want to be there anyway," I say as gently as possible. But even that's gruffer than it should be.

Isola sighs but doesn't respond because the door opens and the others come in.

"Can you at least think about it? For Aero's sake," she whispers. I stare at the water in the pot, wondering if I should suck it up and invite him. But I can't see him. I haven't seen the man since that fateful night when I was fourteen. Even when I came back he never looked me in the eye, he didn't speak to me. Anything and everything went through my stepmother, leaving me a ghost in my own home.

It was torture, after the first few months I stopped trying to talk to him. I wonder if Aero remembers those years, but she was always the apple of our father's eye. So I guess it didn't really matter.

"Isola, please go home. Make sure Aero is fine. I'll figure it out."

"It's what she wants, Vana. We don't have much time, this is all she asks." I nod, my heart breaking for the woman in front of me.

With one last sigh she leaves the house, leaving me stuck in my own head. "Vana?" Layla says behind me.

I turn to her, forcing a smile, glad the others aren't in there anymore. "Hey."

"Are you all right?" she asks, her eyes full of concern.

I nod. "Never better. I have to dye the dress. I have thirteen days to pull this off."

"We'll be here, you know that right?"

I nod, I do know that. But how am I going to tell her that I can't be anywhere near my father without wanting to vomit? How can I tell them why he hates me? Or the fact that Aero wanting him there makes me feel betrayed in a way that hurts me more than the current circumstances.

Layla walks up to me and wraps her arms around me. I sink into her, sighing softly. "I'm scared, La. So scared."

"I know. I know you are." Her hand rubs gentle circles on my back.

"Everything feels like a ticking clock. A timer that's running out faster than I can keep up. I haven't seen her since the doctor told us. I don't want to see her, to see her slip away from me."

"Sweetheart, listen to me, it's going to be hard. I know it will be, but you won't be alone."

It's what Ravi told me, something I didn't believe because even if they are here for me they can't stop the thoughts that run rapidly in my mind.

"Thank you," I whisper instead, pulling away slightly.

"What do you need right now?" she asks, brushing her red hair from her face.

"Um, I need the dress. It's on the bed." Layla nods, sending me a smile of encouragement. I force my own and lift the pot from the sink and move it to the small stove top. I turn it on and wait for it to heat up.

I'm lost in thought when a coffee cup is set in front of

me. I glance at it before turning to Delaney who offers a gentle smile.

"How are you?" I ask.

"I'm okay. What about you? I heard Isola asked about Father Bridges."

I groan and pick up the coffee cup, sipping the rich flavor of carmel and rich coffee beans. "Apparently Aero wants him there."

Delaney scoffs and leans her hip against the counter. "I hope you said no."

I smirk. "Of course I did."

Delaney puts her head on my shoulder, her fingers curling through mine. "Can I tell you something?"

"Of course. You know you can," I reply.

"You're the reason I went into therapy."

I peer at her and laugh. "What are you talking about?"

"You remember what happened in school, with Marcy? You came home and I followed you."

I roll my eyes. "Yes, you're very persistent."

She laughs. "I have to be. You're all very stubborn women."

I laugh with her. "And you happen to have seven stubborn men to deal with when you decided to fall for the big one."

Delaney lightly slaps my arm and says, "Hush. They're not stubborn." I arch a brow at her and she shrugs. "Okay they may be a little stubborn but it's nothing I can't handle," she pauses. "But you gave me the courage to find what I was passionate to do. To help people."

I sigh, staring up at the ceiling. "Did Aero talk to you or something?" I ask.

She nods. "She did. She made us promise we'd look after you once she's gone."

Shaking my head, I scoff. Of course she did. Here she

was dying and yet she worried about me. As if I were dying. "I won't go crazy, Laneybug, if that's what you're worried about," I say. Not any more than I felt like I already was, that is.

"Never thought you would. I just want you to know."

I laugh softly. "I don't need another pep-talk, Lane. This is the third one today and it's not even seven in the morning."

Delaney laughed with me. "Who else gave you pep talks, that's my thing?"

"Layla and Ravi."

Her eyes widened. "Ravi?"

For some reason heat rises on my cheeks. "Yeah. He was here when I woke up and we went shopping to get some stuff."

She hums and watches me closely for a moment before sending a small smile my way. "Well, let's get to planning." Layla walks into the kitchen holding my mother's dress. I turn away from Delaney's astute stare, begin pouring the dye in the pot, and take the dress from Layla.

"This is a beautiful dress," Layla comments.

"It was my mother's," I mutter distractedly as I dunk the dress in the pot. "I think I should've gotten a bigger pot."

"I'm sure we can figure this out. Let's see if there's a bin or something," Delaney suggests.

"Check the backroom. There might be one in there or something. Ask one of the guys to help you. There might be a ton of shit in there that might be too heavy."

They nod and head out leaving me alone to figure out the dress and plan the next few weeks. The creak of the house makes it feel like it once did, alive. I was aware of everyone going through the small rooms. Of Caden and Max working in the bathroom to fix that awful shower handle that broke.

To Sam and Rory straightening up the living room together. Sera and Ophelia weren't here because Ophelia had work and Sera had Darcy. I saw Ravi and Sorrow working on the floor and fixing a cracked tile. I watched the way Ravi's back flexed every time he moved. Delaney went up to them and I saw Ravi glance up and nod, following her and Sorrow down the hall. Hopefully looking for that bin. I don't know if they'll find one, so I go to my bedroom in search of one, hoping these next few weeks go somewhat smoothly. Or as smooth as they can go given the circumstances. I go into the room and search under the beds and see a nearly empty clear bin under Aero's bed.

Reaching under the bed I pull it free, grunting when it got stuck on the bedpost. I pull it harder and groan when I fall on my ass sending the contents of the bin onto the floor. Cursing, I quickly put it all back in only to stop when I saw it was old medical records. *My* old medical records. From when I was sent to the treatment camps. I lift up the old yellowed folder and flip through it seeing the outline of my treatment.

Reparative Therapy.

Aversion Therapy: When a patient is given therapy to rid themselves of a less than desirable habit. A harmful habit.

ECT (Electroconvulsive therapy): When paired with the negative effects of same sex intercourse it will lead the patient away from such desires.

Imagery: Patient must be introduced to the normalcy of a heterosexual relationship.

Patient's guardian wants patient to experience a relationship between a woman and a man.

. . .

Nausea filled me as I read the notes that were written in the margins of the records. Why did Aero have this? Slamming the folder shut I stuff it under the mattress, and stand up quickly leaving the room to go outside and clean the bin. To breathe in fresh air that wasn't coated with dust and the old memories of my time in that camp. To breathe away the betrayal I suddenly felt.

Chapter 10

RAVI

I take the spackle Sorrow holds out to me and try to fit a piece of wood into the cracked tile until the floors can be ripped up and redone. I don't know if Nirvana plans to stay here, but I'd make it at least decently livable for her.

"So you're going to help her plan a wedding?" Sorrow asks, studying me.

"No. I said I'd help her wherever she needed me. It just so happens to involve a wedding."

He snorts. "What about when you get back to work?"

"I'll make time," I grit out.

Soft footsteps sound behind us. "Can you come help me find a bin?" Delaney asks me and Sorrow, drawing me away from our conversation.

"Sure," I say, following her down the hall glancing at Nirvana, our gazes clash and she turns away quickly. I sigh and walk behind Delaney, Sorrow falling into step with us.

"You've been friendly lately," she begins, walking into a

room which was covered in a thin sheet of dust. I wave a hand in front of my face, coughing slightly.

"I'm normally a friendly guy," I say.

Sorrow scoffs, earning a glare from me as Delaney starts searching around the room. "What are you looking for, bright eyes?" Sorrow asks his fiancée. I shake my head at him. Of course he'd change his tune when it comes to his woman. It was comical in a way. Seeing this big, scary man practically melt for this woman.

"A bin big enough for the dress. The pot Nirvana got isn't big enough," Delaney said, pulling open the wardrobe door. She jumped back as a book came falling from the top shelf. It was like a chain reaction and stuff just came falling from the closet. Sorrow grabbed Delaney and pulled her behind him so she wasn't harmed in the sudden rush of books falling.

Dust surrounded us and caused us to cough.

"What the fuck is this?" Sorrow coughed, waving a hand in front of his face.

"Father Bridges is a preacher or pastor. I always get the two confused. But I didn't think he'd have so many Bibles," Delaney said, picking up one of the books that fell open. Each Bible was highlighted to a specific verse.

"They're all the same verses," Sorrow muttered.

I pick up a bottle and grimace when I see it half empty with what looked like water. "Is this holy water?" I ask.

Delaney closed the Bible. "Whatever this is don't mention it to anyone. Especially Nirvana. She's going through a lot as is, so let's find the bin and get the hell out of this room. Makes me feel like I'm in some weird shrine to this man."

Shaking my head I make a path and dig in the closet, pushing past old clothing and sagging boxes until I find a plastic tub. I dump its contents out and grab it. "We might need to rinse it before putting a dress in it."

"There's a hose out back. When you're done bring it in. Rory!" Delaney called loudly, making both Sorrow and me wince.

"Jesus, give a warning next time, Lane," I say.

"Sorry," she apologizes as Rory comes into the room.

"What's up?" Rory asks, glancing down at the Bibles and half empty bottles of holy water. "Are you performing an exorcism?"

"Ha ha, so funny. No, I need you to find some towels, a bottle of some type of alcohol and the decorations. We have a few weeks and I have a feeling it's going to be a tough few weeks. Whatever happens, I don't want Nirvana to be left alone for too long," Delaney says.

"Want me to bring Louise? She has this calming presence about her and Nirvana has always been able to be herself around her," Rory suggests. I glance at Sorrow who just shrugs, as if to say she runs the show.

Delaney thinks for a moment, biting her bottom lip in thought before nodding. "It might help. I, um, did some research on this type of cancer. It won't be long before Aero turns into a different person. I think it's best if we work as fast and efficiently as possible."

"All right you got it. Sera is going to be here after she brings Darcy to school. Cannon sent the address to Layla and I have already started paperwork for the wedding certificate."

"Good. Let's get this done." Delaney bends down and begins putting the books back in the closet and I take my leave to go to the back of the house leading to the backdoor where the hose is.

I walk through tall grass and find the tangle of green hose. Sighing I place the bin down so I can unwind it. For it being so early it is already starting to swelter outside making it almost unbearable. Cursing under my breath I roll up my sleeves.

"What are you doing?" a voice sounds behind me. I turn and see Nirvana sitting against a tree. Her head pressing against the bark watching me. Her voice was devoid of any emotion and colder than it was earlier.

"I thought you were inside," I say instead of answering, not dwelling on it much. It wasn't my business.

"I was. I brought the dress out here in that bin, I'm just waiting." I look at the bin she was pointing to and gave a self-mocking laugh.

"Shit, I guess I took too long finding my own bin." She gave a small smile, some of that cold shifting slightly, and pointed to the spot beside her. Nodding my head, I drop the bin and walk towards her. She looks up at me, motioning with a tilt of her chin to sit down. I do and we sit in silence watching the dusky sky turn to a bright orange and red as the sun rises.

"It's quiet back here," I mutter.

Nirvana looks around us. "Yeah, it is. The sunrise is always better from over here."

I hum under my breath. "How are you?"

"Please don't ask me that. I don't have an answer. Everything is so bleak right now. I just want this all to end." At least she's honest, most people would put on a front. But nothing about this woman was ordinary. She continued to surprise me at every turn. Maybe that's why I suddenly felt so drawn to her.

"Your friends will handle it well," I start, not turning to her, "Delaney already has plans to help you better."

Nirvana laughs. "Delaney has always been the most organized of us."

I huff out a short laugh. "Sorrow, too. He always kept us in line whenever we were in the field."

"What was that like?"

I glance at her briefly before looking off into the distance. "What? Being in the field or Sorrow being organized?"

"Both, I guess."

"It was exhausting and scary at times. But it's what we trained for. To save people," I explain.

"Were you scared?" she asks softly.

I swallow hard. "Every fucking day. But we did what we had to do."

"What were you like?"

Shrugging, I say, "I don't know. I did my job. I rescued those who needed to be rescued. I killed those that needed to be killed. I followed orders. I saved people just like the others."

She hums. "Is that what you're trying to do here, Ravi? Save me?"

I shake my head. "No. I don't believe you need it."

Her head tilts to the side as she watches me. "Why's that?"

I shrug. "You'd have to want to be saved for one."

"And you don't think I do?"

I turn to her and say, "I believe you're in denial. No one can be saved unless they want it. Otherwise you're just wasting your time. I believe, right now, you're stressed, tired, probably hungry. But not in need of saving. At least not yet."

Her lips tilt up slightly. "Even if I wanted it, I don't think I'd survive long enough to be saved." Her words cause my heart to race as she stands up, dusting off her pants before walking away from me. I stand too, watching her. Her cryptic words swirled in my head making it hard to think. What did she mean by that?

Chapter 11

Nirvana

Sighing softly to myself I climb out of my Jeep, and grab the garment before I head towards Aero's apartment. It's been a few days since I dyed the dress and decorating is well under way. I haven't seen my sister but I've talked to her by text keeping her updated. I wasn't sure how to talk to her in person if I'm being honest. After finding that folder I wasn't sure what to say to her. Or if I should say anything at all. There was just so much going on. With the help of everyone things have been getting done a lot faster, and I've never been so grateful for the group of friends I have behind me.

My only problem is Ravi. Well, not entirely, I had that folder to worry about and Aero. But mainly it was Ravi. Not that he's done anything wrong, but I can't get him out of my head. He's becoming a distraction I can't afford and it's becoming a problem. Our talk had me seeing him differently. It gave me a small glimpse of him. Of the silent broody man who stood in the corner. I shake my head, shaking away any thought of Ravi. I had to be present today with Aero before heading to Cannon's aunt's ranch to set up some more. I flip over my keychain and find Aero's house key to let myself in.

When I walk inside, I stop and take in the apartment. The usually pristine space is now messy with take-out boxes on the floor and clothes strewn all over the place.

"Aero?" I call out. There's no answer. Worry slides through me as I rush deeper into her apartment. I don't see her anywhere, and then I hear loud retching in the bathroom. I set the garment bag on the couch and walk towards the bathroom where Aero is currently hunched over the toilet vomiting. I rush forward and pull her hair out of her way, grimacing slightly when my hand touches remnants of vomit in her dark blonde hair.

"Go away," Aero groans. I ignore her and smooth out her hair, pressing the back of my hand to her warm head. "I said go away!" she yells now, moving away from me, ripping her hair from my hand.

"Aero, I'm just trying to help," I say calmly.

Aero doesn't look at me as she stands slowly, her hands gripping the edge of the sink for better balance. I close the toilet lid and flush it hoping it will take away the worst of the smell in the room.

"I don't want you here!" I wince at the venom in her tone, but try not to react. It doesn't stop the slight sting to my heart. Or the tears that want to fall. But I push it all down.

"I know," I whisper.

"Then go away! Just go away! I don't want you seeing me like this." The last word ends on a choked sob. I turn away from her and turn on the shower, making it lukewarm instead of hot.

"Didn't you hear me? I said get out. Get out!" Aero yells, but again I ignore her. I grab her hand and she fights me but I don't care. At the moment I'm stronger than her. I step into the shower, pulling her with me. She screams and fights, but I wrap my arms around her.

"Stop it!" Aero shouts, but I already have her in the shower, letting the water pound down on both of us. Her head thrashes side to side almost hitting me in the face, but I simply angle my head away, letting the water pelt me in the face.

"You stink. Showering will do you a world of good. So take off this god-awful track suit and let me wash the vomit out of your hair," I say sternly.

"Fuck you! I hate you! Let me go!" she shouts, pushing weakly against my chest. I try to ignore her words, try to let them roll off my back knowing it's not her real words. That she's deteriorating before my eyes. Faster than I anticipated, I thought it would be a gradual process, something that would be slow and give us time to process everything, but it wasn't. I wanted to grieve her loss but I can't because I know she needs me, even with her claims of hating me. So I just grab her shirt and pull it off before tossing it to the side. Her nails scratch into my skin as I turn around, causing me to wince. Ignoring the stinging pain, I grab the shampoo and squirt a bit in my hand before pulling her head down and lathering her thinning tresses.

"Stop fighting me, Aero!" I snap, at my wit's end.

She pushes at me again but it's a feeble attempt that stops when I rub my fingers against her skull in firm circles. All the fight has left her now, and she sags against me slowly sinking to the shower floor. I smooth the shampoo through her hair, being careful of the tangles as I slowly and gently clean the vomit and spittle from it.

When she finally calms I tilt her head back. "Lean your head back," I whisper gently. Aero does as I say and leans her head under the spray. I run my fingers through it sighing softly as I wash away the soap before grabbing the conditioner and repeating the process. Throughout the process Aero is silent, no longer fighting me. The only sound in the bathroom was the sound of the water running and Aero's shallow breathing. "You're going to have to help me finish washing you," I say once I'm done with her hair.

"I got it. Thank you," she responds. I nod slowly and help her stand, ignoring my soggy clothes. I climb out of the tub and stand beside it in case Aero needs help. Her movements are jerky and off balance but she manages to take off her wet pants and wash her body. Once she's finished I turn off the water and help her out, wrapping a towel around her.

"I got the dress for you," I say, drying off her body before moving to the adjoining room to get her some fresh clothes.

"Is it black now?" she asks, some of her bright personality seeping back into her. It was startling how fast her personality seemed to change, going from angry and then back to normal.

I nod, a small smile forming on my mouth. "Of course."

"Thanks, Van. I can't wait to see it." I go to the dresser and find some sleep shorts and a large t-shirt for her and make my way towards her. I kneel and help her dress. She presses her hand into my shoulder as I lift one leg to slide the shorts onto her. When she's dressed we move towards the living room. I move the garment bag so Aero can lay on the couch. I unzip the bag and show Aero the dress. Her face brightens as she sees it.

"I love it!" she exclaims. I smile and close it, trying not to notice the way her cheeks are sunken in and how her eyes hold dark bags under them. Her skin was pallid and no longer full of life as it once was.

I look away, clearing my throat from the sudden thickness, and say, "I'm glad you like it." I zip up the garment bag and set it down gently trying to compose myself before turning back towards my sister. But it was harder than I thought it would be.

"Vana?" Aero said behind me. I closed my eyes and took a deep breath before turning to her.

"Yes?"

"Are we okay?" she asked.

"I…" I stop talking as a lump forms in my throat. I have to swallow a few times before I am able to speak. "Of course we are." But I don't know if we are. My mind goes back to that folder and the reason why she has it, and hasn't told me about it. I'm still angry that she decided against the treatments.

"Then why can't you look at me?" Her voice is hoarse and it tears me up inside.

I wave a hand at her, my fingers shaking. "It's hard. To look at you like this," I whisper brokenly.

"I can't help it. I'm sick, Vana."

I nod. "I know, I know that. But it doesn't mean it's any easier. It hurts to see you like this."

Aero narrows her eyes at me. "Like what?"

I throw my hands up. "Dying! It hurts to see you fucking dying!" I shout. "You're fucking dying, Aero! Do you honestly think I'd want to watch you slowly die in front of me?"

Aero's eyes soften and she stands on shaky limbs, taking careful steps until she's in front of me and her skinny arms are surrounding me. "I know. I know you're scared but it will be okay," she whispers, running shaky fingers over the back of my head.

"I don't want you to go," I cry. "It's not fair."

Aero swallows. "It's life, baby girl. We can't stop it no matter how hard we want to."

I nod, burying my face in her neck, taking in her flowery

scent. A scent that I'll always connect with her. "I can't lose you."

Aero lifts my face, her cold hands framing my cheeks as she looks at me intensely. "You can. It will be okay. You'll go on and be happy." I'm already shaking my head, tears running down my face in earnest. "Yes, you can. Once I'm gone you get one month. Only one month of mourning, Nirvana. Then you have to let me go. You have to live your life, find a partner who loves you the way you deserve."

Her words make me cry harder. "I can't! Don't you see that?"

She smiles sadly and says, "You can and you will. I've got everything planned, all you have to do is bury me and move on."

I shake my head and step away, my chest tightening. "Don't you hear yourself? Why are you talking about it like it's easy? It's not easy! I can't mourn you for a month and then forget it as if it's better! It won't be better!"

"You have no other choice, Nirvana," Aero says.

"Yes, because you took it from me! You made these decisions without even talking to me!" I shout, my tears blurring my vision more and more making my sister nothing more than a hazy figure.

"I don't want to put it off! I won't get better! Doing the stupid treatment only prolongs it!"

"It would've given us more time! I need more time!" I couldn't picture a life when she wasn't in it. Where she was just some distant memory that would fade over time. And she would fade, leaving me wondering what she sounds like when she laughs, what inside jokes we have. But once she's gone it's gone. No more late night calls, no more random spa days. I'll be alone. All alone.

I shake my head and walk towards the door. "Where are you going, Nirvana?" she demands.

I don't respond. I don't know how to. All I know right now is that I don't want to think about this. I want to forget just for a little while. I want to pretend that nothing has changed, that I'll still have my sister and we will still be there for one another.

I climbed into the Jeep and pulled away from my sister's apartment and headed to the one place I needed to be right now. To be able to finally forget what is happening around me. Nothing says getting over the thought of impending death like getting plastered in the middle of the day.

Chapter 12

Nirvana

I walk into the empty club and make my way towards the bar where Cannon is cleaning some glasses. "We're closed," he calls out without lifting his head.

"I know," I responded. He looks up and his dark eyes widen.

"What the hell happened to you?" he asks.

I walk up to the bar wincing as my shoes squeak on the dance floor. "Had to force Aero into the shower."

"Tequila or bourbon?" he asks, placing a clean glass in front of me.

"Surprise me and make it a double." I pull myself up onto the stool suddenly exhausted. I put my head in my upturned hands and take a deep breath. He pours the liquor into the glass and slides it over to me. I salute him with it and throw it back, hardly tasting it other than the burn it left as I swallowed. I motion for him to pour another one and he does without question. I throw the drink back trying to ignore his concern.

I don't need it and I know he sees that. So we stay like that for a few minutes, him filling my drink and me drinking it as if it were water. It's not long until I can feel it though.

"Is it bad?" I ask randomly.

Cannon stares at me. "Is what bad?"

"That I'm angry at her? For dying?"

Cannon sighs and leans against the bar, his eyes holding a sadness I haven't seen in a long time. It's the same sadness I saw when he was shoved into that room with me. The same sadness that I carry with me. Only mine feels hotter, more angry than a true sadness. I hated how Aero was just deciding everything. Leaving me an unwilling participant. I was angry at the fact she was sick. I was angry at her obvious secrets. I was just so fucking angry. I motion for him to pour me another drink. When he doesn't right away I hit the bar top with the palm of my hand.

With a sigh he pours the drink, answering my question, "No, no it's not bad. I'd be worried if you weren't a little angry. Fuck, I'd be furious if it were any of you girls or Mark." He shakes his bald head, running a hand through the coarse stubble that slowly grew on it. "I can't say I understand what it's like for you. I can't fucking imagine what you're going through, but I do know you'll get through this. You've gone through hell, you can get through this too. You're a survivor."

I gulp down the drink without responding, then I motion for another drink. He pours it watching me as if expecting me to say something or agree with him. That's the problem, I was tired of surviving. I didn't want to. I wanted peace, I wanted the happiness that Delaney and I talked about all those years ago. I just had to figure out a way to get it.

I don't know how long I've been at the club drinking but it must have been awhile because there is now loud music blaring from the speakers and people are dancing on the dance floor while others are vying for the bartender's attention. And I am still on the same stool as when I got here. Only I'm a lot less coherent and more warm than when I first got here.

Someone brushes against me drawing my attention. "Hey! Why so sad, beautiful?" a man asks me. I snort, staring up at him but it's hard to focus when there's three of him. I laugh to myself. "What's so funny?" he asks, laughing awkwardly.

"I look like a dumpster fire and you called me beautiful!" I'm laughing harder now.

The man and his two clones look confused. "I'm failing to see how that's funny."

I shrug, pushing a hand through my hair. "It would've been easier to just ask me to go home with you. I've fucked guys like you before. It's like charity work." I nod to myself. I should get a medal for the charity work I give them. A great lay plus experience with an actual woman's body. What more could they want? I nod again, yep. I was practically a hero for all women in a thirty mile radius.

The man, men?, glare at me.

"I rather not fuck a bitch who gets around anyway. If that's all it takes to get you to fuck then you're nothing but a whore."

I shrug, I've been called worse. "But I'm a whore who can make women come so..." I shrug again, unconcerned. I wasn't going to let a man talk to me as if his opinions matter. That's what happened last time. Nope, not again. I turn away and almost tumble off the stool and the men grab my arm steadying me with a fierce frown now.

"Nirvana!" a sharp voice says on the other side of me. I glance up as four Ravis come towards me. One Ravi was enough to send me into heart palpitations, but four? That was enough to send me into full blown cardiac arrest. I'm so absorbed in the four Ravis that I lose sight of my surroundings.

"Hate to be the one to tell you, bro, but your girl is a whore and spreads her legs easily with just a few words. You're better off alone," the guy said.

Oh, I forgot he was there. Oops.

The Ravis stop beside me, putting a strong hand on my arm, moving me out of the grasp of the other men. How were so many touching me? I blink rapidly trying to clear my vision. It didn't work. Oh well. I turn away from the conversation and grab my empty glass, growling in frustration as I try to wave the bartender down to me.

"She's not a whore, *bro,*" Ravi one says, emphasizing the word 'bro' while glaring at the man. He takes the glass from me and sets it aside, harder than is socially acceptable. My breathing stops for a second at the harsh way he spoke and how hard he set the glass down.

The other guy shrugs, taking a sip of his drink. "Hey, if you want a loose bitch that's your prerogative. I'm just saying when your piss starts burning you'll know why."

What? I glared at him, offended. "Hey! I'll have you know I do kegels on a regular basis so my pussy is plenty tight. And I get checked you pinheaded prick. I almost had a threesome back here a week ago. Before I was rudely inter-rupted—I draw the word out glaring at the bouncer before turning back to Mr. Bro—unlike you." I flick the collar of his polo shirt, and say, "Who the fuck wears a polo to a club? You're missing your ascot you egotistical pissant. No wonder you don't get laid." My words are slurred but I don't care. I'm worked up and looking for a fight.

Ravi steps between us, grabbing me roughly against him, his eyes hard, no longer that earthy green but a dark ocean green.

"Settle down," he hisses so only I can hear.

"Yo man, control your cunt. She'll end up saying the wrong shit to the wrong person and they won't be so kind," the man shouted, his face turning red. Ravi stiffened and looked at the man. He was shorter by a few inches but made up for it in his build and the menace and violent air he had around him. They're pressed chest to chest and I see the way his jaw tics slightly, I feel his hand clench on my bicep tightly as if holding himself back.

"Watch what you say to me about her. I'm not nearly as 'kind' as you are." With that he grabbed me by my waist and slung me over his shoulder. I squeal loudly and wrap my arms around his hips. He shoulder checks the man sending him falling against the bar.

"Put me down!" I gasp.

He doesn't answer me, just pushes past people who are gaping at him. He has one arm across my thighs and one on my calfs, making it impossible for me to fall on my face.

He pushes open the door and takes us outside, moving through the parked cars until he gets to the one he's looking for. Setting me down, Ravi opens the door.

"Get in," he says.

"I'm good, thanks," I answer, moving to pass him but he stops me with a firm hand on my stomach and pushes me up against the car. The breath whooshes out of me and my heart starts to race.

"What the fuck is your problem, Nirvana?" he snaps.

I wince. "Oooh, you're using my government name. I must really be in trouble."

His jaw clenches making me smile. "Nirvana, I mean it. Get your ass in the car right fucking now."

I press my hand against his chest, pushing slightly. "Who are you to tell me what to do?"

He glares at me. "Do you really want to push me tonight? You're drunk as shit and talking to random men."

I shrug. "I'm a grown woman, Ravi. I'll talk to whoever I want to," I snap, feeling a little more sober than I did in the hot, crowded club.

He closes in on me. "The last fucking time you did that shit a man nearly choked you out." His words were blunt, angry, and his breathing was harsh.

I knew I was provoking him but I didn't care, I wanted to fight. To feel something other than this cold numbness I've been drifting in for the better part of a week. "Maybe I wanted to find someone who could choke me right."

Before I could process what was going on his hand was wrapped around my throat and he was pushing me roughly against the side of the car. His hand flexed against me, cutting off my air supply without pressing down on my windpipe like Blake did.

I'm struggling to breathe and my heart is pounding, not from fear. No from something else. Something darker, more arousing. He leans into me and his spicy scent fills my nose then he whispers in my ear.

"This is how you choke someone, pixie. This is me controlling if you get to breathe or not. You want someone to choke you until you can't fucking see you come to me," he says and squeezes tighter, just for a second before letting go, letting me take a deep breath. "Now be a good girl and get your ass in the fucking car. Right now."

I press my hand into his chest, gripping his shirt in my fist, and ask, "Or what?"

Chapter 13

RAVI

I brace my hand against the car, leaning into Nirvana's space. Her blue eyes widen and her face turns a shade redder making her sparse freckles stand out more on her pale skin. The smell of bourbon wafts toward me followed by the distinct scent of an ocean breeze and roses. A mixture that was more intoxicating than the alcohol Nirvana drank. My palm itches to wrap around her delicate throat again. To see that look of ecstasy on her beautiful features when I tightened my hold on her. Cutting off her air supply. Then she got a small smirk on her face and pressed her hand against me, pulling me into her.

"Get in the car right now, Nirvana. Or I'll put you in it myself," I repeat, my voice lowering. I wanted to pull her closer, to kiss that stubborn mouth of hers. But I held myself back, she wasn't sober nor was she thinking straight.

Nirvana glances up at me, pushing a stray piece of

blonde hair out of her face. "You're not the boss of me, Ravi." Her words are slightly slurred but she's stern.

Shaking my head, I step back from her. I open the passenger door before pushing her inside. Lucky for me, she's caught off guard and easy to put in the seat. It's the buckling her up that's difficult. She flails her arms nearly hitting me in the face as I try to buckle her in, and I almost have the mind to call Delaney up and demand she come take care of this drunk gremlin of a woman instead of doing her a favor. I try to buckle the belt, but with Nirvana's constant movements I accidentally hit the lever between the seats sending the seat unfolding backwards, making me fall against her with a groan.

"Get off of me you giant oaf," Nirvana curses. I brace my hands on the headrest and glare down at her, my patience finally snapped.

"I swear to God, if you fight me anymore I will make sure you don't sit for a week. Do you understand me? I came as a favor, but I'll be damned if you act like a drunken toddler when I try to take you home," I bark.

Nirvana stops moving, staring up at me and breathing heavily. Her eyes search mine and she nods slowly, her hands going to my chest to push me away. At least that's what I thought before her hands moved up towards the back of my neck. I shiver slightly, shocks going through my body.

"Ravi," she whispers.

I shake my head. "Don't do something you'll regret." My voice is strained but I stand by what I said.

"Who said I'd regret it?" she whispers. It would be so easy to press my lips to hers. They even brush ever so slightly, but I pull away. "Let me take you home so you can sleep this off."

Nirvana takes a shaky breath. "Please, please don't bring me back there. Not tonight."

I search her eyes for a moment wondering what I should do. She looks sad, exhausted and so alone that I can't find it in me to take her back.

"Okay," I nod, "Okay I won't take you there."

———

I pull into my driveway nearly twenty minutes later, my heart pounding. Nirvana has sat quietly beside me the entire time, her head pressed against the window, watching the surroundings as we drove. I park in the driveway and take the keys from the ignition, but I don't make any other move to leave the car.

"Are we just going to sit in the car all night?" Nirvana asked.

I sigh. "I didn't expect company so..." I shrug.

Nirvana tilted her head to the side. "You've been in that dump I've been staying in. I'm sure your house is fine." I nod and climb out of the car waiting for her. She's a little slower paced before she's standing next to me, staring expectantly.

Squaring my shoulders, I put the pincode into the system before unlocking the door. I flick the lights on and motion her inside. Her eyes widen and I wonder how she sees my home. It's not as big and showy as some houses down the block, but it's decent. The floors are almost black wood with a deep shine to them and there's a small wood fireplace on the wall surrounded by black bricks.

"Why were you so nervous to let me in? This is a beautiful house," Nirvana said, sounding a lot more sober than she did when I first got to her.

"It's not the house. I, um, live with someone," I say. "Well, not really live, there's an interconnected tiny house connected to this house."

Nirvana arches a brow and I begin to explain when I hear the sound of footsteps. "Ravi? Is that you?"

"Yeah, I'm in here, Gran."

"Oh, you live with your grandmother," Nirvana said, comprehension dawning on her.

"She lives with me," I confirm as my grandmother comes into view. "In the tiny house," I add, feeling my cheeks heat up.

Nirvana gives me a small smile as Gran walks into the foyer.

She's a small woman, smaller than Nirvana and Layla who admittedly are smaller than an average woman in height. My grandmother is hunched slightly with pale thin skin, big green hair, and cloudy blue eyes.

"Is there someone with you, Ravi?" Gran asks.

"Yes, just a friend, Nirvana. Nirvana, this is my grandmother, Flo."

Nirvana stares at me then my grandmother, "It's nice to meet you Ms. Flo. I love your hair color. Green's also my favorite."

My grandmother smiles, touching her hair. "Thank you! Ravi did it for me." I feel my cheeks heat up even more.

"He did an excellent job." Nirvana glances at me, a softness in her eyes that wasn't there before.

"Ravi you didn't tell me you were bringing company, I could've made cookies," Gran scolds.

"It was spur of the moment," I say, "and shouldn't you be in bed?"

Gran puts her hands on her hips. "I was listening to this book. Very good read."

I sigh and take off my shoes, watching as Nirvana follows suit.

"Are you thirsty or hungry?" I ask Nirvana.

"Can I have some water?" she asks.

112

I nod and press my hand on the small of her back to lead her to the kitchen. Gran follows behind us. "It's that *Fifty Shades* book, you know with that rich guy," Gran explains. "I don't know, you young people are so different. The positions in that book seem nearly impossible. I think I broke a hip just from listening to it."

I stop suddenly, gaping at my grandmother. Nirvana on the other hand bursts into laughter.

"I'm serious, how can they do that? The cuffs, the rope? Wouldn't it hurt?"

"Okay, Gran! I think that's enough of that," I say.

Gran rolls her eyes. "Do you hear him? I swear you'd think he's the old prude. I may not see it, but I know when you're glaring at me. I'm going, I'm going. It was nice to meet you, dear, let's chat more when Captain Prude isn't around." Gran gives me a wide smile before turning and leaving the kitchen. I listen until I hear her door open and close before I shake my head and go to the cabinet and pull down a glass before filling it up with water from the fridge. I hold it out to Nirvana.

"Thank you," she says and sips it, staring at the space where my grandma was. "Your grandma is funny. I like her. How come you never mention her?"

I shrug. "No one knows, they never asked."

Nirvana hums under her breath. "Or you've never wanted anyone to know. You're closed off, why?"

I lean against the island, crossing my arms over my chest. "I can say the same thing to you, Nirvana."

"I'm not closed off."

My brows shoot up to my hairline. "No? Then why do you have a hard time asking for help?"

She waves her hand. "That's different. That's not wanting to be a burden."

"You're not a burden. And I don't mention my Gran

because my home life is no one's business. The guys know about her but not that she lives here. She's been here a little over two years. She couldn't be alone anymore, not after she lost her eyesight."

"You don't need to explain anything to me, Ravi. Like you said, it's not my business."

"You're right, it's not. But you met her, I can see the questions rolling through your head might as well get it out there before you start probing."

She snorts, setting her glass down. "I wouldn't probe." I arch an eyebrow and she sighs and says, "Much. I wouldn't probe much."

I shake my head, a grin touching my lips. "Exactly. So I decided to bypass the questions." She's silent for a while and I wonder if she's going to ask all those questions that are rolling around in her head. But she surprises me.

Nirvana nods to herself, twisting her hands together tightly before blurting, "I don't like men." I arch my eyebrow at her, staring intently as she turns away, gasping. I lean against the counter and give her a minute to figure out what she wants to say.

Chapter 14

Nirvana

I gasp, covering my mouth with my hands. Why the fuck would I say that? Ravi doesn't react, he just stares at me. I wish I could read his expressions, but he keeps his handsome face so carefully blank at all times and I don't know what he's thinking. I shake my head. "I... that didn't come out right. I don't like men like a normal woman does. I like women too, and non binary, and well, anyone really. I'm not attracted to just one gender. It's more about how I connect with a person, you know? If we match and it's good I don't care. It's all about how our vibes and personalities match." I'm rambling now, suddenly feeling stuck in a box. I haven't felt like this since I told the others about me. I shouldn't have said anything, and I didn't plan on it either, but he brought me to his home and let me meet his eccentric, yet oddly endearing, grandmother and I knew I should say something.

We stood in silence for so long that I got nearly light-headed while holding my breath, it wasn't like when he was holding my throat, it was panicked. So I snapped, "Well, say something."

"Okay. Are you hungry?" he responds, turning towards the fridge.

"What?" I say confused. I know my eyes are probably bugging out of my head but damn, who is this guy?

Ravi looks at me then places his hand on the fridge, opening it slightly in almost an invitation, "Are you hungry?"

I shake my head, "No, I heard you. I'm just confused."

"About what? Your announcement? Nirvana, you don't owe me or anyone else an explanation on your sexual orientation and what you like or are attracted to. That's your business," he says, closing the fridge with a *clack*. He leans against it, crossing his arms over his broad chest.

"Well, okay then," I say and nod.

Ravi's green eyes pin me with a heated gaze, staring at me so intently it's almost like a physical touch, "Just so you know, I don't care about that. It doesn't change how I view you."

I look at him, my heart pounding, and ask, "How do you view me?"

"You're a strong woman, beautiful, caring. Just because you're attracted to all people doesn't make that any less true. Whoever made you feel as if it is something other than normal doesn't deserve you anyway."

I nod, looking at the ground. If only he knew how much I wished I could be someone other than myself. He steps in front of me and tilts my chin up, forcing me to meet his gaze.

"Don't do that. Don't be ashamed to be you. Be true to yourself. Do you understand me?"

I nod, my gaze going to his full pink mouth. I swallow hard. My eyes trail down to his full lips and suddenly I want to know how it would feel to have them pressed against my mouth. Against my burning skin, easing the ache between my legs. "I really want to kiss you," I whisper. The fact that I want to voluntarily kiss him is astounding to me. I never let anyone kiss me, not after Marcy and not since that prick Blake forced it. But right here right now. With Ravi, I want to feel what it's like to be kissed by a man who's attracted to me. Who feels the same burning need that I do. But does he feel it? That burning desire to taste me as much as I want to taste him? To see if his lips are as soft as they look?

Ravi's thumb traces my chin gently. "I want to kiss you, too, but you've had a lot to drink tonight. I want you to be all in when it happens, I don't want you thinking of spontaneous announcements and the fact your judgment might be skewed because of one shot too many." I wanted to protest, to tell him I was more sober than I was before but maybe there was still a small part of me that was being influenced by alcohol because of the way I was acting, something that I normally wouldn't do. Especially with my no kissing rule. So I nod in agreement. It was better this way.

"Let me get you into bed if you won't eat right now."

"Okay," I whisper following Ravi towards his room. His house was nice and cozy. But his room is exactly what I would imagine Ravi's room to look like. All dark colors. He had a king size bed in the middle of the room with black sheets with red pillows. There were dark mahogany nightstands with black square-shaped lamps. He goes to his dresser, the same color as the nightstands, and pulls out a t-shirt. He hands it to me and looks around us.

"There's a bathroom through that door," he points behind me and I nod. "If you need anything just come get me. I'll be right in the living room."

My eyes shoot to him. "You're not staying in here?"

He rubs the back of his neck, and says, "I figured it would be best if I stayed there so you can get some sleep."

I look at the bed and reply, "There's enough room. I don't mind. Or I can sleep on the couch. This is your room."

He eyes me for a second before nodding. "Okay. I'll just get changed then you can have the bathroom." I nod and watch as he gets his clothes together and goes to the bathroom. I quickly strip out of my clothes and put on the shirt and by the time Ravi comes out I'm folding my clothes. I look at him and notice his hair is wet and steam follows him.

"I put a new toothbrush out for you. And I laid out some aspirin and a cup for water. That way you don't have much of a hangover in the morning," he states, running the towel over his hair. I thank him, trying not to look at the way his shirt rises or how low his sweats hang on his hips. I swallow hard and make my way to the bathroom to brush my teeth and do my business. He's thought of everything and it makes my heart flip a bit and butterflies fill my stomach. I take the medicine and quickly brush my teeth before leaving the bathroom, suddenly nervous to be sharing a bed with him. I stare up at the ceiling as a thick silence fills the room around us.

I'm not really sure how long it's been before I talk. "I've never done this before."

I feel Ravi turn his head. "Done what?"

"Shared a bed with a man."

Ravi is silent for a moment, then asks, "Not even sex?"

I snort. "God, no. It was my one act of rebellion."

"What do you mean?" he asks.

Licking suddenly dry lips I sigh, closing my eyes. "If I've never been intimate with a man, in a bed as was deemed biblically acceptable, I would never have done what my father wanted. I was telling him to go fuck himself without the words, without seeing those hate filled eyes. It was the only revenge I could get."

I feel Ravi sit up, looking at me with too intelligent eyes.

"What do you mean?"

I mimicked his stance, placing my head in my hand so I could meet his gaze. "Whenever you've been villainized and told you're going to burn in eternal Hell for being attracted to someone you're not supposed to be, you find solace in the little things." I roll to my back. "So you're the first man I've voluntarily let into my bed. Or in this case your bed."

"Nirvana," he starts, causing a lump to form in the back of my throat.

"It's nice. Not as awful as I thought it would be," I tease.

He gazes down at me for a full minute, I know because I count silently in my head, waiting for him to say something, anything, instead he just laughs softly. Catching me off guard.

"And how did you think it would go?" he asks in a teasing tone.

Relief fills me as I relax against the mattress before shrugging and answering, "I don't know. I guess in my head I imagined they would grow horns and turn green or some shit."

He laughs, a real belly laugh that sends a shocking wave of warmth through me. "No you didn't," he says, wiping under his eyes.

I feel my own mouth twitch slightly as I nod, "I did. I even told Aero once that if she were to ever get into bed with a boy he'd turn into a small elf with sharp teeth. Little did I know I had nothing to worry about."

Sadness enveloped me, almost like a long lost friend hugging me for the first time in years. Just thinking about her made my heart hurt. It made it all seem as if I was watching everything play out from the sidelines.

"I can't say I've ever heard that type of sex talk before. But I guess it beats spending money on condoms or birth control," Ravi muses.

I glance at him, watching as his brows furrowed leaving

small wrinkles in his forehead. Without thinking I reach out and run my index finger over his forehead, smoothing it away. He grabs my wrist, tensing slightly. We sit looking at each other, waiting for something. I'm not sure what, but I know I'm holding my breath.

"You're making it really fucking difficult to resist you, tinker hell," he said.

"So stop resisting." I lick my dry lips and he follows the movement with his eyes.

"You drank a lot tonight," he tries again.

I shrug and reply, "I've never felt more sober in my entire life." That was the truth, with smoking weed every now and then and constantly on a cocktail of different medications, this moment is the first time I've ever felt truly coherent. I was in control of this, I was choosing to kiss him. My first real kiss. Ravi drops my hand and grabs the back of my neck dragging me into his chest, pulling me so close I can feel his heart pounding against my breasts. Our eyes meet in a heated look. He stared at me as if waiting for me to object. To tell him to stop. But I don't. Instead a small whimper escapes past my lips and he moves forward. He takes my mouth with a bruising kiss, holding nothing back. Claiming what little breath I had left in my lungs. His mouth is hot on mine, taking what he wanted and giving what I needed.

His strong hand fists the hair at the nape of my neck and his tongue pushes into my mouth. I gasped, pressing my hands against his chest, digging my nails into his skin through the soft cotton of the shirt. He growls low in his throat, sending a thrill through me. He grabs one of my legs and throws it over his waist so that I was half straddling him and half lying on the bed. It was perfect.

His tongue thrust into my mouth, tasting every inch of me. He bit on my lower lip, pulling it enough to add a bit of a sting that had me grinding against him. I've never imagined kissing could be like this, so all consuming and hot. Was kissing always like this or was it just Ravi? I don't think for long because his lips traveled from my mouth to my throat, his lips burned a hot trail against the exposed skin until I was whimpering against him. Begging for more. So much more.

Heat spread through me, causing my core to throb and my breasts to ache with a hot and heavy need. I run my hands up his chest to his hair so I can fist my fingers through the silky strands. I pull his head back and attack his mouth. I thrust my tongue in groaning at the way he felt against my mouth, the way he quickly took over the kiss to hold me at his mercy, allowing me to feel his own burning need. It was perfect. Tasting mint and the hint of spice that always seemed to follow him. It was so intoxicating and I wanted more. Grunting against my mouth he grabs my hips and rolls us over so he's on top of me, his weight holding me down against his bed.

I wrap my legs around him and pull him closer. He presses his erection against my throbbing core, thrusting his hips in time with his tongue as if he were fucking me and I loved every second of it. I want more, and as I'm about to ask there's a knock at the door. "Ravi! Ravi! I can't find my medicine!"

Ravi pulls away, breathing heavily as he presses his forehead against mine. "Shit," he mutters.

I chuckle softly, unsure if I should feel upset at the luck or glad that we were interrupted before we could go any further. It was probably the latter. "Go help your grandmother. I'll probably be asleep before you get back." It was a lie, I hardly slept but he didn't know that.

He studies me for a second before nodding and climbing off of me. I know he wants to say something but before he can his grandmother knocks again making him sigh and head to the door. I watch him go, my mind moving a million miles a minute. I cover my mouth with a small gasp and I turn in the bed, shocked that I kissed him. Holy shit, I kissed Ravi. I run my fingers over my swollen mouth memorizing the feel of his mouth on mine, holding it to me like a talisman before turning in bed and falling into a restless sleep while thoughts of death and intoxicating kisses plague my dreams.

Chapter 15

RAVI

I curse my shitty luck as I walk out of my room. I couldn't get Nirvana out of my head. From her half confessions to the stormy taste of her in my mouth, clouding my every sense making me want more of her. Just seeing the way her pale skin flushes with desire, to the way her eyes dilated with need, the black overtaking the blue making her eyes look more indigo and violet than the normal blue.

Just seeing this woman come undone beneath me was enough to send me over the edge. At least it would have if we weren't rudely interrupted. I adjust myself in my sweats, cursing at how little they concealed. Giving up, I followed the sounds Gran was making in the kitchen.

"I'm here. Which medication?" I ask, trying to control my raging hormones.

"Oh you know, the pain ones. For my hip," Gran's voice is oddly high pitched. I raise an eyebrow and spot the exact medication she's looking for in front of her. I grab the bottle and place it in her hand.

"Gran, you may be blind but you're not blind enough to not know where you keep your medication. It's in the same spot as it always is," I scold lightly. I lean against the wall and glare at her, even though I know she can't see me. But I know that she feels my look.

She waves her hand without a care in the world. "My mistake. You know I'm getting up there in age. It must've slipped my mind on where I put it."

I hum under my breath, waiting for her to take the medicine but she just puts it back down on the counter. "Gran, what's going on?" I ask, suddenly suspicious of her actions.

She stands for a moment, twisting her frail fingers together nervously. She closes her cloudy blue eyes, takes a deep breath before turning to the direction I currently stood. "You cannot touch that girl." I'm stunned by the venom in her tone. "She is fragile and I did not raise you to take advantage of a girl who is in need of help."

I stare at her, dumbfounded, before bursting into laughter. "Laugh all you want, Ravi Issac, but I will take you behind the house and teach you a lesson. I taught you to respect women. Hell, I taught you to respect everyone. I'll be damned if you take advantage of that broken girl in there."

I stop laughing, staring at her in complete shock. "First, I would never, *ever* take advantage of a vulnerable woman. Like you said I was taught better than that. Secondly, I had her consent and it was a simple kiss." Well, simple isn't the word I'd use for it. More like earth shaking, soul shattering. Yeah, those words fit better. But then I stopped to actually think. Did I take advantage of her? Of the vulnerable position she was in?

Nausea suddenly churned in my stomach. Fuck, what the fuck was I doing? I knew better than this! Even if she gave me consent she was heavily influenced by alcohol and it was clouding her judgment. Fuck me. I push a hand through my hair and curse again.

"I…" I clear my throat. "I'm sorry, Gran. I didn't take advantage of her." I don't think. God, now I was second guessing everything. I curse myself silently and decide I'd apologize to her. Right, that was the way to go. I'll apologize and hope I didn't somehow make everything worse on her. "But if she felt like I did I'll apologize right when she wakes up and keep my distance." Because God knew I couldn't take advantage of Nirvana. Nor would I want to. Right now she's dealing with a lot of shit, with her sister's quick deterioration and the past that still seems to haunt her. Fuck, I was the worst. Goddamnit. I sigh and run a hand through my hair. She needed a friend, I couldn't fuck that up by wanting to fuck her. Or seeing her on her knees for me. I curse silently to myself. *Fuck, get it together Ravi!* I scold myself. Jesus, since when can't I act like a mature grown man without feeling the need to fuck someone? It was embarrassing.

"I'm sorry, Gran. I didn't realize. I'll make it right," I say through a clenched jaw.

Gran nods, her green hair falling in her face. "Good, that girl needs a friend. Not some horn dog of a man sniffing up her skirt. Do better, Ravi. I raised a gentleman, not another rat bastard. Do you understand me?" she says sternly.

"Yes ma'am," I say, guilt riding me hard and fast. What the fuck did I do? Did I ruin everything with Nirvana? With a shake of my head I say goodnight to my grandmother and head to my room. I had to fix this. I move back to my room, ready to apologize to Nirvana but I stop short when I see her curled up in a little ball, her blonde hair fanned out on my pillow.

I close the door silently behind myself before I walk up to the bed. I don't want to wake her as I climb back onto the bed, pulling the covers over the both of us while trying to keep my distance from her. I'm laying stiffly in the bed when she rolls over and throws her arm and leg over me and snuggles deeper into me. My heart nearly stops there. I glance down at her wondering if she knows what she's doing. But she's asleep, her breathing is even and her mouth is slightly turned down in a small frown. Licking suddenly dry lips I force myself to relax. She's warm against me, her ocean breeze scent wraps around me like her arm and leg holding me hostage to her. And the weird thing is I don't exactly hate it like I thought I would.

My eyes are getting heavy the longer I lie here and I promise myself I'll talk to her tomorrow morning. The last thing I remember as I fall asleep is me wrapping my arm around her, holding her to me. Just this once.

Sunlight drifts through my windows waking me up. I blink while reaching across my bed but find it empty. I shoot up and glance around the room. "Nirvana," I say as I look around. She's no longer in my bed. Did she leave? Fuck. Panic slides through me as I stand up ready to go find her, but I stop when I hear soft laughter. I leave my room and head down the hall where I see Nirvana sitting at the table with my Gran laughing, her face relaxed for the first time in weeks.

"Ravi," Gran calls when I enter the kitchen. Nirvana looks at me, a slight blush stealing up her pale cheeks before she looks away, her hands clenching around the mug that sat in front of her.

"Morning," I say.

"I was just telling Vana about your high school days," Gran says and laughs, tapping her freshly painted green nails on a scrapbook in front of her. "Do you remember when you went into choir because of a girl you liked?"

My eyes narrow on Gran as she goes into her favorite story about my time as a teen. We both knew it wasn't that bad, but I can't help the small curve of my mouth as I notice Nirvana trying to cover a laugh. "Gran, you know I had to do one extra curricular activity," I defended myself, bypassing the women on the way to the coffee pot. "Besides, it didn't even last a month."

"To be fair, they were going to nationals and you couldn't carry a tune if your life depended on it," Gran said turning to Nirvana. "Poor thing couldn't carry a tune to save his life. I swear, I heard him practicing one night and I thought our cat was hurt."

I grimace as I pour my coffee in a mug. "Fluffy was dead well before I was in high school."

"Exactly." Gran laughs even harder. But then so does Nirvana. I lean against the counter watching her for a second before sipping my drink. Letting the hot liquid soothe my throat a little bit.

"Do you think you can take me to get my car? I have to finish setting up today before trying to get ordained online," Nirvana asked after she stopped laughing.

"Yes. I can drop you off before I head to work," I offer.

Nirvana tilts her head. "I thought you were on vacation."

I nod. "I was. But I go back today. A week passes by fast when it comes to work vacations."

Nirvana nods and stands, walking towards the sink to dump the rest of her drink. I stop her and take the mug from her hands. She doesn't meet my eyes and I try not to wince as she thanks me. "Go get dressed. We leave in fifteen minutes."

She nods again before glancing at me briefly, I want to apologize now but I can't, not with Gran being openly nosy.

So instead I turn away first and wash out the mug, effectively ignoring the moment the two of us had. I hear her soft footsteps fading away and I turn around.

"Smooth," Gran says, closing the scrapbook, running gentle fingers over it. Almost as if she was remembering every detail on the white cover.

I glared at her. "I wasn't trying to be smooth."

Gran snorts and says, "Clearly."

I throw my hands up in exasperation, "You're the one who told me to back off."

"No, I said don't take advantage of her. She seems to be very sensitive. I didn't say ignore the girl out in the wild. Jesus, it's like choir all over again." She grabs the book stepping near me. She places a gentle brittle hand on my arm, squeezing slightly. "She needs someone, Ravi. You can still be a kind man and not awkward while she processes whatever she is dealing with. Because there is something there between the two of you. Something great. Don't let it pass you by because you can't get your head out of the sand. Or show some type of emotion—she shakes her head—My goodness you're not a robot, Ravi. Get it together."

I stare down at her, sighing softly, "You're a very confusing woman, Gran."

Gran shrugs, sending me a smile. "I'm old. I earned that right." Shaking my head, I kiss the top of her head before washing my own mug.

"Will you be all right here on your own? It's your first time being here alone while I work." She may live in a separate house, but it was still connected to the main house. Gran hasn't been here that long, so leaving her to her own devices makes me break out into a cold sweat.

Gran snorts. "I may be old and blind but I do know the basics of taking care of myself."

"I know that, Gran. I just worry. There are enough

microwavable foods in the fridge for you. You know where the fridge and microwave are. I have your slippers in front of your favorite chair so you can find them easily," I rattle off, putting the two mugs in the dishwasher.

Gran stops me and says, "Ravi. You're a good boy, I can take care of myself."

I sigh, hugging her. "I know. I just worry."

Gran hugs me back, her eucalyptus scent wafting from her over use of essential oils. "I'll be fine, Ravi. Go on to work. Someone's cat needs saving from a tree."

I laugh then, letting her go. "I don't save cats. I fight fires."

"Sure, sure. Whatever you say, dear boy."

Shaking my head I step away from her so I can go get ready for work.

Chapter 16

Nirvana

I sit silently in Ravi's car, twisting my fingers around Ravi's shirt. My clothes were dirty and I currently sat in just Ravi's shirt and my underwear. There was a tense silence between us making me nervous. Why did it feel so awkward now? I knew I shouldn't have kissed him. Not only that, it's the fact I'm the one who made it strange. My brain told me no but my horniness told me yes. I clearly should've listened to my brain but I didn't. Instead, I now sat here wondering if I should jump out of his moving car and hope for the best or disappear from ever seeing him again when we got to my car.

I glance sideways out the window noticing the amount of cars on the road. "Fuck," I whisper to myself. There goes plan A.

"What is it?" Ravi asks, turning his head slightly to look at me.

I sigh and lean my head back. "I can't throw myself out of the car without possibly dying."

"Why the fuck would you want to jump out of the car?" he demands.

"To get rid of this weirdness between us." It's obvious as to why I'd want to do it.

"And you think jumping out of the car wouldn't make things more awkward?" he asks incredulously.

I shrug. "I mean it'll make a new reason other than the kiss. Then you can actually meet my eyes without feeling sorry for me."

Ravi is quiet for a moment. "You think it's because we kissed?" he clarifies, his hands squeezing the steering wheel so tightly his knuckles turn white.

"Isn't it?" I counter, staring ahead, feeling relief as I see Cannon's club in the distance.

"No. Yes. I don't know," Ravi says. "I shouldn't have taken advantage of you. I knew better than to kiss you. You were drunk and sad and I feel awful and," his hands grip the steering wheel tighter, if that's even possible, and his jaw clenches, "I'm just sorry I did that. You deserved better."

I don't speak. I don't know what to say. The tension in the car rachets up more, making my head hurt before I finally find my voice, "I wanted it. You didn't take advantage of me."

Ravi's already shaking his head. "I did. I know you're going through a bunch of shit right now. I shouldn't have done it and I won't ever do it again. I'm so sorry, Nirvana."

"So you regret it?" I ask.

He sighs, pinching the bridge of his nose. "You're vulnerable right now, pixie. If we continued I would've wanted more and that's not okay. Not in your situation. You were drunk. I knew better and I'm so fucking sorry."

Well that was disappointing, I thought to myself. I wanted him to go farther. I wanted more, I almost needed more.

I honestly enjoyed the kiss. I wanted it and I want it again. But then he's right. I do have a bunch of shit going on right now. Namely the fact that my sister is getting married in five days, and I haven't finished setting up. So I don't argue. I just force a smile and thank him for the ride as he pulls up next to my car.

As I go to get out he grabs my arm, stopping me. I don't turn around to face him and I do my best to ignore the heat from his touch.

"Are we okay?" he asks.

"Of course. No harm done, Ravi." I pull away slowly and climb out. I don't want to look at him, seeing the pity in those earth-green eyes. But then I do something fucking stupid, I point to the passenger's window and he arches a brow and rolls the window down.

Leaning over, I push my hands under the shirt and pull off my panties.

"Just for the record I wanted you. I don't think you took advantage of me, and yesterday I wanted more." With that I threw the lace at him and turned away. I square my shoulders and climb into my Jeep and quickly start it to speed away. Why I did that, I have no clue. I was pissed, I was horny, and fuck it, I was sad. It screamed a recipe for disaster.

I had no time to be hung up on guys or anyone else for that matter. I had one goal in mind, and that's making sure Aero's wedding went off perfectly. I sit in absolute silence as I head to the ranch trying to forget about the heavy weight that's been building in my chest these last few weeks. I pull up to the ranch and sit in the car trying to breathe.

How am I supposed to do this? How can I plan an entire wedding knowing that in a matter of weeks I'll be planning a funeral? I rub a tired hand down my face, hoping that the simple move would erase those thoughts. It doesn't help.

"This is for Aero," I mutter to myself and climb out the car and make my way behind the car to the trunk. I unlock it and see a pair of old scrub pants and sigh as I pull them up my legs, suddenly regretting my half-haired plan to toss my panties at Ravi as if he were David Bowie. I push the embarrassment away and make my way through the tall grass and the broken fences towards the barn. It's not in the best shape, but it'll have to do. I move towards the double doors and push on it, cringing when the hinges squeaked loudly before giving way and swinging open. I glance around and see some WD40 and spray it on the hinges of the door. Hoping that the rusted metal will at least hold up for the next few days. We've done some work to it, cleaning out the old hay bales and trash that got in over time but the barn is still far from being put together.

I was supposed to come in yesterday, but with everything that happened with my sister and getting drunk, I didn't make it. My emotions were all over the place. Yesterday, was the first sleep I had that wasn't drug induced and it had me cursing to myself as I headed back to the car and pulled out the supplies I'd brought with me. Some cleaning supplies, and the stuff to make the arch. It wasn't much and I knew it would realistically take longer than four days to fix this place up, but I was out of time and options. So if I had to stay here day and night I would. Squaring my shoulders I move forward. I dropped the supplies on the floor and stood looking at the wooden arch wondering how I could make this more presentable.

Lifting up the black tulle I have, I hold it up to the wood. I tilt my head to the left then the right before deciding to wrap the tulle around it. Nodding in satisfaction, I pull the step stool towards me, grab the stapler gun and get to work. I work in silence, moving the tulle over one side of the arch, covering the chipped and rotting wood as best as I can. I don't know how long I worked until it's all covered and I'm panting and sweating from the heat. I step down the stool and study my work. There's some bald spots that couldn't be covered, but other than that it doesn't look too bad. Proud of it, I grab the rest of the tulle and make it like a canopy having one side hanging low at the top and stapled at the bottom and mimic it on the other side, before I grab the battery twinkle lights and weave them through the fabric making it sparkle between each arch.

"Looks good," a voice says behind me, causing me to lose my footing and fall from the stool. I fall to my ass, wincing as my foot catches on the last step. A tall body steps over me and I look up at Sam who's grimacing apologetically. "Shit, I'm sorry! I didn't mean to scare you."

"It's fine." I groan, embarrassment sliding through me. Sam holds his hand out to me and I take it, getting to my feet rather clumsily. "What are you doing here?" I ask. Wincing, as I dusted off the back of my pants.

Sam steadies me before stepping back. "Well, it's me and Sorrow. We're here to help. Delaney sent us."

"Is she with you?" I ask looking behind him.

Sam shakes his head and says, "No. She's helping Layla and Spence with the wedding cake. Which they told me to tell you to come taste at three. I do know Rory is on her way."

I nod. "Thank you. I didn't know anyone was coming."

Sam sends me a kind smile and replies, "Couldn't have you doing this all alone."

I nod, my eyes suddenly burning with gratitude for these people I'm lucky to call friends. I turn away as Sorrow comes into the barn carrying a tool kit and another bag of what I'm assuming is decorations, followed by Rory who's carrying another bag and drink carrier of coffees.

"I brought coffee," Rory says. She smiles at me and sets

her bags down before holding out the carrier to me. I grab my drink and sigh with gratitude, suddenly, not so sad or stressed. But I knew that feeling wouldn't last long. It never did.

Sighing softly to myself, I walk into Heidi's where I hear laughter. Masculine and feminine. I move towards the back and stand near the kitchen door watching as Layla and Spencer laugh and talk to themselves, completely oblivious to their surroundings. Ever since the two met they have been as thick as thieves. I often wonder why they don't just go for it, I could see the way they looked at each other when one glanced away. The longing, the desire. They never made a move on each other, and I know it's not my business, but I wanted to see my best friend happy.

But I can see how Layla feels about the man. I want to walk away, leave them to spend their time together, let them figure things out on their own, but I was on a limited time crunch so I stepped inside the room.

"Where's Delaney?" I ask as if I just got here and wasn't watching their entire exchange.

Layla looked at me, her green eyes wide and brighter than I've ever seen them. "Bathroom."

I nod. "So, this is the cake. It's beautiful." I look at the black cake with red roses and feel a twinge in my chest. I press my palm against it, rubbing in soothing circles hoping to ease some of the pain to no avail. "What's the flavor?" I ask.

"Strawberry vanilla," Spencer answers, pushing his black rimmed glasses up his nose.

"It's black which is odd for a wedding," Layla hedges.

I nod again, I've been doing that a lot. I wouldn't be

surprised if it detached from my shoulders, not that I'd mind. "Aero is anything but conventional. She and Isola are both wearing black. Guests come in white."

"And what will you be wearing?" Delaney asks, stepping into the kitchen looking paler than usual.

"Are you okay?" I ask, not answering her question.

Delaney waves the concern away and replies, "Of course. Sorrow said the barn is starting to look a lot better. I can come over there in the morning if you want."

"Oh, it's practically finished. All I have to do is set everything up the way Aero and Isola want. So it shouldn't take too long. I plan on doing it in the afternoon I think. I have to take Aero to the doctor in the morning, so—" I shrug.

That was one thing I wanted to forget about doing. It was one thing when I didn't understand what was happening, it was another to go back to see how much longer she realistically had left. It was like rubbing salt in the gaping wound, never letting it heal properly. No, instead it kept it open, letting infection seep in, festering until it eventually died and fell off.

Clapping my hands, I turn to Layla. "Let's see the other desserts."

Chapter 17

RAVI

I sit down, wiping the sweat off my brow, panting from exertion. "Jesus. You look like shit," Caden says, climbing off the ladder holding the wiggling cat in his gloved hand. The cat was all purrs for him. But when I tried to grab it it was hissing and growling, slashing out with its claws.

I glare up at him. "Shut up. How'd you just get here and you're already showing off?"

Caden smirks at me, handing the little bastard over to the owner who was clutching the feline to her chest as she cried, "Thank you, thank you so much." I try not to roll my eyes, Gran jinxed me or set this up, there is no other reason behind a three legged cat getting stuck in a goddamn tree. That's just not something that happens every day in Texas. At least I fucking hoped not.

The cat stared daggers at me drawing my attention. I glared back and it hissed at me again. Actually fucking hissed, as if I somehow inconvenienced it by it being stuck in a tree. Which sent Caden doubling over with laughter. I stood and shoulder checked the asshole before getting into the truck. I heard Caden follow after me, his laughter mocking as he climbed in behind me.

"Aww, I didn't know you had such an affinity with animals." My jaw clenched as he continued, "Although, you need to work on feline friends because I'm pretty sure that cat is planning your demise."

"Are you done, Caden?" I demand.

Caden touches his chin, tapping slightly as if he were contemplating. "Nah. This is just too fun." I roll my eyes and sit back in my seat tapping my fingers against my leg.

I can feel Caden looking at me, studying me in that weird way of his. I grit my teeth before turning to him. "What?"

Caden shrugs his shoulders. "I don't know man. Looks like you have a lot on your mind. Do you want to talk about it?"

I snort. "You've been hanging out with Delaney too much." Caden doesn't take the bait causing me to sigh. "I fucked up." God, did I fuck up bad.

"Come on, it can't be that bad," Caden says, putting his headphones back on as the truck gets started. I do the same, wincing slightly at the echo I hear between us.

"It's bad."

Cade arches a black brow. "What did you do?"

I rub the back of my neck and take a breath. "I kissed Nirvana. I'm pretty sure she was drunk." Caden's eyes widened and I said hastily, "I stopped it before it went any further." But god, I wanted to kiss her again. Not to mention she admitted to me that she wanted it to go further. Hell, she even threw her damp panties through my car window. Surprising the shit out of me. And turned me on. Like the fucked-up man I am, I have the pink lace on the gearshift of the car. Holding it like some goddamn trophy.

"You kissed her? How the fuck did that even happen?" Caden gaped at me.

Static sounds through the headphones. "What's the ETA of the closest emergency personnel from Huntiting Street?" a 911 operator asked, saving me from having to answer.

Brooks responds, "I'm about two minutes out."

"We have a seizure. A bad one. I need medics there ASAP." Brooks replied in the affirmative and switched on the lights sending the siren on with blaring urgency. Caden and I stop talking, getting serious. We quickly go over our emergency kit searching for the seizure medication we can administer. It doesn't take long to arrive at the apartment complex, and then to get to the unit we need. Cade and I hop out quickly rushing towards the unit.

"Austin Fire Department!" Cade calls, knocking on the door.

"It's open," a shaky feminine voice calls out. Cade opens the door and we rush in, heading in the direction of the commotion. We end up in the bathroom, a small woman with dark hair sitting with another half-covered, naked woman in her lap as her body locks up. Cade says something about meeting the paramedics and I nod.

The alert woman looks up as I enter, her dark eyes wide and red rimmed. "I tried what the internet said. She was taking a bath and just started seizing. She hit her head."

I set the kit down and moved towards the women. "Any medical issues that may have caused this?" I ask, sitting beside them. I turn the woman to her side taking care to keep her covered.

The woman swallows hard, nodding rapidly, and replies, "She's got cancer. Brain cancer." I look down at the woman, doing a double take. I didn't recognize them with the urgent activity and I felt the blood drain from my face.

"Aero." I look at the woman, Isola if I remember

correctly. "Shit. Shit. Did you call Nirvana?" I demanded, as I pulled out the lorazepam and gave it to Aero, keeping her on her side as she foamed at the mouth. I curse, hoping she doesn't choke on her saliva or vomit. "How long has she been like this? Did she hit her head?" It sounded like that's what she said as we were coming in, but her words were fast. But now she's just shaking, holding Aero's hand, not responding again. "Isola!" I snap, drawing the woman's attention.

Isola nods her head, tears forming in her eyes. "I... yes. She did. It happened so fast. I went to get her clothes. She was sitting down in the tub, there wasn't much water in it and then I just heard something falling. She knocked the shampoo off the side and I came rushing in and I stabilized her head."

I check over Aero and see a gash in her head and pull the kit to me, grabbing gauze from it and pressing it to the oozing wound. I don't know how long we wait there, it couldn't be more than three minutes before Aero stops shaking and the EMTs show up. It all happened so fast, but as soon as Caden enters the room and sees the woman, actually sees her, his face loses all color.

Once the paramedics take over, Caden and I leave the room standing off to the side.

We don't speak but I do pull my phone from my pocket and dial the one person I can't get out of my mind. "Hello?" she answers on the third ring.

"It's Aero. She needs you."

———

Nirvana

.   .   .

My heart is racing as I rush inside the hospital. This seems to be happening more and more lately. The call from Ravi had me panicked. Why would he call me? Why didn't Isola? It wasn't supposed to be this fast. I have two and a half months left. My mind was a whirlwind of thoughts, incoherent and chaotic. I was aware that Layla and Delaney were beside me, they were talking but I couldn't hear them.

I only heard a white noise. Almost like a buzzing. The hospital staff was milling around, talking in hushed tones, at least I thought it was hushed tones. A phone ringing made it all come back. Sending a wave of breath rushing through me as I stopped at the front desk.

"I'm here for Aero Bridges. She was brought here thirty minutes ago." That's how long it took me to get here. Thirty minutes. Was I thirty minutes too late? No! I immediately rejected that idea. I wasn't too late. The older woman looked at me, her dark eyes assessing me before pointing to the waiting area.

"Family must wait over there. The doctor will be out shortly."

I don't look behind me. I need answers now. "Is she okay?"

The nurse glances at me and points again. "Family waits over there."

I slam my hand on the desk hard enough to make my palm sting and the nurse jump. "Are you always such a bitch to families?" I snap.

A gentle hand settles on my shoulder making me stiffen. "Nirvana. Calm down. Let's just sit before they kick us out," Delaney's soft voice said behind me. I glare at the woman one more time before letting Delaney and Layla pull me away. I glance to the side and see Spencer and Sorrow, both watching the room but staying at a distance. I let the two women sit me down, waiting in the furthest corner of the waiting room. They sit on either side of me holding my hands, giving me strength to go on.

I don't know how long we are there but I am mildly aware of the others coming in. Rory walks behind my chair and wraps an arm around me pressing a kiss to my head, murmuring how it's going to be okay. It wasn't, we all knew that. But the sentiment meant something. It's the last person that comes in that raises alarms in me. I don't see him. No, I smell him. I feel his stare, that hard disapproval that always came with each meeting.

The strong smell of his cologne was too much. The brittle smell of Irish Spring soap mixed with the thick cloying smell of smoke from that old pipe he used to set on the end table was almost suffocating. I tensed, my bones locking up on instinct. I felt bile rise in my throat.

"Nirvana," Ophelia whispered somewhere behind me but I couldn't hear her because he finally came into view.

He was taller than I remembered, but the cold, hard stare of his blue eyes remained the same. His hair, once thick, was thinning and gray. And he wore his robes, those fucking robes. They swished around his ankles like a cloak, sending shivers through me. I could hear the sounds of his boots hitting the tiled floors, a sound of finality. One I knew too well.

I laid my head against the deflated pillow, tears streaming down my face. My head was pounding, the therapy session went longer than it should have. I can still feel the shocks, hear the whispered prayer and feel the spray of holy water on me. I don't understand why I was here. I don't even know what day it is.

I sniffed, trying to stop the sobs that were contorting my body. It wouldn't do me any good to draw attention to myself. I don't know how long I was there for, but the moment I heard the echo of boots hitting the concrete floor I knew it was too long. But I didn't move. I was too tired, too weak. The hinges on the door squeaked open making me tense but I didn't turn.

The boots came into view moments before I was roughly yanked from my bed. I didn't dare make a sound so I bit the inside of my cheek so hard that I tasted the metallic tang of my blood. I gazed up at the cold blue eyes, meeting them head on.

"Your instructors tell me you are not following the procedures I have outlined for you, Nirvana," he sneers, shaking me hard enough that I thought I felt my brain rattle in my skull. "Answer me!" he shouts, his eyes flashing momentarily.

"I want to go home," I say, trying to keep the whimper out of my tone. He scoffs, dropping me on the cot.

"You will not come into my house while you house the Devil in you," he curses.

I try not to grit my teeth or let the tears burning in my eyes fall. "Please, Father. There's nothing wrong with me. I'm not housing the Devil." Whatever that meant.

But he didn't answer, he just shook his head in disgust. "You are no child of mine." With that he turned and walked away, leaving me alone in that dank small cell-like room. The door locked with a click and panic set in. I scurried from my cot and rushed to the door. Banging on it.

"No! Don't leave me here! You can't leave me here again!" I screamed, my little fists pounded on the door as I screamed and screamed. "There's nothing wrong with me! I'm normal!" They're words I was familiar with, words I cried the first day I was brought here. When those doors were locked behind me, trapped within these four walls, leaving me to a fate I'd never understand. But now... now they were hollow, they meant nothing. I meant nothing. I kept banging on the door, splitting my hands until blood ran down my arms. Leaving me feeling numb.

I don't know how long I screamed for, but I knew after this I'd *never be the same. And I was no longer the girl who was happy and kind. No, I held hate in my heart. Hate for the man I once called father.*

I met his eyes steadily. His steps faltered just for a moment before he glared at me, looking at me as if I was beneath him. I watch him as he sits down, right across from me.

"Nirvana," he said, his tone condescending and grating on my nerves.

I tilt my head to the side. "Father."

His face turns red. "I've told you not to call me that."

I shrug. "What else am I supposed to call the man who spawned me from his loins?" I see the others inch closer. Barely noticeable, but I saw it. I didn't know when they all showed up, but I was glad they were here. Maybe, just maybe, I wouldn't cause a scene.

"I'd never bear such a vile child," he states calmly. "You hardly come from me. More like your mother with the wicked way you act."

I shrug. "Wicked knows wicked. Like they say, the apple doesn't fall from the tree." I glance at him and continue, "Even if that tree is burning from within. But, hey, we can't pick our family."

He scoffs, finally turning away.

"Why are you here? How'd you even know to come here?" I ask.

"I owe you no explanations."

But I knew he shouldn't have any knowledge about Aero or what was going on with her. Unless Isola called him. Which made anger burn through me. I thought we had an understanding about him.

Breathing deeply I nod, I can't make a scene. I'll be civil. "I suppose so. But you're on none of the emergency contacts.

So you nor Doreen should've been contacted unless given permission. I didn't do it. Aero is ill, why are you here?"

My father bristles at my tone. "I came to pray over her soul. It's the last chance to save her before she goes into eternal Hell."

I stare at him a moment before shaking my head. "Eternal Hell. Fucking eternal Hell. You can't pray over her. I forbid it." Aero wasn't even Christian. She didn't have a religious belief, she believed in science more than God. He knows that. Or he should remember when he yelled at her when she refused to bow her head at her high school graduation prayer and she said she didn't believe. So the fact that he'd try and force it over her made my blood boil.

"You cannot forbid me from doing anything. Much less when it's an act of God." He's smug and that just makes my blood burn hot. I stand, brushing off the women.

I step towards him and he visibly tenses. "I have the final say in all things Aero. Me. Not you. I say no, and no means no." I tsk. "Oh wait, I forgot you don't take no for an answer do you, Father? She doesn't even believe in it. Or did you forget? Knowing you, you chose to be an ignorant asshole to push your agenda. No."

The sound of shoes rushing on the floor draws our attention. "I'm so sorry I'm late, honey," a voice says, making my world tilt.

I glance at the waiting room door. "Marcy?"

Chapter 18

Nirvana

You have got to be kidding me. Marcy. Fucking Marcy is standing in front of me after years of not seeing her. The same person who had made my life hell for years.

"Why the fuck are you here?" I turn, shocked at the venom in Delaney's voice. I'm not the only one either. No one but Delaney knows what happened with Marcy. She doesn't know what happened afterwards, or my time in that camp, but she knows what Marcy did. The others know I had a thing for her, but they don't know what happened between us. Not the kiss, not the fact she slapped me in the courtyard at school, or that the kiss was a dare. None of it. But Delaney, Delaney knows. She was there, she was there when I snapped at her to leave. When I thought she was going to hate me for it, too.

She held me instead, held me as I cried for the person I was becoming. For the secrets I held within me. She was angry on my behalf for what Marcy did. She was here now.

When I needed her most. She bailed me out of jail without question, and now I see her staring at Marcy, her eyes a multi-color pool of hatred. And Delaney didn't hate anyone. She didn't even hate her own half-brother who tried to kill her. Or her mother who set off the chain of events that tied us all together.

Marcy pales, placing a hand to her obviously swollen stomach as if Delaney made a threat to her, making me roll my eyes at the dramatics. "I'm here with my husband. If you must know." Marcy barely glances my way when she goes and sits beside my father.

Wait what? I take a step back, suddenly wanting to vomit.

"What the fuck?" I hear Layla whisper a little too loudly.

Marcy swallows hard, glancing at me briefly before looking down. I shake my head, wanting to curse, to cry, to laugh. God, did I want to laugh. Did I do any of that though? No. I just turned away. Wondering what I ever did to deserve such torture. The waiting room is thick with tension and it just keeps getting thicker and thicker as the time ticks by. There was too much going on at once. Way too much, and it was getting harder and harder to process it.

"What's wrong with Aero?" I hear Marcy ask. They don't even care to find out what's wrong with her? Seriously?

"Don't. Don't you ever speak her name again," I snap, not looking at them. I could hardly breathe as I walked back and forth in the waiting room. There was an insistent pounding behind my eyes and my temples. The faded marks there hurt, they hurt bad. I pressed my fingers to them hoping that slight pressure would ease it a little bit, but it didn't.

A cold sweat was beading on my skin making me feel clammy and cold. I couldn't tell if I was hot or cold. "Nirvana," Rory says, but I just shake my head, suddenly overwhelmed. What was taking the doctors so fucking long?

"Nirvana." This time it was Seraphina, but I wasn't listening. I was too far gone, wanting nothing more than to be with my sister. This wasn't how it was supposed to go. I ran a hand through my hair, accidentally pulling too tight and ripping out strands. I shook my hand out, wanting to get the feeling of the hair off me. My skin felt tighter, as if my bones were stretching it to impossible lengths. It hurt. It all hurts. I am hyperventilating now. My breaths were becoming faster and faster and black webs edged my vision. I can't breathe, it feels almost impossible to draw in a deep breath.

Why wasn't I getting any answers? I thought again, pacing back and forth.

"Nirvana, why don't you come sit down?" Delaney asks. I shake my head again, tears burning my eyes. No, no, I need to stand, then I can get to Aero faster. What if she woke up and I wasn't there? I need to go to my sister.

I go to walk to the reception desk, but stop suddenly when I feel a hand grab my arm and I look up meeting my father's hard gaze. "Sit down." His fingers squeeze my arm hard, bruising, but I hardly feel it.

I yank away from him. "Don't you fucking touch me!" I push him away from me but he doesn't even move. I don't care though. I start my pacing again. Wanting to get the feel of him touching me off my skin. I run my hand down my arm as if that would get rid of the feeling of his cold fingers on my skin. His touch always made my skin crawl and I hated it. I haven't seen him in years and now he is suddenly in front of me. God, where was Isola? Why wasn't she here? Was she with Aero? Then it started all over again. Me wanting to know what was happening with my sister and never getting any answers.

I can hear the others talking, wanting me to stop walking back and forth. What don't they understand? Movement is the only thing keeping me sane. That without moving I will break down and do something stupid, something that will cause more harm.

"Nirvana," another voice sounded, stern and commanding, stopping me in my tracks. I glance at the waiting area and see Ravi standing in the doorway watching me intently. Ravi. He was here. And he was staring at me with those earth-green eyes again. Sending my heart palpitating in my chest. A rough *thump thump thump*. A drumming that was louder than it should be. I can't breathe. I need to breathe. I suck in a breath when I see him inhale, almost as if he were breathing for me. Time is suspended in air, leaving just the two of us. I want to run to him, and I'm not sure why. But the moment is broken before I'm turning away and I'm looking at my friends who were gazing at me with worried eyes.

"Why haven't we heard anything?" I ask, my voice softer than it should've been. I was supposed to be strong for her, but I didn't feel strong. Not anymore. I press the heels of my hands to my eyes, suddenly so exhausted.

Ravi

"Nirvana," I called her name, waiting until she looked at me. But it was as if she didn't hear me. I watched her as she paced back and forth, rubbing her head and her eyes, ignoring everyone who called her name to sit down and relax before the other man grabbed her arm a little too roughly for my taste. I take a step forward only to stop when Nirvana snatches her arm from him.

"Don't you fucking touch me," she sneered, pushing at him. The man tenses and his jaw flexes but he doesn't touch her again and Nirvana resumes her pacing and rubbing her arm roughly. Leaving red marks on her pale skin.

"Nirvana," I say again, my voice stern and commanding. She stops then, looking at me with big watery blue eyes. Her chest is heaving as she struggles for breath. And before I realize what I'm doing I inhale deeply. Hoping she will follow suit so she doesn't pass out from lack of air. She sucks in air gazing at me with big eyes. The world around us fades away leaving the two of us. Breathing in and out, in and out. The color comes back to her face and the spell breaks. She licks her full bottom lip and turns away, her shoulders tensed slightly before she turns to the other women who looked at her with concern. Hell, I was concerned.

"Why haven't we heard anything?" she asks in a soft voice looking so defeated and alone.

"Come sit down, Nirvana. We'll hear something soon," Delaney says, standing and moving towards her slowly. Nirvana nods, taking a deep breath and moves towards her friends sitting down silently. The tension in the room was high as we waited. We all stood by Nirvana, crowding around her, keeping guard against the newcomers who watched her with judgmental eyes. Well, the man was. I don't know what I missed, but I didn't trust them. The woman, however, looked at Nirvana with interest before glancing at me. Ignoring them I turned to Sorrow who was standing behind Delaney, rubbing her shoulders but glaring at the other people as if he wanted to kill them.

Honestly, I wouldn't put it past the man. I kind of wanted to kill the man for putting his hands on Nirvana. I didn't like the way he looked at her with a sneer.

"Nirvana." We turn as Drew walks in looking tired. Caden is behind him and I nod to him. He took the rest of my shift for me so I could be near Nirvana. He nods back at me, patting Drew on the shoulder before coming to our rather large group. Nirvana stands and walks to Drew. She stands on her toes and whispers something to him, and Drew's ice green eyes glance at the couple. He nods and motions for Nirvana to follow him.

"Wait a minute! I have a right to know what's going on with my daughter!" the man snaps. My eyes track him. So this is Nirvana's father. I can see why she hates him.

Nirvana stops and looks at her father over her shoulder, "You and Doreen signed your rights over to her a long time ago. I raised Aero, you have nothing to do here. Nor do you have any type of pull over what goes on with her and her health."

Nirvana turns away with that last statement ignoring her father and his attempts to see Aero. A thick silence follows after her departure.

"You can leave now," Seraphina finally speaks up. "Nirvana doesn't need any more stress than she's already under."

Bridges glares at her. "You do know I know your parents."

"Damn, they're still alive? That's a shame," Sera says, gathering her bag. "Next time you see them, tell them I'll see them in Hell." She leaves after that.

Turning away from the couple I look at the others. "What the fuck happened?" Delaney stood and motioned for us to follow her. She sent one last scathing look to the couple, a look I've never seen from her before, and it was unnerving when Delaney was normally a sweet woman.

"That woman was the reason Nirvana was essentially disowned. Her father is a hypocritical creep who uses God as a scapegoat to be a twat," Delaney said, pressing a hand to her stomach.

"Are you all right?" Sorrow demanded. "Do you need to sit?"

Delaney shakes her head. "No. No, I'm fine. I just... I

don't understand why they're here. Someone had to have called them."

I clear my throat drawing their attention to me and ask, "Does anyone know if she's taking care of herself?" I know she slept when she was at my house, but how much sleep was she actually getting? Was she taking care of herself the way she should? I rub the back of my neck annoyed with these thoughts I was having. But I couldn't get that haunted look on her face out of my head.

There was a silence that followed after my question. "I haven't been over in a while. Not since that first day," Layla admitted softly.

"Me either," Ophelia replied.

Well, that answers that. We've all been so preoccupied we haven't taken a second to even check on Nirvana. Fuck. We may have helped her with the wedding and other things, but never once have we checked to see how *she* was doing. Or how she was feeling.

Cursing, I turn on my heel. "Where are you going?" Spencer calls after me.

"To see Nirvana."

Chapter 19

Nirvana

I followed Drew into the room where Aero was currently staying and my heart nearly stopped. She looked so small. Her once glowing skin was now pallid and clammy. Gray even. Her once vibrant shiny blonde hair was now brittle and dry. She was practically a different person. Isola sat in the corner, her eyes puffy and red from crying.

"I'm sorry. I'm so sorry, Nirvana," Isola says. I nod but I don't respond. I don't blame her for what's going on. We all knew she was sick. Granted we didn't think it was as progressed as it is. In fact, we all assumed that we had months before she declined like this. But we should've known. Once her personality began to change and her once bubbly personality turned to anger and sometimes hatred, we should've known she was on a limited time table. I knew it, I just didn't want to admit it to myself. I knew she was going fast but I ignored it and went and got drunk. Shame filled me as I moved closer to my sister.

"Can I have a little bit of time with my sister, please?" I whisper. Isola nods and gets up from her chair letting me pull the vacant chair up to the spot. Drew hovers a little bit, watching me. "What?" I ask, almost snapping at the man.

"How long have you been bipolar?" he asks.

I tense, scoffing, "I have no idea what you're talking about."

"Don't lie to me, Nirvana. It's not a good look on you. I'm well aware of your situation. We all are. Even if they don't know the full truth. You're spiraling. The others are just too polite to say anything. I'm not. You need to take care of yourself for your sister. For the women you claim to love as sisters."

It was none of his business. He didn't know anything about me.

I clench my teeth looking down at Aero's hand. "I don't need you in my business."

Drew scoffs, "Don't be an idiot. You know you have to take care of yourself or you'd be running yourself ragged when you don't need to. Are you taking any medication? Seeing a therapist?"

I run my thumb over Aero's cold hand, not looking at Drew. "You know, for a man who doesn't speak much you sure do have a lot to say to me. Why?" I don't answer him about medication. In all honesty, I don't know when I took it last. Or when I last saw Sherry, my therapist. Could've been weeks or months for all I know.

"Because I can. I don't want to see you wither away and lose sight of yourself in this. You need to be strong, not just physically but mentally as well. How can you do that if you're not taking care of yourself?"

"I'm fine," I reply. I was far from it, but I just had to get through this little rough patch. Then I'll finally be free. I just needed to get Aero through this. Even if I'm on less time now than I originally thought.

"I need to know you won't do anything stupid."

That caused my lips to turn up. "I won't do anything stupid. I still have to take care of my sister."

Drew is silent for a few seconds before he sighs. "You know she doesn't have much time anymore?"

I nod. "I know. I just want to do this one wish for her." I look at him and explain my plan. He looks skeptical, but finally nods. I could get this done in two days. Drew shakes his head before turning to leave the room, but I stop him. "You won't tell the others will you?" I ask.

He stares at me, his green eyes seeing too much on an uncomfortable level. The scar on his face is shiny against the fluorescent lights making his expression all the more dark. Especially when he shakes his head. "I'll decide if they need to know. If you don't start taking care of yourself like a responsible adult, you bet your ass I'm telling them." With that he turns and leaves the room. Leaving me alone with Aero.

"Jesus, he's terrifying."

I glance at Aero who is slowly blinking her eyes. "And you, my dear sister, are a devious woman," Aero says, her voice scratchy and dry. I stand and get her some water from the pitcher by her bed.

"You heard all of that I take it?" I respond, holding the straw to her chapped lips.

Aero nods, wincing slightly. She sighs when I pull away, closing her eyes again. "I did. Thank you. For doing this for me. I know it can't be easy. But why aren't you taking your medicine? You know you're supposed to take it at a set time every day. Are you out?"

A lump forms in my throat and I force myself to swallow it. "Of course not, I just missed a day. I've been busy. Trying to get everything done for you. I'd do anything for you. You know that."

Aero doesn't speak for a long time, I almost fear she fell asleep or worse. But then she does, shattering my world. "Even making up with Father?"

That sense of betrayal rushes through me again. Reminding me of that folder she has on me. I took a breath, breathing in deeply through my nose and exhaling out of my mouth. "He doesn't like me, Aero. And I don't like him."

Aero hums under her breath. "I know what happened. To you. What he did."

I wince. Trying not to lash out at her. But it was so fucking hard not to. So hard. "Then why would you want me to reconcile with him? And how do you have that folder? Why do you have it?" I ask through gritted teeth.

"It's not important," she waves the questions away. "You're going to need someone when I'm gone. Mother is hardly around, at least we know where he is."

"That's a shitty excuse, Aero. And you know it," I snapped, angry.

"Is it? I feel like you need family. I don't want you going off the deep end once I'm gone."

I turn away from her, rubbing at my chest. Just hearing her say she'll be dead soon makes breathing nearly impossible. I can't take it. I don't want to hear this.

"Stop it."

Aero scoffs which turned into coughing. "Why? Can't you handle the truth? I'm dying, Nirvana. Sooner rather than later. The sooner you accept it the better we will all be. You're old enough to know what death means. You're not naive so stop acting like you are and woman up."

"Fuck you, Aero. You don't get to tell me how I should handle this. That's not your right. I've respected your decision on this, I've done everything in my power to make everything right for you. But you don't get to control how I process everything!" I hissed.

Aero sighs. "Come on. You can't keep doing this to yourself. You need to move on. Go out and live. Not for you, but for me, too."

I brace my hands on the sink in the room, hanging my head down. Those tears I worked so hard to keep at bay are coming down freely. "You're only twenty-two. This wasn't how it was supposed to go." I shake my head, sniffing, trying to force myself to calm down.

"Life doesn't go the way we want it to, Vana. It's the way life is. The good die young. I just happen to be one of the unlucky ones."

I turn to her and see her watching me with so much love in her eyes. "Aero, this is the hardest thing I'll ever do. God, I raised you since you were eleven years old. You were and are my best friend. What am I going to do without you?"

Aero sends me a watery smile and holds out a shaky hand. I grab it, wrapping my warm fingers through her cold ones. "You will because you're the strongest person I know. You need to live for me. For yourself. Fall in love. Have beautiful babies, marry a prince or a princess. Live in a castle. Do it all."

I squeeze her hand. "Life isn't a fairytale, Aero."

Aero smiles, a serene smile. "Maybe not. But it doesn't have to be a tragedy either."

Chapter 20

RAVI

I wait outside the room, wanting to give Nirvana and Aero some more time together. I don't want to interrupt them. I don't know how long I wait before the door opens and Nirvana steps out wiping at her eyes.

She stops short when she sees me. "Ravi."

I straighten and stare down at her. "You need to eat."

A small smile touches her mouth, it's sad and watery but it's a smile and I'd take that over her tears. "What is it with you and food?"

"You need to eat, I need to eat. We might as well go together." I shrug. She watches me as I hold out my hand to her, she hesitates but eventually slides her smaller hand into mine. I twine our fingers and pull her into me. Her eyes widen and she presses her palm onto my chest, her fingers digging into the fabric of my shirt. I feel the slight touch all the way to my bones. Wrapping me in all things Nirvana.

"Ravi," she breathes.

I swallow hard, before whispering, "Just let me comfort you. Okay?"

She nods and allows me to wrap my arms around her, pulling her into a tight hug. Nirvana stiffens for a second but quickly relaxes and wraps her arms around my neck, holding me to her. I stroke her hair with my hand and pull her closer with the other, holding her as if I didn't want to let her go. And in this moment I don't want to. I see Drew walk past and he stops, arching an eyebrow at me. I don't say anything and neither does he. He just gives me a look and a nod. He gazes at her briefly and some emotion I can't place crosses his features. As if something happened between them. I tighten my hold on her briefly before pulling away.

"Come on, pixie. Let's go get you some food," I whisper.

"Okay," was her soft response. "Can we have that fish dish you made? It was good." I chuckle softly and nod.

"Sure. Let's go and I'll cook it. Do you want to do it at your house or mine?"

"Yours. Please." I nod and twine our fingers again and walk towards the waiting room. I see everyone is still there, including her father. I meet Caden and Sorrow's eyes and tap a message on Nirvana's hand. The men nod and motion to the others who also look and nod in agreement.

"What was that?" Nirvana asks, as I lead her outside into the muggy heat of the night.

"When we were on a mission we'd tap out Morse code messages when we couldn't talk. I told them to keep an eye on your sister's room. You don't want your father in there, so we'll keep him out," I say, navigating to the crowded parking lot until I found my car.

"Oh. Thank you. I really appreciate that." She slides into the car and I close her inside. I walk around the other side and glance up as her father and his wife exit the hospital. The woman looks at me briefly before turning away, a flash of guilt clouding her features. Her father, however, has an air of superiority around him. As if he were better than anyone and he would always be better. I clench my jaw and climb into the driver's seat.

"Ravi?" Nirvana says as I turn on the car and point the air conditioner towards her.

"Hmm?" I respond, pulling out of my spot.

"Thank you. For being there for me. When I was panicking. You didn't need to do that."

She's wrong, I did need to do it. I'd do it again if she needed it. I glanced at her from the corner of my eye, she was twisting her fingers together. Right now, she wasn't the confident, happy woman I've come to know from a distance. She was fragile, self-conscious, and timid. She was real and broken. So beautifully broken that I wanted nothing more than to help her put herself back together. But I know it's more than that. Nirvana is vulnerable and going through a traumatic event that would alter her life, she's been through things, things I don't understand and not even her friends understand. I wanted to know more about her, to be there when all of this eventually took that turn she didn't want.

Yet I don't say any of that. I just nod and pat her hand, "I'm here for you, tinker hell. Whatever you need."

A small smile graces her mouth at the nickname. "You're a very confusing man. I always thought you were against friendships with women."

I snort, getting on the highway. "No. I just enjoy being alone."

"You must be fun at parties."

"I've had my moments. But you're different." I don't mean to say that last part out loud but it's too late to take it back.

Nirvana leans her head against the headrest, gazing at

me from half-closed eyes. "Different. A good different, I hope."

"It depends who you ask."

She gives a mock gasp before she lightly smacks my arm. "That's very rude. I thought Flo taught you better than that."

I grin. "She did. Gran likes you."

"I like her, too. She's very sweet," Nirvana pauses. "Well, except when she thought you took advantage of me."

My face heats up with embarrassment. "I'm really sorry about that."

"You don't need to apologize again. I would've gone further if we weren't interrupted." She fingers the lace on the gearshiftt. "I'm sorry I threw my underwear at you."

Scoffing, I turn down the road, "No, you're not."

She laughs. "No, I'm not. But I did want you. I still do." Her voice turns husky at the end.

I squeeze the steering wheel tightly. So do I. "You needed a moment to come to terms with everything. Sex would've given you a temporary relief from it all but it would still be there."

Nirvana gives a small smirk. "You don't have a lot of confidence in your skills, do you, Ravi?"

"Make no mistake, Nirvana. I may be acting a gentleman now, but it doesn't mean I'll always be one. Once I have you in my bed, you'll be at my mercy. You'll be mine to play with, to use, to fuck any way I want to. And I promise you there will be nothing gentlemanly about me," I respond as I pull into my driveway.

Her breathing turns labored. "I don't want a gentleman. I want to be used anyway you want. I want to have one moment to myself. Doing what I want."

I look at her, seeing the red rise to her face and spreading lower. "Not tonight. Not when you've had an emotional day.

When I fuck you I want it to be because you want me to. Not because you need a moment's peace. I need you to be sure because once I have you, you're mine. Sleep on it after we eat. And if by tomorrow you still want me, I'll give you what you need."

I wait for her response, she pouts a bit but I can see she agrees with me. She needs time and after today and yesterday I don't want her to do something she'd regret. With a resigned sigh, she nods. I climb out of the car and she follows.

"I like it here. It's calm, not too secluded, and peaceful."

I give her a small smile. "This is the first home I've ever really had. One that I won't have to worry about losing."

"What do you mean?"

I shrug as I walk up the cobblestoned steps. "My parents died when I was really young. Drunk driver hit them head on. My grandparents had to take me in. They didn't have a problem with it, but there wasn't a lot of money back then. Gramps worked at a plant that paid less than minimum wage, Gran was a teacher and they don't make much so we were struggling. Living paycheck to paycheck and sometimes we didn't have enough to pay the bills. We got evicted a few times." I unlocked the door and opened it so Nirvana could go in first.

"Is that why you joined the Air Force Pararescue?" she asks.

"It's part of the reason. I wanted to be able to take care of them once I was able to."

"Where's your grandfather?"

"He died a few years ago." My throat tightens slightly.

"I'm sorry," she says, her voice soft and she touches my arm, a gentle brush of her fingers.

I shrug and walk to the kitchen. "He was an older man.

It's another reason I wanted Gran with me. So she wouldn't be alone."

"What about you?" she asks, sitting at the bar watching as I get the ingredients out for a late dinner before I wash my hands.

"What about me?"

"Weren't you lonely?"

I shrug. "I had my work, the guys. Nothing really to be lonely about."

"Have you always been close?"

I snort. "God, no! When I first enlisted I was paired with Caden and Sorrow. Those two were insufferable. Caden was always upset missing his girlfriend and Sorrow, well, he was Sorrow. A little less angsty though. He actually cracked jokes every once in a while." I roll up my sleeves and get to chopping some onions.

"Can I help?"

I look over my shoulder and motion Nirvana over. She stands and washes her hands before stepping near me. I hand her a small chef's knife and a bundle of parsley. "Just chop about half of it really fine."

"What was it like with the others? Did you like them aside from Sorrow's emo feelings and Caden being a lovesick fool?" I grin at the descriptions.

"Sam was quiet, always reading some book he found. Spencer was, well, the same if I'm being honest. It was difficult not to like him. Max was always standoffish and Drew was broody. Hardly talked then and hardly talks now."

Nirvana hums under her breath as she chops slowly and meticulously. "So how did you become so close?"

"I think it was the first year, after training and our first mission. We didn't know what we were getting into. We were in our early twenties."

"Aww, you were practically babies."

I scoff. "I suppose so compared to others. We were sent in to rescue some troops who went AWOL. Government thought they were runners. Turns out they lost their packs and were turned around in the jungle. It was for training. It wasn't a difficult mission, not by a long shot. We were effective and quick. It drew the attention of the government. Showed what we could do as a team." I shake my head, thinking if I knew then what I know now I wouldn't have entertained the idea. Being some type of double agent, stealing from terrorists, learning secrets that could get us killed.

"Are you okay?" Nirvana asks, halting her knife.

I gaze at her. "Yeah, why?"

"You got this faraway look in your eyes. As if you're reliving something."

I shake my head and finish cutting the onion. "Yeah. I'm just remembering a simpler time."

"Before you went into it?"

"I guess so."

She clears her throat. "Do you regret it?"

"No. It's brought me lifelong friends, a family. But I wish I knew more before I decided to enlist." We work in silence for a while before I speak up, "You're a dentist right?"

Nirvana smiles. "I'm a dental assistant."

"Do you like it?"

"Do I like getting bit by little terrors whose parents don't properly brush their teeth? Oh, I love it," she teases.

"Sounds riveting," I reply sarcastically as I scoop up some butter and put it in the hot pan. I let it melt a bit before I toss the onions and parsley into it.

"Do you like being a firefighter more? You're retired, right? From Pararescue I mean," she clarifies.

"I finished off my contract. I then went into the fire

department. I like the rush I get from it. The action," I explain.

"The rescuing."

"And the rescuing," I relent.

"You have a complex."

I grunt under my breath and reply, "I don't have a complex."

"You do, too. It's a savior complex. White knight syndrome if you will."

Sautéing the onions, I sigh. "I wouldn't say that. I just like helping those in need."

"Which is fine. But it's still a complex."

"You're aware I'm making your food, right?"

Nirvana's eyes widen and she closes her mouth, pretending to look innocent. "I won't say another word. Scout's honor."

Shaking my head, I finish off the sauce before setting it aside and prepping the salmon. I season it and hand Nirvana a lemon to slice up, before I wash my hands to clean the rice and put it in the rice cooker. Once everything is done, I put the fish in the oven to cook for the next fifteen minutes.

Nirvana cleans our area before going to sit down. "Where did you learn to cook?"

"Gramps. He loved cooking." I lean against the counter and watch as she plays with the red placemat on the table. "How'd you become friends with the other women?"

"Seraphina's family came to Father Bridges' church. Then eventually we went to the same elementary school. Delaney became friends with us after Ophelia came. Ophelia was picked on. Delaney stood up for her and I helped Ophelia and we just kind of fell into each other," Nirvana explained.

"It's rare that people stay friends this long after school," I murmur.

"Isn't it rare to have an entire unit survive wars?" she asks, tilting her head to the side letting white blonde hair fall over her delicate shoulder.

"Not if you're a good team. In sync with one another at all times." The timer for the rice went off and I quickly turned away to pull the salmon out before opening the rice cooker and scooping some onto a plate.

"Are you still a team?" Nirvana asks suddenly.

I swallow. "We'll always be a team." No matter what, we'll be a team, and it was slowly including these women who were becoming a part of this twisted family.

Nirvana didn't say anything as I set her plate in front of her, just sent me a small smile. I gathered my own plate and we ate in a semi-comfortable silence. Both of us lost in our own thoughts. I glanced at her and for a moment I think about her assessment.

You have a savior complex. White knight syndrome if you will.

Was she right? Is that why I do what I do? Is that why I'm becoming attached to this broken woman? The more I think about it the more I see that I do have a white knight syndrome but with Nirvana I don't want to save her, I want to embrace her, I want to consume her. Broken parts and all. Because underneath this shattered woman is a survivor, a warrior who needs to break free.

I don't want to fix her, I just want her. But deep down I know that's not possible. Not now, and maybe not ever. She had her own shit to deal with and I needed to know if I was ready to carry those demons with her. I knew the answer already. Yes. Yes, I would. But the real question is, will she let me in to carry this burden with her?

Chapter 21

Nirvana

I stretched my arms over my head as I watched Ravi come out of the bathroom with gray sweatpants hanging low on his hips and a white t-shirt on. Whoever invented gray sweatpants needed to be praised by all women. Because it was simply unfair at how attractive they were.

"What?" Ravi asks, pulling the blanket back to climb into the bed beside me.

I shake my head. "Nothing. Just staring."

He snorts and lays on his back, putting his arms behind his head to stare up at the ceiling. It gave me a moment to study him again. Taking in all the stuff I missed the first time. He had a strong jawline with a permanent shadow on it. His hair was a light brown but I could see strands of blond and gray lacing through the hairs on his face. He had a small scar on the side of his mouth that I hadn't noticed before. The more I looked at him the more I saw. But it was the slight ink that was peaking up the shoulder towards his neck. Without thinking I ran my finger over it.

Ravi turned his head to look at me, those forest green eyes darker than I remember with splashes of brown and gold in them. Kind of like leaves when it was just turning fall. Beautiful.

"You're a beautiful man, Ravi," I whisper, trailing my finger from the small ink on his shoulder up the side of his neck.

He shuddered slightly before he grabbed my hand and pulled me into him, sending my heart racing. "Men aren't beautiful, pixie." I swallow at the name, my throat suddenly becomes dry. At first it sounded condescending, that and tinker hell but when he said it his eyes lit up slightly. He said it with affection, and well, sometimes frustration but it still made me go soft on the inside.

"I beg to differ. You exceed the norm for men."

He gives me a small smirk. "If I didn't know any better I'd think you're flirting with me."

I roll my eyes. "I wouldn't go that far. It was an observation. Don't let it go to your already big head."

Ravi laughs, a deep masculine sound that goes through my body making me feel hot and achy. Needy. He let go of my hand. "Go to sleep, Nirvana."

With a huff I roll over to my back muttering, "Whatever you say, Daddy."

Ravi moves then, leaning up and grabbing my chin so I would look at him. "I don't appreciate your sarcasm. I'm trying to be a decent man here."

I gaze at him. His eyes are heated and his breathing is a little labored. I gaze down and see the tenting in his pants. "Oh," I say, still looking at his growing erection. My eyes widened. "You liked me calling you that?" I ask, staring at his cock hardening before my eyes.

"Eyes up here," Ravi commands. I look up quickly. *Holy shit, holy shit,* I thought to myself, an ache suddenly building between my legs. I squirm slightly, trying to add just a little pressure to ease the need I felt, but it only made it worse.

"Go to bed. Now. I'm at my wit's end and what little control I may have is snapping quickly. So go to sleep, don't move, don't speak. Understand?"

I lick my lips wondering if I could push his limits. Was it wrong of me? Of course. Did I care? I probably should, but I don't. So with a small grin, I whisper, "Yes, Daddy." His eyes flash, heat rising hard and fast. His nose flares as he takes a deep breath. Ravi lets go of my chin, sits up, and scoots to the edge of the bed, his shoulders stiff. I sigh to myself, did I go too far?

I know that I'm pushing, but ever since I've gotten to know him, the real him I can't stop thinking about him. I can't get him out of my head. Even if he's brisk and to the point most of the time, I still want to be around him. I want him. I sit up slowly and glance at the clock on his nightstand and see the time. It's a little after midnight. Taking a breath, I muster as much courage as I can before I speak.

"Ravi," I start, watching as his broad shoulders tense even more. I swallow hard. "It's tomorrow." My voice was breathy and needy when I tried to be confident and strong. "I still want you." *I'll probably always want you.* I don't say that but it's on the tip of my tongue. I don't think he's going to respond, leaving us in a thick, tense silence where I can only hear the blood rushing to my ears. But he stands turning to me.

"Be sure this is what you want, Nirvana. Because once you're mine, you're mine." The thought of being his is terrifying, but it's also exhilarating. That look he got at Club Anarchy is back. That possessive dark look when he gripped my throat was back and directed at me. My heart was hammering in my chest, my throat dry. God, I wanted this man with every breath in my body.

"I'm sure." As soon as the words leave my mouth he's there. He grabs my ankle and pulls me to the edge of the bed making me fall to my back. Ravi leans over me, his large hand going to my throat. The move is so sudden I don't react, trying to breathe in, but then he's there. Taking possession of my mouth. And that's what he does, possesses me. Owns me. I gasp in surprise and he uses that to thrust his tongue into my mouth. Groaning, I wrap my hands into his hair, pulling none too gently. It was too much, but somehow not enough. I need more. Our tongues thrust together, mimicking the moves of sex.

God, men shouldn't kiss like this. That's how women get obsessed and begin doing crazy shit. And I was falling fast into the obsessed category. My hands travel down his back to the hem of his shirt pulling it up. Ravi pulls back slightly and reaches behind himself with one hand and pulls his shirt off, throwing it somewhere behind him. I lean up on my elbows gasping for breath.

"Holy shit. It should be illegal to look like you," I say before I can stop myself. I drink him in. He has tattoos on his shoulders to his arms reaching over his back and climbing up to his neck. Intricate black and red designs I want to study more, but I can't because I look lower. His chest is muscular with a smattering of soft brown hair that disappears down into his pants. Fuck. His stomach looks like God himself chiseled it from the finest stone. So much muscle. I wanted to run my hands down him, to take my fill then restart because I can't get enough. Ravi leans forward again, grabbing the front of my shirt, lifting me up so our chests are flush together. Then his mouth is back on mine.

My hands fly to his shoulders, holding him to me. This kiss is different. Almost urgent and intense. His tongue thrusts against mine, all heat and fervor. Ravi pulls back again and grips my shirt. He doesn't say anything, just rips the material down the middle and throws it aside leaving me in my black bra and sweatpants. He pushes me back on the bed, so he can pull my pants down leaving me in nothing but my bra and panties while he is still in his sweats.

"Beautiful," he whispers. And I feel like I am. In this moment with Ravi I feel like I'm the most beautiful woman in the world. The way his eyes follow every line and curve of my body, to the way he slowly runs his hands up my legs, tracing the slight imperfections I have there. To the way he spreads my thighs wide and leans down to press his mouth against them. Kissing them gently before biting down, marking me. I gasp, wanting him to go higher.

"Ravi, please," I whimper when he kisses up my thigh to my hip where his teeth grab the waistband of my underwear before pulling them down. With. His. Teeth. "Oh my god," I moan. I look down at him watching as he tosses my panties away. He looks beautiful standing there. The sliver of moonlight peeking from his curtains makes him look like an avenging angel. Dark and mysterious. Deadly. And fuck if I didn't die before he actually touched me.

Chapter 22

Nirvana

I lean up on my elbows watching Ravi with a quick arch of my brow. "Are you just going to stare at me?" I ask.

"I will if I want to," he responds. I narrowed my eyes, wondering what kind of game he was playing with me. I watched him as he circled the bed and moved to the nightstand. He pulled it open and reached inside pulling out a row of condoms.

I arch an eyebrow at him. "You know you only need one, right?"

He snorts and looks at me. "It's cute you think I'd stop at just one time."

I swallowed hard, suddenly nervous as a shiver of anticipation went through me. I watched him, my breathing turned shallow and dampness gathered between my thighs reminding me I was practically naked. On Ravi's bed.

"Take your bra off and grab the headboard. Don't move unless I tell you to." I glance at Ravi but his back is towards me as he walks into the bathroom. I lean forward on the bed and reach behind me to unhook the clasp on my bra before letting it fall down my arms. I toss it aside and grab onto the brass headboard, leaving myself fully exposed to Ravi. The cool touch of the metal along with the cool sheets was a stark contrast to the heat that was coursing through my body. Ravi came out of the bathroom then, fully naked. My eyes widened. Holy shit. Holy shit. I've never seen a more perfect man in my entire twenty-eight years on this planet.

I thought his chest was something magnificent but damn, I was wrong. My eyes traveled down his chest, stopping at the V that led towards an erection that he was proudly sprouting. An erection I wanted to run my tongue over, tasting every single inch. He was long and thick with a slightly red head that was already leaking precum.

"Ravi," I breathe out, not too ashamed to beg for him. He climbs on the bed and presses a kiss to my mouth. A quick kiss, nothing more, before he runs his mouth down my neck. I arch into the touch, gasping every time his teeth nipped and his tongue soothed. My hands clenched on the headboard trying to stop myself from moving. His lips kissed every inch of skin before he stopped at my breasts. I squirmed, wanting more.

"You're so beautiful, Nirvana," he whispered before he pulled one of my nipples into his hot mouth. I threw my head back and moaned. His other hand moved up my side to my other breast.

"Ravi. Ravi, please, I need more," I groaned, spreading my legs so he was wedged between them. His cock was pressed against my throbbing clit, brushing ever so lightly that I was nearly sobbing with need. He left my breast and kissed down my stomach moving lower until he was right where I needed him to be. So close, yet it felt so far away.

I felt his breath first, warm air pressing against my

swollen flesh before the first touch of his tongue. I was done for, I just knew it. But it was when he sucked my clit into his mouth that I knew I was ruined for anyone else. Completely and utterly ruined.

He groaned against me as he stroked and tasted before he speared a thick finger inside. I lost all pretense of listening. I dropped my arms and grabbed his hair, pulling slightly. But he didn't seem to mind, in fact he grabbed one hand and twined our fingers together as he fucked me with his other hand and tongue. Owning me. It was too much. His finger curved inside of me, hitting my G-spot sending me into a shockingly strong orgasm. I cried out his name holding him to me as I rode the waves of intense euphoria.

Ravi leaned up and wiped his face with his hand before leaning forward to grab a condom. I watch in a haze as he rips it open with his teeth and slides it on his cock, before he grabs my hips and flips me onto my stomach. Bracing me on my hands and knees. I glance over my shoulder and stare at him breathing heavily. God, he was beautiful like this. Nearly out of control, one hand on my hip as his other lines up his dick against me, rubbing gently up and down causing me to shudder.

His eyes connect with mine, flaring hotly with desire, "You moved without my permission," he says, his voice deep and husky. He rubs his cock up and down my pussy again before pushing in just a little bit. I gasp, arching into him. My head falls forward as he stretches me. My hands grip the sheets tightly. Holy hell, it felt like he was splitting me in two. I tried to breathe through it but I couldn't seem to catch my breath. I pushed against him wanting more. "Fuck. You're so fucking tight," he ground out, his fingers flexed on my hip before running up my back and wrapping in my hair. It happened so fast, he pulled my hair up making my back arch more, then with a growl he thrust forward, seating himself fully inside me.

I scream, suddenly coming again. "Oh my god." I didn't know it could be like this. So intense I couldn't do more than moan and cry his name. I could hardly do more than meet him thrust for thrust pushing myself back against him. It was nearly impossible to move with the way he held me by the hair. I loved it.

Ravi cursed, pounding into me hard and fast, prolonging my orgasm. It was too much. I could hardly breathe feeling the way I came, how the sheets got embarrassingly wet. But I couldn't find it in me to care. Then he moves again, he pulls out of me fast, grabs my hips and flips me to my back before thrusting back in. I can barely react as his hands force my thighs open to accommodate him. I groan as he pushes into me over and over causing my eyes to close involuntarily as I try to breathe.

"Eyes on me, Nirvana." The sharp command has my eyes snapping open and finding him as he pumps inside of me. "See who owns your pussy. See who's making you come."

"Ravi," I moan, as my hands find his hips, urging him on. He leans down and captures my mouth with his own. Kissing me as if it would be his last. And I loved everything about it.

Ravi

I pull away from Nirvana's mouth and slow down, wanting to prolong her pleasure. God, she was so tight and hot, and I didn't want this to end. But she shocks the fuck out of me when she grabs one of my hands and leads it to her throat.

"You said to come to you when I wanted this," she whispers.

I did, I know I did but she looked so vulnerable. "Please. Please, I need this," she begs softly. Fuck.

"If it's too much, squeeze my wrist. Do you understand?"

She gives me a smirk, "Yes, Daddy." My cock jerks in her and I know I no longer have the control. That belonged to the woman under me. Arching forward I squeeze her throat, cutting off her air just enough to make her coming orgasm more intense. I pump into her hard and fast, feeling the way her pussy clamped down on me, tightening against me. Leaning down I pull a taut nipple into my mouth. Pulling in time with my thrusts. I hear her gasp and watch as her eyes close. She squeezes my wrist ever so slightly and I let go of her throat. Gripping her hips tightly as I thrust into Nirvana a few more times before I felt her tense in my arms. Her back arches and her tits press against my sweat slicked chest as she gets ready to come again. She sucks in a deep breath and comes. Her voice goes hoarse as she calls my name on a low husky groan that sends me into my own release. I press my forehead to hers and groan her name, my hands flexing on her hips as I empty myself inside of her. Her hands find my back rubbing soothing circles on it as we both attempt to catch our breath.

I press a kiss to her damp cheek, holding her to me.

Hell, I've never had sex like this before. So intense that my body is shuddering as if it were my first time. But once I left the bathroom and I saw Nirvana laid out naked on my bed, her hands gripping the headboard making her breasts jut out like an offering I couldn't stop myself. She was like a dream. One that I never wanted to leave. I glance down at her and see a small smile touch her lips.

I give her my own smile before pressing a kiss to her lips and turn over to discard the condom. When I lie back down, she rolls over and lies on my chest. I wrap an arm around her and run my fingers up and down the smooth column of her back. She sighs contentedly leaving us in a comfortable silence.

"Are you asleep?" Nirvana suddenly asks, her voice softer than I've ever heard it.

"No."

She gazes up at me, her blue eyes bright. "I never knew sex could be like that."

I grin, lifting my hand to her hair to smooth it out of her face before replying, "It's never been like that for me before. This was different, it was..."

"Intense?" She finished the sentence. I nod. Yeah, it was intense. I never knew it could be like this. Like two souls coming together. It was hot and breathtakingly beautiful. Something I didn't know was possible.

"Did I hurt you?" I ask, trying to shake those thoughts out of my head.

Nirvana shakes her head. "No. It was perfect. It was everything."

"You did so good. So fucking good," I whisper fiercely.

I grip the back of her neck to pull her down for a kiss. She eagerly moves forward pressing her lips to mine. Tasting herself on my tongue. An intoxicating combination. My cock stirs between us and Nirvana reaches forward and grabs the other condoms. She pulls one free and sits up to unwrap it and slide it down my cock. I stare at her. She sends a little grin and straddles me, grinding herself against me. I groan, grabbing her hips so she can slide down on me.

She throws her head back and moans, "Ravi."

I sit up and pull one of her nipples into my mouth. Tonight is going to be a long night. And it was. Leaving my room with condoms littering the floor and the sheets strewn all over the room.

Chapter 23

Nirvana

I groan as I walk down the hospital hallway twisting slightly to ease the ache between my legs. I should've stopped after round three but I couldn't help it. Not when Ravi worshiped me over and over again. I blush thinking about it. I press a hand to my throat still feeling Ravi's hand there and how he sent me spiraling over and over again.

"Why are you walking like that?" Layla asks, sipping her coffee as Rory pushes an empty wheelchair towards Aero's room. I shake my thoughts out of my head.

"I'm not walking like anything," I defend.

"You're walking as if you've been bull riding and got knocked off and kicked in the vagina twelve times," Rory comments, ignoring the looks from nurses who've overheard her.

I give an apologetic smile before glaring at the two women beside me. "Will you keep it down," I hiss. "And no, I'm not." I might as well be. God, Ravi was insatiable. I didn't know men could go more than once at a time but Ravi exceeded all expectations. Just thinking about it had my body heating up. The way he held me afterwards, or went to get us snacks and water. To the hot bath.

"Nirvana," Layla said, snapping me from my head.

"What?"

"You okay?" she asked, as we made it down Aero's hall.

I nod, trying to subtly fan myself but stop when I see the rather large love bite on my shoulder. "What was that?" Layla asked, stopping me. I quickly fixed my shirt, but Layla pulled it back, her gaze falling on the bite, her green eyes growing wider than should be humanly possible. "Oh my god! You were fucking!"

I put my hand over her mouth. "Shh! Do you want the entire hospital to know my business?"

Rory turned to us. "What are you doing? We have a small window."

Layla licked my hand causing me to pull away in disgust. Smiling smugly, she turned to Rory. "Vana has been holding out on us."

Rory arched a black brow. "Oh? How's that?"

Layla pulled my shirt down. "She's been hooking up with someone."

I slap at her hand, glaring. "It just happened you redheaded stepchild."

She shrugs. "Who was it? Do we know them?"

I start walking again muttering, "Ravi."

"What?" Rory says, following after me. Trying to keep up with my strides because she was laughing and hardly paying attention to anything around her.

"Ravi," I repeat, speaking lower.

"Speak up, Vana," Layla says in exasperation.

"Ravi! It was Ravi!" I say a little too loudly. Wincing when people looked at me as if I was crazy.

"What was Ravi?" a deep voice asks behind us, making me jump.

I turn quickly, almost falling, but strong hands catch me. "Ravi! Hi!" Rory says, her face turning a little red. Layla turns away and rushes down the hall. I shake my head, my heart pounding rapidly. I stare at him and nearly melt on the ground. He wore a suit sans the tie. His sleeves were folded up showing off his muscular forearms. I didn't know I could be attracted to forearms until this man and it was a tad surreal to even think about it. But I couldn't help but remember what they looked like holding me tight as he fucked me. My body heated at the reminder.

"Hey," he says, dropping his hands from my hips, making me miss his touch.

"What are you doing here?" I ask. Did I sound as breathless as I felt, I wonder, glancing at him.

Ravi looks at me a small smirk playing on his kiss swollen lips. "I'm the getaway driver today. Drew called me to pick up the van."

"Oh. Right. Well, let's get to it. We don't have a lot of time." I turn and wince at the twinge I felt between my legs.

Ravi steps beside me, brushing his fingers over my hip. "Are you all right?"

"Looks like she went horseback riding," Rory said, trying to cover her laugh with an obnoxious cough.

"Bull, you said bull riding," I say through clenched teeth that makes her laugh a little harder. Ravi gives a small laugh beside me and I feel my face heat up. Not in embarrassment, never that. I'm not embarrassed about sleeping with Ravi. But with the fact I want him again and I can't help thinking about it. Ignoring the two beside me, I walk into Aero's room where Louise, Ophelia, and Delaney are doing Aero's hair and makeup. I stopped short seeing her in our mother's wedding dress.

Tears fill my eyes. "Oh, Aero."

Aero turns and smiles at me. I can tell she's exhausted and that she was getting sicker but I could still see the excitement in her eyes. "What do you think, Van Van?"

I clear my throat and step into the room, "You look beautiful."

"Do you think Isola will like it?"

I scoff, pressing my hand to her cheek gently, "She's not going to be able to take her eyes off of you."

Aero's smile brightens even more and she points to the bed where a garment bag rested. "Your outfit is in there."

I walk over to the bed and shake my head, a small smirk playing on my lips. "You are a diabolical woman."

Aero smiles at me. "Go on. Put it on. Bathroom is over there." I grab the bag and walk to the bathroom. My eyes meet Ravi's briefly. Seeing the heated look he sent me made my heart speed up until I locked myself into the bathroom. I took a breath and put the bag on the door and opened it, seeing a long flowy gold dress. I swallow hard and strip out of my clothes glad I decided to shower at Ravi's this morning before coming here. I quickly put the dress on. It hugged my body like a glove with its long shimmery train that sat neatly behind me with one strap that hung on my shoulder thankfully covering the mark Ravi gave me.

I turned towards the mirror. I hardly noticed the woman staring back at me. My eyes were brighter than they have been in weeks, my cheeks had more color and I looked content. Albeit sad and tired but better than I have. I can't see the marks on my skin which I was glad about. My hair hung in neat waves down my back giving off goddess era vibes. I nodded to myself and dug into the bag where there were black strappy heels and a garter. I put both on and stepped out of the bathroom.

The room quieted and everyone stared at me. "What?" I ask.

"Wow. Nirvana, you look stunning," Louise said, speaking first. She was Ophelia's mom and kind of adopted the rest of us. She wore her long curly black hair in intricate braids with gold accessories in it. Ophelia and her often times got mistaken for sisters. Both had smooth dark skin, and onyx eyes that shined whenever they were smiling or happy. I wasn't surprised Louise was here, especially for Aero.

"Thank you," I say, slightly embarrassed to have them all looking at me.

"You look like a ball of sunshine. I love it. Come on now we're on a time crunch," Aero says, coughing slightly. I nod, and notice that Drew is in the room helping her into the wheelchair and making sure she's still hooked to machines. He glances at me as if trying to gauge my mental health and I turn away, looking towards Ravi.

Ravi gazes at me, staring me up and down with desire burning bright in his eyes, making me highly aware of what we did yesterday. I lick my lips and turn away catching Delaney watching me, but I don't say anything.

"Okay, we can't be there longer than three hours. This is expensive equipment so the longer it's gone the more likely my ass gets arrested for theft," Drew says looking out the door. "We're clear." We move out together and see the elevator waiting open with Sam and Spencer standing in it.

"Guards?" Ravi asks, putting his hand at the small of my back to push me inside.

"I hired a few guys I know from a while ago. They owe me a favor," Sam says, not explaining anything.

"What if the doctors try to check on her?" I ask, panic rising inside of me.

"I have a nurse who knows. She'll go in the room and check her vitals. I'll be texting updates," Drew says.

"Aren't your machines connected to some system?" Rory asks.

"Yes. Sam and Max overrode the system to show her vitals even when we're gone. But it only lasts so long, so let's get a move on."

The elevator takes us down to the garage. Ravi leaves us, quickly coming back with a larger black van. Caden pops out of the back and helps Drew get the medical equipment in followed by Aero. Delaney touches my shoulder and smiles. "We'll meet you there. Be careful." I nod and hug her quickly before climbing into the front with Ravi.

"Do you know where you're going?" I ask.

Ravi nods and pulls up the GPS plugging in the address for Cannon's barn. I twist my fingers in my lap trying to take calming breaths that did nothing to calm my racing thoughts. Ravi gazes at me briefly before looking ahead.

"Are you okay?"

I scoff under my breath, "I don't know. Not really."

He nods, and the car ride after that is silent. The clouds are darkening and the slight rumble of thunder sounds in the distance as we get to the bar. Cars are already lined up and Caden and Drew help Aero out so the hospital machines don't get ruined. I climb out slower than the others not wanting to go inside just yet. Ravi steps beside me, his fingers trailing gently down my arm.

I shudder at the contact, moving a little closer to his warmth. It's mid-June and I feel cold, perhaps it's the fact that after this I know there's nothing left I can do for my sister. Or that I'm watching her marry the love of her life knowing there is hardly any time for them to be together. Those happy thoughts from earlier vanished like smoke, leaving me feeling numb. Desolate from everything around me.

Ravi doesn't speak for a long time before he says, "We have to go in. The wedding is starting soon and you're needed at the front."

I nod before peeking up at him. I stand on my tiptoes and press a gentle kiss to the side of his mouth, inhaling his spicy scent. "Thank you. For yesterday. For these last few weeks."

I go to pull away, but Ravi wraps his hand around my throat and pulls me in for a kiss. An earth shattering kiss that has me sinking into him. His tongue moves lazily against mine, stroking a fire within me. I pull away first, breathing heavily. I press my hand to his steady beating heart letting my breathing match his before I step in front of all of those people. "Your lips should be illegal," I mutter, earning a cocky smirk from Ravi. Shaking my head, I step back from him, putting a little distance between us.

"I'll see you inside?"

"I wouldn't miss it." I give another shy smile before turning away squaring my shoulders as I went. I could do this. For Aero I could do anything.

Chapter 24

RAVI

I step inside the barn, shocked at how different it looks. There were people mingling with each other, a bar stocked and manned by Cannon. Black chairs were set near the arch where Nirvana was setting up. I could see the stiffness in her back as she opened a small notebook and set it on a podium. The arch held twinkle lights making it look like the night sky filled with stars. I move to my seat sitting beside Caden and Max.

The chairs slowly began to fill up, guests sat all dressed in white. Sorrow slid in the seat beside me and Delaney was at his other side. It filled up quickly making the barn feel smaller than it was.

"I didn't realize so many people would be here," Max said beside me.

"Aero has a lot of college friends. Her bridesmaids flew in this morning," Rory explained as she took her seat in front of us. The sound of music filled the air and the bridesmaids began to walk down the aisle all wearing white. But I didn't watch them, I watched Nirvana. She stood in front of the arch looking reserved and sad. Alone.

I didn't get a chance to think ahead because the wedding march started. We all stood and Isola came down the aisle with her parents beside her. She wore a black suit and held a bouquet of flowers. She stood with her side and smiled when the barn doors opened showing Aero. Drew held her carefully and somehow he and Caden found a way around the medical equipment. I looked at Nirvana and saw her eyes filling with tears as she looked at her little sister.

Nirvana smiled at her sister when she stopped at the arch with Drew. She touched her sister's face so gently it made my heart twist. Drew stepped away but stood close enough in case something happened. "You may be seated," Nirvana's soft voice filled the space around us.

There was a thick silence, filling what should be a happy day into a bleak darkness. Thunder sounded in the distance, but that didn't stop Nirvana. She plastered a smile on her face and looked at the couple in front of her.

"I'm not exactly sure how to start this. I don't really know much about love, I've only seen real love a few times in my life." Our eyes met briefly a look passing through her before she looked at her sister. "One of those being Aero and Isola. I've seen these two grow up together and slowly fall in love. I'm talking real love, the one that country singers write songs about and authors write books about. It's inspiring and I've never felt more proud to see two people get married as I am today."

Nirvana looks around the crowd of people, her gaze falling on someone behind us and narrowing. "If there is someone who doesn't believe these two should get married, speak now or forever hold your peace." There is a slight pause, a cough in the distance but no one stands or speaks.

"Good. Now off to the vows." Nirvana clears her throat grabbing her little notebook. "Marriage is a bond between two people. A unity that is strong and can't nor should be broken. This is sacred and precious." She turns to her sister, giving her a watery smile, "Aero, please repeat after me, I, Aero Lorraine Bridges, take thee Isola to be my lawfully wedded wife."

Aero smiles at Isola, her own tears filling her eyes, "I, Aero Lorraine Bridges, take thee Isola to be my lawfully wedded wife."

Nirvana takes a breath and says, "In sickness and in health."

"In sickness and in health."

"Till death," Nirvana's voice chokes up slightly and I see a tear come down her face. Clearing her throat she continues, "Till death do you part."

"Till death do I part," Aero whispers, grabbing Isola's hand. Both women were crying now. Hell, I'm pretty sure I saw Caden dab his own eyes.

Nirvana takes the ring from the large man behind Aero and hands it to her sister.

"Place this ring on her finger."

Aero does so and smiles, "I love you, Isola. You were my first, my only, and my last love." A sob leaves Isola and she pulls Aero into her, holding her tight.

I watch as Nirvana turns away wiping under her eyes and I want to do nothing more than hold her. I hear Delaney sniff delicately beside me and see Rory bow her head. Layla is holding onto Seraphina and Ophelia is dabbing her own eyes. All feeling the same emotions that are going through Nirvana. It's intense, shit, I even feel my chest tightening.

Isola pulls back and Nirvana asks her to repeat her vows and she does, putting on Aero's ring and squeezing her hand. "Aero, do you take Isola as your wife?"

Aero smiles proudly. "I do."

"Isola, do you take Aero as your wife?"

Isola smiles. "I do."

Nirvana nods, "By the power vested in me by some sketchy website I found on the internet, I now pronounce you wife and wife. You may now kiss your bride." Isola grabs Aero's face and kisses her, a long kiss. A goodbye, one that we all knew could very well be their last. Nirvana looks forward, her eyes finding mine as I clap with the others. Aero pulls away from her wife and looks at Nirvana who smiles sadly. Aero pulls her into her arms and I see Nirvana tuck her head in her shoulder, hugging her tightly.

I sit back down with the others as the guests move to get food and drink and congratulate the brides. I watch as Nirvana closes her notebook and looks over at Aero who said something to her. Nirvana gives her a small smile and takes her hand. Music plays in the distance and Nirvana pulls her sister into her holding her tightly. Neither woman cares about the guests and I don't blame them. This is their only chance for this moment. Nirvana buries her face against Aero's shoulder and I can see her shoulders shaking. Aero holds her close, swaying then she whispers something to Nirvana that has her looking up and shaking her head.

Aero nods firmly then moves away leaving Nirvana alone.

"Aero, I said let it go," Nirvana calls following her sister. I stand and move in behind her, grabbing her hand.

"What's wrong?" I demand.

But she doesn't get a chance to say anything when we hear yelling. Loud yelling.

"Shit, shit, shit," Nirvana pants, pushing through the crowd of people. I push them out of our way when we see Aero arguing with her father.

"I have no idea what you're talking about, Aero," he says, his voice void of all emotion.

"When you sent her to "Bible camp" that one summer. I remember that day! I was there. I was there and heard it all," Aero says, adding sarcastic air quotes to Bible camp.

Nirvana tenses and steps forward. "Aero, it's okay. It's all right. It's your wedding day. Let's just let him go home."

Aero shakes her head, "No! No! He needs to know what he did!"

"Aero!" Nirvana shouts.

"You were alone, abused, and scared. You were barely fourteen. Fourteen! I was eight and I remember it. You screamed when they dragged you out of the house. Remember that, Father? She screamed and cried for you and you let them take her."

My blood runs cold and I glance at Nirvana seeing her face is red with embarrassment or anger. I can't tell which, but that doesn't stop Aero as she screams at her father, uncaring of the audience.

"I wanted you to make up, be a family once I'm gone. But I saw you stand when she said if anyone objects. Or you began to," she says and laughs and it sounds almost manic.

"Aero, enough. You're drawing a crowd," her father snaps.

"Oh you don't want people to know you sent your four-teen-year-old daughter to a conversion camp where she was tortured. I found Vana's records, you know. You kept them out studying them to make sure she got her "treatment." Electric shock therapy, Aversion therapy. I looked it up, aversion therapy, that's where they immerse you into learning to get rid of habits that they shouldn't like. That's what you did isn't it? You forced her to be treated for her liking women, what they did was assault. On a minor. You allowed it to happen!"

Their father turns to Nirvana, his face turning red. "You've corrupted her mind. I told you this is what would happen if you lived your lifestyle. Now she is bound to a woman no less. All because of your influence."

He was getting into her face shouting louder and louder. I pull Nirvana behind me. Putting myself between her and her father. "I need you to back up," I say, keeping my voice even and calm.

He turns towards me and glares. "Do you know who I am?"

I shrug. "I don't really give a fuck who you are. You're not going to talk to Nirvana like that." Aero is still yelling behind him cursing him out, but he's standing in front of me, turning red from anger.

Nirvana snapped, then stepped out from behind me, "Aero Lorraine Bridges! Stop right fucking now!" Aero glared at her sister.

"Don't defend this creep!"

"Aero stop it. Now."

I glanced at Caden and Sorrow beside me and lowered my voice, "Get everyone out of here. They don't need to see this."

Aero is shouting at Nirvana but she's not looking at her, she's looking at her father. "Leave. Now. You've caused enough damage," Nirvana said.

Aero turns to him and yells, "I hope I see you in Hell when I die!"

Nirvana grabs her sister, not rough but pulls her into her. "Stop it. Stop it right now."

"Fuck you! I hate you! You left me alone! I hate you so much!"

"I know. I know," Nirvana says, stroking her sister's hair. Drew moves through the crowd holding a syringe and walks up to the pair and presses the needle into Aero. The sedative works quickly leaving Aero unconscious against Nirvana who is gently rocking her.

"She didn't mean it. She's sick, she's not the same person you once knew," I hear Drew say.

"I know," Nirvana repeats. I walk up to her and crouch down beside her. She doesn't look at me and I sigh.

"Nirvana, look at me."

Her eyes lift to meet mine and all I see is shame and humiliation. "She didn't mean it," Nirvana whispered.

"I know. I know she didn't, baby." The endearment falls from my lips involuntarily and I see Drew look at me but luckily he doesn't call me on it. Not that I'd care. "Let me take you home."

Nirvana looks down at her sister and nods, pressing a kiss to her head. "She didn't mean it," she says again, holding her tightly. "We need to drop off Aero first."

"I got it. Go get some rest," Drew says, he lifts Aero in his arms and Caden comes forward with the wheelchair. I stand and hold a hand out to Nirvana. She places her hand in mine and I pull her up. "Take Sam's car. He'll get it tomorrow," Drew says. I gaze at Sam who tosses me his keys and I catch them, grabbing Nirvana I turn her around and walk in the direction of the cars. I know our friends are watching us, but I don't care.

I have questions, so many questions about the outburst, but I don't ask them now. Not yet anyway. I need answers, but I have a feeling I won't like what I'm told.

Chapter 25

Nirvana

I sit in the car, my heart heavy and my head aching. This wasn't what was supposed to happen. It was supposed to be a happy day for the couple. I scoff to myself. It was hardly going to be happy considering one of them was dying. How could it have gone so bad, so fast? I didn't even know he'd be there. Aero must've invited him. Or Isola. It went well until I was dancing with Aero. It was fine, then she told me she was confronting our father. Demanding why he did what he did. I told her no, but did she listen? No. No, she didn't. She went haywire and stalked over to him shouting and cursing. Spilling everything, things I never wanted to be said out loud in front of a lot of people. In front of my friends who knew nothing about what happened. Groaning, I put my hands over my face. I knew it would be bad if he came. Ravi stops the car and I see he brought us back to his house.

He doesn't say anything, just climbs out and comes to my side of the car. "Come on before it starts to rain," he says when he opens the door, holding his hand out to me. I sigh, unbuckling my belt and letting him help me out.

I couldn't even look at him. How does he see me now? Tarnished? Used up? Disgusting? Probably all of the above, not to mention I threw myself at him yesterday. I pause in the doorway. "Maybe I should go to my house," I say. Grimacing at saying it was my house, it wasn't my anything.

He stops and looks at me. "Is that what you want?" No, but I won't tell him that. I don't want to see what he thinks of me now. That I am truly broken and that he's wasting his time with me. He walks up to me and pulls me deeper into the house and closes the door, locking it behind us. He grasps my hand and walks me to his bedroom where I see he changed the sheets from last night, these ones are a crisp white making the usually dark room seem lighter.

"Do you want to talk about it?" he asks, taking his coat off and going to the closet to pull down a hanger to hang it back up.

"No," I whisper, watching as he slowly unbuttons his white dress shirt. He nods, tossing the shirt in the black hamper leaving him in his pants and shoes while I'm just standing awkwardly in the center of his room.

I didn't know what to do, I've never been in this type of situation before. So, without knowing what else to do I just watch as he undresses. He toes off his dress shoes as his hands go to his belt. The sound of the buckle clinking against itself made my legs shake. He drops his pants, leaving himself completely naked.

"You've been freeballing all day?" I gasp, earning a soft chuckle from him. He walks towards me, all masculine energy and desire. Adding fire to my already growing heat. He closes and locks his door before stopping behind me, his calloused fingers going to the zipper of the dress, letting it pool at my feet, leaving me in my underwear, heels, and garter.

"You looked so beautiful today," he whispers, brushing my hair to the side so he could press a kiss to the mark he left on my shoulder. I draw in a shuddering breath as he kisses down my spine to my ass. His touch is gentle as he goes lower, pushing my panties to the side so he can spread my cheeks, running his fingers between my legs, spreading my pussy to his viewing. He kneels behind me. "Turn around, Nirvana," he murmurs against my skin. I do as he says looking down at him, a strong proud man, kneeling in front of me.

My heart is pounding as he runs his hand from my ankle to my thigh spreading them farther apart. "Such a pretty pussy. So mine." He leans forward, running his tongue over my sensitive folds, dipping between to circle my engorged clit. I moan softly, lifting my right leg to place it over his shoulder.

He groans in satisfaction as he pushes the panties to the side again and spreads my lips apart so he can feast on me. And that's what he does, feast. He's treating me as if I'm his last meal and he was starving. His groans vibrate against my clit making me shudder.

"Ravi," I moan, spearing my fingers through his hair arching my body so he can lick me better. "I'm so close," I gasp. He stops then and stands, licking his lips wet from my arousal. He walks towards his made bed and lies down.

"Come sit on my face," he instructs, his hand going to his thick erection. I swallow hard, slowly peeling my underwear off. "Leave the rest on." His voice is thick with desire spurring me on. I walk towards him and straddle his chest looking down at him.

"You're sure?"

"Wouldn't have said so if I wasn't. Now be a good girl and come fuck my face."

I nod, moving up until my pussy is directly above his mouth. When I don't sit directly on him he grips my hips and pulls me down on him, his tongue thrusting deep. I moan his name arching my hips riding his tongue like he demanded.

"Fuck, Ravi," I groan, my body trembling. I look behind me and see his cock, hard as stone, straining up with the head red and leaking precum. Without thinking I turn over so my stomach is pressed against his. I wrap my hand around him, squeezing tightly causing him to give an almost pained groan.

His hand comes down hard on my ass making me yelp in pain. I glare at him from over my shoulder but he's already back to licking me. I gasp his name, rubbing myself against him.

"Be a good girl and suck my cock," Ravi says against my clit.

I lean forward and run my tongue over the swollen head, tasting the saltiness of him and what's uniquely him. Ravi. I groan at the taste, swirling my tongue around him again. He growls low in his throat before slapping my ass again. "Now, Nirvana."

I smirk against him and say, "Okay, Daddy." Before he can respond I take him into my mouth. Ravi curses low in his throat going back to my pussy. It's almost too much, feeling the way he sucks my clit into his mouth before going lower so he can thrust his tongue inside of me, fucking me. Bringing me closer and closer to release. I hollow my cheeks and suck him harder. His hips arch up pushing his cock deeper into my throat causing my eyes to water and drool to fall from my mouth. He's bigger than I remember causing my jaw to ache. I love every second of it.

Ravi

I curse as Nirvana pulls me into her hot mouth. I've never felt anything so good in my life. I thrust my hips higher pushing my cock down her throat, pushing her limits. I hear her gag slightly and I almost lose it then.

"Fuck, pixie," I groan, my hands going to her pale ass cheeks, spreading her to my view. I run my tongue up her pussy reveling in her taste. I can feel her getting closer as I thrust my finger in her tight cunt, thrusting it gently inside her. The lights flickered as the sound of rain bursts through the clouds but we were too far gone. Lost in the pleasure of each other.

Nirvana pulled away to breathe, gasping, "Ravi, I'm so close."

I add another finger and hook them inside of her, thrusting gently before going higher up her body. She tenses and says, "Ravi." She's panting now, unsure and nervous.

"I got you, baby. Relax." With my other hand I spread her cheeks and run my thumb over the puckered ring while thrusting my two fingers inside her pussy. Nirvana moans low in her throat before taking me back into her mouth, sucking harder and harder as I fuck her pussy and ass with my fingers. I pull her clit into my mouth, tugging it gently before scraping my teeth over it. That sends her careening over the edge. Her pussy convulses around my fingers as she comes letting her juices run down my hand and mouth. I curse and sit up fast, sending my cock deeper down her throat.

I pull her off of me and reach for a condom, frantically searching. I open the nightstand and grab the box with an urgency that sends the drawer falling to the floor. I don't care though, as I pull out the condom, quickly open it with my teeth, and slide it down my aching cock.

I pull a trembling Nirvana up pulling her back against my chest. "Lift your hips," I demand. She does and grabs my cock to position me at her entrance. I didn't wait, I needed to bury myself inside her. I thrust up and she screams my name, her hands going to my thighs and squeezing.

My hands move to her tits, squeezing and pulling her nipples causing her to gasp, and grind down on my cock. Her head falls back on my shoulder, the pleasure taking her over. Her heels are digging into my hips as she moves on me making it more intense. I move one hand up her chest to her throat, holding her as I thrust my hips up, fucking her.

"Oh God, Ravi," she moans, the sound a sob that has my cock thickening.

"I saw your face at the wedding. I don't want you to be ashamed of yourself. Of what happened," I grunt out. She tenses and I squeeze her throat a little so she'd look at me. "You were going to leave. I saw it in your beautiful blue eyes. The self hate, the disgust. You thought I'd see you differently, didn't you?"

She doesn't answer, just moves her hips harder and faster, but I stop her with another squeeze of her throat. "Answer me."

"Yes. Yes, I was going to leave," she sobs. I reward her by thrusting into her harder and faster. I move my other hand to her clit and pinch it making her scream as her orgasm hits her. Her pussy clenches around me as her orgasm moves through her, milking my cock in the process, sending a strong orgasm through me. I grunt her name before claiming her mouth in a bruising kiss, claiming her.

Chapter 26

RAVI

I fall back on my bed pulling Nirvana with me. She's gasping for breath and trembling against me. I pull her into my arms as she curls into herself, sobbing. I press my forehead against her back, kissing her shoulder, just holding her.

"How can you still want me?" she gasps, sobbing.

"Because you're someone special," I say honestly.

That only makes her cry harder. Her body is trembling so hard that I fear she'll snap in half. I pull back a little and discard the condom in the trash bin by my bed before wrapping my arms around her again.

"I can't do it. I can't, it's too much," she sobs.

"Baby," I whisper. She's shaking her head, sending her hair flying in all directions.

"I hate him so much. And I hate her for what she did to me. What she said, but she's fucking dying. Why does she have to fucking die?" Her words nearly shatter my heart. "It's not fucking fair. She's hardly old enough to drink, let alone die." She shakes her head. "Was it something I did? Maybe I didn't take her to the doctors enough. They could've caught it sooner. They could have given her more time. Me, more time. I just need more time!"

"What do you need? Tell me what you need and I'll do it," I say, rubbing her back.

"Girls," was all she said. I press a kiss to her spine and get out of the bed and grab a pair of sweatpants from my dresser. I pull them on and head to Nirvana who was still silently weeping, and pull the blanket from my side of the bed to cover her naked body. I press a kiss to her head and leave the room.

"Is she okay?" Gran asks softly.

I sigh. "No. We are about to have more company. A lot of it." I grab my phone from the charger where I'd left it at home, pull up the number and press call. She answers after the third ring, "Hello?"

"I need you. Nirvana needs you."

Nirvana

I don't know how long I lay there, huddled in a ball. I should be basking in the afterglow. Holding Ravi to me. But he saw right through me. How could he still want to touch me after all of that? After admitting I hated Aero for what she did? But I knew I didn't. I was angry, embarrassed, ashamed. The door opened and I glanced up and saw Delaney. She walked in with Layla and Rory behind her. She shut the door and gave me a soft smile.

"Hi," she said.

I sniff and say, "Hi."

She walks to the bed and climbs on behind me, wrapping an arm around me, and then I start crying again. Layla comes on my other side and climbs on and Rory scoots in by my legs and they all hold me. The door opens again and Ophelia and Seraphina come in joining us on the bed. All of them holding me as I cry.

"It hurts. It hurts so bad," I cry out, burying my head into the pillow, inhaling Ravi's scent.

"Honey, talk to us. Let us help," Ophelia says, rubbing my ankle only to stop when she gets to my heels. "Why are you in bed with heels?" she asks. Rory sits up and lifts up the cover beginning to take off my shoes.

I sink deeper into the pillows. "I slept with Ravi." God, Ravi, he must think I'm crazier than he originally thought.

"How was it?" Ophelia asked, running her fingers through my hair. Leave it to her to try and ease into the rough topic. It was one of my favorite things about her.

I laugh softly and say, "I'm pretty sure the dude lodged into my cervix. Best I've ever had. Don't tell him that though. Somehow I feel like his head would get bigger than it already is."

"Clearly that's not the only thing that gets bigger," Layla muttered, making me laugh until I was crying again. Only I don't know if it was from laughing, or if my emotions had finally broken and I was stuck in a state of utter chaos. That I was stuck like this until I drowned in my own sorrow. I bury my head into the blankets again, trying to force myself to breathe deeply, to do something other than cry. And they let me. No one says anything, no one rushes me. We sit in silence until I finally calm down enough that the tears dry. Why am I like this? Why can't I be a normal woman whose sister isn't dying of a rare brain cancer and a father who sends her away to a camp that is supposed to make me straight?

"So he really sent you to that camp?" Seraphina asks, her voice strained.

I didn't even realize I had said that out loud. I curse myself and cover my eyes with my hands. "He hates me so much. I didn't tell him. Marcy kissed me and he caught us. It was a dare from Brody."

"What? I thought Marcy had a thing for you?" Layla says in disbelief.

I shake my head. "No, it was a stupid dare. One I wasn't in on. Fucked my life up. When I got back she blamed me for her parents grounding her and taking her phone." I laugh bitterly, swiping at the tears falling from my eyes. "At least she wasn't sent there. I wouldn't wish that on my worst enemy. I met Cannon there. He was my only friend there."

"Oh, Nirvana," Delaney said. She pulls me into her arms, uncaring that I'm naked. Layla covers me up and cuddles into me saying nothing. They just hold me, they don't ask for answers, they don't ask questions, they simply lie there and hold me. It's what I need and what I think I'll miss most.

Chapter 27

RAVI

I sit on the couch as Gran tells the guys stories. I called Delaney and somehow they all showed up. The storm rages outside and we are currently sitting in the dark. I didn't even realize the power went out until they showed up. Which shows I'm not paying as much attention as I should be.

"Then he fell right in the middle of the concert," Gran was saying as I tuned back in. "My Fred thought he'd cracked his skull open."

"I can't picture you in choir, dude. It just doesn't sit right with me," Caden comments.

"It was only for a month," I grumble, tapping my fingers against my knee.

"A month is a long time for someone who can't sing," Max mused. I glare at the man who just shrugs.

"So you and Nirvana?" Sorrow says, leaning against the wall, his gaze going down the hall towards the closed bedroom door. I don't answer, I'm not sure how to. I mean, I like her. I enjoy her rather dark company and twisted humor. I enjoy the feeling I get when I'm inside of her. And the way she teases me. But we haven't talked about it. Shit, it all happened so fast I wasn't even sure what she wanted.

Sorrow shakes his head, a sly smirk gracing his mouth. "I can't believe she was right. Shit, now I owe her forty dollars."

"What the fuck are you talking about?" I demand.

Gran gasps, clutching imaginary pearls dramatically. "Ravi, language. You've got ladies in the house."

I roll my eyes. "Gran, I'm pretty sure those women swear more than a sailor."

"Don't roll your eyes, Ravi. It is common courtesy to not swear around a lady." I fight the urge to roll my eyes again, and don't.

"Delaney and I made a bet to see how long it would take you to fall for her. Didn't take long," Sorrow tsks under his breath.

"I don't know how I feel about being bet on," I reply.

Sorrow shrugs, pulling his phone out of his pocket. "How long do you think we should wait before checking on them?"

I stand and head to my room, aware Sorrow is behind me as I open the door to the room. I'm not sure what I was expecting, but it wasn't the women being cuddled up to Nirvana and sleeping.

"I swear they're like toddlers sometimes," Sorrow whispers.

"I heard that, Stevens," Delaney said back, easing herself up slightly so as to not jostle Nirvana. She looks down at the small blonde and caresses her hair, a sad look in her eyes.

"She's so broken," she whispered.

"Come on, bright eyes. We need to get going if we're going to make the appointment," Sorrow says, going into the room and helping Delaney off the bed so she didn't disturb the other women.

They walk towards me and Delaney stops. "Don't hurt her, Ravi. She's had enough to last a lifetime," she turns and looks over at the women, "and more is coming her way."

"I don't intend to." And I didn't. But how could I help a woman who didn't want help? Delaney squeezes my arm before following Sorrow out. I leave the room and go back to the living room waiting until the others finally got up and left, leaving just Nirvana, Gran, and me home.

"Go check on her, dear. She probably needs you."

I nod and get up, heading to my room. The storm was still going but not as strong, our lights were still out leaving the house sort of muggy and hot. I walk in the room and see Nirvana sitting at the edge of the bed with the blanket wrapped around her. Her head was bent down allowing her hair to curtain over her face.

"Nirvana," I say. She looks up at me with red rimmed eyes.

"I'm sorry. I shouldn't have reacted like that." I walk deeper into the room, closing the door behind me. I walk towards her and pull her up, sit in her spot, placing her on my lap, blanket and all.

"Shh. It's okay. You're overwhelmed with everything that's going on. It's understandable." I press a kiss to her head and rock us back and forth, soothing her as best as I knew how. And to be honest it wasn't much. "I'm here, I'll be here."

She wraps her arms around my neck and burrows herself against my neck, crying softly. I hold her to me, whispering sweet nothings and rubbing soothing circles against her back. A part of me is afraid I'm falling for her. The other part is terrified that I might've already fallen. Either way there's no going back. For either of us.

"I want to go check on Aero," she whispers against my neck after she finally stopped crying.

I nod, stroking her hair. "Get dressed and we can go." She stands on shaky legs and wipes at her eyes.

"Why are you being so nice to me?" she asks.

Leaning back on my hands, I stare up at her. "Because I can. Is that a problem?"

Her shoulders rise slightly as if she's genuinely perplexed as to why someone would be remotely kind to her and that pissed me off. "No. It's just... weird. What do you want from me?"

"Your father is a dick. He should've treated you with the love and respect you deserved. Both of your parents did not. But don't lump me up with them. As for what I want from you? I just want you. I want your body, I want your tears, I want your laughter. Shit, I don't know, Nirvana. Being around you these last few weeks has fucked me up and I'm not sure if it's a good thing or not."

She snorts, pulling on her shorts and t-shirt. "That's not very convincing."

"I'm not here to convince you to be with me. You either want me or you don't." I shrug.

She turns to me. "What about what you know? That I've been sent to that camp? Doesn't that disgust you?"

"Yes," I reply honestly and her face fades of all color. "But only because he sent you there. He made you think there's something wrong with you. That it made you fear sleeping in a bed with a man. That's what disgusts me. Not you. Not what you've been through." I step up to her, cupping her face gently, "It makes you so much stronger. Stop thinking that every man is like your father."

Her eyes widen but she nods slowly. I press a kiss to her lips pulling away slightly. "Now let's go. It's storming and I would rather not be stuck in this all night."

Nodding, she turns on her heel and moves away. Leaving me looking after her.

Chapter 28

RAVI

Grunting I lift the barbell above my head. Caden stands behind me to spot me, making sure I don't drop the damn thing on my chest.

"Just one more then you're done," he encourages. I breathe deeply and pull it down then push it back up, feeling the way my muscles are burning in my arms and back. Once I'm done with my last rep he pulls it into place allowing me to sit up and breathe.

I grab the towel next to me and wipe off my brow, panting from the workout.

"How're things with Nirvana going?" Caden asks, opening the water and handing it to me. I drink it down in a few gulps, trying to find a way to answer his question as I look around the near empty gym.

"There are no things. She's got a lot going on without me coming into the mix." I've made my feelings known to her. I made no secret that I wanted her. But I knew she wasn't in the right headspace for anything more and I was fine with that.

"From the sounds of it you already came into the mix," he wags his eyebrows making me toss the towel at him.

"Real mature." I roll my eyes at him.

He laughs and sits next to me on the other bench press. "I'm not wrong though." He wasn't, but I don't need him to know that.

"She has too much going on," I say again. What else can I say? She had to watch her sister die, not to mention all the other shit she holds close to her chest on a regular basis.

Sighing, I grab the back of my neck and rub trying to ease the sudden tension that's building. "Nirvana is a good woman. She has her issues, but don't we all," Caden says, bracing his arms on his knees.

I nod but don't respond, stuck in my own head. I know she's a good woman, it's obvious in the way she cares about the people in her life. It's clear in the way she spends every waking moment with her sister, taking care of her, planning a wedding in two weeks. It's in the way she dropped everything when Delaney needed her after her attack. It's in the way she looks out for everyone. But who looks out for her? Who is really there when she needs it?

I glance at Caden who looks just as lost in his thoughts as I was. "How would I know what a woman wants?" I ask, breaking his concentration.

Caden looks at me, arching a black brow. "Are you asking me for woman advice, Banks?"

I roll my eyes. "Not anymore I'm not."

Caden looks at me for a moment before throwing his head back and laughing. "I'm sorry. Okay, women are simple creatures. You wine and dine them, then make sure their backs are properly cracked after you fuck them. Make sure they can't walk the next morning and you're golden."

I gaped at him. "Are you serious?"

He laughs again before getting serious. "Nah. What you need to do is be their rock. To love them even through the bad. You have to be their partner not their dictator, you have to have the patience of a saint because they will push your buttons until you can't tell if you want to kiss the hell out of them or strangle them. You have to anticipate their needs before they even know what it is they need or want. You have to be their best friend, their lover, their protector."

I glanced at my friend, shocked at how insightful he was being, and confused as to how he was acting. "How are you single?"

He shrugs, sending me a cocky, well practiced grin. "I'd rather not settle for less than I deserve. Plus, I'd rather not commit to something I wasn't a hundred percent about. And it's fun to fuck when and who I want, when I want."

"You're a strange man," I commented.

"You still love me though," he teases, pretending to toss hair over his shoulder. I shake my head, my own grin tilting my mouth. But his words echo in my head, *What you need to do is be their rock. To love them even through the bad.*

After leaving Caden, I made my way home to shower before going into the kitchen and throwing together a quick meal of steak and vegetables before packing it up. Then I make a quick fish dish for Gran and cover it with plastic wrap and put it in the fridge. I head down the hall and see Gran in the living room listening to another book on the TV. I'm not sure what book it is, but I hear, *cock* at least three times.

"Gran?" I call out. She jumps and turns down the audio, her wrinkled face turning red at being caught listening to whatever it was.

"Child, make some noise when walking. I'm blind not deaf. Get it together before you give an old woman a heart attack," she scolds, dramatically rubbing her chest above her heart.

Trying not to laugh, I walk into the living room. "I left your dinner in the fridge. Top shelf, it's in plastic."

"You won't be home for dinner?" she asks, running a hand through her green hair.

"Not tonight, but I'll be back before ten. Do you think you'll be okay?"

She waves a dismissive hand. "Of course. I have your friends' numbers. Especially the broody ones. What were their names again?"

I arch a brow. "Are you talking about Sorrow and Drew?"

Gran sighs dreamily. "Yes. Such strapping young men. The lot of them."

"Sorrow is engaged, Gran." I laugh.

Gran nods. "Yes, to the nice lady who always smells like apple pie. Makes me want to take a bite out of her. She's as sweet as can be, too. Such opposites those two. I like it."

"I'll let them know you're rooting for them," I deadpan.

Gran smiles. "You do that. Now leave me to my stories. I'll see you later if I'm still awake." I nod and walk over to her and press a kiss to her head before turning and grabbing my stuff to head out the door. I lock up and set the alarms making sure she's safe and head to my car. I don't really have a plan as I head to Nirvana's house. It doesn't take long to drive there.

As I pull up I see her sitting on the porch. Her face perks up when I pull up, and she gives me a little wave as I climb out of the car bag in tow.

"Hey," she says. "I didn't know you were coming over."

"Hey tinker hell," I say, smiling when she scrunches her

little nose at the nickname. "I didn't either." I stop in front of her so she has to lean back to look up at me.

"So why are you here?"

I stare down at her, meeting her blue eyes. "Because there is nowhere else I would rather be." And I meant it with every fiber in my being.

Chapter 29

Nirvana

My heart is pounding so hard and fast as I stare at Ravi, then let him into the small house. After Marcy showed up to the hospital I waited until Isola came before leaving. Then coming to the one place I probably shouldn't be. But for some twisted reason I felt like I should be here. And it solidifies as I watch Ravi put the old throw blanket on the cold floor and set out some plates before staring at me.

"What are you doing?" I ask, standing against the wall.

"Food."

I arch a brow. "I can see it."

Ravi sighs, sits down and pats the spot next to him. I regard him cautiously before making my way to him and sitting down on the tattered blanket. He doesn't speak as he hands me a plate with steak and vegetables. I don't remember the last time I ate and my stomach rumbles at the smell.

Thoroughly embarrassed, I take the fork and knife from

him with a small 'thanks' and dig in. I sigh softly as the flavors of the meat hit my tongue and close my eyes enjoying the food.

"How is it?" he asks.

I open my eyes and notice he's watching me. I clear my throat, a flush stealing up my face. "It's delicious, thank you."

"You're welcome." We sit and eat in a comfortable silence and it makes me nervous how comfortable I feel with him. Once we finish, Ravi takes the plates and packs them away before turning to me. "How are you doing?"

I laugh softly. "I'm pretty sure I threatened a pregnant woman today."

His eyes widen and it makes me laugh harder. "Yeah. Marcy showed up at the hospital to apologize and I guess I just snapped."

"Who's Marcy?" he asks. Oh right. I forgot he doesn't really know what happened. Not really anyway. A part of me wants to tell him, to lay everything bare for him, another part of me, however, didn't see the point of it. But I figured he deserved the basics.

"Marcy is someone who I used to be friends with. She's married to my father now."

Ravi takes a breath. "Damn. So that's who was there that day."

"Yeah. Pregnant bitch," I mutter.

"Why'd you threaten her?" he asks with interest, leaning back to study me.

"She touched me," I reply honestly.

An emotion I can't figure out moves over Ravi's face, but he quickly masks it. It looked like anger mixed with something else I couldn't put my finger on. But anger was definitely there. "Did she harm you?" His voice was low and deadly.

"No. Of course not. It was just my shoulder," I say

honestly. At least, she didn't harm me physically. Emotionally was another story, however.

Silence descends again. I glance down at my hands and sigh. "Are we going to be awkward now that I cried in front of you?"

"No. Crying is a natural response and emotion when you are dealing with grief."

I smile to myself. "You sound like Delaney."

He snorts, "She's rubbing off on everybody it seems."

I glance at him. "How do you mean?"

Sighing, Ravi leans back on his hands, and says, "Gran described her as smelling like apple pie and she wants to take a bite out of her. And she is Sorrow and Delaney's number one fan."

I look at him for a moment before laughing my ass off. "She does smell like pie. Warm and lovely. Like home. I love it." It was one thing Delaney did when she was old enough to leave home. She found a scent that she described as being homey. That and strong enough to wash out the smell of old cigarettes, body odor, and stale beer. I'm not sure if anyone knows that about the woman but it was the first thing she told me when I got my own apartment.

I glance around the depleted apartment and smile, showing the others. "What do you think?" I ask.

"It's a decent size but it needs a little work," Seraphina says, rocking Darcy in her arms as she slept.

"Yeah, the landlady was nice and said I can paint. It's not much but I think I can make do with this."

Ophelia nods. "It's good for a first time home. It's not the best neighborhood, but I think we can work with it. I know a locksmith who can give you really good locks on the doors and windows."

I nod and look at the area. It wasn't much, but it was mine. It was a small two bedroom one bathroom apartment, it was perfect for me and Aero. Once I got her here it would be fine. The others slipped outside and began sifting through the small things I brought with me, leaving me alone with Delaney who held out a pink bag to me.

"You didn't have to get me anything," I say.

"It's not much. But open it." I smile at my friend and open it seeing a Yankee candle that was scented as an ocean breeze. I take it out of the bag and smell it, inhaling the strong oddly comforting scent. "When I moved, I found a candle that smells like home. My own home. It's supposed to be soothing. It helped take away bad memories, especially the first night alone."

I glance at her and set the candle back in the bag before pulling her in for a hug. "I love you. Thank you."

Delaney laughs hugging me back. "I love you, too. Now, let's get this place perfect."

I still had the candle. It was nothing more than wick now, but I still had it stashed away. I never told her how much it meant to me. Or still means to me. I feel Ravi looking at me and I glance at him. "What?"

"You're just unexpected," he says softly.

"What do you mean?"

He shrugs. "You just light up whenever you think of them."

"They're family. You're supposed to get all bright and happy when you think of them." Most of the time. If I think about the sperm donor and the bank that housed me as a child I feel nothing but disdain and anger.

"That's true. You have a great family," Ravi says. I smile at him, a sense of peace settling over me.

"Thank you for coming over tonight, Ravi. I didn't

realize that I needed this." Ravi leans forward and tucks a piece of hair behind my ear, stroking my face gently.

"Of course. Like I said, I wouldn't want to be anywhere else."

I lick my lips, staring at him intently. "Why?"

His thumb trails over my wet bottom lip. "Because there's something about you that draws me in. You're fucking captivating and I want to know more. I want to know everything." My heart stutters in my chest and butterflies fill my stomach. Everything about this man had me feeling needy. Made me want things that weren't possible. Shaking my head, I leaned forward and pressed my lips to his so I didn't have to think. I could just feel. Ravi's hands went to my hips and squeezed tightly, so tightly I knew I'd have his marks on me. And that just spurred me on.

My tongue thrust fervently against his and my hands found my way into his soft hair, pulling gently. I ran my nails down his neck moving my hands slowly to the hem of his shirt so I could pull it off. He let me, helping slightly by lifting his arms leaving him shirtless in front of me. I sat back on my haunches and stared at him. Taking him all in, from the broadness of his shoulders to the soft hair on his chest that leads to his stomach. I place a hand on his chest and he shudders. I glance at Ravi and see him watching me intently, his green eyes bright with desire, burning with a heat that seared me all the way to my soul as I traced the muscles of his chest to the abs on his stomach. Trailing my fingers over him gently, I lean forward and press my lips against his chest.

"Nirvana," Ravi said on a breath.

I push him back, kissing down his body. "Shh, let me explore you." Ravi presses the palms of his hands flat on the hardwood and nods stiffly as I circle my tongue over his nipple before going lower. My fingers find the buttons to his pants and I slowly pop them open. One button after the other. Arousal surrounded me as the last button opened letting Ravi's cock pop out.

Holy shit, this man. I didn't have the words to describe how beautiful this man was. And I've seen plenty of naked men and never have I thought a penis was even remotely attractive. With shaky hands I pulled his pants past his hips, freeing him completely. I run my nails down his sides, scratching slightly causing him to hiss out a breath and his hips to arch up. I smirk to myself, wanting to tease him more I lean forward and brush my lips, just a featherlight touch across his stomach. Nothing more.

"You're killing me, Nirvana," Ravi groans.

Laughing quietly I grab him in my hand, and say, "We can't have that." But fuck, the moment I grabbed him I was lost. He was hot and thick and I could barely curl my entire hand around him. I pumped him slowly, moving up and down watching in fascination as precum beaded on the engorged tip. I circled my thumb against it, wetting it before sliding my hand down again, squeezing. "Fuck," he groaned. I saw his hands fist at his sides before I finally took mercy on him and leaned forward to pull his cock into my mouth.

I had him like this before, but then his hands were on me and I didn't get the chance to savor him, to make sure he felt the pleasure he was giving to me. Now, I had my chance and I took it. Boy, did I fucking take it. I moan at the first taste, slightly salty with his spicy scent. All Ravi. I loved it. I trace the underside of him with my tongue, tracing that one vein that pulses with each touch before I swirl it over the sensitive head. Ravi gave up on all pretense of letting me explore. His hand wrapped in my hair and pulled tightly. I reveled in it. He pulled my head back staring down at me with a flushed face and heated eyes.

"If you're going to suck my dick, Nirvana, do it like you mean it. Otherwise, I'm going to take over and fuck that pretty little mouth of yours without mercy. Do you understand me?"

Hell. Heat unfurled between my thighs and my clit began to throb. "Yes, Daddy," I tease before taking him deep into my mouth. He curses as I bobbed my head up and down, tasting him. My hand slid up as my mouth slid down. Just the feel of him in my mouth was enough to make me wet and needy with want. His fingers flexed in my hair.

"Look at me," he said gruffly. I did, my eyes met his in a heated dance. Ravi's nostrils flared and what little control he had snapped as he pulled me across his lap and took my mouth in a deep kiss. His tongue thrust into my mouth, taking me over. His teeth nipped and bit making me moan. My hands push at my pants and he reaches forward only to stop.

"Shit, I want to feel you bare."

I whimper in the back of my throat. "I'm clean and on the depo shot. I just got it last month." Especially after my little escapades with that couple, though we didn't actually have sex but one couldn't be too cautious.

"Thank fuck, I'm clean. I'll send proof tomorrow." I go to respond but Ravi is pushing my pants the rest of the way down and rips my panties, leaving them hanging on one side. I lean up, grab his cock and line it up at my entrance. Without preamble he thrusts up, making me scream in shock at the intrusion. Holy shit, holy shit.

"Goddamn, baby. You feel like fucking Heaven and Hell." I lean forward arching my hips, taking him deeper. We groan in unison. Ravi's hands moved up my hips, gripping my shirt and pulling it over my head. I reach behind myself to unhook my bra letting it fall forward. Ravi grabs it and tosses it to the side. Placing a hand on my chest he pushes me back to where I have to grab his jean clad legs and ride him slowly. He leans forward pulling a nipple into his mouth making me moan softly as I arch my hips up and down slowly.

It was slow, almost loving. It was too much, too intense.

"Ravi," I gasp, moving my hips in a rhythmic motion. Up and down, up and down. One of his hands moved up to my throat squeezing until my air was cut off. I clenched around him and he groaned, moving to my other nipple to lick and pull. To torment me. My hips moved slowly against him, taking more of him. Taking all of him. And he gave it.

"You take me so beautifully, Nirvana. So fucking beautiful seeing your tight pussy squeeze down on my cock." His words spur me on, making my body heat up and my moans to come in short gasps. My vision blurred slightly before he let go; letting me take a deep breath. It was intense, earth shattering, really. Pulling me up, Ravi kisses me again. His hips drive up, fucking into me hard. My hands grasp at his tattooed shoulders meeting him thrust for brutal thrust.

With a growl, Ravi rolls us over so he's on top. He grabs my legs and pushes them apart, so far that it aches, but I love it, groaning into his mouth. He pounds into me until I feel my body tighten.

"Be a good girl and come for Daddy, pixie," he whispered darkly against my mouth. Fuck. Holy shit. My body tightened against his and I was done for. My back arched and I screamed his name as the release hit me. My back arched as I cried out his name. I didn't know I had a daddy kink until this man. Which I guess could be seen as toxic, kind of weird but my god. The way he owned my body, my mind, and slowly my soul, it was too much. But then he could disarm me when he changed it up. When he slowed down, when he wasn't being rough and commanding, like now. He was moving slower inside of me now. The movements of his thrusts almost gentle as he looked down at me. My eyes met his in a hazy daze. He smoothed the damp hair from my face and made love to me. As if he were savoring this moment between us, drawing it out. It brought tears to my eyes. He leaned down pressing the gentlest kiss to my head as he grabbed my hands, linking us together. This wasn't just sex, this was different. So completely different.

"Kiss me, Ravi. Please, please kiss me," I breathe out on a whimper and he obliges taking my mouth tenderly. We rock together chasing oblivion until neither of us could breathe without the other. The change from rough to gentle was life altering. I just knew that after this I wouldn't be able to survive him. Not without being hurt in the process and that nearly broke something in me. So pushing those thoughts away I embraced him, squeezing his hands in mine as we found release. Such a sweet, sweet torturous release.

Chapter 30

RAVI

Something happened last night. Something changed between me and Nirvana. I wasn't sure how to feel about it. I wasn't sure how to act now. I wanted her, I had developed some sort of feelings for her. I never made a secret about it. But how the fuck was I supposed to go about it? Leaning back against the chair I sat in, I took a pull of my beer, staring at Nirvana as she sat laughing with her friends.

I have no idea how I ended up here. Or whose idea it was, but here we were, all together for a "family" night as Delaney put it. Sorrow sighed beside me, rubbing his temples. "You good?" Spencer asks, shuffling the deck of cards in his hands.

The big blond snorted, "I have a houseful of people. What do you think?"

Sam snorted, drinking his own beer. "Not our fault you got engaged to a very social woman."

"I heard that Samson!" the woman in question called

from the living room. Sorrow chuckled beside me as Spencer dealt out the cards.

"What are they even doing?" Caden asks, looking into the living room where the women sat on a pile of blankets eating snacks and drinking what Layla called Tipsy Juice. Whatever the fuck that meant.

"Watching some movie series. I don't know," Sorrow replied absently.

Delaney came into the kitchen with one of those headbands from her self-care kit and smiled at us. "I offered you to join us, grumpy. But you said no."

Sorrow sighed exasperatedly and tossed his cards on the table before wrapping an arm around her waist. "I want you to enjoy time with your friends, bright eyes."

Delaney rolled her eyes. "Come on. You know you'd rather do self-care movie days with us than play whatever you're playing."

Caden put his cards down and stood. "You have more strawberry masks?" he asks, almost excitedly.

Delaney laughed. "Of course."

"Yeah, it sounds good. I would rather do that." The man left the kitchen and we heard a whoop in the living room from the women and I shook my head laughing.

"Come on. Don't be a bunch of wusses. Just come join. We'll even let you pick the next movie," Delaney said, grabbing Sorrow's hand and pulling him from the chair. And that's how we ended up here, seven men wearing weird ass fuzzy headbands and watching *Twilight*.

"So what's with the team Jacob, team Edward shit?" Max asks, drinking his own drink, a weird glittery pink concoction that Layla cooked up. I can see why she calls it Tipsy Juice, the damn thing doesn't even taste like alcohol.

Seraphina sips her own drink before answering, "Bella has

a thing for both. Jacob is a werewolf and Edward a vampire while Bella is a human. Both want her but she's struggling to choose between the two, though she loves Edward more."

Ophelia nodded. "Then teen girls everywhere were drawn into who they would pick, thus team Edward and team Jacob were born."

"Who'd you pick?" Spencer asks, pushing his glasses up on his nose to study the TV.

Nirvana answered first, "Charlie and Carlisle."

That stopped everyone and we all looked at her. She turned a pretty shade of pink and forced a glare. "What? Maturing is realizing you'd rather be railed by Charlie Swan and Carlise Cullen opposed to Eddie and Jake." The women tilted their heads in unison as the men in question came onto the screen. Nirvana shrugs and says, "Plus, I have unresolved daddy issues." She glances at me and wags her blonde brows, making me think of all those sarcastic remarks of her calling me daddy. But after last night when I called myself that... Shit, I feel my cock stir in my pants and a flush rise on my cheeks. Nirvana laughs under her breath looking back at the screen.

"Yeah. I see the appeal as an adult. But as a girl, give me Edward any day," Layla said, fanning her face.

"Nah, Jacob was so much better. Edward was always the woe is me type and it was annoying," Seraphina argued. "He has the personality of a mop."

"No, no, Jacob tried to kiss Bella without her consent though. We can't get past that," Delaney added.

Sera winced. "Oh shit, I forgot about that part. But then she kissed him when Edward proposed to her. Like right after. And Edward was weird, he kind of blackmailed her into marriage because she wanted to be a vampire."

"Not to mention she cuddled up to Jacob, while he was

practically naked, right in front of Edward," Nirvana points out, sipping at her drink.

"So is she fucking Edward or Jacob?" I ask, thoroughly confused.

Nirvana turned to me and smiled. "No. She's a virgin. So is Edward I believe."

Me and the men scoffed. "There's no way Edward is a virgin," Caden argues.

"He is, too. He went to school for most of the time of his life," Rory added, speaking for the first time.

Caden shakes his head. "There's no fucking way. He's well over a hundred years old. You mean to tell me in all of his hundred some years that man child never once fucked?" he asks and tosses his hands up in frustration. "Besides, what kind of sadists want to repeat high school over and over again?"

"Well, sex with a human would hurt the woman. He wasn't human. And they want to blend in. That's why they go to high school," Ophelia said.

Max scoffed and said, "You mean to tell me, this hundred year old vampire would be around other people who are obviously fucking and not get a stiffy? Not even a little bit? And there's no fucking way people think they're teenagers. Not with those sideburns."

"Well, she's like seventeen for one. And he likes his hair, makes him all the hotter to them," Delaney argues.

"So he's a pervert with bad hair," Sorrow surmises, earning a glare from his fiancee. "And why the fuck did he act all dramatic when she walked into that classroom?"

Delaney throws her hands up. "Because he wants to drink her blood which makes him feel like a monster."

"That makes no sense," I say.

Nirvana laughs. "Okay, so a run down since you boys are clearly uncultured." She flips her hair over her shoulder.

"Edward is technically mated to Bella. She's a human, while he's a vampire so, where he's from it's unheard of. The others were all vampires so nothing made sense to them until later on down the road. Bella wants to fuck Edward, he doesn't want to fuck her because he's scared he'd hurt her, and wants to be married first. Which happens in movie three or four. Since she's a human her body is weaker... blah... blah... blah.... Jacob doesn't want her with a vampire because then she'll be a blood sucking demon like the rest of them. Although they only hunt animals, not people like other ones."

"So what you're saying is Edward is lame?" I state.

Nirvana shrugs, a smile tugging at her mouth. "No. He's broody and mysterious. Drives the women crazy." She shimmies a little bit before drinking down the rest of her drink earning mocking glares from the women.

The night goes on like this and honestly I don't think any of us have ever laughed so much. Even with Caden and Rory arguing over who was better or Drew correcting all automatically inaccurate information. It seems like the first time we all hung out and actually relaxed in a long time. If only it stayed like this.

Chapter 31

Nirvana

The buzzing of a phone woke me up. Groaning, I turned over on the floor bumping into someone beside me. Blinking, I look over and blurrily see Ravi sleeping soundly beside me, his arm over my waist. Holding me close to him. The buzzing finally stopped, making me sigh with relief and roll back over and close my eyes. Until it started again. Cursing under my breath I feel around until my hand connects with the buzzing phone. Which is mine. I pull it closer to me and I feel my heart stop. It's three in the morning and Isola is calling me. I sit up slowly trying not to jostle Ravi or wake one of the others. I sit up on my knees and with a shaky hand I answer the phone.

"Hello?" I whisper into the phone.

"Nirvana. You're going to want to come before it's too late," Isola sobs out. I pull the phone from my ear and press it to my chest. My heart was pounding so hard and I lost the ability to breathe momentarily. I took some deep breaths, sucking in as much air as I could before putting the phone back to my ear.

"I'm coming now." I hang up and stand, trying to gather my stuff as quietly and quickly as possible. I walk to the door and without thinking open it causing the alarm to go off. Next thing I know the lights are on and everyone is looking at me and I have a gun pointed at me.

"Sorrow, put the gun down," Ravi orders.

"Shit. Sorry. Habit," he muttered.

Delaney blinks slowly as Sorrow stands and shuts off the alarm. "Where are you going?"

I swipe at my eyes, cursing myself for the tears that were forming there. "Um, Isola called. I need to go to the hospital. I didn't mean to wake you all." I don't say anything else, I can't. I just dash out the door to my Jeep and climb in. I couldn't form any words, I could hardly breathe. I knew they would come, that's the type of people they are. But I couldn't wait. I couldn't lose this little bit of time I had. My hands clench on the steering wheel as I speed through the nearly empty streets to the hospital.

Blood was rushing in my ears when I parked. It was crooked and in another spot but I didn't give a shit. One night, I had one last night of happiness. It didn't last long. Not at all. I opened the car door and jumped out, uncaring of anything as I ran across the parking lot. Uncaring that I was almost hit by a car, or the honking. I didn't care when I rushed through the automated doors and the security guard that was there. I didn't care that nurses tried to stop me as I ran down the halls.

I ran towards my sister's room, tears already forming in my eyes as I pushed open the door. Isola was there with her parents, crying. She saw me and gave me a sad nod.

"Let's give her a moment," she whispered and her parents saw me, giving me sympathetic looks before they gently guided their daughter out of the hospital room. Leaving me alone with my sister. The machines were still beeping slowly but I could hear the labored breathing of Aero. The death rattle that people have read about or witnessed themselves.

With a heavy heart I stepped forward until I was on the bed with her. My beautiful sister. I climbed on the bed, uncaring that I'd get scolded by nurses or doctors. I didn't care about anything but holding my baby sister in my arms for the last time. And that's what I did. I wrapped myself around her, stroking her hair as I placed a kiss on her temple.

"I don't want you to go," I whisper brokenly against her cold head. "What if I never see you again?" This moment made me remember one of our late night talks together.

I tuck the blankets around Aero and smile at her.

"Goodnight, I'll see you in the morning," I whisper and press a kiss to her head.

Aero sighs and looks up at me. "Vana?" Her voice is tentative as I straighten.

"Hmm?" I say, sitting on the edge of her bed.

Aero sits up. "Do you think there is a place in the afterlife? Like when we die?"

I stare at her. "Do you mean Heaven and Hell?"

She shakes her head. "No, no. For people who don't believe? Is there a place for us?"

I brace my arms on my knees and take a deep breath. I don't know how to answer this question. It's deep and thoughtful. But I know she's genuinely asking, even at eleven she's always been curious.

I glance at the door and hope our father doesn't hear us, but by the noise on the TV I'm pretty sure he's asleep so I answer.

"I think there is a place for everyone. Not necessarily a Heaven or

Hell but some place in the afterlife that we go to when we die. To find peace."

Aero nods. "Do you think you'll be with me when I die."

I grab Aero's hand in mine and squeeze. "You wouldn't die before me. I'm older so I'll go first. And even if I were to die I'd always be with you. In your heart and in your memories."

She sniffs. "But will I ever see you again?"

I nod smiling at her. "Of course you will. My love for you will always bring you to me."

"If I die first I'll be in your memories too. And we'd see each other again. I promise. Then we can haunt people together."

I laugh and pull her into a hug. "Deal. But you can't go before me."

Laughing, Aero holds out her pinky to me, "I promise." I wrap my own pinky around hers and kiss my thumb waiting for her to do the same. She does and we press our thumbs together sealing our promises.

"You promised me," I choke out. "You promised you wouldn't go before me. You promised you wouldn't leave me alone, Ree." I knew realistically no one could predict when they'd die, that anything can happen. But it wasn't supposed to be like this. She was supposed to grow old with her wife, build a family of love and support. She was supposed to grow old and gray, not go out like this.

Rocking back and forth I whisper to her, "I'm not ready. Please, please, please don't go yet. Please, Aero." My vision is cloudy as tears fall uncontrollably now.

Sobs wrack my body as I hold her. I place my head on her chest, directly against her slowing heart. "Aero, please. Just give me one more day." That's all I needed. One more day. One more day to talk to her, to hold her hand. One more day of being her sister. But I knew it wasn't going to happen. I could feel it as the breathing in her body slowly stopped, I felt when her heart gave one last shuddering beat. I heard it when she gasped her last breath, when the machines finally went off and the line went flat and her body grew limp. I knew instinctively that she was gone. My heart shattered and even though I knew it was going to happen I couldn't breathe. I couldn't accept it.

I didn't want to accept it. I rocked her, held her as if that would somehow get her to wake up and smile at me. But I knew she wouldn't. And I knew I couldn't go on like this. I knew whatever piece of humanity and love I had in me died with my sister. I couldn't breathe, I couldn't go on. I was barely processing and when the doctor came in and announced her time of death, I screamed. I screamed and pleaded for a life that no longer existed. A light that slowly burned out leaving me in a sea of darkness and grief.

Chapter 32

RAVI

As soon as Nirvana ran out of the house we all sprang into action. We knew what this meant, we all knew as soon as we were in the hospital and saw Isola standing outside of the hospital room crying. We all knew when the alarms were blaring and the doctors rushed in. As the door opened, I had a quick peek of Nirvana holding her sister whispering and crying.

I heard the doctor say the time of death. I knew it was going to happen, these last few months we all saw how quickly Aero declined, how little time she had. We knew it was coming, but nothing, and I mean nothing, would've prepared me for the scream of anguish that came from that room. I've heard and seen people lose a loved one. I was there with my Gran when she lost Gramps, but even then it wasn't like this. The hairs on the back of my neck stood up and the raw pain that scream held would forever haunt me.

I'll always remember the doctors coming out of the

room, crying. I'll always remember seeing Nirvana clutching her sister's lifeless body to her chest and rocking her back and forth. She screamed until her voice was hoarse and no sound came out, but the sound of sobbing still was heard through the cracked door.

"I'm sorry for your loss. And as much as it pains me we need someone to get her sister," a nurse said from beside us.

No one moved right away, it must've been a full minute until Rory walked towards the room. She walked in and moved over to Nirvana saying something to her. Nirvana shook her head and flinched when Rory reached out. I watched from the side as the other women moved into the room. Ophelia gently pried her fingers from Aero's body and it took Layla, Rory, Seraphina, and Delaney to pull Nirvana away from her sister as doctors came in and covered her up and slowly began wheeling the bed out.

"*No! No!*" Nirvana screamed, fighting against Rory's hold on her. Nirvana twisted and arched but that didn't stop Rory from trying to calm her. They fell into a heap on the floor and I heard Rory groan as her back hit the floor, but she didn't say anything, she just wrapped herself around Nirvana.

"Vana. Shh, it's okay," Delaney whispered, kneeling in front of the woman. The sight was almost too much, seeing the fight slowly fade out of her. Nirvana rolled to her side and Rory stayed with her, uncaring that they were on the hospital floor.

"What do you need, Nirvana?" Seraphina asked softly.

Nirvana sniffled slightly and whispered, "Ravi. I want Ravi." The men turned and stared at me watching closely as if to gauge my reaction and I can feel my heart pounding. I walk towards the room as if by some tether and her friends slowly move away from Nirvana watching me as I kneel beside her.

"Nirvana," I mutter.

She looks up at me, her blue eyes swollen and her nose is red from crying. She blinks slowly. "She's gone," she whispers brokenly.

I don't think, I pull her into my arms, and stroke her hair. "I know, pixie. I know," I mutter. She wraps her arms around me and sobs softly, her body heaving as she tries to draw in a breath. "Shh, I have you. Take a breath."

Nirvana tried, but it just came out in short gasps. I grab her face and force her eyes to mine. "Breathe. Follow my breathing." She nods, following every breath I took. In out. In out. "Good. That's good." My thumbs wipe gently at her tear soaked cheeks.

We sit like that, alone in an empty hospital room, working to calm her down. She takes a few more gulping breaths before nodding. "I'm sorry," she whispered, her voice hoarse and nearly inaudible.

"Don't do that," I whisper to her. "Don't apologize for your emotions, ever." She nods but I don't think she really heard me. But I knew deep down that the grief hasn't sunk in. At least not yet. I stood, pulling Nirvana with me, and tug her against my chest, holding her to me. Her arms wrap around my waist and she burrows herself against me. She doesn't cry though. She just holds on and I let her. Needing her to know she's not alone. That she'll never be alone.

After a few minutes, she pulls away. "I want to go home," she whispers. I nod and twine my fingers with hers before leading her out of the room. There wasn't any sign of our friends until we got to the waiting room and saw them sitting. And one by one they stood when they saw us. No one said anything, there wasn't much to say. But I knew they would be there for Nirvana. So, without prompting, they fell into step with us as we walked out of the hospital. I felt Nirvana tense when we saw her father walking towards the hospital. She didn't say anything, however. Just tilted her chin up and walked forward. I felt the men surround us separating Nirvana from her father, as the women walked in front of us, cutting him off from even seeing the daughter he disowned. Nirvana squeezed my hand in hers and I squeezed back. She wouldn't be alone. Never again. Not if I had anything to say about it.

Chapter 33

Nirvana

I stare down at my hands sighing softly. It's been three days since my sister's death. Three days since my heart stopped beating. At least theoretically. I was currently in my childhood home alone and stuck in my own head. I sat in my old bed and looked over at Aero's. It sat empty, covered in dust. I grip the neck of the Patron bottle in my lap before pulling it up to my mouth and taking a deep draw from it. The liquor burned down my throat, filling my empty stomach with the fire that had simmered for the last few days.

It was the only thing I could feel at the moment. That burning sensation that settled over you to the point you felt you were floating somewhere between this world and the next. Scoffing to myself I stood, throwing the bottle as hard as I could at the wall. It shattered, slinging glass in every direction. I was breathing heavily, watching as the puddle formed on the dingy rug, a dark stain that would soak down further and further until there was no getting it out. I watched it, the way the liquid spread slowly, so fucking slowly, stuck in an almost trance-like state before something in me snapped.

All that frustration, that anger just erupted from me. The anger at Aero for not attempting the treatments, at the doctors for not pushing for it more. At myself for not being enough. I slapped my hands on the dresser sending the contents scattering across the room. I screamed in frustration. I wasn't enough. Never enough! I gripped the edge of the dresser and pulled, grunting as it crashed to the floor splintering the aged wood into hundreds of pieces. But it wasn't enough. I needed more, I needed to find a way to get this anger out. I walked to Aero's bed and pulled that folder out before I stepped over the broken dresser and made my way to my father's bedroom. I threw the folder watching as the papers flew down the hall, scattering in every which direction. I was angry. So angry that it happened, that Aero knew. "Fuck!" I shouted, pushing the end table in the hall away. Sending that damned little lamp crashing to the floor. Breathing heavily I moved down the hall to the one room I haven't been in the entire time I've been here. My father's. I push open the door, wincing at the eerie creaking that came from it. I stepped in, sucking in a breath as I haven't been in here in years. The air was musty with that hint of Irish Spring and old tobacco. Stepping into the room was like stepping into some morbid shrine. The ode to hypocrisy and hate. Walking into the room I made my way to the closet, opening it and watching as those old Bibles fell to the ground. Without thinking, without one fucking thought in my head I started throwing them. Tears were running down my face as I tossed the books watching as old yellowed pages floated down to the ground.

All while shouting, "I hate you! I hate you! I hate you! You took her from me!" I was tearing at the leather that bound the pages, that bound the scripture that made it okay for my father to hate me. "'If a man lies with a male as with a woman, both of them have committed an abomination; they shall surely be put to death; their blood is upon them.' Fuck you! Fuck you!" I recited the damned verse from the memory of that camp, shouting it over and over again. I walked out of the room, searching for the old bat that was hidden in the hall closet. I tossed out old coats, tattered shoes and old board games before I found it.

I gripped the wooden handle, my fingers digging into the dented grooves before I walked back to the room. I wasn't in my right mind, I knew that. But I didn't care. Not anymore. So after years of holding onto a burning soul searing hatred I swung. It connected with the vanity mirror splitting it almost instantly. I barely spared a glance at the deranged woman staring back at me. Messy blonde hair and dark bruises under sallow eyes. I just swung again, grunting as the impact jarred the bones in my arms. I swung, relishing in the way the glass cracked slowly, then with each swing those cracks got wider and longer. It splintered until finally it shattered sending glass flying.

It was almost euphoric the way I felt with each swing of the bat. It connected with the wooden vanity, hitting open drawers, sending contents to the ground. And I just kept going, letting the anger fuel me until I physically couldn't hold the bat anymore. It dropped from my leaden arms falling with a *thwack* on the floor. I fell to my knees beside it breathing heavily, drawing in panting breaths that seemed few and far between. Sweat was sliding down my back bathing me in shame and anger.

I closed my eyes, trying so hard to breathe, but I can't. My heart is pounding loudly in my ears and black webs are edging my eyes making the room spin. I swallow the bile that threatened to come up as I drew in a breath of musty air.

The room seemed to tilt until I was lying flat on my back, staring up at the cracked ceiling, those webs getting thicker and thicker until finally unconsciousness overtook me.

"Nirvana," a deep voice said from beside me, shaking me gently. I groaned, batting them away. I hear a deep sigh before I'm lifted up. I don't even fight it, hanging limply in the arms of the person carrying me. I don't have the energy to fight. My mouth is drier than a tumbleweed in the Texas heat and my head feels like twenty tiny jackhammers are pounding at every crevice of my skull. That is until cold water is beating down on me.

"What the fuck?" I shout, my eyes popping open to stare into the stony green eyes of Ravi. He's holding me in the shower letting cold water pound down on us fully clothed. "What are you doing?" I shriek, wiggling in his arms. He holds fast, his large arms holding me tightly under the spray.

"Stop fucking moving, Nirvana," Ravi snaps. I just struggle more, flailing against him. He moves forward, pressing my chest against the shower wall smashing me directly under the spray. His chest pressed into my back caging me in. "Enough. E-fucking-nough," he gritted against my ear, uncaring of the water hitting us directly in the face.

"Let me go, Ravi," I say through clenched teeth. His hand comes up to the nape of my neck, holding me. Stilling me.

"Stop fighting me. I don't want to play these games with you, Nirvana. I know you're grieving. Baby, I fucking know how heartbroken you are. But you are going to get into this goddamn shower, you're going to clean yourself up and you're going to get it together."

"Get out of my house," I snap, tears brimming my eyes.

"It's been five days. Five fucking days. Your sister's funeral is in three hours. I gave you time, I did. But when you weren't answering your phone I was worried." His hand squeezed on my neck slightly and his breathing was labored. "You were unconscious. The fucking house was destroyed, and you were in a fucking heap on the floor."

My breathing stills in my lungs. Five days? I've been unconscious for two entire days? I guess it checked out considering I haven't slept much in weeks. Hell, months. But this was still a little alarming.

"I'm sorry," I mutter, pressing my head to the wall. I almost missed my sister's funeral. Fuck. Ravi loosens his hold on my neck but doesn't let me go. I'm hungover, stinky, dehydrated and almost late. One month. I have one month to grieve. That's what Aero wanted and it's what she'll get. I straighten my spine and nod. "I'm fine now. I'll be at the funeral. I swear. Just give me an hour. I'll be there." I nod again, not sure if I was nodding to the burly man behind me or to myself but I knew what I had to do. I could do this. I would do this. I had to for my sister, for her wife, for her friends. I had no other choice. So, squaring my shoulders I lifted my soiled shirt over my head and tossed it into a soggy pile on the floor. Ravi stepped back and out of the shower watching me. Not that I cared. He's seen me naked before. I shimmy out of my jeans and panties and tossed them on the pile. I didn't bother changing the setting of the shower, nor did I bother adding hot water.

I put my face to the cold spray and let it soak into my heavy bones. I had to make a plan. A thorough, well thought out plan. I ran my hands down my face and closed my eyes. I had twenty-five more days. I could do this. Shaking those thoughts away, I quickly shower as I hear Ravi pick up a bag and leave the room, probably to change out of his soaked clothes. I took a little longer in the shower than I would've liked but it hardly mattered. Once I was done washing my body and hair I climbed out to wash my face and brush my teeth. I grimaced when I ran my tongue over my teeth, usually one for dental hygiene in my profession. I brushed them a second time and rinsed my mouth before flossing. It wasn't much, but it was all I could do. I dried off and walked naked to my room. I ignored Aero's side of the room as I walked to the closet and pulled out the outfit I made sure to get for this moment. No one would know what it meant. But I did. Taking a deep breath, I dressed quickly before leaving the room. Ravi was in the kitchen dressed in all black.

"Hey," I mutter. Ravi turned to me and with a serious expression he slid over two little white pills, probably thinking I was still drunk off my ass or hungover. I glanced down at them before looking up at him. His gaze tracked down my outfit, but he didn't say anything just waited for me.

Huffing out a breath, I grab the pills and pop them in my mouth taking the glass of water he held out for me. I swallowed them down and sarcastically held out my tongue to him.

He doesn't take the bait, just dumps the remaining contents down the drain. "Go pack a bag. You're staying at my house. I don't want you to be alone."

My eyebrows rose to my hairline. "No, I'm not." I'd rather be alone, to plan, to come to terms with it. I don't exactly know. But I knew I couldn't be around him.

"It wasn't a request, Nirvana. Not after walking in to you passed out alone." His back stiffened as he talked and I felt heat rise to my cheeks in embarrassment wishing he never saw me in such a state.

"I was fine, Ravi."

"What if you had choked on your own vomit? What if you had hit your head?" I don't answer and I don't think he's expecting one. He just turns to me, his usually cool earthy green eyes blazing with heat. With anger. "I won't tell you again. Go. Pack. Your. Bag."

Sighing in defeat, I trudged back to the room and gathered what little bit of clothing I had and my toiletries. With that done I made my way back to Ravi who grabbed the bag without a word and led me out of the house. I took in a breath of fresh air and warmth slid through me. I had to go on, at least for now. I could be strong. I was always strong. What was one more day?

Chapter 34

RAVI

When I had walked into the house I knew something was wrong. The house was dark and trashed. Absolutely trashed. The hall table was knocked over and the lamp was shattered on the hardwood floor, ceramic scattered all over. Papers were strewn all over the floor and when I picked one up I could see it was the folder Aero shouted about. I read the one sheet and everything inside me turned cold. It took everything in me not to hunt down every doctor who "treated" Nirvana, and kill them. To find her pathetic father and put him out of his misery. But I knew that's not what Nirvana needed right now. She needed a rock. So, when I found her I was shocked, terrified. Angry. I can remember seeing Nirvana as soon as I walked into the room. Her unconscious body laying in a sullen heap surrounded by destroyed Bibles and a broken vanity. My heart was still in my throat and my palms were still sweaty from the nerves. I don't understand why I acted the way I did. Why I forced her under that cold spray, but I knew I had to do something. She'd hate herself if she missed the funeral, and after she's been secluded and unresponsive for five days I knew I had to check on her. I didn't even think twice before telling her she was coming home with me. I needed her in my sight at all times.

But when I told her about the funeral it was like something inside of her switched. In a blink of an eye it was as if she were a new person. It was honestly terrifying to see such a change take place in a mere second. Her back had straightened and she nodded at me, stripping out of the dirty clothes she wore and showering. I also didn't miss the fact that she didn't even bother turning on the hot water. She just soaked it up. After I left her to change into my clothes I went and found her aspirin for the undeniable headache I knew she had. She reeked of alcohol.

Shaking my head I made my way to my car. "We'll get your car afterwards," I murmur as we climb in. Nirvana nods, but doesn't say anything. It gives me a minute to study her. Her hair fell in soft waves over her shoulders, her blue eyes were dulled of their normal vibrancy and held dark circles under them. She looked slimmer and there was no color on her normally rosy cheeks.

But the main thing I noticed, she wasn't wearing black. No, she wore a multitude of colors. A long, corseted dress that cinched at her trim waist and fell to the ground, following her around like a cape with each movement she makes, making her the living embodiment of a rainbow. All bright colors, yet so little shine. Shaking my head, I start the car and drive us to the funeral home. Isola and Aero already had it planned and everything was set up. From the gravestone, to the casket. All of it. It broke my heart for Nirvana and I could see the way she ran a shaky hand down her skirt as we pulled into the lot that was already filling up. Nirvana took a deep breath as she slowly unclipped her seatbelt looking out into the cemetery.

"Do you need a moment?" I ask.

She shakes her head, taking in a deep shuddering breath. "No. It's fine." She climbed out of the car and straightened her shoulders. I follow after her and step beside her holding my hand out. She glances at it for a second before wrapping her small hand into mine, twining our fingers together. We were a little late, but no one would hold it against her.

We walk through the cemetery where the ceremony was to be held. My gaze landed on Nirvana as she walked, her head held high. She was like a beacon of light in a sea of gray in her dress. The gloom of the day followed by the people dressed in all black made her a startling contrast to everyone. Isola looked over to us, and her eyes widened, a small smile tilting on her mouth. Nirvana gave her a small smile of her own, but didn't go to her. We made our way to the seats that the others had saved for us, all of them watching us with different emotions, none I wanted to acknowledge right now. Delaney patted the seat next to her and Nirvana sat down slowly, crossing her legs. She sat stiffly as the priest stood up at the podium. I sat next to her and she grabbed my hand, squeezing it hard.

"Good afternoon, all. We are gathered here today to celebrate the life of Aero, a young soul taken far too soon." Nirvana moved slightly in her seat looking ahead. "Aero has been a bright light in this world, always willing to help those in need. She is survived by her wife, Isola and her older sister, Nirvana. Two individuals who loved her more than anything. This ceremony is one that is a little less conventional than what I am used to. As it was requested that there not be a prayer. More of a moment of silence for the dearly departed. Please if you will close your eyes in honor of Aero."

There was a silence in the cemetery, the only sound being

that of birds that were chirping high above us. Nirvana doesn't have her eyes closed, no, they are staring at the shiny black casket. After the silence someone else stands up, a man who I recognized from the wedding as one of Aero's brides-maids. He was a large man with a happy smile on his face but it didn't reach his eyes. He had a large black beard and a fade haircut to match. He stood and cleared his throat. "Hi all. I am, Nev, one of Aero's best friends from back in the glory days also known as middle school."

"Oh no," Nirvana whispered, clasping her hands over her mouth.

"What's wrong?" I ask.

She shakes her head and Nev continues, "Now, Aero is a special breed of person. One of the best. She left this little tidbit in her funeral arrangements for me to sing. Now, I'm no Beyonce, but I'd do anything for Aero. Even if it is mildly amusing. So without further ado a song, for the best. This one's for you, Aero."

"Please don't," Nirvana whispered. I want to demand answers from her on why she was silently whispering to herself, but I don't need it because Nev clears his throat and starts singing.

"Amazinggggggg Grace… how sweet the sound," I stop in my tracks. Stunned speechless. This man let out the most shrill sound I've ever heard. I look beside me and I see Caden sitting straight up staring up at the sky. We are luckily far in the back, but fuck. Nirvana has her leg bouncing up and down and I see Delaney squeezing Sorrow's hand hard. *"That saved a wretch like,"* Nev stopped taking a deep breath.

"Oh my fuck," Nirvana whimpered her sides heaving.

"He's going to do it," I hear Rory mutter.

"He wouldn't," Ophelia countered.

Nirvana lifted her hands to her ears just as Nev did as he sang, *"Meeeeeeeeee."* Nirvana bent down covering her face, her body shaking in silent laughter. *"I was once lost now founddddd,"* he mixed up the lyrics and Nirvana was losing it.

"Fucking stop," Caden said, trying his damndest to not laugh at a time like this but that just made Nirvana laugh harder. With every lyric he sang Nev made it longer than it should've been and mixed up the words, but Nirvana was laughing and honestly, I was close to losing it too. It was working until my eyes collided with Caden's and I was done for. Someone shushed us and we all sat up straighter as if we were children being scolded. I see Ophelia motion to her mother up front and the older woman nods, standing, and pushing her dark braids out of her face as she gently touches Nev's shoulder.

"Thank you, honey. But we have so much more." Nev nodded, bowing dramatically before sitting down.

"Vana, can you go up and say a few words?" Isola says, coming up behind us and hunching down to Nirvana's level.

Nirvana's eyes widened with panic. "I didn't write anything. I thought you were doing it." Her voice was almost a plea and Isola shook her head.

"She'd want you to do it. I'll speak, I just need a moment before I go up there. Please?"

"Right, right. Okay. Okay," Nirvana repeated, then stood drawing everyone's attention to her. "Okay," she whispered to herself and moved past us to the front. She looked at the casket and then at the people in front of her. I wanted to go up there and take her away from this pain. But I knew she'd want to do this, need to. So I sit silently until her eyes connect with mine. I give a subtle nod and she nods back.

"Hello. I'm Nirvana, um Aero's sister." She twists her hands in her bright skirt and takes a breath. "These things are a little difficult for me to do, so bear with me," she explains and gives a nervous laugh. "Aero was a special person," she starts. Clearing her throat she stares at the casket again with a sad smile on her face. "She wanted me to wear rainbow to her funeral. It was her first request when she teased me about dying. I told her she'd be fine. I was so sure she would be." She shakes her head, wiping under her eyes while taking a breath. "I wish I was right. That maybe she was just overworked or something but I wasn't, not this time." She finishes in a whisper, as if she were talking directly to her sister. "I'm not good with these things. Preplanned words, it isn't my thing, will never be my thing. That was all Aero. She was the planner out of the two of us. She used to say to me, *'Vana, you need to start planning for things. What are you going to do without me?'*" Nirvana's voice chokes up slightly. "The thing is I don't, I don't know what I'm going to do without her. I don't know how to go on without her. She was my best friend. The other half of my soul, and now she's just gone."

For the first time she looked up, her gaze going to the group of people who sat there, some dabbing their eyes while others tried to hold back tears. Her gaze went back to that shining casket and I saw a sob wrack her body.

"My sister is in there. I'll never hear her laugh, we'll never be able to call off work and get day drunk together while planning world domination." She gives a soft laugh. "Aero was a special person. A great friend, a great sister, a great partner and she deserved better than this. She deserved to grow old and gray with the love of her life. She deserved to be a mom, an aunt," another sob, "God, she deserved so much more than this. Aero was a great fucking person, she was my person. The world won't be the same without her in it. A bright soul taken too soon." She looks at the priest and says, "Sorry I said fuck a lot." With a nod, she made her way back towards her seat. The rest of the funeral goes by without a hitch until there's no one else here but us. Our makeshift family, sitting there watching as they lowered the casket into the ground.

"I'm surprised Nev didn't try to throw himself into the ground with her," Nirvana murmured, her eyes distant.

"Are we going to the wake? Or do you just want to go home?" Seraphina asked gently, holding her sleeping daughter in her arms.

"I should probably go for a little bit. You can take Darcy home. Poor thing looks tuckered out," Nirvana assured her, standing.

"Oh, Louise is taking her. I can come. I want to."

Nirvana gives a small nod. "I've got to meet with Isola and Aero's lawyer there so I need to get going. Thank you all for coming. I appreciate it." She turns and walks away, her arms wrapped around herself.

"We'll be right behind you," Sam mutters, clapping a hand on my shoulder.

I nod and follow after her.

Chapter 35

Nirvana

Leaning back I sigh, pressing a hand to my pounding head. Ravi and I were currently sitting in front of Isola's parents' home where the wake was taking place and I wanted nothing more than to go to Cannon's and get drunk and forget this day. But I knew I couldn't do that. Instead, I glance at the man beside me. Such a wonderful man who has stood beside me these last few months, who cared and helped when he didn't have to.

My heart skipped a beat before it began pounding. Without thinking I reach out, pressing my palm against his stubbled jaw. He glances at me, his eyes softening ever so slightly when he meets my gaze.

I run my thumb over his cheek and say, "Thank you. For everything you've been doing for me, Ravi. I can't tell you how much it means to me." My voice is low and he sighs, leaning into my touch almost as if he couldn't help it.

"You don't need to thank me. I like being around you."

I snort under my breath and say, "I'm not the best person to keep company with."

"And you think I am?"

I arch a brow, running my thumb over his full bottom lip. "I don't know. Caden and Delaney seem to love your self-care dates."

Ravi rolls his eyes. "I told those two never to speak of it."

I laugh, a small one, but it was genuine. "I think you lost any anonymity when you binge watched teenage vampire movies with us and drank sparkly juice. It's cute."

"Men aren't cute, tinker hell," he scolds teasingly.

"I don't know. I think you're adorable, you remind me of a pug."

Ravi gapes at me, before throwing his head back and laughing. "Did you just compare me to a dog that is the embodiment of a living potato?"

I gasp in mock outrage, "I'd never do such a thing." I sigh, leaning back in my seat. "I'm kidding. You're more like Henry Cavill. Clark Kent though. I can't imagine you in a leotard type of thing."

He scoffs, "I'll have you know my thighs look amazing in a leotard. I was Superman in tenth grade."

I laugh, leaning my head back to watch him. "I don't know if I'm ready to face those people yet."

Ravi turns to me, a serious look on his handsome features. "You don't have to. I'm sure they'd understand if you wanted to wait a few more days."

I look out the window, watching as the sun slowly sets on the horizon. "It's okay. I'd rather get it over with." With that I open the car door and step outside.

Ravi isn't far behind me. In fact, he presses his palm on the small of my back and motions me forward. The touch is gentle, but I can feel it to my very soul. As if he were trying to give me his strength and I appreciated it a lot more than I should have. But that doesn't matter. I'd take any and all strength I could get. I walked up the cobblestone steps and opened the door where I saw people talking and mingling with one another. I see Isola talking to her mother and father when I walk in. Her eyes land on me and she excuses herself to come towards me.

"Nirvana, that was a beautiful speech today. Thank you."

I nod, I wouldn't have wanted anyone else to speak for my sister. "Thank you."

"Justin is in Dad's office waiting. We can go on in there. People will be here for a while so we should get this done."

Nodding, I look up at Ravi. He gives my hip a slight squeeze. "I'll be here. I see Sorrow and Delaney coming up the drive now."

"Okay. Thank you," I whisper. Ravi nods and surprises me when he presses a gentle kiss to my head before leaving me alone with Isola.

"He seems to like you a lot," Isola says.

"I like him a lot, too." More than I probably should, but I don't want to talk about him right now. I look over at my sister-in-law. "How are you holding up?"

Isola sighs, looking tired. "I wish she were here, Vana. I miss her so much."

I reach out and squeeze her arm gently. "She loved you so very much."

Isola gives a small nod and swallows thickly. "I know." She pushes forward and opens the door to a small office where I see the last two people I'd ever want to fucking see. My parents. There they are. Standing and glaring at each other.

When the door opens they turn and face us.

"Ahh, we're all here," a stocky older man says, swiveling in a chair which made me think of a toddler in a high chair, because of how big it looks compared to the man.

"You're the lawyer?" I ask warily.

"Yes. Justin Van. It's a pleasure to meet you, Ms. Bridges." He stands and holds out a hand to me.

I step forward and shake his hand. "Nirvana. Just Nirvana is fine." Justin nods, pushing his dark comb-over out of his eyes.

"I was just looking at the will. Let's all have a seat." I stand to the side not wanting to sit anywhere near the two people who brought me into the world. Hell, aside from me walking in, neither really looked at me. Not that I cared. Both washed their hands of me early on. I wish it didn't bother me as much as it did, but I'd be lying if I said it didn't hurt.

Justin cleared his throat, feeling the growing tension in the room, his face was red and perspiration dotted his brow, and began, "On behalf of Aero Lorraine Bridges, beneficiary Nirvana Caroline Bridges hereby inheirits a lump sum of 3.5 million dollars in the form of crypto currency dating back to 2009."

My heart stops and the blood rushes to my ears. What the hell? When did Aero have time and money to do this? She would've had to start at fifteen-years-old, when she'd told me she found some coins online that make a profit. I didn't know anything about it, but she had saved up her allowance so she invested. But to know she had this much was jaw dropping.

"The home that Aero owns with Isola has been deeded to Isola and her alone. However, the family home that was purchased as of a year ago under the name of Aero Bridges has been deeded to you, Nirvana." Justin leans down and pulls out a little safety deposit box and a small ring of keys to open it. "To the parents: Mrs. Bridges, Aero left you a stack of photos. Father Bridges, a Bible and rosary." He then turns to me and opens the box. I peek inside and see an old, well-used Gameboy.

I reach inside with shaky hands and grab it. "The best Christmas ever," I whisper to myself. I ran my thumb over the worn stickers on the back of it, surprised she still had it. It makes our last conversation all the better and special.

"Now, wait a minute. I want to contest this will because it's not right," Father snaps and, for once, my mother was nodding in agreement.

I scoff, figures.

"I apologize, Father Bridges but this is ironclad. You signed away parental rights of Aero to Nirvana, when Nirvana was eighteen years of age. This made Nirvana Aero's legal guardian. Aero also married before her death and leaves a widow. There are no grounds for you to contest Aero's will. It's set in stone."

Father slams his hand on the desk jostling the small knick knacks on it. "She is mentally unstable. I wouldn't trust anything in the hands of this woman let alone my house, or that amount of money."

I roll my eyes and see my father's jaw tic. But my mother interjects, "He's right. Nirvana has been on medication for years, and in a mental institution. Therapists and psychiatrists can attest to that."

"You two are unbelievable," I grit out. How dare they? How fucking dare they use my issues against me to get money? "Why the fuck are you even here? Neither of you have tried to see Aero since she was thirteen. Neither of you gave her birthday gifts or Christmas gifts. You didn't take care of her when she was sick. When she was heartbroken. Why the fuck do you think you're owed anything? Because you fucked once upon a time and that turned into a child? You're not owed anything because you brought her into this world."

Father's face turns red. "Don't you dare swear in front of me, girl."

Scoffing, I grab the will from Justin and the Gameboy. Holding it close to my chest as I leave the room.

"Nirvana, get in here now!" Father shouts, drawing attention to our drama. He always loved an audience.

I turn towards him, facing off with the man who ruined my entire life. Who ruined me and my soul. I can see my friends from the corner of my eye and see that everyone is watching. "You will not cause a scene at this funeral. If you can't behave like an adult you will be escorted out," I say sternly, when all I really wanted to do was turn and leave, and never see these people again.

"I will bring this to my own lawyer. I don't know what kind of lines you fed your sister, but I won't let you use this money or my house for your sinful acts," he sneers.

"Hate to piss on your parade, Father, but Aero also likes women. She married a woman. You think she didn't know what she was doing, but you're wrong. You're fucking delusional. See, unlike you and Mommy over there, I don't give a fuck about the money."

He grabbed my arm and pulled me into him, whispering under his breath, "I did everything I could to make sure your soul and your dignity was saved. And this is the thanks I get?"

I snatch my arm away from him and I meet his stare with a hard one of my own. "You're right. The one good thing that camp was good for, Father Dearest, is it made me an expert when I'm on my knees."

His face turned bright red and without warning he back-handed me, hard. My head snapped to the side and I tasted copper in my mouth. Laughing, I looked up at him and I licked my lip as all hell broke loose. Everything happened so fast, I'm pulled back and away and my father is lying on his back, his nose bleeding, with Ravi standing over him breathing heavily. Ravi leans down grabbing the front of my father's shirt, pulling him roughly up from the floor, and getting within inches of my father's face.

"I don't give a fuck what God you worship, you put your hands on her again and I'll send you straight to Him." He doesn't wait for an answer, just pushes my father away from him and stalks towards me. His hand is gentle when he lifts my chin and swipes his thumb gently over my tender cheek. "I want to fucking kill him," he says.

And I believed him. I could see it in the way his eyes burned with barely concealed rage and the way his chest heaved. "Well, don't do that. You'd end up behind bars for a very long time. I was in jail once, you wouldn't make it, trust me." I try to play it off but it doesn't work.

Ravi rolls his eyes, his jaw clenched as he looks at my face. "Are you okay? Are any teeth loose? Can you move your jaw?"

I flick my tongue across my teeth testing them, then open and close my mouth. "No. I'm good. Nothing but a small bruise."

"His entire hand print is on your fucking face, Nirvana. I'd hardly call that a small bruise," Ravi growls, tossing a look over his shoulder as Marcy helps my father up, her eyes downcast. I see a young boy, well, boy is subjective, he is probably nineteen or twenty but I stare at him as he steps up to my mother, his hair nearly white. Like my mother's. Like Aero's. They had the same features.

I turn away, staring down at the floor, my hands clenched onto Ravi's arm. He looks at me, but doesn't make a sound, just moves closer to me.

"What do you need?" he whispers. It was as if it were just us. No one else was around, just me and him, surrounded by his spicy scent that had my heart racing. But when I looked over his shoulder and saw that kid, I can see myself. I saw my mother. I see her. Taking a shaky breath I shake my head.

"I want to leave. Now." Ravi nods and grabs my hand and taps out a slight beat on the back of it and the others surround us. Large men who form a protective circle around us. No. Not us. Around me.

"Caroline," Father says. I tense. God, I hated that name. It was his mother's name, and being named after that old bitch made me want to jump off the nearest overpass until I was nothing more than a pile of goo. Never to be identified again. He knows I hate that name. Hell, he hasn't directly addressed me since the hospital. Not really anyway. Aside from those dirty looks and that sneer of disapproval he didn't acknowledge I was even born from his decrepit loins.

"You'll be hearing from my lawyers." He's holding his handkerchief to his nose, glaring daggers at me.

I don't respond. There was no point. Whatever he wanted, he wouldn't get. Not if I had anything to say about it. We walked out of the house. The sky was overcast now and the wind was picking up causing my hair to fly in all directions. I stare ahead, my head starting to ache and my stomach to cramp. I was over today, over the pain, the humiliation. The anger. I just wanted to close my eyes for a few minutes and sink into a deep sleep where nothing happened. Just a semblance of peace. At least for a little bit.

"Nirvana!" a voice calls out. I stop and look behind me. The men stop and glare at the boy and I see the other women slowly following after.

"Do I know you?" I asked, but I knew the truth. He may be younger, but I knew who he was. We had the same features, only he had our mother's dark eyes. He looks at the men and the women who were around me, nervously running a hand through his hair. He looked ready to piss himself, but then he swallowed hard and stood up straight, standing taller than me by a foot at least.

"I wanted to say I'm sorry for your loss and see if you were okay."

I stare at him. "How old are you?"

He clears his throat. "I'm eighteen."

I shake my head, scoffing under my breath, "This whole time she had another family." Well, if that wasn't just another 'kick you when you're down' moment.

"I didn't know where we were going. Not until we were already here," he explains in a rush.

"She didn't tell you that you had sisters and you were going to one's fucking funeral?"

"No. Up until today I thought I was an only child. I'm really sorry."

"Name," Ravi says, his voice cool and calm.

The kid pales even further, he clears his throat, and says, "August. My name is August."

"You're a shit liar," Drew states, his gaze on the house where I see my mother come out onto the porch. "What's your name, kid?" Drew asks, staring at him, the side of his face was scarred and his eyes held very little emotion in them. Just a hardened exterior.

"I'm really sorry," he whispers.

"Aero, let's go. Now!"

I feel the blood drain from my face and bile burns my throat. Ravi sees my face and he steps out of the way as I lose whatever contents I had in my stomach. What the fuck was happening?

Chapter 36

RAVI

I hold Nirvana's hair from her face as she vomits. "Ugh. I'm going to kill that bitch," she groans, wiping her mouth with the tissue Drew handed her.

"I'm sorry you had to find out like this, Nirvana," Nirvana's mother said. She walked up to us, her dark eyes settling on Nirvana in judgment. Her hair was turning gray showing her age, but other than that she looked eerily similar to Nirvana. "I should've told you. Warned you. And for that I apologize." But I could tell her apology was anything but genuine.

"For fuck's sake! Get away from me!" Nirvana shouts.

"I just buried a child, Nirvana Caroline. I will not be spoken to like this." The entitlement in this woman's tone grated on my nerves.

"Shut the fuck up! I buried her. Me, not you. I took care of her as a child, I raised her. While you were out there living a completely different life. Don't come here with that, 'I buried my child' shit. I did it. Me. Not you, not that bastard in there. I did it. I held her as she died, I did that. Don't come at me playing the grieving mother. We all know you never fucking cared," Nirvana said, sniffing slightly. "I've had enough drama. I want to sleep. I'm tired, my head fucking hurts and I'm ten seconds away from committing homicide. Someone take me home." I don't think twice, I pick her up and carry her away.

God, she couldn't catch a break today. I take her to the car and help her in, watching as she settles into her seat, sighing softly. I lean inside and pull the belt over her and buckle her in.

"When's the last time you ate?" I ask, concern running through me at how pale she was.

"I'm not hungry," she muttered.

"I didn't ask if you were hungry. I asked when you last ate. Since you can't give me a direct answer I'm going to assume it's been a while."

She rolls her eyes. "You know what they say when you assume things."

"Yes, you make an ass out of you and me. But we both know it's been a while since you've eaten. So we'll go pick something up." She opens her mouth to protest but I stop her. "And you're going to sit there and eat because I told you to do so. You're wasting away right in front of me. Once you've eaten you can clean up and get into bed."

She sighs, turning her head away from me. "Fine." I nod and pull away from her, closing her inside.

"I'm going to take her home. I'll be in touch," I say to the others as I head to the driver's side. I could feel them watching me, but I didn't care. Right now my only concern was the broken woman beside me.

Driving down the highway in complete silence was stifling. I could hardly breathe in the damn car. Let alone think. I kept glancing over at Nirvana but her face was directed towards the window, and she gave nothing away. She kept her face carefully blank. I put on the turn signal, turned off on the nearest exit, and found a Wendy's so I could get her some food.

"I didn't take you for a fast food type of guy," Nirvana says.

I shake my head as I pull into the parking lot. "I'm not. The very thought of eating this makes my stomach twist."

"It's food, Ravi. You're being a bit dramatic don't you think?"

I snorted. "No, in my line of work I have to keep a healthy diet, and this doesn't exactly scream health."

"They probably have lettuce," she teases, her mouth tilting up slightly. Pulling up to the drive-thru speaker, I'm ready to ask Nirvana what she wants, but she leans forward, her breasts pressing against my side, her hand balanced on my thigh, and says, "Hi, can we get a six piece nugget, medium fry, and chocolate frosty." The nearly inaudible speaker told us to pull up. I get to the window and pull out my wallet and pay. We wait for a few minutes before the food is out. I grab the bag and thank the kid who handed me the bag.

"There's a park up the road. We can park there," Nirvana says, taking the bag. Humming, I pull away from the drive-thru. It doesn't take long to get there and park. Nirvana opens the lid on the frosty and digs in the bag before pulling out a fry, dipping it into the frosty, and popping it into her mouth.

"What the hell are you doing?" I ask in disgust.

Nirvana laughs. "You've never tried fries in milkshakes?"

"No. That's what ranch and ketchup are for."

Tsking she dips another fry into the frosty and holds it out. "If you don't take it it'll melt and ruin your fancy seats."

Cursing, I open my mouth letting her pop the fry in. I feel my eyes widened as the flavors coat my tongue. The richness of the chocolate along with the saltiness of the fry oddly works together.

Smiling smugly, Nirvana pops her own fry into her mouth. "Told you. It's delicious."

"Yeah, yeah, yeah. Whatever you say." But she was right. Not that I'd let her rub it in my face.

"Where'd you get the idea from?"

She sits in silence, chewing thoughtfully before passing me the bag to get some. "I've always been doing this. When Aero would have a bad day at school or something we'd make our own fries and shakes and dip. On special occasions we'd go to iHop or something. It's the sweet and savory aspect. Always so good."

"You loved her a lot," I noted.

Smiling sadly she nods, "I practically raised her. Our parents' marriage was awful. They fought a lot," she says, then shakes her head. "No. They fought every single day."

"Why didn't your mother take you when she left?" I ask. Because if it were my children, I wouldn't want them staying with someone who was as abusive, angry, and entitled as Nirvana's father was.

"She didn't want ties to him. At least that's what I've always thought. Now, I'm not so sure. She didn't have a job, she was the preacher's wife, a mother, a homemaker. Maybe she just wanted a complete break from her old life."

I scoff, "Your parents are dicks."

She looked at me and for the first time in days she laughed. "That they are. They're pissed."

"The will?" I ask, remembering what Aero said to us. How once she dies shit will hit the fan because of it.

"Yup. Apparently, Aero was one of the few who invested in bitcoin or something. To be honest I have no idea what that even is. But she left me the house and a couple million dollars."

I gaze at her, my jaw dropping. "Millions?"

"Yeah. A few." She shrugs nonchalantly, continuing to eat. "Aero always was smart. She didn't need to leave it. What the hell would I use it for? She should've donated it. The bitch. What if I had a gambling addiction? That money would be gone by now."

I chuckle softly. "Do you have a gambling addiction?"

"No. But it could happen. Who am I kidding? I suck at poker, my face gives it all away. I'd lose just by walking past a damn table." Sighing, Nirvana rubs a tired hand down her face. "Why'd she have to go and die? I don't know what to do. Not now. Probably never."

"She'd want you to move on," I say softly.

Scoffing, Nirvana closes her eyes, "She gave me a time limit to grieve. A damn month. As if after a month I'd just magically be okay with her being gone. As if she wasn't a big part of my life. Like she wasn't the reason I'm still here. Then she goes and dies." Her fingers pull at the threads on her skirt and I can see her trying to compose herself.

"It's okay to be hurt and angry. It's okay to cry. You're human, Nirvana. You're not going to be okay ever again. She'll still be there, in your heart, but the pain will only numb over time. Not go away completely." I push a strand of hair behind her ear, stroking her cheek gently with my thumb.

"It hurts worse than I thought it would, Ravi," she says with a small catch in her throat. "I'm so mad at her for not getting the treatment. It would've given us a little longer. I could have mentally prepared myself."

I grip the nape of her neck. "But would you have been

prepared, Nirvana?" There was no way to accept the death of a loved one. It was never something people could just accept. Your own death was more acceptable because you knew it would come eventually. But when it comes to family or those you love it's as if you need to take care of them. Protect them from everything. Even things that aren't preventable. I could see Nirvana knew she'd never be able to prepare for it. I see it in the way she gazes down at her hands, in the way her chest heaves with each lungful of air she takes in. A part of me wants to take her pain away, to make her feel better but realistically I knew it was impossible.

"No, I wouldn't be prepared," she finally says. "But I miss her like crazy. I keep thinking she'll show up or text saying she was just being dramatic or something. She's not though. She's really gone." Tears gather in her eyes that she tries to blink away. Glancing away from me she presses the heel of her hand into her eyes.

"Tell me what you need, Nirvana. Let me help you," I whisper.

Sighing softly her shoulders droop. "I'm so tired. I just want to sleep for a little bit." I don't say anything, just pull away from the park. The ride to my house is silent and longer than it should've been but I don't mind. I can see the fatigue slowly seeping into Nirvana. When I finally get home she's leaning against the window fast asleep. I climb out grabbing the trash on the way and toss it in the garbage can before heading to her.

I open the door, lean in and unbuckle her. I pull her into my arms and ease her out. Careful not to bump her head. She curls into me, resting her head on the crook of my neck breathing out a soft sigh. I press a kiss to her head and walk up the porch steps. I pull the keys out of my pocket and unlock the door trying not to jostle her.

"Ravi," Gran calls.

"Yeah, it's me. Just give me a few minutes," I say in a hushed whisper before heading to my bedroom. Nirvana still hasn't woken up as I set her on the bed. Nor does she move when I pull her shoes off. Glancing at her I pause, wondering if I should take the dress off of her or not. Cursing, I go to the dresser and pull out a white t-shirt and go back to the bed, pulling her up to unbutton the corset letting it fall open.

I make quick work of her clothing making sure she's comfortable before dressing her in the t-shirt.

When I go to stand, her soft whisper stops me, "Please don't go."

I stare down at her, but her eyes remain firmly closed. Cursing under my breath, I strip myself and climb into bed behind her, pulling her against my chest. "I'm not going anywhere. I promise." I kiss her neck squeezing her slightly. "I'm not going to leave you," I whisper again. And I meant it, with my entire heart. I wouldn't leave this woman. Not unless she asked me to. And even then I'm not sure I could do it.

Chapter 37

Nirvana

Rolling over in the bed I hit a warm, strong body. Gasping, I sit up looking around the dark room. My mind is disoriented and all over the place. I remember being at Aero's funeral, then meeting my mother's son and leaving. I pull my legs up to my chest and sigh, rocking back and forth slightly. I can feel the panic settling in. It was a heavy weight that hung over my head, hanging precariously by a thin thread. The finality of it wasn't lost on me. I press my head to my raised knees and take a deep breath. Breathing in and out slowly, I glance to the side where Ravi is sleeping soundly. I ease myself away and grab my shoes, uncaring that I was in just a t-shirt and panties. It hardly mattered to me. Casting one last glance at him I leave the room, shutting the door silently behind me. The house was dark and quiet, I wasn't even sure what time it was other than it was dark outside.

I gaze at the alarm system and notice it was disengaged from when Ravi brought us inside. I open the door and lock the knob before stepping into the humid, damp heat. I don't bother putting on my shoes. I just hold them in one hand before I embark on wherever I am going. I had no plan, no phone, no money. I just was. The walk on the road was bumpy and I felt rocks cutting into the soles of my feet, but I hardly felt the pain. The pain in my chest was worse than any type of pain I could physically feel. It was like living in agony every day since her death.

Tears welled up in my already swollen eyes causing me to angrily swipe at them, I was so tired of crying. I want it to just stop. But I knew I had so much to do and I'd do it. I made a promise and I intended on keeping it. I walk and walk and notice the sun starting to rise from the horizon and I'm standing at the edge of my property. And it was mine now. All mine. It was depleted, parts of the porch were rotted off and the shingles were hanging on by a prayer and a rusted screw. Not that it truly mattered. The house was nothing more than four walls that held memories of utter hell.

Not wanting those memories to surround me I climb the stairs and walk inside. It was silent, stuffy. It was too much. Dropping my shoes at the door, I make my way to the bathroom and turn on the shower. The handle for the hot water was broken and I didn't want to pull out the pliers so I was stuck with the cold spray. I didn't mind though. It woke me up. Once I finished my shower I climbed out and went to the room I shared with Aero. I averted my eyes and saw my phone on the pillow. I must've forgotten it yesterday. Shrugging, I grab it and see a ton of messages from my friends. I ignore them and pull up Ravi's number sending him a quick text.

I had things to do and not a lot of time to do them. My eyes go to the time and I see that it is barely even six in the morning. Great, I had enough time to figure it all out.

Dressing quickly I drop my phone on my bed, gather what I need, and head out the door. Pausing, I notice my pill case. Debating on it, I shake my head. I didn't need it. Not now. I yank my keys off the key holder and rush to my Jeep. First stop was the lawyers. The drive is a little out of my way and by the time I get there it is seven-fifteen. I tap my thumbs on the steering wheel waiting impatiently.

"How long does it take to get to work?" I mutter to myself. Not that I'd know, I haven't been to work in weeks. I lean back and finally see a black sedan pull into the parking lot and see Justin Van exiting the car, a briefcase in his hand. Quickly climbing out of my car I rushed towards him.

"Mr. Van!" I call, running through the street. I ignore the horn honking behind me until I'm beside the man who jumps, startled by me.

"Nirvana! You scared me. What are you doing here? The office isn't open yet. Nor do you have an appointment."

I nod. "I know. I'm sorry. But I really need to speak to you. It's urgent. Please." He studies me through beady eyes before nodding.

"You have ten minutes." Perfect. That's all I need. I follow him into the office, pausing when he gets to a desk, motioning for me to sit. I sink into the leather seat stiffly and wrap my hands together. "Well, what is it you need?"

I sit up straighter. "Right. I just have a few questions. Um, you said the will is concrete, right? Nothing can be done unless I approve it, right?"

Mr. Van sits up straighter. "Yes. Everything is left to you. It might take a while, but you are the beneficiary to every-thing aside from what was left to Aero's wife."

Nodding I lean forward. "I didn't get all of the paper-work. I left because of the drama, which I apologize for. Can I have it now, please?" Mr. Van sighs and digs into his case. He signs papers, leaving us in silence for a few minutes, before he hands it to me. I gaze at it, stand, and without a goodbye, leave the office to run back to my car.

I drove quickly to the bank Aero and I used and rush inside towards a teller. There weren't any lines thankfully and I was able to get to a teller.

"Hi!" I gasp, taking in deep breaths. The poor woman looked as if she were concerned as she looked at me. "Sorry, it's been a busy morning. I was wondering how I would be able to split a large amount of money into six trusts?"

"Well, it depends on the amount, the funds available, and when it comes. It takes around six months to complete such a process. Even then taxes need to be paid and debts."

Cursing, I run a hand through my hair. "Am I able to set it up? Then once the six months are up they will be set to go?"

The young woman looks at me before nodding. "Let me go get my manager and see if they can help you better than I can. Just a moment please."

I wave her away calculating in my head. Six months wasn't really that long. If I were to put the money under a different name and to put in writing that I am giving it up maybe then I will have it all settled. The woman comes back with a large man with gray hair and a mustache to rival the monopoly man. He gives me a customer service smile and ushers me to the back room.

"I heard of your situation. How can I help you?"

I sat down at the table and explained everything. Me wanting to convert the assets to different accounts so my father doesn't have a chance to contest the will and try to get the money for himself. And the fact that Aero had just died and I knew it would take a long time, but I wanted it to be situated beforehand because, knowing my father, he really would fight it.

"Any specific reason other than that?" he asked me. I

shook my head, pasting on a fake smile. The man, who's name I learned was Carl, nodded and set up the paperwork. Since I technically didn't inherit it yet I figured it was better to set the money in different trusts. It took a couple hours and by the time I had it all semi-situated I was exhausted. I thanked him and left the bank feeling hopeful. I climbed into the car and headed towards a small bar I knew was up the street.

Was it too early to drink? Yes, but it was five o'clock somewhere and I just needed a moment of silence. Just to let everything sink in. I saw it was open and parked before heading inside. There was no one there and it was just a normal western style bar with cow heads on the walls and country music blaring from the speaker. I made my way to the bar and sat down.

"You do realize it's only one, right?" a voice said beside me. I glanced up at a woman who was wiping down the bar. She had bright blue hair and tattoos on her neck.

"I'm aware," I say, turning away.

"Okay, what can I get you?" she asks, tossing the towel over her shoulder.

"Something strong," I reply. "Do you also have a pen?" The woman raised a dark brow but handed over a pen. I pull the napkin holder towards me, pull one free, and begin to write. I don't really know what I'm writing, but I write until the napkin is full and a drink is set in front of me. I nod in thanks and drink it in one go. Feeling the burn of the alcohol was enough to tell me I was still alive. That the warmth would be enough to sustain me. At least for a little bit. The silence was nearly deafening as I took out another napkin to write some more. I just sit there, not wanting to do anything other than sit alone. That is until a large body plops down beside me.

My gaze travels to the side and I see Spencer sitting

beside me, waving to the bartender. "Hey, Con, let me get a beer please."

It doesn't take long for a beer to appear in front of him and he sips it. Sitting silently beside me. As if he didn't have a care in the world.

I turn back to the napkins and cap the pen before folding them gently and stuffing them into my shorts pocket. "What are you doing here?" I ask, lifting my glass for another drink.

"I can ask you the same thing. Everyone is worried about you. You disappeared and aren't answering your phone. Imagine my surprise, when I came here for a consultation, to find you here. Drinking."

I roll my eyes. "That's a bit dramatic. I texted Ravi."

Spencer sips his drink, nodding slowly. "You did. Ten hours ago."

My eyes widened. "What? I texted him at like six. It's not even past one."

"Actually, it's almost five. Have you not noticed that the bar is filling up?" I feel my cheeks heat up as I look around the bar. Damn, it is filling up. I sat here all day? "No. I was lost in my thoughts I guess."

Spencer stares at me, studying me intently. "Do you need help, Nirvana?"

I reel back. "Help? What are you talking about?"

He shrugs. "Maybe see a therapist. Or counselor or something. Talk to somebody about your loss." The drink is placed beside me and I drink it down without a thought, suddenly angry at his audacity. I don't need help. I can handle this. I slam the glass down harder than intended but I don't care.

"I don't need, nor do I want, help. I'm fine."

He scoffs. "Could have fooled me. You were sitting in here drinking before noon."

I stand, pushing away from the bar. "I appreciate your

insight, Spencer, but I'd worry about your own issues before mine. I don't want help. I'm fine. I've been through worse and came out fine. I'll do so again." I don't spare him another glance as I leave some cash on the bar and turn on my heels leaving the bar. I don't need or want this. I've never wanted this.

It was too much, but not enough. It made me angry that he'd even suggest such a thing. "Help?" I scoff to myself. What would a therapist give me that I can't give myself? I knew better than they would about how I was feeling. Shaking my head, I head to my car and drive home. When I pull up to the house, I sigh. This was it. This was my life now. Getting drinks during the day and snapping at friends. I want to care, and a part of me does, but I'm so tired. Leaving the car I move towards the house. It felt like my legs were weighed down by heavy weights with each step. One more agonizing than the other.

But I made it. Stepping over the threshold, I head to the bedroom ignoring the broken dresser and bottle. Scooping up an old notebook and broken-in-half pencil, I sit on Aero's bed. I pull her pillow into my lap and begin writing. The words blur together making my heart hurt. Seven letters, seven apologies, and not enough time. There's never enough time. Sniffing slightly I push through, holding out hope for something better. That this hurt would fade away. But I knew, deep down I knew it wouldn't end. Not anytime soon.

Chapter 38

RAVI

Sighing, I toss my phone on my bed anger coursing through me. How the hell could she just up and leave? Then go radio silent, not answering anyone's phone call for hours? We would've called the police if Spencer hadn't found her alone in a bar. It was past eight now, and she still wasn't here. Not with me, not with her friends. Not at the cemetery. She was just gone.

I rub a hand on my chest and sigh. Fuck. Fuck. Where was she? Standing, I grab my keys and head to the door. "I'll be back, Gran!" I shout, hoping she was napping on the couch or something, and pull open the door, stopping short when I see Nirvana standing there with her fist raised ready to knock.

"Ravi," she breathes, her eyes wide with surprise.

"Where the fuck were you? Are you hurt?" I don't give her time to respond. I'm already pulling her inside, patting her down and checking for injuries.

"I'm fine. I just had stuff to do. To make sure everything was in order. My father is trying to contest Aero's will and I just wanted to get a headstart on it all." Her small hands cup my cheeks and she gives me a sad smile.

"We checked everywhere for you. Where were you?" I demand. My heart was still racing. All day we checked, I called and texted. I went to her house and her car wasn't there. She was there at some point but then she left, according to Mrs. Murphy and she wasn't there for long.

Nirvana shrugs, dropping her hands. "I just went for a drive. To clear my head a little bit."

Breathing deeply, I pull her against me. Holding her tightly in my arms. She burrowed against my chest holding onto me tightly.

"I'm sorry. I just needed time to myself, to take every-thing in, I think," she whispered. I press my lips to her hair, breathing in her ocean breeze scent. I hadn't realized how much this woman has gotten under my skin in such a short amount of time.

"Have you eaten?" I asked, my voice gruff. It was all I knew to do. I wasn't good with words, I wasn't good with romantic gestures. But I could make sure she was taken care of. That much I could do.

"I ate. I swear," she whispers. I nod, and take her hand in mine leading her to the bedroom.

"You should relax. Gran is down for the night and you look tired," I say, rubbing the back of my neck nervously.

"Want to take a bath with me?" she asks, taking her shoes off and setting them on the floor. I saw raw scrapes and cuts on the soles of her feet, she gave a soft laugh and said, "I walked home and didn't put on shoes. I cleaned them when I got to the house."

I want to lecture her, tell her it was incredibly dangerous of her to do that. What if she was attacked, or stepped on glass or a nail? But the words die on my tongue as she looks up at me with those sad blue eyes. So I give a stiff nod and head to my bathroom and towards the white clawfoot tub and turn on the water. I hear soft footsteps behind me and slender arms surround my middle.

"I really am sorry, Ravi," Nirvana says. "I should've brought my phone with me. I don't know why I didn't."

"We were all worried, Nirvana. We still are."

"I know," she whispers.

I turn around and cup the side of her face, watching her intently. "Let me help you."

She gives a sad smile. "I'm fine. Just sad. I'll be okay. I promise." She pulls away and tugs her shirt over her head. She folds it neatly and her pants and underwear follow, leaving her naked. "Can we turn on some music?" I nod and head to the stereo and turn on my music, letting it fill the bathroom. Turning, I strip my own clothes and help Nirvana into the tub before following her. We sit in silence. Me just watching her and her leaning her head back as if she doesn't have a care in the world.

But I knew better than that. She was tense and exhausted. She was also hiding something. "Are you just going to stare at me?" she asks. Stating the same words she said to me when we had sex for the first time.

"I might," I reply. I tug her foot causing her to look up at me. "Come here." She scooches forward until she's in front of me and I pull her into my lap. "How are you?"

She shrugs, bracing her hands on my shoulders. "As well as can be expected, I think. Numb. Tired. I'm so tired."

My hands move to her hips and I pull her closer, just holding her. We sit like that until the water turns cold. I unplug it and pull her out, wrapping a white fluffy towel around her.

"Let's dry off and watch a movie. We can just relax,

okay?" Nirvana nods and dries off heading to my bedroom and grabbing a shirt. I keep the music on low and turn on the TV. I know neither of us really cares about a movie, but just allowing her to ease her mind off of anything and everything would help calm all her thoughts.

At least I hope so.

Nirvana

Ravi is fast asleep and the TV is off leaving the room dark, the only sound in the room is the soft sound of music. I'm sitting up with my back against the headboard. The song changes and *"Never Let Me Go"* by Florence + the Machine begins to play. I sit silently for a moment, taking a deep breath and looking down at Ravi. My beautiful Ravi.

His arm was wrapped around my waist and his head was turned away. Swallowing thickly I whispered, "I like you a lot, Ravi. So much. More than I probably should." Tears burn the backs of my eyes. "I don't deserve you. You're one of the best men I know. I'm not good at feelings. It's difficult for me to even put into words what I feel. But maybe it's more than like. It's something I can't afford to have with you. I'm a messed up person. I have these wild feelings, bursts of panic, sometimes I feel like I'm slowly losing my mind. I do stupid shit and I don't know what else to do. I'm scared. I'm selfish, so selfish. But I can't keep doing this anymore. I'm so tired. Not physically, I'm not physically tired at all. Mentally? Mentally, I can hardly stand up. I'm dead on my feet."

I sniff and wipe a lone tear from my eye. Wind sent leaves hitting the window. "It'll be better off this way though. No one will have to worry anymore. I'll be free." That's all I ever wanted. The freedom to be myself, to love and be loved however I wanted. But if I stay it'll never happen. There was this constant pressure on my chest, so much pressure that it was slowly pushing me down until I knew I couldn't get back up.

"I hope you find someone who can love you the way you deserve. The way I wish I could've loved you." A sob chokes me. I cover my face and I feel Ravi's arm squeezing me.

"Are you okay?" Ravi asks, his voice deeper with sleep.

I nod. "I just can't sleep." He blinks up at me, green eyes focusing on me.

"What do you need?"

I lick my lips and lean down pressing a kiss to his lips. My hand cups his face gently and my tongue moves with his, a slow dance. He moves to his back letting me straddle him. Our lips don't part as he pushes the shirt up, grabbing my ass with both hands, holding me against him. I gasp, arching into his touch. I pull back slightly to grip the hem of the shirt and pull it over my head. Ravi sits up then, his arm is an iron band around my back as he pulls one pink nipple into his mouth. His mouth is hot against me making it feel as if I were burning from the inside. Burning for him. His touch.

"Ravi," I groan, arching my hips up, feeling his hard erection pressing into my belly. My hands go to his hair, holding him to me as his tongue flicks and tastes my skin. As his teeth bite down, marking me as his. And for now, I was his and he is mine. He'll always be mine.

Reaching between us Ravi circles my clit with his finger. Moaning, my hips jerk forward. His lips moved from my breast to my neck, biting down gently causing me to shudder in anticipation. "You're mine, Nirvana," he whispered.

I nod. "Yours. I'm yours." Then his mouth is back on mine. I lean up and position myself above him, rubbing myself against his cock. Back and forth, back and forth teasing him and myself before slowly sinking down. Sheathing myself on him. My breath hisses out as I glance down, watching as he stretches my body. Pressing my hand against his stomach I move experimentally. Just an arch of my hips.

We moan in unison at the contact. We weren't fucking this time. No, we were making love. Embracing each other. I wrap my arms around his neck and grind down on him. Taking him as far as he'll go. His hips arch up, thrusting in deeper. Forcing me down his dick as he pushed up.

I gasp his name, holding him tighter. Not wanting to let him go. Not yet. Our bodies moved together as if we've done this our entire lives. Taking and giving pleasure. Tears burned in my eyes and I pressed my head against his shoulder moving against him slowly.

His arms tightened around me almost as if he knew. I couldn't have that. I press my lips to his throat and whisper in his ear, "Fuck me. Please. Please, I need you." He groans against me and shifts us until my back is pressed against the mattress and he's above me, holding my gaze as he pounds into me.

My nails dig into his forearms as I meet him thrust for thrust. My body tightens around his and tears leak from the corner of my eyes. He notices and leans down, pressing his forehead against mine. "Whatever you're thinking, knock it off," he grunts.

I don't respond, just moan his name. Taking him deeper. It was raw and primal. Intense. He pulled my legs over his shoulders and fucked into me harder. My body tightened even more with each brutal thrust until I snapped, crying out his name. He pushed forward catching the sounds with his own mouth. This was it. The feeling I'd always remember. My Ravi.

Chapter 39

RAVI

I knew before I opened my eyes that she was gone. I could feel her absence. Blinking slowly I gazed around my room. Sunlight pierced through the gap in the curtain leaving the room bright. I sat up, groaning at my sore muscles. The sound of crinkling paper drew my attention. Gazing towards Nirvana's pillow I see a small piece of yellowed notebook paper. I unfold it and only see two words. *Thank you.*

I don't know why but that has my blood turning cold. Almost a gut feeling. I jump from the bed with the note still in my hand and dress quickly. I grab my phone and keys and leave the house. My heart is racing as I rush to my car and hop in. In a matter of minutes I'm speeding down the road towards Nirvana's house. When I get close I don't see her car and curse. Where the fuck is she?

I slam my palm into the steering wheel and head to Sorrow's house. Maybe she sought out Delaney. I keep that thought in my head as I head there. I grab my phone and put it to my ear dialing Nirvana's number.

"You've reached Nirvana. Please leave a message and I'll try to get back to you. Bye!"

When the line beeped I cursed to myself and started leaving a message, "Nirvana. Where are you? Please tell me where you are and we can figure it out. Baby." I can feel my throat tighten. "Let me help you. Let me take some of this burden for you." The line clicks indicating my message stopped recording. Cursing, I speed up hoping like hell she's there. But as soon as I pull up, I know she's not, I don't see her white Jeep. Cursing, I climb out and bang on the door uncaring that it's early as fuck in the morning.

"Sorrow! Open the fucking door!" I call, pounding on the door. The sound of dogs barking gets louder and the door is swung open showing a shirtless and angry Sorrow.

"What the fuck, Ravi?" he snaps.

I push him aside and step into the house. "Where is she? Has she been here?"

Sorrow sighs, rubbing a hand down his face. "What are you talking about?"

Ignoring him I call out, "Delaney!" My heart is racing and panic is coursing through me.

"Hey! Shut up, she's sleeping," he snaps, grabbing my shoulder. I push him away, slapping that yellowed paper against his chest.

"What's going on?" Delaney asks, wrapping a robe around herself.

I turned to her. "Nirvana. Have you seen her?"

She opens her mouth to speak, but stops when knocking sounds on the door.

"Fucking hell," Sorrow curses. The sound of paper crinkling is loud against the pounding of the door. I can feel the blood rushing to my ears and my heart is pounding.

Sorrow opens the door and Rory and Ophelia rush inside both looking frantic.

"Did you get a note?" Was the first thing out of Rory's mouth.

Delaney shakes her head going to the bowl by the door and flips through the mail. I can hardly breathe when she pulls out an envelope and opens it, showing the same yellowed paper that was left on my pillow.

"I can't find her," I say. But as I say it my phone vibrates and I see Mrs. Murphy's name flashing on the screen and dread fills me.

<hr />

Nirvana

A sense of peace washes over me as I park my Jeep behind the house far enough away that no one would see it. I walk up the steps to the backdoor and open it slowly, letting the creaking sound fill the silent void. The sun was just now rising, leaving the house in an overcast of shadows.

This would be my last time here. There would be no more memories of this house. Nothing would be left here. I step inside and close the door making my way to the dining room where I grabbed a chair and jammed it under the door handle, stopping it from opening and I repeated it with the front door. Effectively locking myself inside.

Stepping inside I head to my bedroom. I stand in the doorway and I sigh, seeing me and Aero as kids. Laughing softly to ourselves as we told secrets. I heard my own screams from the night I was dragged out from under my bed and taken to that van. Panic slowly invaded my senses but I pushed it down and sank down to the floor, feeling under the bed until my hand connected with the small bottle.

I lean back on my haunches and pull out the small pill bottle. Nodding to myself, I stand and head to the kitchen to get a glass of water. My movements are slow and precise as I make my way to the living room where I have the note, and a lighter.

A part of me was scared, terrified even. But the selfish part of me was free. I sit on the ground and open the bottle, dumping half the contents in my hand. All the small pills I'd collected over the last few months. Pills that were to help me sleep, to keep me awake, to calm whatever demons were housed in me. They were all here, varying in different colors and sizes.

Uppers and downers. I knew it would end. My story was coming to a close. One where I'd be reunited with my sister. With a shaky hand I brought my hand to my mouth allowing the pills to fall in. I lifted the glass and forced myself to swallow them down. My heart was pounding rapidly in my chest. I forced myself to calm down and lifted the letter. My final goodbye.

I want to start this off by saying how sorry I am. It's not fair to any of you. I'm aware of that. I am selfish, I'm taking this one last thing for myself. I don't know where I'll end up, but I'll be free. Finally free. But in turn it means I have to leave you all and for that I am sorry. I'm sorry I can't watch you grow, to watch you succeed. But I'll never regret the fact that I am free, free of pain, of hurt.

My tears are running down my face as I look at the letter. This was it. I can feel my body start to shake, my breathing became unsteady and the room was spinning. But I pushed on. I needed to. I grabbed the rest of the pills and took them all, swallowing them dry. I stood, pacing the living room, one hand gripping the letter, the other finding the lighter.

I love you all. I wish you nothing but the best. Aero left me a lot of money. I had it transferred into funds for you all. Delaney and Sorrow, whenever you decide to have children I put up an extra fund for college. Rory, this fund is to pay off your student debt. Layla, you'll have enough to open another shop. I'm so sorry my drama got in the way of your opening, but know I'm extremely proud of you for what you did. What you've accomplished. Sera, I made Darcy a college fund too. She's a brilliant little girl and she deserves the best education.

Ophelia, your trust is to get you the dream house you've always wanted. You deserve it. I also had a trust made for my brother. It's not his fault that our mother is unfit. But it won't be accessible until he's twenty-five. I put you all in charge of it. There is some set aside for taxes and stuff that needs to be taken care of, but that's all in this letter. My will, whatever. I may be gone but I still want to take care of all of you. This is my gift to you. I know you'll be angry, and hurt. I get it, but I just can't go on. I don't want to go on.

I'm glad you all have the guys with you. Someone strong to lean on. You're a family no matter it is one of random circumstances. But the moment Delaney chose Sorrow was the moment they all became family. I'm just sorry I can't see you all succeed and be great. No matter what happened in the past you pushed forward. I just wasn't strong enough. I'll never be strong enough.

To Ravi, I'm sorry. For everything. Thank you for teaching me to love. You deserve nothing less than the care you've shown me.

Goodbye,

Nirvana.

Crumpling the paper I dropped it into the old fireplace. Which was nothing more than brick at this point. I leaned down, groaning as a wave of dizziness hit me. I grabbed the wall, holding myself up as my thumb flicked the starter. It took two times before the flame started and I put it against the old paper, watching as the flame licked over it, spreading quickly. I drop the lighter and move towards the old carpet and sink down, lying on my back. The room is spinning and smoke starts to fill the small area, choking me. I don't breathe, I just stare up at the ceiling. Remembering the first time Ravi came over. Remembering Delaney following me home to make sure I'm okay. To Aero being brought home when she was born. A single tear slid down my cheek and a sad smile curved my lips. I knew I was selfish. I knew I should want to survive. That was the problem, though. I was tired of surviving. I didn't want to. I just wanted peace. This was the only way to get it. I wanted to wait the month, but the crushing weight of being alone was too much to handle. I was tired. I missed her, I missed the person I used to be.

This was my way to get her back. My only solace is the fact I was taking this fucking house down with me. I don't know how long I sat there until oblivion finally swallowed me. Leaving me in a darkness surrounded by smoke.

Chapter 40

RAVI

When Delaney read those words, *I want to start this off by saying how sorry I am.* I knew the rest of the letter was pointless. She'd made her decision, there was no talking her down I just had to figure out where she was and hope I got there in time. Then Mrs. Murphy called, her voice was frantic. I knew I had to find a way to save her. I knew it. I didn't wait for anyone, I just ran out of the house to my car. Taking off fast. I drove with my heart pounding rapidly in my chest and I did one thing I've never done, prayed that I wasn't too late. It felt like it took longer than it probably did for me to get to Nirvana's house. I barely parked when I pulled in, seeing Mrs. Murphy banging on the door. Screaming Nirvana's name over and over again.

"The house is on fire," the older woman exclaimed. I don't respond. I press against the door, jiggling the knob hoping to budge it open. "I called the fire department but I'm afraid it might be too late."

"Something's blocking the door." I could feel it when I pushed against it. Cursing I moved towards the window and kicked at the window, watching it crack little by little. Frustrated, I raised my fist and slammed it against the window pane. Desperation filled me when the ominous crack of wood sounded. I continued to punch it, ignoring the burning sharp pain as the glass shattered against my skin. When it was open, I kicked all the glass out of my way, and wedged my body through it. Grunting slightly when my shirt snagged on the glass and scraped my skin.

I pushed myself in and fell on the floor. I stood and raised my shirt to my nose. The smoke was thicker inside and panic set it. Seeing the flames brought me back to that last mission where the others were trapped, surrounded by dirt.

Forcing myself to push those thoughts away I move deeper into the house. The smoke burned my eyes and made my lungs feel as if they were restricted. I saw her right away. Nirvana. She lay in the middle of the living room as fire rose on the walls from the broken fireplace. She was oddly still and pale. Cursing, I ran forward. I knelt beside her and saw her mouth was tinged blue. I looked around and saw an empty pill bottle and a glass of water tipped over. No. No. I grabbed it and put it in my pocket hoping I could pinpoint what pills she took.

I grabbed her limp body and pulled her into my arms. The fire was getting precariously closer to us and I didn't like that. At all. I tore my shirt off and covered her head, hoping it'll help stop any more smoke inhalation. Blinking rapidly, I ran forward towards the door. Which she had blocked off by a chair. She made sure no one would be able to get to her. That pissed me off. I angrily shoved it roughly away and snatched the door open, running outside to the open air. Mrs. Murphy scurried off the porch with us, panicking. I ignored her, setting Nirvana gently on the grass. Her hair was covered in soot and she wasn't breathing. Coughing slightly, I tilted her head up, opening her mouth to see if something was blocking her airway. When I didn't see anything, I pressed my head to her chest. Hoping for a pulse, a flicker of something that would let me know I wasn't too late. With shaky fingers, I press my hand over her heart and lean down, trying to hear that soft beat. At first I didn't find it, and I was frantically running my hands over her body looking for a pulse.

I felt it then. The gentle flutter of her heart trying to work overtime to keep her alive. I want to rejoice that she has a pulse, but I can't. How long would she have one? Panic was coursing through me now. I pinched her nose and blew my breath in her mouth, a laboring sound because my own lungs were struggling. I blow into her mouth and pull back pressing on her chest starting chest compressions.

"Come on. Don't do this, baby, please don't fucking do this," I plead, leaning down to blow more air into her body. Then I do it all over again. Air, chest compressions, air, chest compressions, air, chest compressions. I don't know how long I do this for before Nirvana gasps and I see her body jolt violently as vomit comes up. I turn her to her side as she's sick and shaking. The sound of sirens are suddenly blaring around us. Nirvana's body shakes again as EMTs show up. I heard the pounding footsteps as they ran to us. Brooks was directing the unit to the house as the EMTs headed towards Nirvana and me.

"Overdose and smoke inhalation. I don't know how long. I gave CPR," I say, taking an oxygen mask handed to me breathing in as much air as I can. It's chaos around us. Fire-fighters are working quickly to contain the house fire and paramedics are working to stabilize Nirvana while another tries to work on me. I pushed him away needing to be near Nirvana. I've felt fear before, but nothing would ever top this feeling I have now. This anger, the hurt, the feeling of betrayal. It was too much. I could hardly breathe myself. My ears were ringing, bringing up shit better left alone.

"How far off are we?" Max asks into the radio. I glance at the small tracking device and sigh.

"It's a dead end. We should move back and reevaluate where we are going," I say.

Curses sound through the radio. "We won't have time to get them out if we do that," Sorrow snaps.

Clenching my teeth, I respond, "We won't be any good if we go in blind. It's a dead end."

Spencer curses beside me, pulling at his own radio, "Move out. This doesn't feel right. Move now!"

But it was too late. A series of gunshots and explosions surrounded us. Boxing us in. Sam fell beside me holding his side and cursing loudly. "Were you hit?" I demand.

"Grazed. I'm fine," he gritted out. Spencer kneeled beside us checking us over.

I shake my head, indicating I wasn't hit before grabbing my radio, calling in the others, "Sorrow, do you copy?" Nothing but static. I try again, "Drew? Caden? Max? Do you copy?" Panic was settling like a lead ball in my stomach.

"Son of a bitch. It was a goddamn trap," Sam muttered. I glance at the two men beside us and know we are fucked.

Blinking, I stare up at the bright lights above me. The sound of beeping is loud in my ears. "Where the fuck?" I groan, my throat sore and raw.

"You're in the hospital. Passed out cold when glass was

taken from your hand," a deep voice said beside me. I glance to the side and see Max and Sorrow sitting by the side of my bed.

"Nirvana?" I ask, my voice hoarse. Where was she? Did she make it? She had to have made it. She had to.

Sorrow stands, grabbing a small pink cup and pouring some water into it before answering. "She had to get her stomach pumped. Had a shit ton of uppers and downers in her system. Some sleeping pills. Had to have a breathing tube from smoke inhalation. Right now she's stable." He brings me the cup and lifts my head to help me drink. I do so greedily letting the cool liquid soothe my sore throat.

When I'm done I lie down, sighing softly. "Anything else?"

The two men looked at me then each other, then said, "Her heart stopped. A minute later and she'd be dead. She's resting now."

I close my eyes. "Fuck. Why the fuck would she do this?" Anger burned inside of me.

"She's grieving. With her past, and her mental health issues, she snapped," Max said.

I push myself up, wincing as the stitches in my hand pull taut. "What mental issues?" I ask, confused. I knew grief could bring on depression that wasn't uncommon, but the way Sorrow said it made me think there was more.

Sorrow sighs and says, "Bipolar disorder. Came out today. She was supposed to be taking medication every day, going to therapy. Her therapist has been notified and she said Nirvana hasn't been to a session in over four months."

I shake my head. "Why the fuck didn't she ask for help?" It wasn't really a question for them, more like to myself. I thought she was comfortable enough with me to discuss anything with me, but she left out something so fucking big.

Something that would lead her to wanting to take her own life.

"Ravi, I know you're upset and scared but she needs a strong support system right now," Sorrow starts.

I laugh darkly. "I tried helping her. We've all fucking tried. But she goes and does—" I'm stammering now, anger making it difficult for me to form coherent sentences. "She goes and does this dumb shit." I shake my head, wiping a hand over my face. I knew it wasn't technically her fault, she had a lot of trauma lately, I knew that. But she almost died. She was angry at Aero for being sick, angry at her for dying, but she'd willingly die? She'd kill herself knowingly leaving people who cared for her behind?

"Delaney said it's a symptom of bipolar and manic disorder. We should've noticed. The way she was acting in the hospital, day drinking, partying. They'll have ups and downs and then do reckless shit. They'll have suicidal thoughts and attempts. Delaney doesn't think she was on the right medication. Or had the right doctors," Sorrow explained gently. I shake my head again, my eyes burning, the tears I've been fighting off threatening to spill.

I clear my throat. "What's next?"

Max sighs and says, "Once she's clear to go they plan to put her into a 72-hour hold. Then it's up to her next of kin to decide what happens from there."

Dread fills me again. "Who's her next of kin?" I already know, I can see it on their faces, but I need the answer.

"Her father. He'll be the one to decide what happens from here," Sorrow says, his jaw ticking slightly.

Fuck. Fuck. I push a hand through my hair forcing myself to take a deep breath. Wondering if there was something I could've done to prevent this. But I already knew, last night, that Nirvana was telling me goodbye. Now I wasn't sure what to do. How to act. Because I had nearly lost the woman I have fallen in love with and I wasn't sure how to go from here.

Chapter 41

Nirvana

Binds were tightened against my wrists, holding me strapped to the bed. Constricting every time I struggled. And boy, did I struggle. I pulled, I fought. I did it all. But now I was just stuck. Staring at the white peeling wall, listening to the consistent beeping. My lungs burned with each breath I took, my head throbbed and my throat was dry. I wasn't supposed to be here. Why was I here?

"I knew you were stupid, but I didn't think you'd go to such extremes," a deep voice said from the doorway. I didn't respond. Just stared into nothingness.

"What, you won't even look at me? What you did, Nirvana was selfish and reckless. Your sister just died. Did you even think of the people who would be affected by such a stupid action?" I glanced at the door where my father stood, glowering at me. His arms crossed over his chest.

"Like you or Doreen actually give a shit about what happens to me," I mumble. And we both knew they didn't care. Hell, if it was up to them I would be six feet under by now. "Why are you here? Don't you have a sermon or some shit?"

He scoffs, walking deeper into the room. "You're being transported to St. Rowe Hospital. A mental institute to take care of whatever is going on in your head."

I stare blankly at him. I figured once I was conscious enough I'd be sent somewhere. But to a secluded hospital near San Antonio wasn't it. I feel panic rise in me, but I carefully keep my face blank.

"They will keep you where you need to be. Make sure you're taking your medications because clearly you're not capable of taking care of yourself. Which includes the inheritance."

I laugh softly, the sound grating due to how sore my throat was. "The inheritance is no longer in my name. It's gone. Signed over. Do you truly think I'd kill myself and allow you anything? I may be stupid by your standards, Father, but I do know some things about life. For one, you're a greedy prick who deserves to rot on the streets. You don't deserve an ounce of goodness. I've planned ahead. You're fucked if you think you're getting anything from me or Aero."

He walks up to me, that signature red finding its way onto his wrinkled face. I stared up at him arching an eyebrow. "You've always been ungrateful. Never listened to your parents. I'll make sure they bury you under that hospital, Nirvana. Even if it's the last thing I do."

"Have you always been an evil man, or did you become this way because you think being a preacher at a church gives you some sort of power?" I arch up, staring directly into his eyes. "Newsflash, no one gives a fuck. You hold no power. You're an egotistical prick."

"Yet, I hold your life in my hands," he whispered,

pressing a kiss to my head. I yanked away from him, cursing at the binds on my wrists. "She's ready," he calls. My eyes find the doctors and I see Father Brent in the back. It's almost like I'm back there that night. My breathing is elevated and panic is overtaking me as I begin pulling at the binds. Hell no. Hell no.

"No. No!" I scream. Kicking my legs out to get away from the group of men in front of me.

"I'll see you in a month's time, Nirvana. Hopefully by then you're in a better state."

I scream, fighting it. "I hate you! I fucking hate you!" I shout. Pain was radiating from my head as I was wheeled away. I wanted to be free. This wasn't what I meant. Tears fall down my cheeks and I'm hyperventilating. I'll never understand why he had such an intense hatred for me, why he'd leave me to such a fate.

"Nirvana, please calm down," Father Brent said, trying to be soothing but only making it worse.

"Get away from me, you creep!" Was I making a scene? Yes, yes I was. And it wasn't my proudest moment. I was pissed, I was hurting, and I wasn't supposed to fucking be here. I was supposed to be with Aero. I squeezed my eyes shut. I didn't want this. I don't want help. I don't want anything aside from being where I was supposed to be. It's my own fault. I knew better, but I still did it. The fight slowly seeps from me, leaving me exhausted and crying.

"Where are you taking her?" I hear. I open my eyes and see Delaney standing to the side anxiously wringing her hands with Sorrow beside her glaring at the passing doctors. "We were told she'd be here for 72 hours for observation. Are they allowed to take her?" she asks, she's talking to Drew who looks angry.

"Private insurance and going against medical advice is allowed if her beneficiary makes the call. She's being brought to another medical facility. I'm not sure which one yet. But as it's being done by her insurance and her father there's not much we can do. Especially not with her condition. They are saying her mind snapped. Psychosis or something." His words are bleak and he's looking at me with anger, sympathy and guilt?

Delaney gasped, in outrage. "She's not dealing with psychosis. She's bipolar. She needs the proper medication and therapy in order to help her. They can't know what she has without a thorough screening and medication trials..." Her words drift away the farther down the hall we get. So she knows now, no wonder Drew had guilt in his eyes. But that can't be right because he wouldn't feel bad about telling. My head is too fuzzy to think about it all. My eyes lock on Delaney. "I'll get you out. I promise," she calls.

I want to believe her, but I wasn't sure who to believe anymore. I couldn't trust myself, so how could I trust others? I arch my back fighting the bindings, screaming loudly.

"Let me go! I want to go!" The fabric of the bindings digs into my wrists, rubbing the sensitive skin raw. I'm kicking out my legs, but it's all futile when my body is weak and my voice damaged. It doesn't stop me from trying though. One of the medical staff from St. Rowe moves closer and I kick out and connect with his balls, sending him to the ground, cursing. Father Brent moves closer holding a syringe, shaking his head in that disappointed parent type of way.

"You should've been calmer, Nirvana."

I growl low in my throat, arching away as best as I can but I feel that telltale pinch on my neck. "You should've been put on a list," I mutter. My eyes are becoming heavy. Breathing became a struggle for a second as my vision became unfocused, blurring the people around me.

My eyes connected with earth green eyes for a second

and the last word on my lips before sinking into darkness was, "Ravi." Then nothingness.

Groaning, I turned over in bed. Well, I tried to. My movement was limited and I was stuck solidly in the middle of the bed. Blinking open my eyes I stare down at myself, seeing my hands bound to the sides of the bed.

I glance around the room and see nothing but slate gray peeling walls and a metal chair sitting in front of a chipped wooden desk. Nothing else. There are no windows, there's no toilet or bathroom. Just four barren walls, a desk, and cot that I was now currently held down to. There was a sense of peace settling over me though.

I didn't have to deal with the passing of Aero, I didn't have to feel like my own mind was fighting against me. It was just me and four walls. But the moment I closed my eyes I was right back there. Taking those pills that would inevitably end my life. The fire that would turn me to ash along with the house that was the source of torment for years. There was Ravi who held me and whispered sweet nothings to me. Who worshiped my body sending me into a sea of pleasure. There was Aero who died, no longer in my life. I was alone. Forever alone.

A hysterical laugh bubbled up inside of me. Tumbling from my mouth on its own. If this wasn't karma I didn't know what was. I laugh so hard until I'm crying, and those tears turn to screaming. I wanted to go home. But I didn't have a home. Not anymore. The screaming wasn't helping, in fact I'm pretty sure my vocal cords are severed at this point. Sagging to the bed I choke back another sob. How did I end up here? I'm not sure how long I've lain there until the door of the room finally opens.

And when it does I see a small brunette standing in the doorway, watching me.

"Hi, I'm Nell. I'm one of the orderlies at St. Rowe. I'm here to give you your medication and make sure you eat something. Help you to the bathroom if you need it."

Nell comes deeper into the room pulling a small cart with her. I watch her warily as she pulls it to the side of the bed. Nodding in satisfaction, she picks up a small dixie cup and shows me the contents.

"This is your new antipsychotic medication and anxiety pills. It's going to calm you down a little bit. This is Tylenol that will get rid of the headache and inflammation. And a beta blocker to slow your heart rate into a normal range."

I shake my head. "No thanks."

Nell gives me a small smile. "I'm sorry, Ms. Bridges but you don't really have a choice. I know it's difficult right now, but it will get better. I promise." I snort, turning my head away from her. It would never get better. Places like these never got better. Being on medication for the rest of your life didn't exactly strike me as "better." I didn't want that dependence. I wanted to be normal.

"I want to go home," I mutter.

Nell pats my hand gently. Her touch is almost motherly. "I know you do. Give it some time and you'll be right back where you belong." She lifts me up from under my shoulders making it easier for me to take the medicine. I glare at her, but she just smiles. She is a little older than I would've guessed, probably in her late forties. She had kind brown eyes with laugh lines. Tilting my head back, she drops the pills into my waiting mouth before holding a straw to my lips. I take it greedily, my mouth obnoxiously dry.

I drink for a few minutes before she pulls away letting me settle back into the cot.

"How long will I be here?"

Nell shrugs. "You did hit an orderly. So it could be close to a week."

"How long have I been here already?" I ask.

Nell moves back to rearrange her cart. "Three days. You were in the hospital for a week before you were transferred to St. Rowe. We've had a doctor come and check your vitals and all is well. But your medication has to be strictly monitored now."

I hum under my breath staring at the wall. "Whenever you are allowed to socialize you will be getting a sleeping buddy."

Turning my head slowly I stare at her and ask, "A sleeping buddy?"

Nell nods, sending brown hair bouncing over her shoulders. "Yes, ma'am. At St. Rowe we like to integrate our patients into society and to be better people by adding sleeping buddies. That goes for group meetings too."

"I am already integrated into society. I don't need that," I mutter, closing my eyes.

Nell turns silent, I could feel her gazing at me. I peek at her from one eye, waiting for her to say something. She finally sighs and sits at the edge of the bed. "You almost killed yourself, Ms. Bridges. You're going to need supervision at all times. Even when you go to the bathroom. You are not to be trusted alone. We can't have a repeat of you trying to commit suicide. Especially with other patients around."

"I wouldn't harm anyone," I say sullenly.

"Ms. Bridges, someone was hurt in your attempt," Nell said.

Whipping my head sharply to her, I gape. There was no way. I had my car out of the way. The house was as secluded as can be apart from Mrs. Murphy's house but she wouldn't have been there until the fire was well on its way to toppling that godforsaken hut to the ground.

Shaking my head adamantly, I say, "That's not possible. No one would've known until it was too late."

Nell looks at me with sympathy. "Ma'am, your boyfriend pulled you out of the fire. From my understanding his hand was pretty busted up."

I shake my head in denial. "No, that's not possible. I saw him. I saw him when they were taking me here. He was there." Was he there? Did I really see him or was I seeing him through a drug induced haze? Was it real?

"Yes, he was injured. Smoke inhalation and glass in his hand. He pulled you out of the fire. The nurses can hardly stop talking about it." Nell fans her face, but I can hardly focus on that. What if Ravi was hurt or worse? What if he would've died with me?

I twisted my wrists trying to free my hands, but it didn't work. "Can you untie me, please?" I ask on a sob.

Nell winces. "I'm sorry. I have strict rules that I can only allow you to go to the restroom and then put you back in the bed with your hands bound. For your safety." Frustration beats down on me like a battering ram. But I nod in defeat. Nell helps me stand, holding on to me after my legs nearly buckle under me from lack of use. She brings me to the bathroom right next to the room and helps me inside, watching me intently.

"I can't even piss in private?" I snap. Nell grimaces and gives a quick shake of her head.

Embarrassment washes over me as I do my business not making eye contact with the other woman. I've been to an institute before, after the camp but it wasn't like this. It was different. Maybe because I didn't attempt to off myself, but the way I was being watched over like a prisoner made it ten times worse. I pressed my hands to my eyes and sobbed. Why couldn't I have succeeded?

Chapter 42

RAVI

It's been nearly two weeks since I've seen Nirvana, heard her laugh, or talked to her. No one knows where she was taken or when she'd be out. "Can't we just ask her father?" Caden asks for what feels like the tenth time.

Spencer sighs, leaning back in his chair. We were currently at S Security searching through Nirvana's closed off records to find out where she was taken with no luck.

"Yes, Cade, because that self-righteous prick is going to tell us where he sent his daughter who he hates with a passion. I'm sure he'd get right on that," Max said sarcastically.

I stood, moving away from them as they bickered back and forth. A part of me was still angry at her. At the fact she'd do this, that she's been gone and I can't see her, see for myself that she is alive and well. The last time I saw her was in the hospital when she was screaming and fighting with the people wheeling her away before she was sedated. Her eyes met mine briefly before she went unconscious. Then her father was there looking smug as fuck without a care in the world before he turned and left. Now she was just... gone. I can't even work with my hand being busted and they still worry about my lungs due to smoke inhalation. So every moment of every day I'm in a perpetual state of worry morphing into anger.

I hate it. I hate that Nirvana was hurting so bad that she thought the only way out was through death. I hate that none of us realized it.

"Perhaps it's best she's there," Drew spoke up.

I scowl at him. "And how the fuck is that best?"

He shrugs. "She needs help, Ravi. Serious help. Help that none of us are equipped to handle," he holds his hand up stopping me from speaking, "and before you say Delaney, Vana hasn't been in her office in well over a year. She's not equipped to prescribe her medication she needs, nor can she give her extensive therapy without bias being involved."

My jaw tics and I have to force myself to breathe before I do or say something I'm bound to regret. Logically, I know he's right. I know it. But the fact that she could be anywhere alone and afraid bothers me. "We still don't know where she is. What if something happens?"

"There's nothing to be done by us. She's getting help. That should make everyone feel better."

I step forward. "Do you know where she is?"

Drew stares up at me, his eyes cold and harsh. "If I did, I'd tell you. I'm just being realistic."

I shake my head, this was getting me nowhere. Not wanting to get into a fight with him, I grab my phone from Spencer's desk and leave the office. I just needed to know she was safe.

Nirvana

Nell leads me down a hall of the institute and rambles on, "Your new room has a shared bathroom with the other four rooms down this hall. There are orderly shift changes from morning to night so you won't always see me."

I hum under my breath rubbing at my raw wrists. These people left me tied to that cot for an entire week. Only letting me up to use the bathroom and eat. With one shower. After that week I was deemed 'sane' enough to move to a normal room. Which I guess meant I was one step closer to getting out of here. So that was a plus. Or so I told myself. Nell stops at the last door and knocks. A raspy voice calls out, "Come in."

Pushing the door open Nell smiles and says, "You've got a roomie now." The woman in the room turns her head and looks over at me. She is a stunning woman with tan skin and dark straight hair, reaching down her back in a thick braid. She had almond shaped dark brown eyes.

She stares me up and down and nods. "Hey."

I nod back without saying anything as Nell puts a single bag on the bed. "Group therapy starts at one on the dot. Don't be late." With that she turns and leaves the room. I stand by the door unsure what to do. The woman stares at me and tilts her head to the side. Almost feline like, studying me intently. She has this air about her, cold and calculating. As if she's not meant to actually be here. Which strikes me as odd because every person we passed on the way through had this distant and defeated look in their eyes whereas she was completely aware and determined.

"I'm Misery."

I nod and move to my bed, sinking down on the thin mattress. "Nirvana."

Misery snorts. "Your parents must've hated you," she said.

"As opposed to Misery?"

She smiles then. "My parents are dead I'm afraid."

"Lucky bitch," I say without meaning to. I gasp and cover my mouth. "Oh my god. I'm so sorry."

Misery looks at me for a full minute before she starts laughing. "I like you, Nirvy. Can I call you, Nirvy? Oh well, I'm going to do it anyway."

My brows furrow, well I guess there was a reason she's in here after all. "So what are you in for, Nirvy?"

"Suicide attempt and fail."

Misery winces. "Damn. Brutal."

"What about you?" I ask.

Misery looks at me and smiles. "Murder. So if you need someone to take you out just ask and I can."

Dumbfounded, I stare at her, my jaw dropping. Then she bursts out laughing, "Oh you should see your face! I haven't murdered anyone. Yet."

Laughing awkwardly I scooch away a little bit.

"So why'd you do it?" she asks, changing the subject and not directly answering my question.

Clearing my throat I mutter, "Overwhelmed, I guess."

Misery stands and moves towards my bed, crouching in front of me she meets my eyes. "I don't like liars, Nirvy. And if we're going to room together you'll have to learn that quickly."

I swallow hard. "My sister died. She was my only family." A look passes over her features, almost agony before she stands and turns away.

"I'm sorry for your loss."

I nod. "It's okay."

Misery clears her throat and heads to the door. "We can't be late for group. They'll send someone to get us." Standing, I follow after her. The walk to group seemed shorter than I would've liked. Granted, it was in the common area. Just a circle of chairs surrounding another chair set right in the middle of the ring.

I sit in the nearest chair and Misery sits directly beside me. "Who runs it?" I ask.

"Stassia, she's kind. If you're into the overly bubbly and bright type of person." I hum under my breath and watch as people start to fill the chairs. I sit stiffly wanting to be anywhere else than here. We don't wait long before another woman comes into the room. And like Misery said, she was bright. Overly bright. She wore bright orange and green. I grimace, my eyes burning at the color after seeing nothing but gray for a week straight.

"Hello everyone!" she says, her voice high pitched. She had on cat rimmed glasses with pink dots on them and her hair was a bright red. She kind of reminded me of Flo. My heart pitched in my chest thinking of the elderly woman. Was she okay? Was Ravi okay? I shake those thoughts out of my head. I didn't need to think of him. Not right now.

Stassi sat in the chair with a flourish and smiled. "Oh, we have a new bird in the nest," she said when she saw me. She set a tote bag on the ground beside her chair and leaned forward. "Welcome. It's good to meet you. I'm Stassi, I'm the counselor at St. Rowe."

I give an awkward smile, you know the one when you make unwanted eye contact with someone? Yeah, that's where I'm at. I'm unsure of what to do, or say. But for some reason Misery speaks for me.

"Nirvana just got here," she says.

Stassi nods in understanding, giving me a smile. "That's

okay, Nirvana. No pressure. If you want to speak you're free to do so when you want. All I ask is that you wait for the talking stick. Having everyone talk all at once can be a little much," she laughs and pulls out a bedazzled stick from her bag. "So who'd like to start?"

Chapter 43

RAVI

Flames. There were flames everywhere. Crawling up the walls surrounding me on every side. I couldn't breathe. The black smoke was thick and impenetrable. Pulling my shirt above my nose I move slowly forward. As if something were pulling me through it. Thick swirls of smoke choked me, sucking the air from my body. I couldn't breathe. My steps faltered and tears burned in my eyes, streaming down my face.

I couldn't see, I couldn't breathe. I was stuck. Panic sank in. Turning around I saw it. A small light. Hope unfurled in my chest as I sprang forward. I reached for the light and it pulled me in. Dropping me onto a patch of grass. I sucked in as much clean air as I could, coughing roughly when I couldn't. Turning onto my stomach I propped myself up with one hand, coughing and hacking. The crackling of flames drew my attention. Turning my head I see that little house, burning from the inside out.

In the distance sirens sounded but all of it fell on deaf ears when I saw the lone figure at the opposite side of the yard.

"Nirvana," I breathe. I clamor to my feet, shaking slightly. "Nir-

vana!" I call my voice louder now. I stumble forward, struggling to stay on my feet. But I do it. "Nirvana!" I had to get to her. But the more I walked, the farther she'd become. It didn't matter how much I ran, it didn't matter if I screamed until my voice was hoarse. She wasn't there. Nirvana was gone. I fell to the ground and screamed. Those sirens became louder and louder and a soft touch to my shoulder had me jerking.

———

I jerked awake, breathing heavily. "Hey, you're okay," a voice said beside me. I glanced around me until my eyes landed on Caden.

"Why are you in my house?" I ask, my voice hoarse. I clear my throat and take a deep breath. The smell of smoke is still stuck in my nose and the scent makes me nauseous.

"Flo called me. When I got here I heard you screaming from outside."

Rubbing a tired hand down my face I fall back on my mattress.

"You must really love her to be reacting like this," Caden murmurs.

I scoff. "I don't know what love is, Caden. We weren't even in a relationship. We hooked up a few times, I helped her with her sister's death but that's it. And clearly I didn't do a good job." My words are bitter even to my own ears. It was a lie. I know I love Nirvana. But I knew it wasn't what she needed. Not now.

"Stop being a dick. We both know you love her. And no one could've predicted this, Ravi," Caden says.

"We should've noticed," I snapped.

"Maybe. But she was grieving. How the fuck were we supposed to know she was dealing with bipolar on top of all of that? Her friends didn't even know, Ravi. She kept it under wraps for fucking years. This was just her breaking point. Her sister fucking died. She had to watch her die. That's not easy to do. It wouldn't have mattered if you were there or not, it would've ended the same way."

I shake my head. "You don't know that."

He nods in agreement. "You're right. If you weren't there she'd be dead. You saved her life."

Yeah, and she probably hates me for it, I think to myself. I glance at my wrapped hand and wince. "You didn't need to come here, Cade. I'm fine."

"Well, that's bullshit. But think whatever you want. Go shower. We have places to be, people to see, and all that." He pats my knee and stands. Nodding, in a job well done. But I'm thoroughly confused and don't move. Sighing, he puts his hands on his hips. "Well? Get the fuck up. We're going to go find your girl to ease your poor little mind. We can't do that with you lying in bed." Shaking my head I get up and head to my bathroom to shower.

An hour later, Caden and I are sitting beside Sorrow and Delaney with Nirvana's brother sitting nervously across from us at the local diner called Andy's.

No one speaks for a long while. We just stare at the boy, until I can't any longer. "Well?" I demand.

"Right. Right. I just want to apologize for the funeral first," he starts, but I wave him away.

"You can't pick your family. We hardly care about that now. Where is she?" I ask, losing patience.

"I overheard my mother talking. Bridges sent her to St. Rowe. It's on the outskirts of San Antonio," he said.

"Is she okay, Ae..." Delaney pauses. "I'm sorry, I don't know what to call you."

"August is fine. It's my middle name. I don't go by Aero, I've never actually been called that by anyone until the funeral." His jaw clenches and he looks away. "As for Nirvana, from my understanding they had her in isolation for a week."

Interjecting, I lean forward, "I thought it was 72 hours."

"It usually is. Unless the patient is a danger to themselves or others around them," Delaney explains gently.

"Do you know this place?" Sorrow asks.

Shaking her head she replies, "No. I'm not really familiar with institutions. I worked in a clinic but never a place like that. I can make some calls and see."

August shakes his head. "She's not allowed visitors. Not unless you're on the list. And probably not until after a few weeks. It can disturb any progress she has made or something along those lines."

"And how do you know this?" I ask with suspicion.

He smiles, his dark eyes brightening with mischief. "I have an in."

Chapter 44

Nirvana

I sit silently as another group member talks about their day. I hardly listen though. This is my fifth meeting and I swear it gets longer and longer each time. Sometimes people don't talk at all, it's just a silent group sit down and it makes me want to rip my hair out. "Nirvana?"

I glance up quickly when my name is called. "Hmm?"

Stassi stares at me with a kind smile. "Would you like to share?"

"Share what?" I ask.

Stassi shrugs and says, "Anything you want. Tell us how you're feeling. Anything is fine." She nods encouragingly as the bedazzled stick is passed to me. I grab it and look at it, twisting it in my hands. Wondering how long it took her to glue these plastic gems to the wood.

"I'm fine," I finally say.

"Are you sleeping okay?" I nod, but it's a lie. I hardly sleep. I wake up from nightmares every night. And when I do, I look over expecting to see my temporary roommate, but she is never in the bed. I don't know where she goes, nor do I ask. It's not my business and I'm simply floating by until I can get out of here.

"And your medication? How are you doing on it?"

Shrugging I say, "Fine. I don't feel any different. Maybe slower. Or well, tired, but not physically." Before Stassi can ask more questions I'm already passing the stick to someone else. I don't want to sit and talk about my feelings with anyone I don't know. It makes me uncomfortable. Sighing in disappointment, she nods and turns to the other patient. Talking to him about his anger and the fact he wants to run away. I tuned them out after that stuck in my own head. Time drags on until finally we are dismissed to our own activities. Standing, I quickly make my way back to my room.

"You know, you could make more of an effort. It might do you some good," Misery says following me into the room.

"Why does it matter? It's not like anyone actually cares what I have to say or what I feel. I'm here to do my treatment and go. Nothing more nothing less."

She scoffs, "Treatment hardly works if you're unwilling to try."

I turned on her then, and said, "Why do you care? You don't participate. Hell, you leave the room in the middle of the night. Why are you here, Misery?"

She looks taken aback by my questions, but she doesn't back down. "I'm here for an orderly."

Laughing, I shake my head, "You're here to fuck an orderly?"

"No. I'm here to kill an orderly," she corrects me. I look at her, expecting her to laugh but she stands still, staring down at me with hard serious eyes.

"You're serious?" I gasp.

"As a heart attack. He's taking advantage of drugged patients. Did you know orderlies sometimes abuse the patients they take care of because of the lack of power the patients have?"

"What?" I say with a stunned squeak.

Misery nods. "Yes. I'm not a real patient here. I'm here to kill that bastard and then I'm gone," she says and steps towards me. "And if you mention this I won't have a problem killing you either."

Tilting my head back, I glare at her. "Do you think I care if you're taking out an abuser? I don't give a shit. What you do is your business. That doesn't give you the right to pry into my life."

"Listen, I'm sorry about your sister. I am, but you're here because you tried to kill yourself because you couldn't stand the thought of being alone."

Gritting my teeth, I pushed her away from me, and she let me. I wasn't dumb enough that I thought I could take her. The woman had five inches on me and was a lot stronger than me. "You don't know me."

"Well, I highly doubt anyone truly knows you since you were so ready to off yourself. What, you didn't have a part-ner? Friends? A job? Or are you just that selfish that you didn't think about anyone else? I bet you left a pretty little note too," she taunts.

My face heats up. "Fuck you."

"Mental illness is treatable. Did you even try to get help? Or was your sister's death the perfect excuse to pull the trig-ger? Oh wait, you didn't pull the trigger. If you did you wouldn't be here. Almost like you hoped you'd live. Why? Why'd you do it?" she pushed.

"Go to hell!" I yell.

Laughing hysterically she says, "I'm already there."

Turning away, I run my fingers through my hair. "I hate

it. I hate it. She left me. Alone. They always leave. Always! Why would I want to stay?" I don't know who I'm talking to at this point, her or myself.

"You were saved. By that man, Ravi." My eyes widen at her words and she smiles. "Don't look at me like that. I know things. I ask around. He jumped through a fire for you. Saved you. He clearly has feelings for you. Yet you didn't care about what this would do to him. Why'd you do it?"

Screaming in frustration, I explode, "I can't! I can't do it! I never wanted this! I never wanted him! I've lost one person I care about and I can't do it again! He'll leave, once he knows me. He'll leave because no one wants to be with a broken fuck up! And if he leaves I won't know what to do! I won't survive him. So, I decided to leave. I decided not to hurt anymore!"

Misery sighs softly. "That's not something you get to decide, Nirvy. Your actions don't just affect you." I sink to the ground and wrap my arms around my knees, rocking back and forth slowly. I told Aero something similar. When she decided to go without the treatments. When she told me to mourn for a month then move on with my life. I did exactly what she did. Only I knew I had a choice.

Misery crouches down in front of me. "It seems bad now, but this could be good for you. You don't have to be alone. You have a man who cares, I'm sure you have friends who care. You have to learn to fight. I was where you are. I wanted to end it, too."

I glance up at her through teary eyes. "Why?"

She smiles sadly and I think it's the first real emotion I've seen on her face. "My little brother, he was assaulted and killed. Murderer got away. I was alone, so alone, then I met my sisters."

"What kept you going?" I ask, my heart hurting for her. That I assumed that she'd never understand my loss, but hers was worse. I had my time with Aero. She lost her brother suddenly in a brutal way.

"What kept me going was hate, the need for revenge. You have to find what it is you need in order to keep going. You can't let this get you. Whatever holds you back, let it go. Get stronger, get even, do what you need to, and get the fuck out of here," she advises, her hands going to my shoulders and shaking me.

"Why are you so adamant?" I ask.

"You remind me of my sister, Anarchy. Broken and hopeless. You have hope though. People like us, Anarchy and myself, we are better left alone. Gone. But you? No, you have something worthwhile. I'm making my move in two weeks time, Nirvana. Then I'm gone. You better be gone, too." She stands in a fluid motion, leaving the room. I sit in a sort of stunned silence. I used to be normal, I used to have my life together. Now I was stuck in a mental institute with a roommate who openly admitted to being here for the sole purpose of murdering an orderly. If I was sane I'd report her. But if I was sane I wouldn't be in this situation to begin with.

Chapter 45

RAVI

"So what are you going to do?" Max asks, peering at me from the passenger's seat.

I gaze up at the large building in front of us. It was a hospital rebuilt within the ruins of an old church. Which was fitting knowing Nirvana's father. The bastard probably spent hours trying to find it. I scoff to myself. As if that piece of shit did any research for the best place to send Nirvana. "Ravi," Sorrow snapped from the driver's seat, drawing my attention.

"What?"

"Plan. What is it?" the bastard says.

"I'm going to go in there on the pretense of being a janitor. They are doing interviews for the job. Sam made me a resume." I opened the folder, and was holding up the sheet of paper Sam handed to me before we left. After our talk with Nirvana's brother, August yesterday we made a plan. We put in an application and somehow Spencer was able to fast-track my application to the top of the list, and I was called in for an interview.

"How are you going to explain your hand?" Sorrow asks.

I glance down at the bandaged hand in question. "I had surgery from a previous work injury that comes off tomorrow." Not technically a lie, my cast comes off tomorrow. It's going to be replaced, but they don't need to know that.

"And when you don't show up for work?"

I grunt in frustration. "I'll say another offer came up. Can I go now or do you want to braid each other's hair before I go in?"

"Don't be a dick. Get in there, get your answers, and let's leave. This place gives me the creeps," Max says.

Pulling on a hat, I climbed out of the car. This could be a dumb plan, but I needed to know she was okay. If no one could visit or call then I needed another way. Squaring my shoulders, I move forward, climbing the cobble steps to the institution. There is an eerie feeling to the place. Cold. Shaking off that feeling I opened the door, wincing when it creaked.

"Oh, hello!" a cheerful voice said. The voice was out of place with the dark gloomy atmosphere of the building. In fact, it didn't belong at all. I glanced up as an older woman in a nurse uniform came towards me. "I'm Nell, are you a visitor? We don't have visitation until Saturday I'm afraid."

Clearing my throat I shake my head, "No ma'am. I actually have an interview for the janitor's position. My interview is supposed to be in thirty minutes but I don't like being late." I force a laugh and she smiles.

"Oh! Right! You're Mr…"

I hold out my uninjured hand, "Carter. Xavier Carter." I introduce myself with the identity we came up with last night. Nell smiles kindly and shakes my hand before ushering me to a waiting area.

"I'll go let Silas know his next interview is here. Please have a seat."

I nod and go to sit down, but stop before I touch the seat. "I'm so sorry. But can you tell me where the restroom is?"

"Of course, it's down the hall, last door on the left," Nell says. I nod and smile politely and make my way down the hall. I see her walk away from the corner of my eye and I wait until I hear her footsteps disappear before turning back to the main area. I tap my fingers on my leg five times and I feel my phone buzz. The cameras are off. Now, I can go find her.

I move down the empty hallway peering in closed doors until I come to a common area where there are multiple people sitting or talking. Some are painting, some are reading. My eyes move around the room, searching for the small blonde who's haunted me for months. When I don't see her, I move on. I don't know how long I've looked before frustration begins to set in. I know I'm running out of time when I finally see her. Walking alone towards the common area.

I fall into step behind her and grab her.

"What the—" her sentence is cut off when I cover her mouth with my palm. She fights me, kicking out her legs but I don't react. I just pull her into the closest empty room and shove her inside. She yanks herself out of my arms, turns on me, and punches me in the stomach. I grunt at the force, but don't react as I close and lock the door.

She tries to hit me again, but I expect the move and grab her, pushing her stomach against the door and holding her fist in my hand. "You got your one shot, tinker hell, but you won't get another."

Her struggles stop and she sags against the door. "Ravi."

"Are you calm?" I ask, breathing in her ocean breeze scent. She draws in a shuddering breath, but nods. Slowly, so slowly, I let her go and take a step back, putting distance between us.

She turns, staring at me with wide eyes. "You're here."

"I am. So are you."

She gazes at me, her eyes roaming over my body before stopping on my broken hand. "Yeah. Thanks to you."

I fold my arms over my chest and stare down at her. Taking her in. Her eyes have more bags under them and her face is slimmer. Her hair hangs loosely down her back and she's wearing gray sweats, but she's never looked more beautiful to me than at that moment. But I'd be lying if I said anger didn't still simmer low in my chest. I didn't know which I wanted to do more, kiss her breathless or strangle her. So I stood away from her.

"How are you?" I ask.

She shrugs a slim shoulder. "I'm breathing. Not for the lack of trying."

I shake my head, anger snapping like a loose thread. "That's not fucking funny, Nirvana."

"I'm not being funny. I'm being honest. You're not supposed to be here."

I pace, breathing deeply, in and out. "You're impossible. So fucking impossible."

She's silent for a moment before she whispers, "I'm sorry, Ravi."

I laugh sarcastically. "You're sorry?"

Nirvana

I swallow hard, unsure of what to say to him. I was sorry. But how was I supposed to convey that to him? Seeing him after weeks without hearing his voice, seeing his face made my heart hurt. It was so unexpected to see him here. I don't know how to react right now. My conversation with Misery yesterday made me see things differently. And seeing him in person made it clear I didn't deserve him. He deserved someone better. Someone who wasn't broken. Insecure in their past. He shakes his head again. "You're sorry."

"I am. I'm truly sorry," I say.

"You're sorry for trying to kill yourself? Or sorry that it didn't work?" he asks.

I look at the door. "I'm sorry you saw me like that." It's the only thing that came to mind. "I'm ashamed of how it all went down."

"You almost died, Nirvana."

I nod, closing my eyes as tears burn behind them. "I'm sorry."

"Will you at least look at me when you give me a half-assed apology?"

My eyes snap open and I glare at him. "Fuck you, Ravi. You don't get to come here and insult me. I'm sorry you had to see that. I really am."

He throws his hands up. "It has nothing to do with seeing you like that, Nirvana."

"Then what is it?" I snap. "You saved my life. Thank you. Is that what you want?"

He huffs out a laugh. "I walked through fire for you. I'd do it all over again, too," he snaps.

"I didn't ask you to, Ravi! I was content with dying!" Was I though? I wasn't so certain anymore.

"You didn't have to ask me! I'd do it a thousand times over!" he shouts.

"Why?" I demand, because I certainly don't deserve it.

He shoves a hand through his hair. "Because."

"Because why?"

He turns away breathing deeply.

"Because why, Ravi? Why would you risk yourself like that?" I press him, almost desperately.

"Because I fucking love you, Nirvana! I love you so much it hurts!" he says.

My heart nearly stopped and a soft gasp escaped my mouth. He couldn't love me. "Ravi," I breathe out. I don't get to finish because he's there kissing me deeply. His hand wraps in my hair tightly, angling my head back so he has better access to me. I want to resist, but I can't. With a soft whimper I wrap my arms around his neck and pull him closer to me. His tongue pushes into my mouth, stroking against mine. It's hot, it's rough, and it's perfect. God, I missed him. I missed this. I missed him. God, did I miss him.

He pushed me roughly against the door, pushed my legs apart and wedged himself between them pressing his erection against me. Groaning, I ripped my mouth from his, arching into his touch. He kissed and bit down my throat. Claiming me, branding me as his. My hips thrust against him searching for that pleasure I know he'll give me. His cock pressed against my throbbing clit making me moan, wanting more. I stare up at him, wanting to feel his soft hair. With shaky hands I pull his hat off and toss it onto the ground, threading my fingers through his hair.

"I'm so sorry, Ravi," I whisper again.

He stares at me, his eyes dark and swirling with emotion. "I know. Why didn't you tell anyone you were struggling?" he asks, pushing forward again.

My breath caught in my throat. "I don't know," I groan, rubbing myself against him wanting more.

Ravi doesn't take the hint though, he just stays still. "You do know, pixie. I want to help you."

I shake my head not wanting to talk about it. Misery already wrung me dry with her pressing, but this was Ravi.

He was different. I owed him that much. Leaning forward I press my head against his shoulder, taking a breath, letting his spicy scent surround me. To comfort me. "It's not something people volunteer. It's embarrassing."

He pulls back slightly. "Embarrassing? You shouldn't be embarrassed by being bipolar or any other mental illnesses."

I shake my head. "It's different. When I was ten I was sent away for being too difficult. For being unstable. I had moments when I'd have tantrums without even meaning to. I would go without sleep, and walk around my house. I'd stop eating. Stop drinking. They sent me to an institute. Granted, not like this one, but similar."

It was odd talking about this with anyone, even the girls didn't know. "My parents hated me when they found out. I had something that couldn't be dealt with through prayer. It was something I heard about a lot. Then they began fighting. My father wanted to send me away. The problem child. Aero was really young at that time. Their fights escalated to hitting and then she left. She tried taking Aero with her, but he wouldn't let her."

The hand in my hair fisted and he lifted my head with it. It didn't hurt, in fact it sent a slight thrill down my spine. I swallow hard at the harsh look on his face. "You have nothing to be ashamed about. This is something out of your control, if they did any amount of research they'd know."

"That may be true for back then, but I'm an adult. I should be able to deal with it. Not get so fucking overwhelmed I want to die. I wanted to go so bad, Ravi. I was ready." I plead with him to understand. "I wasn't scared of dying. I'm not scared of it. I'm scared of what will happen if I survive. I'm scared of forgetting my sister, of living."

He sighs softly and presses his forehead to mine. "Your sister would want you to live, pixie. Even if it was difficult."

"I know she would," I whisper. And I did. Logically, I

knew Aero would want me to live, to do all the things she couldn't do. Clearing my throat I pull back a little and finally ask, "Why are you here?"

"I wanted to see for myself that you were okay. I don't trust your father not to send you to one of those awful places again."

I scoff, "I'm surprised he didn't. I'm kind of surprised I haven't seen Father Brent either. Not since I was brought here."

"Are you treated okay? No one touches you or forces you into anything?" he asks, studying my face.

I shrug. "That first week was brutal. They had me tied to the bed so I couldn't harm anyone else. I accidentally, on purpose, kicked an orderly in the balls." Ravi grabs my hands, pushing up the sleeves looking for marks on my arms and hands. There were a few scratches from my struggling, but nothing major was done. "It was more embarrassing than anything else."

"I should kill them for putting you through this shit," he muttered. For some reason that sent a flutter through my heart and made me smile for the first time in weeks.

"It's okay. I'm in a normal room. I have a roommate. She's good." Apart from the fact that she's a killer, but that's not really important to mention.

"I'll get you out of here soon. I can make some calls."

I grab his face, forcing him to look at me. "No. I need to stay. I need to get some help. Please understand, I need this. I need to work on myself and my mental state. I need to figure out what to do about that house. If I'll be in trouble or not." I run my thumbs over his stubbled jaw and admit, "I want to win you over."

"You've already won me," he says softly.

Shaking my head, I lean forward, pressing a gentle kiss to his mouth. Savoring our time. "No. I wasn't in the right mind. I will be. Come back in two weeks. Or well, thirteen days I guess."

"Nirvana."

"Please, Ravi. Please come back then." His chest heaves as he takes a breath. His eyes roam my face and he gives a clipped nod.

"Fine. But if you're not ready at that time I will drag your ass out of here kicking and screaming."

I smirk at him and say, "Don't tease me with a good time."

Rolling his eyes, he grabs the nape of my neck pulling me into him. "Shut up." With that he takes my mouth in a bruising kiss. It wasn't a goodbye kiss, though. It was a promise for something more. Something darker, maybe brighter. It was a promise for the future.

Chapter 46

RAVI

I left Nirvana in that little room and made my way down the hall. Leaving her was the hardest thing I've had to do. Leaving her in this unknown place alone. But I could see the sincerity in her eyes as she pleaded with me to come back after she got help. I could see she needed it. I knew it, and even if I wanted to be the one to help her I knew I couldn't. Not in the way she needed.

Ignoring my interview, I leave the institution. Clouds have begun moving in, darkening the once bright sky, leaving it dreary. I make my way towards the truck and climb in without a word. "What happened?" Sorrow asks.

Sighing, I lean back in the seat. "I found her. She's lost weight but she's not as bad off as I feared. She told me to come back in two weeks. Well, thirteen days."

"That's specific." Max snorts, then turns to look at me, "Where's your hat?"

I reach up and feel my head, cursing. "I must've dropped

it." Max looks at Sorrow and the two smirk. "Grow up," I grumble.

"So did she tell you anything?" Sorrow asks, pulling away from the building.

I shrug. "Nothing that August didn't mention. Other than wanting to get help and she thinks she can get it there." What she mentioned about her parents, I don't share with the men. It couldn't have been easy for her to share with me. The ride from San Antonio back to Austin is silent. Then the rain started, making it difficult to see.

"Shit. I might need to pull over in the next gas station, I can hardly see." Sorrow curses and pulls over into a small gas station. Sighing, I lean back in the seat hoping the rain doesn't last long.

We sit in silence for a while, watching as the rain pelts against the windows and I can't stand it anymore. "Do you think Delaney would help me learn about bipolar disorder and how to help Nirvana?" I ask.

"You really want to learn?" Sorrow asks.

I arch a brow at him. "Why wouldn't I?"

He shrugs. "It's just you've always said you wouldn't settle with the woman. You were adamant that you weren't serious."

Rubbing the back of my neck I grimace. "Things change, Sorrow. You of all people should know that."

Sorrow nods, pushing a hand through his long hair. "I do." They're silent for a moment and I sigh.

"I love her. All of her. I want to learn to be a better partner. To understand her situation more."

I see Sorrow smirk, and hear Max curse while reaching into his pocket and handing Sorrow a bill. Leaning forward, I snatch it out of his hand. "Twenty dollars? Seriously?"

"He bet me you'd come out admitting your feelings. You told her, didn't you?" Max asked.

Tsking, I shoved the twenty into my pocket, "Shut the fuck up and drive. The rains have slowed down and I would rather not be stuck in this truck with you assholes any longer."

Laughing, Sorrow starts the truck and says, "For what it's worth, I'm happy for you, man."

A small grin tilted my mouth. Everything seemed to be looking up after all.

A knock sounded on my front door hours later pulling me from my laptop. Standing from the table, I walk to the door and peek through the peephole and see Delaney standing there. I pull the door open and she smiles up at me.

"Hey, I heard you requested my expertise." Nodding, I motion her inside. "I'm glad you want to do this, Ravi. It'll mean a lot to her, and it means a lot to me. Nirvana is a special woman."

"She is," I say. "I want her to know she has support."

Delaney sits at the table. "I agree. I know the girls have been wanting to do more for her. Sorrow said she wants to stay. That means she wants to get help which is step one."

"Can I get you anything, a drink or something?" I ask. She shakes her head, so I take a seat in front of her. "I did a little research when I got home. It said that a lot of the support comes by listening and being understanding."

Delaney nods. "Yes. Not a lot of people listen to those who suffer from mental illnesses. In all honesty, I don't know how I didn't realize she was suffering. I have a degree in this, she showed signs but I never once reached out to her."

"She's embarrassed, Lane. She was always told she was messed up in some way and she hid it," I say to try and console her.

"We wouldn't do that to her. But I can see how it came to be like this. Her parents and Marcy fucked her up."

I clear my throat, pulling my laptop close to me. "Has she had any episodes before?"

Delaney pauses, thinking, and says, "Once. That I can remember. It was in high school. At that time I guess we just thought she was fun and easy going, always hyper. But she went on a bender for a week. Jumping from college party to college party. She drank a lot, did some drugs. Nothing hard, I don't think. She smoked a lot of weed."

"When was this?" I ask.

She sighs, running a hand through her hair. "After everything went down with Marcy. The start of our sophomore year."

"After that camp." I could see how that would break her. Her mind was still processing the trauma she had to deal with. Nirvana had to learn to deal with the betrayal of not only her parents, but also a girl she had feelings for, one she thought reciprocated them.

Pushing those thoughts away, I stare at Delaney. "What can we do to make sure this never happens again?"

Chapter 47

Nirvana

Staring out of the window in the common area, I sigh. It's been two days since I last saw Ravi and I felt worse when he left than I did before I got here. Maybe it was the nerves of being around the others soon, or the fact that I continued to push my feelings to the side, refusing to talk about them. Or the shame that was circling inside of me more and more.

"Nirvana, would you like to share today?" Stassi asked gently. Turning my gaze from the window I stare at the eccentric woman in front of me. She wore another bright colored dress today, only this time it was a pristine white with cherries on it. It went well with her red hair, I thought. Misery sits beside me and nudges me with her foot, nodding sharply. Right, sharing.

I take the talking stick from Stassi and hold it in my fist, tightening it ever so slightly. "I'm not sure where to start," I say under my breath, more to myself than to the group around me.

"Start wherever you want to. There's no rush." I guess not, we were all trapped within these walls; it's not like we had anywhere to be.

I straighten in my chair, give a definitive nod and begin, "Right. Um, I'm Nirvana. Well, I guess you all know that by now. I am here because a few weeks ago I tried to kill myself after my little sister died from an advanced brain cancer." My throat tightened. This is the first time I said those words as if I was accepting them. I wasn't going to fool myself into thinking that I wouldn't ever break down when thinking about her. But at least maybe not every time. It hurt, it hurt then and it hurts now. I was sure it would always hurt, but right now I didn't get that soul crushing pain in my heart whenever I thought of her.

"When I was eighteen years old I fought with my father. He kicked me out and I fought for custody of my little sister," I say.

Another patient, Pammy, an older woman who was there for her own manic depressive episodes raised her hand, and asked, "Why would you want to get custody of your sister? You were eighteen and could've done anything. Did you get custody?"

I swallow hard remembering what led me to getting custody. "My sister was thirteen when I got custody. My father signed over his parental rights. I had caught my sister holding hands with another girl. Now, you may not think it's a big deal. I didn't, and I still don't, but my father is a homophobic twat. And I wouldn't let him do to her what he did to me."

Stassi leaned forward, and using a gentle tone she asked, "What did he do to you, Nirvana?"

I look down at my lap twirling the stick in my hands. "He sent me away when I was fourteen. An old friend of mine was dared to kiss me and she did. My father walked in and he freaked out. He's a preacher, you see. So he called me all kinds of names and said I was going to Hell for all my sins and misdeeds. The next day I was dragged from under my bed, where I was hiding, and taken away to a camp. It was a conversion camp that would take all the gay out of me, he'd said. I'm not gay, I'm what you'd consider pan; I don't require a certain gender. I fall for anyone if we are compatible."

"Sexuality is a construct that was put upon people based on a book that has changed so much over time," Misery says beside me.

I close my eyes. "But that book made my own father hate me. I didn't get to come out when I was ready. I didn't know what was happening, and I was so scared when I got there. I can still remember the screams, the way I begged over and over again to be let go. The promises I made to be a better person, a better girl. How it wasn't my fault. But those went unheard. Ignored.

"I hated it. I hated that book. I hated my father. I hated what they did to me. I hated myself. I still hate myself."

"Your dad sounds like a real prize," Misery snorts.

I shake my head, a small smirk falling to my lips. "He married her. The girl who kissed me. God, when they showed up to the hospital to see my sister, I was so angry."

Stassi crosses her legs and asks, "What did you feel?"

"Angry. I was so fucking angry. I wanted to rage, I still want to. To know that the reason I was sent to that fucking place is now my new stepmother. God, I never felt so angry, so hurt." I could feel that anger in me now. Slowly simmering in the pit of my stomach.

"But you didn't," Stassi said it like a statement.

I nodded anyway. "I didn't."

"What stopped you?"

"Ravi." He was the only person to break through that

haze which was surrounding me. He penetrated my chaotic thoughts, breaking through the betrayal I felt. He held this power over me. Like a soothing balm on a burn. While he was there it was like I forgot everything around me. It was just me and him.

"He stopped you? How?"

"I don't know," I say, honesty ringing from my tone. "He was just there and it was like everything bad was suddenly so trivial."

"How'd you meet?" Ronnie, another patient, and a large burly man, asked.

I smile sadly. "My friend, well she's more a sister than a friend. Anyway, she was attacked by her stalker. And I was running through the hospital and he caught me. Pulling me away from the chaos when I was almost run down by the doctors. After that I stayed away from him. But Delaney decided to hitch herself to one of his best friends and suddenly he was always there."

"But you never got with him until now?" Pammy asks with wide brown eyes.

I gave a short laugh. "No. I try not to be around men I don't know. Unless I was fucking them, or at some sort of function with Delaney and the others, I stayed away."

"But you somehow found your way together," Misery says.

I nod. "The night we were alone it was due to unforeseen circumstances. I was attacked at a club my friend owns." Some patients gasp but I hold up my hand and say, "It's okay I was fine. I busted his balls so I doubt the dude is getting it up ever again." I wave it away with a flick of a wrist. "Anyway, Isola, my sister's wife called me. I had just woken up from a nightmare and was getting ready to take a shower, and she told me my sister was in the hospital. I dropped everything and went. We didn't know what was wrong and she seemed fine, so my sister sent me home. When I got back I heard my shower was still on. Water was everywhere and it was a mess.

"When I went to shut it off, I slipped. I lay there. I was tired, and worried about my sister. I was attacked. It was a shit day. But I pulled myself up and I went to turn off the shower and the fucking handle broke. It wouldn't turn off, so I called Delaney. I figured she'd send her fiancé or something. But nope, Ravi showed up."

I remembered, it was the first time since the hospital that I was alone with Ravi. I was so tired and when he opened that bathroom door and I saw him my breathing stopped. He filled the doorway with his muscular form and glared down at me with those forest green eyes and sighed as if I somehow inconvenienced his night. As if I had personally called him.

But then he looked at me, at the busted lip and bruises and something changed. That hard look turned to anger, to concern. For me. Then he kicked off his sneakers and pushed me out of the way, protecting me from the excessive spray with his body when he finally shut off the water.

"I was a bitch when we talked and he was an asshole. But he kept coming around. Especially after the diagnosis my sister got. He became more in those few weeks. My rock, my person. I became a real fixture with them, not just him but the other guys. Sort of like brothers. I was spiraling and I hated how I couldn't control it. But they were there. Not only when my sister was sick, but for the wedding. They helped me plan a wedding in two weeks. Ravi is the first man I've slept with. Not just sexually, but actually slept with. Then he saved me. When I tried so hard to end it he pulled me out of that house. He walked through fire for me. He brought me back to life."

And I don't mean that he just resurrected me when I tried to overdose, I thought. I mean, he did that too, but throughout those weeks he slowly brought me to life. He made me smile, laugh. He watched teenage dramas with me, wore those god awful fuzzy headbands and sat in the middle of the room as we did facemasks and drank fruity drinks. He held me as I cried, he punched my father in the face after he slapped me. He was there when I buried my sister, giving me the choice to go to that wake or not. He somehow got in here and checked on me.

And by some miracle he loved me. Even broken and bruised he loved me.

"Who is Ravi to you, Nirvana?" Stassi asked.

Taking a breath I respond, "Everything."

Chapter 48

Nirvana

I stare up at Stassi, my eyes wide. "I don't…" I shake my head. "I don't know what to do."

She gave a gentle smile to me. "Love is difficult, Nirvana. It's messy, it's exciting. It's hot and it's cold. It can even be toxic and scary. But from just the little you told me it seems like this man loves you, yet you're hesitant. Why is that?" She tilts her head studying me. Waiting for me to respond.

I don't answer right away. I hardly know how to. "People like me don't deserve men like him." I finally decided on.

"Do you care to elaborate?"

I swallow hard. My throat was suddenly dry and my heart was pounding. This was the thing that freaked me out most about these meetings. Admitting to my flaws, on what goes on in my head. But I knew I had to. To be better. For myself, for my family. For my sister.

"I am broken. What man would want a woman who tried to kill herself? Who can go through periods where I'm riding a mechanical bull and two handing shots until I black out? Someone who can very well go to jail for arson when I get out of here because I tried to burn down my childhood home with me in it?" I ask almost desperately.

There's a silence and Pammy speaks, her brown eyes sparkling, "Probably the same man who would walk through said fire."

Stassi leaned forward, her dark eyes kind and understanding, "The things you went through were traumatic. You suffer from bipolar disorder. It's going to be hard at times and that's to be expected. After everything, you still find it in your heart to think of other people. What your father did to you is awful, and I promise you not all members of the Christian community think or act like that. But like everything else we'll have our good ones and our bad ones. Your father, he is a bad one. He doesn't preach the word of God because he hasn't listened to the actual words. He depicted the book to fit his agenda. You deserved a family who loved you. And you seem to have a good one now."

Tears fill my eyes and I nod. "Yeah. They're great. Some should probably be in here with me, but they're great, nonetheless." That got a few laughs, but I meant every word. We were a misfit bunch who probably needed more help, but we were all going with the flow and seeing where life would take us. Even if, at times, it led to killing abusive stepfathers and being stabbed by a half-brother we didn't realize we had.

Or it led you to trying to kill yourself and taking the house that caused all your pain with you. Or it led you to fighting for your country, saving people who needed it. To falling in love with people you never would've dreamed of.

I push a hand through my hair. "I can't love myself let alone another person."

Stassi smiles widely. "Well, that's what I'm here for. I'm here to help you realize you can get help and still find love.

Even if that's from yourself. People oftentimes dismiss people with mental illnesses, but that's not what we do here. I want to show each and every one of you that there's nothing wrong with you. You're all strong and just need a little extra time and help."

I hand her the stick and she gives us an assignment to write what we hate about ourselves and what we like about ourselves in order to prepare for tomorrow's session then dismisses us.

I sit back for a moment, giving myself a chance to breathe. This was the first time I ever talked about what I went through. Maybe not in all the gory details but enough that I felt a physical weight being lifted off of my chest. I felt a hope that I thought was long gone by now. A hand fell to my shoulder drawing me from my thoughts and causing me to jump in my seat. Glancing up I see Misery.

"Oh, hey," I say.

She nods and sits down beside me. "You did good today, Nirvy."

I scoff. "Why do you call me that?" I ask.

She grins at me. "You're here for essentially a nervous breakdown. Your name is Nirvana. It felt fitting."

I gape at her, wondering if I should be offended or not. But in the end I decided not and burst out laughing. "That seems fitting."

She hums under her breath and stretches her long legs out in front of her. "Do you want me to kill him?" she asks randomly.

I glance at her, arching an eyebrow and ask, "Who?"

"Your father. I will."

I glance around, making sure no one is close, before I lower my voice and ask, "Are you a serial killer?"

She just shrugs, making my eyes widen. "He is a waste of

space. The planet is dying enough without one more entitled prick sucking up the oxygen."

Shaking my head I laugh. "No. No, I'm pretty sure when he finds out his wife's kid isn't his he'll have a heart attack and die."

Laughing, she pats my knee and says, "Let's hope it's soon. We've got some homework, so we should get on it before dinner. I've got planning to do." I arch an eyebrow and watch as she leaves like a thief in the night. These last few weeks here I often find myself wondering if she's serious about her reason for being here.

But then I think to myself how we all reacted to that night at Delaney's with her stepfather and I decide it's not my business. I'm only here for another week and a half, I could do it. Standing from my chair I move closer to the windows and watch as the wind picks up and rain begins to splatter across the field. I'm lost in my thoughts when I see a reflection standing behind me.

"You don't need to sneak up on me, Pammy," I say to the older woman.

Pammy snorts and replies, "If I wanted to sneak up behind you, I doubt I'd do it through a window of all things."

My lips quirk up, she has a point. Giving her my full attention, I nod and say, "What's up?"

The older woman motions to one of the worn couches and I sink into it. Wondering why she was suddenly so talkative when she's been as shut in as I have. "I wanted to say your story really touched me."

I stare at her, meeting her light eyes. "Oh. Is that good or bad?"

She rolls her eyes and says, "You remind me of my granddaughter."

"Oh. You have kids?" I ask.

Pammy nods, her gray hair bouncing against her withered face. "I used to. My daughter got in trouble with some drugs. You know the tales, a working mother falls in with a bad crowd. She neglects her children, blah blah blah."

I nod. "Yeah. Yeah, I know some of those."

Swallowing thickly she stares out the windows, watching as the rain falls faster and harder. "My Gemma, my granddaughter," she elaborates, "was a bright girl. Sweet and kind. But she wasn't always happy."

The way she talked about her granddaughter had my heart racing and dread fill the pit of my stomach. "What happened to her?"

Pammy sniffs, wiping under her eyes. "She couldn't handle it anymore. Her mother was never present. I tried to be there as best as I could, but in the end it wasn't enough." Clearing her throat she turns to me and begins, "Her mother's boyfriend of the week was angry. Gemma had this way about her. She'd be sarcastic and witty without meaning to and her mother's boyfriend snapped when she replied in a way he didn't like. He beat her to death while my daughter watched. Did nothing to protect that child. Too high off her ass to do anything."

My eyes widen and my heart stops beating. "Pammy, I'm so…" I stop, I don't know what to say. Sorry didn't feel good enough, but then that's what you usually say to such revelations. But this didn't feel like enough. I reach out slowly and put my hands on hers, squeezing slightly. That's what Delaney did when we were stressed or were close to panic. Said it would bring a person on the brink back. At least for a little while.

She squeezed back. "It's okay. It's okay. At the trial my daughter didn't even look remorseful, just out of it. So I lost all sense of control. It was too much for me. I was angry. I was hurt, I was mourning. It wasn't fair."

"It's not fair. You had every right to react the way you did. I can't imagine what that must've been like."

Pammy nods. "So, your story made me realize that my granddaughter would've wanted me to keep fighting. Much like your sister would you."

I nod. "She would. Your granddaughter sounds like she was a great girl. I'm sorry for your loss."

"Thank you," Pammy says and stands, then pins me with a serious stare. "Whatever happens with your father, don't let that bastard break you. Don't let him win. You fight and you fight like your life depends on it because it very well might. You don't belong here with the rest of us. You belong with your family, with your man. You need to do anything and everything to get out of here." With that she turns and walks away leaving me feeling more determined and hopeful than I've ever felt before.

Standing, I make my way back to my room. I had a list to make.

Chapter 49

RAVI

Staring out at the burnt house I sigh. Only the living room and the kitchen were affected by the fire Nirvana started. Honestly, if Mrs. Murphy hadn't called the fire department before me, this house would've been in shambles and nothing more than ash and broken plywood. The sound of gravel crunching drew my attention as Drew walked towards me.

"What are you doing?" he asks, crossing his arms over his chest. I shrug, turning back towards the house that has caused Nirvana so much pain and heartache.

I move up on the porch, careful of my steps due to the crooked steps and rotted wood. "You were right," I say, catching the other man off guard.

Drew arches a dark brow. "About?"

"Nirvana needing to stay in the institute. She wants to get help."

He sighs. "So you found her." It's a statement.

I nod. "August told us."

He hums under his breath and looks at the rubble, then asks, "How is she?"

"She's as to be expected. Better than she was." It's been almost a week since I've seen or heard anything about her and a part of me was itching to break her out of that damn place right now, but I knew she wasn't ready yet. "She said to come back in two weeks."

"Are you sure that's wise?" he asks.

I stare at him from the corner of my eye, rubbing my fingers at the top of my cast. "Why are you acting weird about her?"

"I'm not acting weird about her, Ravi," he says and sighs.

I scoff, "You could've fooled me. When we were trying to find her you said to stop."

"Because she needs help, Ravi. She tried to kill herself."

I round on him. "You don't think I fucking know that? I was right fucking there." I was having nightmares about it. I glare at him and ask, "Do you think that no one wants what's best for her?"

"She needs help. She needs to stay there and get it. It won't help seeing everything she was trying to run from," he says.

Stepping up to him, I stand toe to toe with him. "She needs someone. She needs a family. She almost died."

"What she needs is medication and therapy."

The way his eyes glanced to the side and his jaw ticced had me on edge. He was hiding something. And that was pissing me off.

"What did you do?" I ask quietly.

"Nothing, Ravi. Just stating facts."

I shake my head. "You're hiding something. You've always been shitty at it. For as long as I've known you. What. Did. You. Fucking. Do?"

A look of guilt crossed his face before it was gone. It was so fast that I thought I imagined it. But with the way he inhaled and looked at me, I knew I was right. "I knew she was bad off. I guessed it when Aero was brought back. Before she died."

I reel back and he stands straight, not shrinking from my stare, not that I'd expect him to. It takes me a minute for his words to register before I'm lunging forward, my fist connecting with his face. "You fucking knew she was dealing with this mania and didn't say a goddamn thing?"

"I talked to her and I thought that was that," he sneered. But he didn't make a move against me and for some reason that made it worse. It made my anger spike. Anger I didn't realize I was still hanging on to. I pushed him and he hardly budged.

"Fight back, you prick," I demand.

"Fuck you. I'm not fighting you, Ravi." Drew wipes at his mouth, at the blood that dripped from his teeth. I wanted to feel bad, but I couldn't. Not right now.

I punch him again, this time in the stomach causing him to hunch over and expel a gust of breath. "You should've told someone! We could've prevented all of this!"

He shakes his head. "She would've done it anyway. She didn't want help at the time. She was grieving her sister, she was angry, sad. Scared."

I grip the collar of his shirt, getting in his face, saying, "Don't talk to me about her as if you know her."

He chuckles sarcastically. "I know her better than you, Ravi."

"The fuck you do." I push him away from me, stepping away. "You should've told us." I shake my head and say, "You should've told me."

"She didn't want me to. So, I didn't. Not until she tried to commit suicide."

I shake my head. "I can't believe you." I say it more to myself than him.

"You wouldn't have stopped her. No one could've. Her mind was made up."

"Stop talking, Drew. The way I feel right now I'm bound to kill you with my bare hands."

He scoffs, "You don't like hearing the truth. You never have. Even all those years ago you hated hearing the truth. You hate not having some ounce of control, but you fucking can't. You know damn fucking well she needs help."

"Since when do you give a shit?" I demand.

He snaps then, whatever hold he had on his temper was gone. "Because I feel the same fucking way! I've seen those symptoms before! Nothing would've stopped her during an episode, not you, not her friends, not me. Nothing. You're angry at her, at yourself. You feel guilty for missing the signs. Nirvana covered it up for years, this time was just too much for her. So if you want to fight then do it. But after that you need to get it together and let it go. You want her out, I get it, but you aren't going to get the same woman you had."

I'm breathing deeply, he's right. I am angry at myself and at Nirvana. Where I understand from her perspective it was too much and I don't blame her. But I am still angry at her. That she would just rather die leaving me alone than to go on. To live. She would've left me alone. Always alone. Cursing, I plop myself on the ground.

"Fuck. I'm so angry with her," I mutter, wiping at my face.

Drew settles next to me, working his jaw with his hand, wincing slightly. "I'm sorry I didn't tell you right away. I should have, but I was worried about you, about her."

I glance at him, at the jaded look in his cold, ice green eyes. "Do you really feel like she does?"

He shrugs. "Sometimes. Not in the same way, I'm not

bipolar. But I have moments where I feel panicked. Scared out of my mind."

I stare at the house. "I panicked. Going into the house. I almost stopped myself," I whisper.

"But you still went in."

I give a short laugh. "Of course I did. I love her. The thought of losing her outweighed my panic."

"You still think of that night?" he asks. I stare ahead wanting to deny it, but I can't.

I nod. "I was terrified. In all my career I've never felt terror like that. And I haven't since. Not until Nirvana. All those years ago, when that cavern was burning I thought we'd lost you all. I can hear the screams, smell the flesh melting from the bones. I can feel the heat on my skin. I almost turned back then, but the thought of losing my brothers was too much." Drawing in a shaky breath I admit, "I have nightmares, but instead of those screams I hear Nirvana's. I hear yours, Sorrow's, Max, I hear Caden. And I can never get to any of you. I'm just stuck."

"Yet you willingly go into burning buildings. Why?"

I shrug. "Probably the same reason you are an ER nurse. Or why you go to third world countries to administer medical care to those who can't afford it." He doesn't deny it. Not that I'd expect him to. Sighing, I climb to my feet and hold my hand out to him. He takes it and I glare at him. "If you keep anything about my girl, as important as this, from me again, I will kill you."

He smirks. "I'd expect nothing less."

Nodding, I let him go. "Good. Now let's go gather anything that might be Aero's and see if it's salvageable. This place pisses me off." We walk together into the house, the smell of burnt wood and carpet still heavy in the air.

"I'm surprised the house didn't combust," Drew murmurs, kicking a piece of broken furniture out of his way.

I was surprised too. When I got here the house was almost black with smoke but when I looked at the interior, only some parts were burnt. Most of the damage was due to the smoke. Shaking off the eerie feeling, I move down the hallway to Nirvana and Aero's childhood room. It was the same as it was the last time I was here.

Dust filled, with the broken dresser and end table, but nothing else. I glance around the room and my gaze falls onto the dress. More specifically what was under it. Crouching down I pull up an old VHS tape. Turning it over in my hands I saw a neat scrawl written on the front, *'For the bad times'*. The marker had faded over the years, but I could still make out the words.

"Do you think the TV in the living room still works?" I ask.

Drew snorts and says, "No. But I think Sorrow and Delaney have a VCR. I don't think there's much else here that we can find."

Nodding, I stand.

"Let's go."

It's not long before we are at Sorrow and Delaney's. I grab the tape and leave the car, walking up the drive to the porch where Sorrow stands drinking a cup of coffee.

"Little late for coffee don't you think?" I say.

Sorrow rolls his eyes. "There's not enough caffeine in the world to deal with your antics, Ravi." He looks past me to Drew. "What the hell happened to you?"

"You know, the usual," he shrugs.

"Is Delaney here?" I ask.

Sorrow sipped from his mug, tilting his head towards the living room. Nodding, I walk inside where I hear arguing.

"It's called buddy reading, that means you read as a buddy," Delaney snapped.

"Lane, it moves along with reading speed," Max sighs.

"You read the entire book!"

I walk into the living room and see Max holding a book above his head glaring down at the woman who is glaring right back at him.

"It's not my fault you read slow," the redhead said, shrugging.

Delaney groans in frustration. "We picked it out yesterday!"

"Hey, Lane," I called.

She turns her head and smiles at me, before glaring at Max again. "This is far from over, Maxim."

He rears back, stunned. "You do know it's just Max right?"

"Today it's not. Now go sit down and think about what you did," she says, pointing to the couch.

"Hell, no. I'm a grown man…" Max starts.

"Now! I'm upset and I will cry and Sorrow will most likely shoot you," she says. I raise an eyebrow as Max sighs, sitting on the couch.

"What the fuck just happened?" I ask. "Nevermind. I don't interfere in your weird book wars. Do you have a VCR?"

Delaney looks at me, then at my hand. "Are we watching a movie?"

"Sure. Can we?"

She nods and moves towards the TV, opening a cabinet and pulling out an older VCR. "Why do you have a VCR?" Max asks.

Sighing, Delaney leans forward and replies, "I have an older copy of My Girl that I watch from time to time," she explains. Then as if remembering she's mad at Max she glares and says, "No talking. Think about what you did." Max turns wide eyes to me and I shrug. It wasn't my business.

I hold out the tape to her and she pops it in without looking at it and rewinds it. Standing she grabs the remote and turns the TV on, putting it on the right channel before sitting down. The picture is fuzzy at first, like a home video before clearing slightly.

"Laney should be Belle. She likes to read," a tinny voice said *through the TV as a small little blonde walked up holding another blonde child. "Plus she has brown hair too."*

"She wears glasses, Belle doesn't wear glasses," another girl *argued.*

Another girl, Delaney by the glasses, sighs through the screen. *"It doesn't matter, Marcy. If you want to play Belle then you can."*

"No, Ms. Vern said you were Belle in the play. You can't give it up just cause Marcy wants it." the redhead child said. Layla. It's all of the women as young girls, probably no older than eight or nine with Aero being a toddler.

"Where did you find this?" Delaney asks softly.

"Under the dresser at Nirvana's house," I reply, still watching the home movie.

"Just cause she reads doesn't mean she should be Belle," Marcy *snarked.*

Sighing, Nirvana sets her sister down. "It's how the teacher wants it. We all have our parts." I can see how agitated she is becoming. Looking over at her sister and taking a breath. This had to be before she was sent away the first time. The time she told me about when I saw her last.

Marcy rounds on her. "You always side with them. Never me."

Nirvana shrugs. "It's how the teacher wants it so we go by that."

Marcy screeches, stomping her foot. "She's too big and wears glasses. If anything, she should be the clock!" Nirvana stops and with her own little screech she launches her smaller body at Marcy, knocking her to the ground.

"Laney is not big!" I reach forward and take the remote from Delaney's hand and fast forward until the girls are a little older. The only difference is that Nirvana isn't in this video.

Ophelia sits down in the living room and points toward the camera, "Is it on, Mama?" she asks. The camera moves up and down.

"What do we say?" Layla asks, tossing a pink bear up and down, catching it every now and then, then dropping it on Rory's head.

Rory grabs the bear and holds it in her lap, shooting a glare at her, "Stop that. We gotta show our cards then go to school before we're late."

Delaney talks first, "Hey, Van! We miss you. We made you some cards for when you get home." She held up a piece of red construction paper with blue glitter all over it. "We wanted to bring them to you but your mom said you were too sick for visitors yet, but maybe soon!"

"Ree is fine," Seraphina interrupts. "She misses you, but she know's you've been too sick to visit. We sometimes play dolls with her after school. She doesn't let anyone play with yours though. But we don't mind."

"I remember this," Delaney whispers. "Right after she attacked Marcy she was gone. We didn't get to see her, but we were told she was really sick. Louise let us make this video for when she got home. She was the only parent who bothered to make home videos."

I sigh, Nirvana wasn't sick. She was sent away. Alone. She was hardly ten when she was sent away. I couldn't imagine how scared she must've been. I move forward and stop when Aero pops up on the screen, older than when the tape first played.

I press play and sink into the couch beside Max.

Aero reaches forward and adjusts the camera, "Okay, I think it's on. Otherwise that would be really embarrassing," she glances behind her at the closed door before turning back. "Hi, Van Van. I found this video a few days ago. Father never showed you," she rolls her eyes, "But I wanted to make this video for you. You're not here anymore. They sent you away. Again. It's not fair. What they did to you. I'm sorry if you were hurt. I miss you. I tried calling Mom but she didn't answer. Your friends are worried about you. I didn't know what to tell them. I just said you went to summer camp. I don't know where you are. I just saw Father Brent and the others push you into that van."

Aero reaches under a book on the bed and pulls out a piece of paper. "I know it has something to do with Marcy. I don't like her. She's rude all the time. Don't worry, I got her back for you," smirking slightly she says, "I cut the brakes on her bike. She sadly fell down a steep hill. Broke her arm. Father was mad. They blamed it on you, but it wasn't your fault."

A door opened and closed. "Dang it. Father's home I've got to go, I'll be back later."

The camera shut off and we sat in silence until Delaney spoke, "Huh. I always wondered how she broke her arm."

"Serves the demon right," I mutter under my breath. The TV screen wavers a bit and the camera turns back on and Aero is standing in front of it, breathing heavily and wet.

"Hey Van! I told ya I'd be back," she gasps out, hunching over slightly holding up a finger. "Hang on. I ran all the way home." After taking a few deep breaths she looks at the camera, her eyes bright, "It's raining here, Van. Today was an eventful day. Guess what? Sera is dating Phil's brother! They got caught kissing by her mom! She was in so much trouble but I think she is staying with Rory and her family for now. Anyway, we'll come back to that in a minute. I've got bigger news," Aero lowers her voice and pulls out a polaroid from her pants pocket, "I went to the church today. Also I found out you were sent away for kissing Marcy." She grimaces, "I feel like you could have kissed anyone else but I won't judge too much. Anyway, I went to find father and I saw him. Kissing someone." With a shaky hand she shows the camera the picture.

I lean forward as Aero tries to focus the picture. It's a

little bit blurry but it's clear the picture is of their father in a rather compromising embrace with another man. "Holy shit. Holy shit," Delaney says, cupping her hands around her mouth.

Aero nods and smiles proudly, "He was kissing Marcy's dad! Can you believe it? After he sent you away. I don't know who to tell. I can get in trouble for being nosy, but look at this." She points to the picture, "How can they send you away when they did it too?" She shakes her head. "I wonder where they sent you. Maybe I can show them and you can come home. School starts soon. I wish you were here," she looks behind her, "I gotta go. Love you."

The video stops again and we all sit in stunned silence. Holy fuck. No wonder he was so against Nirvana's sexuality. He was ashamed of his own. Of the secret he's held on to for all these years. The camera turned back on and I expected to see the young Aero again but I was surprised when I saw her now. She smiled at the camera and I swear we all held our breath.

"Hey, Van Van. I haven't done this in a while. I think my last entry was a day before you got home. I haven't even shown you this tape before. It's been hidden under the dresser for so long. I don't even know if this works. I got this camera from Bill. He was excited about my interest in it," she laughs, smoothing out her yellow dress.

"I snuck in while you're at work. It's only ten in the morning. My appointment is in three hours. I'm a little scared if I'm being honest. I gotta tell you the truth though, after I got home I had two more seizures. I haven't felt the best but I don't want to worry you too much."

She sighs, "I just want to tell you I love you. Just in case I can't say it again. I know you'd think I'm being a drama queen but I don't think this time is the same. I feel sick a lot lately. Tired, weak. The works. But I put it up to exhaustion. Maybe not to worry as much. It's okay though. I'm fine with it. If this is my last ode to you though, I want you to know I love you more than anything. You're my best friend. I just hope for your sake it's nothing. But if it is, you have to promise me you'll be strong. You have to take your medicine on time. You have to keep going to therapy even if you hate it. I know we've always talked about not wanting the other to go first. I know you. You'll fall off that deep end."

Taking a breath she leans forward, "Don't let those thoughts win. If they do, I'm going to kick your ass. The world needs you. Your friends do. You're going to get your happy ending. Maybe you don't think so but I know you will. You have other sisters. They're great, you have your patients. They love you there. Let's face it no one goes to that dentist because of fucking Brad. He's practically a wisdom tooth with legs and gelled hair. Fucker is weird I can't believe you tried to set Delaney up with him. Well, it worked out for her though."

Aero links her fingers together, "If I do die, I want you to know that you're amazing. That your future is bright and exciting. If you ever marry, know that I'll be there with you. That I am so proud of you. And don't forget, at my funeral you have to wear a rainbow. Don't tell anyone. It'll be between me, you and Isola. You'll be my passing light to the other side. I know I don't believe in Heaven or Hell but I know I'll be free, waiting for you. But don't come so soon. Fall in love, travel, have pretty babies and tell them all about Aunt Aero. Be the rainbow you were meant to be. Not the storm cloud I know you'll become."

I stop the video and turn off the TV, not wanting to know what else is on the tape. That was for Nirvana. A parting gift from the one person she loved more than anything.

Delaney sniffs beside me, "Oh Aero." We sit for a while, none of us saying anything, just sit and process what we learned. What Aero put into place for her sister, never knowing if she'd even see this video. She knew about her father, but never said anything about it. Why?

Chapter 50

Nirvana

Tossing in the bed, I groan, pushing my thin blanket off of me and sitting up.

"Oh good. You're up, I thought I'd have to wake you up." Gasping, I turn in the bed seeing Misery standing over me with specks of red on her face. She's no longer in the gray sweats we are usually wearing but a black corset with a leather jacket and black leather pants and heeled boots. I narrowed my eyes at her.

"What the fuck? Were you watching me sleep?" I demand, pressing a hand to my pounding heart and drawing in a breath.

She arches a neat dark brow. "I'd hardly call what you were doing sleeping. Looked more like a body invasion. Or possession. Anyway, I'm done with my job. By the time I'm gone it'll be like I was let out. The perfect redeemed patient. You remember our deal. You get out."

I lean against the wall, pulling my knees to my chest.

"You make it sound as if it's easy to just go. I didn't put myself inside here."

"Don't worry. You'll be out today," she says, digs into her pocket and pulls out a small white card. "Remember, if you need something give me a call." Leaning closer she drops her voice making it a mere whisper, "But remember this is for a one time favor. So make sure it's a good one." She grabs my hand and puts the card into it, closing my fist around it.

"Thank you. For what you did for me."

She smirks. "I didn't do anything for you, Nirvy. Just gave you the kick in the ass you clearly needed. Don't do anything stupid. Go be happy with your man. You have a second chance, don't blow it." I nod slowly as Misery pulls away from me. She sends a small salute towards me then slips out the door. Closing it so silently that I didn't even hear it. If I wasn't looking directly at her I would've never known she was here. Sighing, I lean my head back staring up at the ceiling. The thought of going home was terrifying, but exhilarating at the same time. I had so much to make up for and I knew I had to do it soon. I don't know how long I sit there but soon it becomes too much. The silence is louder than it has been in weeks. Standing, I move over to the small desk in the room and pull the chair out. Grabbing a sheet of paper and a very dull short pencil I begin to write, to plan for my future because suddenly I had one. And it looked brighter than it ever has.

A knock sounds on my door jolting me from my seat and sending me toppling to the floor with a soft *hmpf.* Wincing from the impact on my side, I grasp the side of the desk and pull myself up. The process is slow and sluggish. Had I fallen asleep? I glance at the paper on the desk with a list written on it. Grabbing it, I fold it neatly, and stuff it into my pocket before going to answer the door where Nell was already raising her fist to knock again.

"Oh. Good morning! I have your medication ready and you have a visitor, so you can get ready afterwards." I grab the little cup from her and toss the pills into my mouth before accepting the water gratefully and tossing it back. Once done, I lift my tongue to show her that I actually did take the medication I needed.

Nell smiled brightly and motioned me towards the bathroom. I nod and go back into the room to grab a change of clothes and my toothbrush before gladly walking across the hall. I enter the white bathroom and quickly do my business before hopping into the shower. The water is lukewarm but settles the aching muscles from falling asleep in the stiff wooden chair. Washing quickly, I climb out so I can change and brush my teeth in record time.

Feeling a little better, I open the bathroom to see Nell still standing there waiting for me. "Sorry if I took too long," I mutter. Though I wasn't. Not really. It was like something inside of me eased a little bit. Just the thought of being out, with the people who cared about me. Maybe it was finally opening up with the group, or just the thought of being outside these walls. Who knows? Either way I had this sense of peace around me.

Nell waved me away, "It's all right, dear. I understand. It's been a month since you've been here, so I get it. You're still adjusting and it takes time." Nodding, I fall into step beside her as she leads me down the hallway. "This is our meeting room. It'll give you and your guest enough alone time." The hall is practically empty and cold. It reminds me of something, but I can't put my finger on it. As if I had been here before. I felt the same way when I first got here but chalked it up to being on medication while being transported here when I was supposed to be in the hospital.

"Thank you," I say. When I walk into the room, I stop in my tracks seeing my father standing by a mostly empty book-shelf. He turns at my voice and I curse to myself.

"It's about time you joined me. I don't like being kept waiting, Nirvana." I roll my eyes and move deeper into the room closing the door behind me.

"What do you want?" I demand, looking at him with my arms crossed over my chest.

He pulls out a chair and sits, waiting for me to join him. And knowing him he won't speak until I've taken a seat. Another power play to him.

Grinding my teeth, I sit down as far from him as possible. I clasp my hands on the table waiting for him to start. He just stares at me with his beady eyes. Waiting for me to start. But I was tired of his manipulative mind games, his god complex. If he wanted to talk then he could do so. I mean, I knew how much he loved hearing himself talk. Meeting his stare head on, I move my hands, tapping my fingers against the peeling wood. He hated when I did it, and I took pleasure in seeing that vein on his head throb. I counted the seconds until it would explode, leaving me in a false sense of content. Sadly, it never happened.

He slams his palm down wanting to startle me, but I anticipate the move and quirk my brow. "You make me wish you were never born," he grits out.

Shrugging, I lean back in the chair. "What? No stairs were available? A wire hanger perhaps?"

"How can you say such vile things?" he demands.

I laugh bitterly. "If I remember correctly, God was pro life. You could've opened that book of yours, found that little recipe and sent me right back to the sender. You two chose to have me. That's your problem."

He stands towering over me with disgust in his eyes. "You think I didn't consider that? That I knew your mother was making a mistake birthing you? God, I knew at the moment in the hospital what an evil creature you'd be. Promiscuous, reckless. Ungrateful. Yet your mother was determined to keep you."

His words stung and I felt my heart tear a little bit more, but I didn't show it. I couldn't. Where my parents were concerned I no longer felt anything but pity for them. But one thing I was tired of was him disrespecting me. I was tired of him thinking he was better than me. As if he had never sinned a day in his life.

Straightening in my seat, I tilt my head to his vacant chair. "Sit down."

He huffs, "You don't speak to your father that way, Nirvana."

"No. I wouldn't. But at eighteen you officially disowned me. So you're no father of mine. Now sit down and shut up. You've had your chance to speak, now, it's mine." He still stands and that irritates me. "Sit the fuck down!" I shout and reluctantly he does. I take a deep breath and stare at the wall over his shoulder. Looking at the peeling yellow paint. "You shamed me. Called me disgusting and sent me away." My words were hollow, detached. And my father just sat there. Not saying a thing. He just sat there stiff and stoic, not a single expression on his wrinkled face.

It angered me. To see him sitting in front of me not uttering a word while I sat in a dingy room where people saw me as insane. A danger to myself and to society. Then again, the assessment isn't that far off. I can be crazy, I can go from one mood to another quickly. But it was all thanks to the man sitting in front of me. I'd never hurt another person, it wasn't in my nature, but a person could only be pushed so far before they couldn't handle it anymore.

"Where's the money, Nirvana?"

I laugh, muttering under my breath, "The money. There is no money. She left you with none of it. You have no legal claim on it." I smirk at him, "Neither do I."

His eyes widen and he slams his hand on the table again, shaking its already rickety stature more. It made an ominous creak then settled. "You had no right! Especially someone like you."

That snapped something in me. It was almost as if I were the strings on a violin, fragile and with one pluck too strong, the string just… snaps.

"People like me? What? A person? Someone who struggles mentally from shit you did? From what you put me through?"

He sneers at me, his eyes twin blue flames. Eyes like my own, like my sister and I hated seeing them. "You're an abomination. A disgrace!" He shot up again, towering over me as I sat. It used to terrify me, but now it was just a normal part of our routine. "You go against every grievance and every moral code for what a woman should do. Do you not realize how you make me look in front of the congregation?"

Was I supposed to care? I look up, staring him in the eye. "Like the hypocrite you are?" I ask.

His nostrils flared. "You will not talk back to me. You will show me the respect I am due."

I huff out a sarcastic laugh. "Respect is earned, not given. I don't owe you shit."

His teeth snap together so hard I can hear it. "I am your father and you shall honor me as such."

Laughing, I shake my head. "Yeah, no. I'm disowned remember. I just mentioned it, but of course you weren't listening. You're nothing but a sack that I happened to be unlucky enough to be fertilized from. Nothing else qualifies you as a father. You destroyed me when you sent me away."

He shrugs. "Do you think you're the only person who's been to that little camp, Nirvana? You're not. You were sick and needed help, so I did what I had to do."

"I was not sick!" I yelled, standing up so we were now toe to toe. "I simply didn't fall into your picture perfect world. I did not want to marry a church boy, nor did I want to be a preacher's wife."

My father stood taller, glaring at me. "No, you'd rather be a used whore like your mother."

Scoffing, I tilt my head back to look him directly in the eye. "I love people. I don't care if they are women or men or non-binary. I don't care what they are as long as they love me. The real me. Not some fake stuffy version of myself."

Shaking his head in disappointment he sighs, "I sent you to that camp to find God. To pray over your sins."

"What about your sins? The ones you carry with you every day of your pathetic life? You act as if you're this godly man who would help anyone in need. But the truth is, you're a hypocrite. We both know you sent me to that camp to hide your failures. The one child who was not perfect." I take a step back, "You know, they say the more you push onto a person the more you're hiding. So tell me, Father, what are you hiding?" His face pales slightly and I know I hit the nail on the head. "You know. It would make sense if you were pushing your own narrative. Were you sent away as a child? Who was it?"

"What my life was like is none of your concern. You'll stay here as long as you need it. You can die here for all I care. It would save the world from your type of evil."

I rolled my eyes even though tears burned, threatening to flow down my face. "Get out." He doesn't move. "I said get out you ignorant fuck! I don't want you to ever come near me again or I swear to God I will report you to the police for harassment and indecency. I will bury you under that church you value more than you ever did your family. Now get the fuck out!"

"It should've been you who died. Never your sister," he sneered at me.

I laugh hysterically, "Don't you think I know that? That I rather her be here? Because I do. Not because I want you to have the perfect child, but because she was the epitome of warmth, of sunshine." I walk towards the door and open it, never taking my eyes off of my father. "Oh, that little brat your wife is carrying isn't yours. She told me herself. Now go." He still stood there. "Go!"

Sighing, he moved towards the door, but suddenly stopped. I knew why, I could feel him behind me, smell his spicy scent. I glance up and I see Ravi. Staring at my father with what looked like a murderous stare. "Shit," I mutter.

There goes any sort of peace I felt.

Chapter 51

RAVI

"Go!" I heard as I rounded the corner. It was sharp and filled with pain and it had me rushing forward just as the door opened and I saw Nirvana staring at her father. Her eyes were red as if she were trying not to cry. Nirvana tenses slightly before tilting her head back to stare up at me. Her blue eyes widened and she muttered under her breath.

"Are you okay?" I ask, not taking my gaze from her father. Everything about him made alarms go off inside of my head. Made me want to push her behind me and protect her.

Nirvana nods. "He was just leaving. Weren't you?"

Father Bridges sighs. "This conversation isn't over." He goes to walk out of the door, past the two of us, but I stop him. Bracing my arm up on the door hinge.

"It is over. Don't come near her again," I say. "I already warned you about what would happen if you came near her."

He rolls his eyes. "Please. I'm her father. I'll talk to her if I want to. She has something that belongs to me."

Moving my hand I push him back into the room until he falls on the concrete ground. I pull Nirvana in with me, slam the door closed, and lock us inside. "The money. Yes I'm aware of that. However, it doesn't belong to you or your ex-wife. Nor does it belong to Nirvana. Not anymore. Once she signed it all away it was dispersed in the way she wanted." He goes to get up but I push him back down with the toe of my shoe. "Did I say you could move?" I demand.

He shakes his head, his gaze going to his daughter as if she would help him. "No. You look at me when I'm speaking to you. Not her, me."

He grimaces. "I'll have you arrested for assault."

I shrug. "I hardly give a fuck. I wonder though… how would your wife feel when she finds out you're fucking her father?" He pales and I nod. "Yeah, I know your secret. You sent your daughter away because her father threatened to stop funding your church. To stop sleeping with you. Quite the kettle if I do say so myself." Crouching to his level, I whisper, "You'll never contact Nirvana again. Do I make myself clear?"

He nods quickly. "If you do I'll slit your throat without a moment's hesitation. If any word that was said in this room comes out I'll know it's from you. Are we understood?" He nods again. "Words, Bridges, I need the words."

Swallowing hard he says, "Yes. We're clear."

Straightening, I nod to the door, "Now get the fuck out." He scurries to his feet and rushes out the door, opening it in a rush so it hits the wall with a loud bang. There was a long silence between Nirvana and me. She stared at me before going to the door, closing it and relocking it. She leans back against it, crossing her arms over her chest. Staring at me with heated eyes.

"Well, that was interesting," she says.

I look at her. "If you're expecting me to apologize it won't happen."

Nirvana scoffs, "I had it handled. But I wouldn't make you apologize for it. In fact, it was kind of hot." Her voice turns husky and her pupils dilate.

I feel my cock twitch in my pants and my heart starts to pound. "Nirvana."

She pushes herself from the door, walking towards me, her hips swaying slightly. "It's been almost two months, Ravi. I've missed you." Stopping in front of me she runs her fingers down my chest.

Grabbing her hand with my uninjured hand I stop her movements. "Don't test me, Nirvana." Because I was well on the cusp of exploding from need.

Her mouth tilts up in a small smirk. "What?" she says innocently. "You didn't think about me at all?"

Gritting my teeth, I pull her flush against my body. "You know I fucking have. Every day I've thought about you. How you feel against me, how you sound when you're close to coming. How you feel with me inside you. I thought about you so much."

Her face flushes a light shade of pink. "Tell me, Ravi. How many times have you fantasized about me?"

Leaning down my lips brushed the shell of her ear. "Do you really want to know, pixie?" I bite down on the lobe of her ear and she moans, tilting her head back.

I can see the pulse in her neck pounding, hear the way her breathing hitched.

"I want to know. Tell me and maybe I'll tell you how many times I've pictured you between my legs since I've been here," she answers.

Wrapping my hand in her hair, I yank her head back so she was looking at me. "I want to fuck you like I hate you.

Then make love to you like I can't live without you." And I couldn't. This woman owned me. She owns my body, my mind, my heart, and my fucking soul. Tightening my hand in her hair I slam my mouth down on hers. Her arms come around my neck, holding me to her. My hands move to her ass and I heft her up so she could wrap her legs around my waist. Her taste is intoxicating, mint with that ocean breeze scent surrounding me. My tongue thrusts into her mouth and my teeth nip at her bottom lip. It's frenzied and hot, all consuming.

"I need you," she whispers against my mouth. Her hips undulated against me, rubbing her hot core against my throbbing dick. Searching for that friction that was bound to send us both careening over the edge. But I needed more. I needed her at my mercy.

Groaning in need, I lower her. "Then get on your knees. Show me how much you need me."

A small grin tilts her swollen red lips as she sinks slowly to the floor. Her hands find the button of my jeans and she pushes it slowly open, before lowering the zipper and letting my swollen erection spring free.

"So beautiful," she whispers, wrapping her hand around me, squeezing tightly. Cursing, I wrap a hand in her soft hair, watching as her tongue swirls around the swollen head, teasing me.

"Fuck," I murmur, staring at her through hooded eyes. Waiting for that glorious moment where she'd take me into her hot wet mouth. She glances up at me, her eyes meeting mine before sucking me deep into her mouth. The breath rushed out of my lungs as I watched her sliding down on me deeper and deeper until she pulled away. It was too much, but not enough. I needed to feel her body wrapped around mine, I needed to taste her need for me. I just needed. "Tighten your hand," I instruct. Her fist tightens at the base, squeezing just enough that my balls tighten. I didn't want to come in her mouth. Not now.

With a curse, I pulled her off of me and pushed her face down on the peeling table. "Ravi," she breathes out, wiggling her hips.

"I need you, Nirvana," I whisper, pressing a kiss to her throat, nipping at the sensitive skin between her shoulder and neck. Marking her as mine.

With a sobbing plea she nods, "Please. Please I need you too." Kneeling behind her I pull her sweats down her legs and push her thighs apart before taking her into my mouth. She cries out, pushing against me as I thrust my tongue into her wet pussy. "Ravi," she calls out my name, her body shuddering as I run my tongue over her swollen clit. I pressed two fingers into her, thrusting them in deep heightening her pleasure as she rocked against me.

I could feel how close she was as I pulled away. I grab my cock and line it up with her drenched entrance. Leaning down, I whisper into her ear, "You're mine, Nirvana." Then I thrust into her inch by agonizing inch before I thrust deep, sheathing myself deep inside of her.

"Yours. I'm yours," she gasps, gripping the edges of the table pushing back to meet me thrust for thrust. Heat races up my body as her body clamps down on mine, holding me in her like a tight vise. Shit. It was perfect. Grabbing her hips I push forward, fucking her hard. Taking everything she had to offer.

But that wasn't enough. I needed to see her as she exploded around me. Pulling out quickly, I flip her to her back and spread her thighs to thrust myself in again. She screams my name then, her back arching on the old table. Her hands fist in my shirt and she pulls me down to take my mouth in a burning kiss. Our tongues moved in sync with my thrusts. Reaching between our bodies I ran my thumb around her clit before pinching it, sending her falling over the edge, groaning into my mouth. Moving with a fury now, I thrust harder and faster drawing out her orgasm before mine took hold of me.

My hips jerked against her as I came, groaning her name. It was euphoric and intense. We stayed like that for a few minutes, letting our bodies calm down, just holding each other. Once my body calms I slowly pull away from her.

"Are you okay?" I ask.

Nirvana stares up at me. "Never better. I missed you."

Smiling softly, I walk towards the small tissue box on a bookshelf and pull a few free. "I missed you too, tinker hell. More than anything." I clean myself up before straightening my clothes and moving back to her to help her clean up. I glance up at her as I wipe between her legs. She didn't have such dark bruises under her eyes now and she'd gained a little more weight since I've seen her last. "How are you feeling?"

Nirvana smiles at me, running her fingers through my hair. "Better, I think. I still have to get therapy and take my medicine, but I don't think it's so bad."

Nodding, I toss the tissues in the trash and pull her pants up. "I'm proud of you, Nirvana. Really proud."

"Thank you. That means a lot to me." Pushing herself from the table she moves to the door, "I want to leave, but I don't know how to sign out or what to do. I don't remember what Misery said."

I arch a brow, "Misery?"

Waving a hand, she opens the door and sticks her head out. "Nothing. Let's go."

Before I could protest she was already walking out of the room. Shaking my head, I followed after her, a silly smile on my face.

Chapter 52

Nirvana

I peer down the hall and see it's empty and it makes me wonder where everyone is. I got so distracted by my father, then Ravi, that I didn't even realize how silent it had gotten. My heart began to race at the thought of the man behind me. I could still feel him between my legs and taste him on my tongue. Shaking those thoughts away, I focused. I had to get out of here.

"It's quiet," Ravi muttered behind me.

So it wasn't just me. We move down the hall, the only sounds are our footsteps. Well, mine. I would think I was alone if I wasn't highly aware of the man behind me. I don't know how he walks so silently, but I just chalk it up to his military background. We make it to the reception desk where Nell is sitting in front of the computer, her brow furrowed.

"Miss Bridges? I didn't think you were still here," Nell says, her eyes widening when she sees me.

"Oh. Um, I got caught up with my visitors. Why wouldn't I be here still?" I ask, hoping that Misery kept her word. That I could go home today.

"You're supposed to go home today. Stassi gave the all clear. Your room was even cleaned out. I thought you knew," the older woman says and shakes her head. "It's been such a crazy day. I'm sorry. You'll have to sign some paperwork. Hang on."

She moves away from the computer and goes to get some paperwork. Ravi and I sit there for a few minutes and it's still oddly silent. "Here we are," Nell says, handing me a packet of papers.

Thanking her, I sign the papers promising to stay in therapy and take the medications on time every single day. I have the number to a suicide hotline read to me and then put on a sticky note before Nell takes the papers. "Why is it so quiet today?" I finally ask.

Nell turns to me. "You didn't hear?" I shake my head. "An orderly was found dead this morning. Suicide."

Clearing my throat I ask, "Who, who was it?"

"Father Brent of all people. Apparently he had quite the guilty conscience," Nell says, shaking her head as she angrily files the papers. "What he did to those patients is awful. He confessed in a note. Asking for forgiveness for the ones he hurt. Can you believe it? Someone who was devoted to God and helping others only to be a monster. It's disgusting."

I stood there, stunned. He wasn't the one I expected to be killed, but then again, after he brought me here I didn't see him again. "We didn't even find out until this morning. All the patients have been relocated, staff are in a meeting waiting for answers. I thought you had left when your father did. But I guess not." She looks over my shoulder at Ravi.

"I'm her ride," he says smoothly. As if we both weren't confused until now.

I nod. "Right. Sorry, my mind is all over the place right now." It's not a total lie and Nell gives me a sympathetic look.

"The press is out there. We tried to get everyone out before it got bad. I don't know how we are going to get you out."

Ravi takes out his phone. "Don't worry, I'll handle it. Nirvana," he motions for me and I walk to him, gasping as his arm wraps around my waist. Pulling me into him. "I feel like we'll need to have a long talk when we're out of here."

"Hey, I didn't know this was going to happen," I object.

He shakes his head and says, "Not about this, but about everything. Because your name is one of the top names that's on this list of people who were hurt," Ravi said, showing me a picture of the note that Sorrow sent him. And yep, there was my name. In bright red ink, right next to Cannon's. My eyes widen and I look up at him. "I don't think this is a good way to start recovery," I mutter.

"Probably not, but there are cameras and they just found out you were still in here."

I glance at where Nell was, but she's gone. Leaving just me and Ravi here. Alone. Well shit. I figured I'd just get in and out but damn, Misery could've warned me before she went killing Father Brent. Glancing up at Ravi I ask, "What do we do?"

"Sam and Max are coming in through the back," he states.

"I thought Sam was being deployed again?" I asked with confusion. What the hell happened since I've been here?

Shaking his head, Ravi grabs my hand, leading me away from the front door. "No. It was delayed for some reason. He'll leave when he's called." I hum under my breath trying to distract myself from what was happening outside. Who knew this would happen once I defended myself from my father, then got distracted by dick? It was ironic really. Being seen as a godly man to being killed for what you really did. No wonder Misery offered to kill my father.

I declined because a part of me didn't truly believe she was here for such a reason, but now I know she was. A shiver ran through me at the thought of her being a serial killer. But I knew deep down she was only doling out the justice that many people like me and Cannon and Delaney, hell, even Misery herself never truly got. It would be hypocritical if I judged her for the very thing that I helped my friend do.

"Did you find it?" Ravi asks, drawing me from my thoughts.

I glance up and see Max and Sam walking into the dimly lit hall with Drew behind them. "It's starting to storm, but the cameras don't look like they are leaving anytime soon. This is a scandal, dating back years, that no one saw coming. A priest who has a penchant for working with the mentally ill only to abuse them. Can you imagine that headline?" Max deadpans.

Well, when it's put like that I guess anyone would want the inside scoop. It was those types of things you see in movies or TV shows, not real life.

"Can't you just call the cops?" I ask, drawing their attention.

"Cops are already out there. So is a crowd of people demanding answers from the owners. The staff is trapped in the office waiting it out. God only knows how long that'll take," Ravi says, wrapping an arm around my waist.

The lights flickered on and off briefly making my heart stutter in my chest. "Okay, so I saw a scary movie like this before and I'll be honest this is not how I want to die," I say.

The men all looked at me as if I had grown two heads. Looking at me in various expressions of amusement, and annoyance. Not that I'd expect anything less. "Can't we go out the way you came in?" I ask. Then say, "Or go out the front?"

"No. It's been blocked off. And I doubt you'd want to go into every single detail of your life in front of cameras being broadcast around the world," Drew said. He had a point, I'd rather not relive my past in front of strangers, let alone the world. So I had to think.

Sighing, I glance up at the flickering lights. This was an older building, with nooks and crannies that aren't in a lot of buildings, especially places like Texas and all the other southern states. "Basement," I mutter.

"What?" Max asks, looking up from his phone.

The lights decided to flash again, blinking rapidly before going out altogether leaving us in the dark. In a mental institution. My heart speeds up and I take a deep breath so I don't panic. "This is an older building, we can go out of that little cellar. Then make a run for it. No one knows it's there," pausing, I add, "I think."

There's a silence making the thunder off in the distance sound more ominous and terrifying. "We might not have another way," Ravi mutters.

"Fuck. All right, I'll have Caden and Spencer meet us. Just in case someone else sees," Sam says.

Grabbing my hand Ravi turns to me, "Hold onto me. We can't have you getting lost in here."

I scoff, "I won't get lost." They look at me and I can feel my face heat up slightly. "Shut up. Let's go. This place is creepy during the day. Imagine it at night."

Taking out their phones, the four men light up the halls with their flashlights, waiting for me to direct them. "I think it's past the infirmary. Off to the side should be some steps that lead into the basement." Ravi places me between him and Max matching my steps so I won't get separated from them. It's nice, in theory, but everything I've ever learned from books or movies tells me this is a dumb idea. This is where the monster comes out and you realize you're fucked, but still try to run even though it's pointless. This was that moment.

Not to mention the dark, being stuck in the dark makes me physically ill. It reminds me of being locked in that small room when I was at that camp. Especially when I didn't follow orders. I can hear the blood rush to my ears, sounding louder than ever and my breathing turns erratic. "Breathe, Nirvana," Ravi says, his hand squeezing my side tightly, showing me I wasn't alone. Right, I wasn't alone here. Not anymore. I could do this.

Breathing deeply, I nod and push forward. We walk slowly watching the walls for the 'Infirmary' sign. I don't know how long we walk until we find it. And just like I said there was the basement, only instead of it being clear there are four people standing there holding guns pointed directly at us.

The men with me pull out their own weapons and point them in response. I can't really see what the people look like because they are dressed head to toe in black. But I do see one tilt their head to the side before stepping to the side. The others follow suit, stepping away so we can leave. "Go."

The men are hesitant, but move forward. Max grabs my arm pulling me forward but stops when a gun is pointed at his chest. "Not the girl. You can leave. She stays."

My eyes widen and I'm shaking my head. "No, she's leaving. Now," Ravi says, his hold even tighter than Max's.

"Do you think we'd hurt her?" Another one asks, stepping close to Ravi and pointing their gun into his chest. "You're a lot smarter than you look. Grandma Flo seems like quite the woman, Ravi Xavier Banks. The only child to

Corrine and Denis Banks. Such a sad story to know they died because of that drunk driver." The speaker turns their head to look at Max. "Max Reid Casen you did all you could for your family, it'll be such a shame for them to bury you with your father, Reid Micheal Casen. A low income family who would be survived by a little sister and mother who is just trying to make ends meet." Tsking, one points a gun at Max's chest, pressing deeply. He doesn't make a noise but stiffens. "Such strong men. Fought for your country, held captive, betrayed by the country you fought for. Why die for one measly woman?" The other two raised their guns, pointing them at Sam and Drew.

Panic began to settle like a lead ball in my stomach. "I'll stay. I'll stay," I said in a rush when I felt the two men tense beside me. How these people knew about them was beyond me, but I didn't want them to be harmed because of me.

The leader gave a small laugh. "I thought so. Come along, pet, we've got business to discuss." A hand reaches out, grabbing my arm and pulling me forward until I'm pressed against a chest and a pistol is pointed at my temple. Ravi goes to reach for me, but the sound of the gun cocking stopped him. "Leave or I'll blow her brains out right here, right now. We all know how much she would rather be dead." They pause, staring at me, then at Ravi. "But I feel like blood red would look good on you. It's your choice, it matters very little to me." I meet Ravi's eyes, seeing the burning rage in them, the helplessness. I give a short nod and he curses. "Bye bye," the leader said, watching as the men walked down the steps leaving me in the darkness with these four people. When the door closed it was loud and obnoxious. As was my breathing. But it didn't last long because the gun was pulled away and I was free.

"Nirvy, good to see you!" I turned around shocked at the voice that was no longer muffled by the mask. Instead of the masked figure I'm now staring up at Misery. The roommate who left.

"What the fuck? I thought you left and why are you holding me at gunpoint?" I demand, rubbing at my throbbing temple, glaring at her angrily.

Misery shrugs, pushing her hair over her shoulder. "I needed to have a little chat with you as I have unfinished business here. Turns out this place has more skeletons in its closet than a gay biology teacher. But I digress."

I gape at her, wondering if she actually is a bit more unhinged than I originally thought, but I look at the other three people and know they are here for a reason. "Okay," I say slowly. "What is it?"

"Your information has been leaked to the world. Your past stay in that camp was recorded, and it was done here, only changed into something else." She waves her hand around the dark hallway. "This mental institute."

"Huh, no wonder it felt familiar," I mutter to myself. It also explained why the nightmares were so constant here, causing me to have trouble sleeping until I had no choice but to get sleeping pills. "So why are you back?" I ask.

Misery points to the others and says, "I need to know you won't rat me out when it gets too much. If you feel under pressure now you might as well tell me, so I can put you out of your misery. I can't have loose ends. I wasn't supposed to have a roommate until you showed up. So tell me now, Nirvana. Are we going to have a problem?" Her voice hardened and I knew she'd kill me without a single thought.

Shaking my head I hold my hands up. "What you do is none of my business. As far as I'm concerned I didn't have a roommate."

Misery nods in approval. "Good. Now take this," she shoves something in my hand, "and find your man and leave.

I'll give you five minutes. If you're not out of here you'll go up with this building. Understood?"

"Yes, ma'am," I said quickly.

Misery nods to the person beside me. "Open the door and lets go," she turns to me, "Five minutes."

Just like that the door is open, I'm pushed through, and they are gone. Grabbing the bannister to catch myself, I fumble with what's in my hand. I find a button and press it, turning on a light. It's a flashlight? Shaking my head I move down the stairs slowly. "Ravi?" I call, my voice shaking slightly.

"Nirvana?" His voice sounds from the bottom of the stairs making me sigh with relief. Gripping the bannister harder, I rushed down the stairs seeing him arguing with the others. He turns and I throw myself at him, wrapping my arms around his neck. "You're okay?" he demands.

"Yes. Yes, I'm fine, but we need to go." There is a distinct sound *pop pop pop*. Followed by screams. "We have to go now!" I say urgently. Ravi nods and we rush towards the back of the basement where the cellar is.

Sam speaks into his phone, "Okay, Spence, pull it now. We don't have a lot of time."

The sound of a lock breaking is overly loud followed by the brightness of the clouded light coming from outside. Drew goes out first, followed by Sam, then Max. Ravi grabs my hips and pushes me up, allowing Spencer to grab my arms and pull me out of the cellar. Then Ravi pulls himself up leaving us in the open field that I've only seen from the common area. "We've got three minutes," I say, breathing deeply as I look at the stop watch.

"How do you know?" Caden asks.

I hold up my hand where the flashlight is beeping showing the time that is slowly ticking down. "That crazy bitch," I mutter.

"They made you an accessory. So you can't tell what happened," Ravi said, cursing. He grabs it, tossing it into the basement before pushing us forward. "Tell Sorrow to book it, we need to be gone in less than two minutes now." With that he yanks my hand and runs forward. The others follow suit.

Chapter 53

RAVI

So much for a simple get in - get out mission. We were supposed to grab Nirvana, not be running for our lives as a building is getting ready to explode. Or the fact that a priest had committed suicide and confessed his sins.

That wasn't on the list for today. I didn't expect this. None of us did. Now here we were running for our lives in a storm. Cameras were still stationed in front of the building and that timer was still going down. And Nirvana was now an accessory to this shit. A van comes turning into the field sending grass and dirt flying up. Caden moved in first opening the door and we rushed inside. I push Nirvana in rougher than intended, but Drew catches her as I jump in.

"Go!" I commanded and Sorrow gunned it, sending us all flying backward just as the ground shakes. Turning, I grab Nirvana into me and cover her head as the hospital explodes in the distance. The van lurches slightly, but Sorrow has it under control and we are far enough away that we aren't in striking distance.

"Holy shit," Nirvana mutters. Her body is shaking and she's clutching a fist into my shirt. "What the fuck just happened?" she asks, speaking to herself.

"The institute exploded," Drew said, not helping at all.

Nirvana lifts her head. "Well, I was there and I saw that," she replies snarkily. "And to think they said that would've helped me, but I think it only added to the trauma."

We sat in a long silence, all of us wondering what the hell happened. What about all the people who were outside? Did they get away first? All these questions circled around my head, questions I didn't have the answers to.

After a few hours we are finally back home and I have Nirvana dressed in warm clothes as the storm rages on outside. We are all in my living room as the news plays out what happened at the institute.

"This is one of those things you never expect to happen, Larry. A coveted church turned mental institute exploded today. Following the suicide of revered priest, Father Brent. The institute was relocating patients left and right, before it was covered in flames killing the remaining health care officials," the news anchor says in a monotone voice showing coverage from the scene.

"Jesus, I didn't realize there were people still inside," Rory mutters from her spot beside Nirvana. None of us say anything about the gunshots that we heard. The ones that most likely ended their lives before the explosion did.

"It's an awful situation, Joyce. The church, in the past, had been used as a conversion camp for the youth. There was a confession in the note left by Father Brent. In the midst of same sex marriage becoming legalized this is a topic that needs to be discussed more. Not only for

those who have been subjected to this type of therapy, but to the youth who are scared to come out for this very reason.

"There are no state laws, at this time, banning the practice. Only a few select states and countries have banned it. With the progression in this world you'd think we'd have more safety laws for the LGBTQ+ community protecting them. Knowing this practice still happens today is appalling."

Nirvana sighs softly, rubbing her head. "It's not like they'll do anything. These types of camps are privately owned. Not state or government owned like some places."

"Who owns it?" I ask gently.

She shrugs, pulling her knees to her chest. "Who knows? Probably someone who has an in with the church if I had to guess. The only thing is the parents make up a loosely based treatment plan to better "cure" their wayward child."

"Christ, and in these treatment plans they…" Caden drifts off as if too afraid to ask the question.

Nirvana tilts her head to the side, her eyes firmly on the television, and answers, "Touch you? Rape you? Yeah, sometimes. They call it aversion therapy or something. Words get lost on me. The worst was the shock therapy. I still get headaches from it. Or being locked in a small room without the light on. We were often paired up with the opposite sex. Taught the ways of a woman and man relationship." She shudders. "Some treatments were terrifying. Some were ganged up on. Some were stripped in front of everyone when they didn't do as they were told. I think what was worse was seeing everything done to the others and being helpless to do anything. To help in some way."

My heart breaks for her, and I want to reach out to her, to hold her, but I don't move. "It got better though, when Cannon came. He was paired up with me. We found a way to fake it until we pulled off being "cured." It wasn't hard though. I don't think they honestly cared about helping people, it was a power they held over us. Being able to decide our fate. In there, they were our gods. Whether we liked it or not."

"How'd you trick them? From my understanding Cannon is very much still gay," Drew asked.

"We aligned our bodies just so to make it look realistic. We stayed together at all times, as if we were together. But at night we'd leave scriptures on their pillows, bloody hand-prints on the walls and mirrors. Telling them the devil was rampant in the camp. Drugged one caretaker and made it seem as if they were going to be possessed. Stupid shit like that. It's interesting what the fear of the Bible would put into people actively trying to change us through it. It's as if they never read the damn thing."

"What happened after that?" Delaney asks softly.

"A nurse jumped off the roof," she said and sighs, pressing her head to her knees. "We didn't mean for it to get that far. But we were kids, being abused for being attracted to the same gender. After that it was closed down and I came home. I had to pretend that nothing happened. Then Cannon was enrolled into the school, he knew what happened and I wasn't so alone."

We sit in silence. It was a heavy subject. I couldn't under-stand how Nirvana was feeling, the guilt she probably carried. A heavy burden that no one should have to go through life with. I had my own demons, the guys did too, as did her friends. None of us got through life with clean hands. One way or another, our hands were stained with blood whether it be ours or others. There was no getting around that. It was one thing we were bound by. Blood. It's one thing we all knew and understood well.

"Sometimes justice is best when we take it into our own hands," Delaney whispered. Nirvana shook her head, protesting. "Yes, Vana. It's not ethical in any way, but we know how the system works. We are overlooked, we are the outcasts who suffer. You should've gotten real help, not whatever that was. Instead, you were subjected to a lot of abuse. Whatever happens or happened to them was all due to their actions."

Nirvana swallows hard, and says, "I led someone to suicide. That's the worst thing a person can do."

"No, the worst thing a person can do is use, abuse, and torture someone. While I sympathize with her family, I don't sympathize with her. I hope they all rot in Hell. You've carried this guilt with you for fifteen years almost. It's time to let it go," Ophelia said, her voice soft but sterner than I've ever heard it.

Rory perked up, "I know what will cheer you up." With a wicked grin she pulled her phone out and dialed a number. "Rio! I need a favor." She glances at Nirvana and says something in Spanish before grinning wider. "Perfect. I'll need a lot. Yes. I owe you," she listens again, "I suck at math. No, no. Ophelia will totally do it. Great. Thanks!" With that she hangs up.

"Ophelia will do what?" Ophelia asks.

Rory stands, pulling Nirvana up with her, "Rio has some advanced calculus homework he needs help on."

"He does know that I never did it right?"

Rory shrugs, "He said he needs it done, not that it has to be right." With a slightly evil laugh she rushes forward, "Let's go!"

Chapter 54

Nirvana

Rory sits behind the wheel of her car as we pull up to my childhood home, where her three brothers are standing and arguing about something. I glance at her. "What are we doing?"

She sighs, turning sad hazel eyes on me. "Your hatred for life and for yourself started right here. You need to cleanse it. You need to get these memories out of your head and embrace life with a new light. You need to tear it down and build it up again, *amar*."

I stare at her as she climbs out of her car and moves towards my side, opening the door for me. "We tear it down, tonight." I step out of the car and stare at the burnt house. There was only a little damage compared to what I was hoping for, and maybe Rory was right, this is what I need. The others park and come up beside me. I see Ravi and he gives me a slight nod, I take a deep breath and walk up to the three brothers.

"Nirvana, good to see you," Rio says, smiling down at me.

I smile back. "Good to see you, too, little brother. I heard you're struggling in math."

He sighs dramatically, "It's the devil's work, honestly." His other brothers Nico and Marco nod their hellos before handing me a sledge hammer.

"Where do you want to start, Vana?" Layla asks, staring up at the house.

Wrapping my hand around the hammer Rio gave me, I motioned towards the house, "Main bedroom."

Layla nods and takes her own hammer. "All right, but if it gets too much you drop your hammer. Okay?"

A small smirk tilts my mouth, "Of course. I won't hit anyone. I promise."

"Should we cover our balls?" Rio asks, covering his dick. Rory smacks him in the head, grabbing a crowbar and slinging it over her shoulder.

"Watch your fucking mouth. Or I'll tell Mom what you're doing to the neighbor's daughter while she's supposed to be at college."

Rio pales. "You wouldn't."

Rory shrugs, "Guess we'll find out."

"You're *un demonio*," Rio hisses. Rory just smiles and skips inside.

Shaking my head, I walk in after her. "The neighbor's daughter?" I whisper.

"Yeah, they've been hooking up since graduation. I caught them once. You know how her mother is with education." She shoulders her way into the room and scrunches her nose, "It smells like moth balls and soap. I hate it."

"Me too," I mutter. "I might scream. A lot."

"Screaming makes it more fun," Seraphina says.

"Just us?" I questioned.

Delaney nods. "Nothing scares men more than feminine rage."

I look at my friends, my family, tears burning in my eyes. "I'm sorry. For what I did. I shouldn't have done it and I'm really sorry."

Ophelia steps forward dropping her hammer. "Don't, don't apologize. Your feelings are valid and we should've realized you were struggling. After this we'll talk more and find out ways to help you. Okay?"

Nodding, I give them a watery smile. "I love you guys."

Layla smiles and says, "Let's tear this place down."

I give my own smile and step back gripping the hammer, hitching it back, and sending it flying into the wall. The room was already trashed from the last time I was here, but this is different. This is freeing. Watching as the sheetrock and wood splinter around me, it was like my worries, my sorrows, my grief were leaving my body. I scream loudly letting that anger and dread out.

My friends were there with me. Letting out the burdens of their own lives. The trials that we went through, that we will continue to go through are all coming out in this one moment as we tear down the walls of my own personal Hell. Taking away that pain.

I no longer heard my screams and cries as I was ruthlessly dragged out from under my bed in the middle of the night. I no longer hear my father yelling at my mother for my behavior. I was free. Finally, I could breathe. Almost simultaneously we drop our tools, breathing heavily. Glancing at my sisters I see they are also breathing as deeply as I am, covered in a fine sheen of dust, sheetrock, and wood.

"I've never been this glad to be in this house than I am right now," I say.

Laughing, Layla moves towards me wrapping her arms

around my waist. "Destroying shit is always Rory's go to and she always feels better."

Rory shrugs. "Come to a rage room one day and I bet you'd feel even better."

"I'm sure we will. We should try it one day. But now, I'm just tired. Emotionally and physically. I'm pretty sure that hammer weighs more than a horse," I say. We leave the gutted room, all our arms wrapped around each other. If there's one thing I can count on, it's these women always having my back. When I step outside, however, my gaze finds Ravi. My Ravi. He's leaning against his car talking to Caden and Drew, but, as if he feels my gaze on him, he glances up. His gaze travels up and down my body before arching a brow. I nod, and he motions towards his car with a tilt of his head.

"I'm going to go. I have things to do. I'll call you tomorrow," I say.

Following my gaze my friends smirk at me. "So this thing with Ravi?" Sera hedges.

"I love him," is all I say as I rush forward and into his arms.

He catches me to him. "Are you feeling better?" he asks, against my neck.

"Much. Apparently screaming and destroying things is a miracle medicine." He glances down at me and pushes my hair out of my face with his uninjured hand.

"Ready to go home?" I nod, liking the sound of that. Home. With Ravi.

———

Leaning back in the bed I sigh in content. "I missed you so much."

Ravi laughs softly, running his hand over my waist. "I missed you too, pixie. So fucking much."

My eyes went to his and my breathing turned labored. "You kept me going. Even though at first I felt a little angry that you saved me."

"I know you were angry. I'd say I'm sorry, but it would be a lie. I don't regret saving you. You're part of my life. Thoroughly entrapped inside my soul, Nirvana. I don't think you'll ever be out of it."

Turning onto my stomach I drape myself over him. "I want to take you on a date," I say randomly.

His eyes sparkle with amusement as he stares at me, "Oh yeah?"

"Of course. Tomorrow night. I'll even pick you up."

"I've got to get my cast off and speak to my boss. So you'd have to pick me up at the station. Say four?"

Leaning up, I press a kiss to his lips. "Four it is. I have to meet with Cannon in the morning and before you ask, there will be no drinking. I can't with my new medicine."

He hums under his breath, threading his fingers through my hair, massaging my scalp. I sigh softly, closing my eyes, relishing his touch. The comforting feeling of him lulled me into a peaceful sleep free of nightmares and worry.

Chapter 55

RAVI

A warm body is wrapped around me as I wake up. Looking down I see the top of Nirvana's blonde head nestled on top of my chest. Letting out a soft breath, she turns her head and blinks up at me, a small smile tilting her mouth.

"Good morning," she mutters, snuggling closer.

Smiling back, I kiss her head. "Morning."

She turns to stare at the clock before turning back to me, asking, "What time is your appointment?"

"Ten thirty. I have a little time." Humming under her breath she stretches her arms over her head, smiling at me.

"Want to take a shower with me?" She wags her eyebrows, making me laugh. Standing from the bed, I grab Nirvana and toss her over my shoulder, and make my way to the bathroom. Laughing, Nirvana swats at my back before I set her on her feet and turn on the shower letting it heat up. The sink turns on and I watch as Nirvana takes her medicine and brushes her teeth holding out my toothbrush to me. We sort of fell into it naturally as if we've been doing this our entire lives.

It was normal. Comforting. Once done, I stripped her clothes off and pulled her into the shower where I proceeded to kiss down her body, worshiping every inch of her. I was late for my appointment.

"You're late," Drew says as I walk into the exam room.

Apologizing, I sat on the table. "I got distracted." Drew scoffs and puts out the brace and different instruments for my hand.

"You're lucky I could squeeze you in at short notice. Even though I told you to make an appointment with your surgeon multiple times," he scolded.

Tsking, I pick up a gauze pad. "I had a little glass in my hand. Nothing major."

"You could've cut a finger off. Hit a nerve. Severed your hand," Drew lists the things that could have happened, while pulling on his gloves. I wince. I know it could've been worse. I was more worried, frankly, about infection from the dirty glass, but everything was up to par. Leaving me with scars and some mild pain.

"I know. It's fine, though."

He snorts, grabbing the scissors and cuts off the cast. Leaning over, I grab the antibiotic cream and lather it onto the healing scars. "How are things at home?" he asks.

I glance up at him. "Good. Gran loves Nirvana. And she loves Gran. It's still new, so we are navigating together but it's almost natural."

He nods, wraps the gauze around my hand and puts the brace on, then says, "Flex your fingers." Doing as I'm told I flex them a bit, wincing as the skin pulls slightly, but it's not too bad.

"Good. You can probably do menial work at the station. I don't suggest going into fires anytime soon. You'd be a liability."

Standing, I head to the door only to stop before I could open it. "Have you thought about therapy?" I ask.

Drew stares at me. "Therapy? I'm not Sorrow, Ravi. I'm quite capable of keeping any and all types of emotions in check without issue."

Leaning back, I meet his stare. "You don't see the problem with that?"

He shrugs. "Not for me. I've been doing this since before I enlisted. My emotions are different from yours and the others. I don't feel the same way as normal people."

I study him. I've known him all my adult life and I don't truly remember him conveying any type of emotion except for guilt for Nirvana's situation. Other than that he is aloof and controlled. Robotic. "What happened in your life, Drew?" I ask softly.

He turns away and sighs. "Nothing. I'm fine, just tired. There's been a lot going on lately."

I don't move right away, watching him, waiting to see if he has any of the behaviors that Nirvana had been exhibiting.

"Ravi, I'm good. I'm not offing myself any time soon," he says and sighs loudly.

I nod, conceding. "If you need anything you know we're here, right?"

"I know. Thanks. Now, get out. I've got real patients to see."

Snorting, I open the door and leave the room. But a heavy weight settles on me. I need to talk to the others about Drew, just in case he was heading in the same direction as

Nirvana. But it didn't feel the same as her. This felt different, darker. Almost dangerous. I made my way down the hall, stopping when a woman stepped in my way.

"You're Nirvana's boyfriend," the woman says.

I barely spare her a glance as I try to push past her, but she grabs my arm stopping me. "What Marcy?" I sigh.

Her brown eyes widened. "So you know who I am?"

I nod. "Yes, you're the little bitch who got her sent away to that camp. Then married her father. It's kind of hard to miss when you're showing up here to support your husband and his dying daughter." My gaze roams over her and I notice she's no longer noticeably pregnant. "So you had your baby, I see."

Marcy nods, pushing her dark hair behind her ears. "A few weeks ago." Pointing to the waiting area, she asks, "Can we sit? Please?"

I arch a brow. "I'd rather stand. What do you want?"

Marcy huffs, but nods. "I want to see Nirvana. To explain."

Laughing, I turn, and make my way to the door.

"Please! I just need to tell her what really happened. She owes me that much."

My shoulders stiffen as I round on her. "Nirvana doesn't owe you shit. She never fucking has. I don't care what sort of explanation you think you need to give her, but I couldn't give one single shit about it. You're a manipulative, whiny, and toxic bitch. I won't have you messing up her recovery to appease whatever childhood guilt you harbor for her. Get over it."

Finally done with this conversation, I step out of the hospital. But does that work? No, she follows. "It might help to know the real reason she was sent there. To that camp. If I were you, I'd ask her mother. Maybe you can learn the truth behind all of this and why Martin is actually after that money."

I make my way to my car, my mind whirling with a hundred questions. Everything was getting so turned around making it more and more complicated. Shaking my head, I pull away from the parking lot and make my way to the station.

Chapter 56

Nirvana

Climbing out of my Jeep I head up the stairs to Cannon and Mark's small townhouse. I haven't been here in a while. The trim of the house is now a soft green and the brick has been repainted a coal black, contrasting with the pastel trimmings around the house. The flowerbeds were neat and held a variety of flowers giving the house a homey feeling. I haven't seen Cannon since the news broke about our stay at the camp and a part of me was nervous to see him again.

What if he hated me for it? Would he see it as my fault since I was sent back? The sound of the door opening drew me away from the melancholy thoughts and I glanced up staring at Cannon. His head is now freshly shaved again showing off his tattoo of a demon skull sitting at the top of his cranium. How he did that, I don't know. It hurts just to look at it.

"I know I'm sexy, but you don't have to stare," he teases,

his lips twitching. "I'd be happy to model a few pictures for you."

Expelling my breath I smile. "You know what they say, a picture is worth a thousand words and you're a whole book."

Cannon laughs easily, opening his arms. Without hesitation I move towards him, wrapping my arms around his sturdy build. "I'm so sorry, Can," I say softly.

His arms tighten around me, holding me as close as he possibly can. "Shh. Don't do that. Don't take the blame for something you had no control over."

Pulling away, I sniff and say, "Your secrets shouldn't be shared with the world like this."

He snorts, lifting one dark brow. "And yours should?"

I shrug. It was better than him. He was the kindest, purest soul I'd ever met aside from my sister. He didn't deserve to have the most traumatic event he'd ever lived through broadcast all over the television because of an apparent suicide. It wasn't fair to him or the family he was building.

Taking my hand in his, he pulls me inside. "How's Mark? This can't be easy on him."

Cannon shrugs, pushing me gently into his soft recliner. "He's as can be expected. It put our adoption process on hold though," he says sadly.

"Oh Cannon, I'm sorry." He shrugs, giving me a small smile. Trying to show he wasn't hurting when we both know he is. It's bad enough that adopting as a same sex couple is difficult, but for this to be added on top of it made it worse.

Standing, I start to pace. Trying to find a way to center my thoughts. "This isn't fair. Why do we have to suffer for the choices others made for us? Why weren't we protected like other kids?"

Cannon leans back in his chair, rocking back and forth watching me with his dark eyes. "Because no one likes different, Vana. You know that. Especially here. We just got the right to marry, the world isn't going to become progressive overnight nor are we going to be treated as equals with a hetero person."

I wave my hand, dismissing his notion. "We could if we did something about it."

"Such as?" he questions.

Smiling widely I sat on the glass coffee table in front of him. "What if we made our own sanctuary. A safe home for kids who are part of the LGBTQ+ community. A safe place where they can do therapy, learn self defense. Learn how to sustain themselves in a world that hates them. Where they are no longer prey but equals."

Cannon leans forward his eyes bright with excitement, "Shit, Van. That sounds awesome. What about everything going on with you and your inheritance?"

"I have money saved up. I can talk to the others, see if they'd want to help. Maybe buy a little space and make this safe haven and bring these people into a space where they can safely be themselves. Free of judgment, of ridicule."

Cannon smiles at me, "Are we doing this?"

I nod, ideas churning in my mind, "We're doing this."

After leaving Cannon's house I head back to Ravi's and quickly dress in a light blue dress and grab a blanket and a small cooler before packing what I got for the date. Nodding to myself, I make my way out the house and set my things in the back of the Jeep, before climbing into the driver's seat. After the storm last night the sun is high leaving it hot and humid. Rolling down the windows I speed away. There's something about driving with the windows down and the wind in your hair. It's freeing. I smile to myself feeling... happy.

I turn off the intersection to the fire station and my heart does a slow summersault as my stomach tightens with nerves. Pulling up outside the station I slowly climb out of my seat to make my way to the front of the station. Nervously I wipe my hands on my skirt, trying to wipe away the sweat. Shit. Who would've known that dating was this nerve wracking?

I sure as hell didn't. But I wanted this and I was going to see it through. Squaring my shoulders, I walk inside. Maneuvering myself through the trucks I hear voices. Stopping in my tracks I listen.

"I heard she tried to burn the house down while she was still in it. Heard Banks saved her," one man said.

Another snorts. "He's a better man than me. I would've left her there."

"That's why you're single. You only care about yourself," someone replies.

He answers with a scoff, "Please. Banks hasn't stayed with a woman longer than two weeks."

There's a silence, as if they were all nodding in agreement, before the first voice states, "But I heard she's crazy. You know crazy pussy is the best pussy."

Nausea roils in my stomach as I turn away. Fuck what they thought. They didn't know me. Nor what happened. I go to walk away, but stop when another voice pipes up, "She does have good pussy. Little bitch is a freak too. Likes being choked, and bitten." The voice lowers, "She likes two at once. Me and my roommate took turns on her."

Chills slid down my spine at that voice. I know that voice. Why do I know that voice?

The men laughed. "She seems like the type. Did you hear she tried to seduce her step mother? Bitch is practically in heat 24/7. I just hope Banks is careful and wraps it up before his dick falls off." Heat rushes to my cheeks. Mortified, I turn away running into a solid chest. Gazing up I tense, meeting Drew's dark gaze.

"Drew, what are you doing here?" Ravi says, walking out of an office, Caden and Brooks close behind him.

"Dropped your wallet. Brought it back to you," Drew says, his voice cold. He doesn't even attempt to move. He tosses Ravi his wallet and I watch as he puts it in his pocket, but Drew still doesn't move. He just stands in front of me. Staring at the now silent men who caught on to the fact they were no longer alone.

Ravi steps closer and sees me, his gaze going over me quickly before stopping on my face. "Nirvana, you're early," he turns to Brooks before gazing back at me. "It'll only take a few more minutes if you'd like to wait."

I start to answer, but Drew cuts me off, "I don't think that's a good idea, Ravi."

Shaking my head, I step past him, stopping when Drew grabs my arm. His touch isn't rough, nor does it hurt. In fact, it was gentle, but I knew I wouldn't be able to break away unless he let me.

"Drew, what the hell is going on?" Ravi demands, stepping closer to me, grabbing my other arm. Drew moves his gaze from the men and looks at Ravi.

"I think your crew can explain better. You choose Ravi, correct?" He doesn't look at me when he speaks, but I nod. Without hesitation. "Which one?" he says. My heart plummets.

"Drew, it's fine," I say.

"Answer the question, Nirvana. Which. One?" Drew asks. He doesn't raise his voice, no, he's scarily calm. I gaze at Ravi, but his eyes were no longer warm, they were just as cold as Drew's, if not more so. Yeah, whoever said dating was fun was full of shit. This was the last thing I'd want.

Chapter 57

RAVI

Seeing Nirvana in front of me in a blue dress had my heart racing, but seeing her watery eyes and crestfallen face accompanied by Drew's stone-cold eyes made all the alarms go off in my head.

I didn't really know what was going on, but the way Drew was acting and the pale ghost-like look on Nirvana's face was all I needed to know. Whistling loudly, Caden called the other crew members to us. Nirvana flinched at the loud noise. Brushing my thumb over her wrist I try soothing her. Not that it helped. The men moved in slowly, none of them meeting my eyes nor looking at Nirvana.

"Answer the question, pixie," I say, looking forward.

She shakes her head, staring at me with wide eyes, and says, "It's okay. I think we should go."

A snort from the men draws my attention. "Something funny, Wilcox?" I demand.

The man shakes his head, but I can see a smirk playing on his face, smug. Mocking. "Not a thing, sir," he responds.

Letting go of Nirvana's hand, I move forward, looking at the men in front of me. Men I've worked beside. Trusted at my back. "Logans," I said and turned to the newer member of the crew, a small kid who was just learning the ropes. He was smaller than most of us, wearing wire rimmed glasses and a crew cut, but he'd showed loyalty thus far. "What joke seems to be stuck in Wilcox's head?"

Logans swallows hard, looking toward Wilcox, to me, to the small group behind me. "Now, Logans."

"Brooks, you're not going to let him talk to us like this are you? He hasn't worked in weeks," Wilcox states.

Brooks shrugs, "I'm quite curious about what's so funny myself. I like a good laugh every now and then."

Never taking my gaze off of Wilcox, I ask again, "This is your last chance, Logans. The joke. Now."

Logans turns red, clears his throat and pushes his glasses up on top of his nose. "They were, umm, laughing about," he clears his throat, turning even redder if that was at all possible. "They were talking about how Wilcox and his roommate took turns on..." He tilts his head towards Nirvana, "On your girlfriend."

I hum under my breath, staring Wilcox up and down. "I fail to see how that's a funny joke."

Wilcox shrugs, looking proud of himself. "What can I say? I'm sorry you found out this way. Can't help it if shes—"

Raising my hand I silence him, turning to Nirvana. "Which one, Nirvana? I expect an answer this time."

Nirvana lifts her gaze to me before moving it to Wilcox. Clearing her throat, she nods and says, "It was Blake."

Nodding, I turn back to the crew and say, "Dismissed." They turn to leave and I say, "Not you, Wilcox. Stay a minute." The man visibly pales and shakes his head. "Brooks, I need a moment alone. Now, please."

Brooks hesitates briefly. "Ravi, I don't think that's a good idea."

"He tried to force himself onto my woman. Busted her lip and left his handprint around her throat. I don't really give a fuck if it's a good idea or not."

Brooks doesn't respond right away, then sighs. "Don't kill him."

"No promises."

Shaking his head, Brooks walks past us giving Wilcox a disgusted look. "Disgusting."

Wilcox gapes at him. "You're going to believe a whore over me? Are you fucking serious?"

Without thinking I grab his throat slamming him against the truck, squeezing his throat tightly. "I saw the marks, Drew saw the marks, Caden saw the fucking marks you left on her when she told you no. Saw you limping too. She told me she busted your balls." His face turns red the harder I squeeze. "Then you sit here and lie to my goddamn face and expect me not to do anything about it?"

He's gasping for breath now as my hold gets tighter. Disgusted with him I toss him to the floor. Coughing, he grabs his throat, rolling to his side. Lifting my foot I kick him in the stomach, sending him flailing to his back wheezing for breath.

"One thing about me, Wilcox, I don't take too kindly to abusers." Crouching low I stare into his eyes, watching them widen in fear. "But you abused someone I care about. Someone very dear to a lot of people, then brag about said abuse to other men."

"Sorry," he groans.

Shaking my head I point towards Nirvana. "Don't tell me. You didn't touch me. You touched her."

"Sorry. I'm sorry," he says.

My eyes connect with Nirvana's. "Do you forgive him, pixie?"

Swallowing hard she shakes her head. "No. No, I don't."

Tsking I tap his cheek hard and say, "There you have it." Grabbing his hair, I yank his head back and I stare into his eyes. "What you did you receive tenfold. Caden, pliers." Caden moves forward and hands me a pair of pliers from the truck. Wilcox struggles against my hold but Drew steps forward and grabs his head, forcing it still as I grab his chin and place the pliers on his mouth. He's sobbing now, but I don't care. I can only see Nirvana's swollen mouth. The haunted look in her eyes. Without much thought I cut down, splitting his bottom lip. He screams as it breaks through his skin and I pull away, wiping the blood on his shirt. Grabbing the bottom of his shirt I rip part of it off and stuff it into his bloodied mouth. Muffling the screams.

"Hush now. None of that is necessary," I say. "We're almost done." A part of me wants to punish him more. To take any threat away from Nirvana. It's not an emotion I'm used to and I'm letting it control me. The pent up rage that's been simmering in my stomach for weeks. So without giving it much thought I grab his right hand and bend it back. Watching emotionlessly as the bones snapped, breaking at his wrist leaving it at an odd angle. He screams, jerking in my hold but I barely move, focusing on my task. Once I'm satisfied, I drop his arm and say, "Now you will think twice before you touch someone without their consent, won't you, Wilcox?"

Whimpering, he nods, his face red and sweaty, mixing with the blood and tears soaking his cheeks.

"Good. Get the fuck out of here. If I see you again, I won't be as gentle." Standing, I don't look at the other men, I just grab Nirvana and pull her out of the station, stepping on Wilcox's broken hand as I pass.

She doesn't say anything as I shove her into the Jeep's passenger seat and I go to the driver's side and climb in. The keys are still in the ignition, I turn them and pull away from the station. The drive home is silent and I have to force myself not to look at her. To see the horror that would be there. Pulling up to the house, I climb out and walk to the door, aware of Nirvana following me.

"So, that was something," she says. "Not really the date I had in mind."

I don't say anything as I walk to the sink and wash my hands, careful of the new brace.

"You're not going to say anything?" she demands.

I don't respond as I flick the water off my hands before drying them, and walk past her towards my room. Ignoring her. Which she doesn't like. At all. She follows after me and slams the door closed. Her cheeks are red from anger and she's glaring at me. Such a beautiful sight, but I can't help the shame running through me. If I'm willing to harm a man like that in front of her, what else am I willing to do? Would she grow to hate me? Fear me? I don't think I could handle seeing that look on her face.

Chapter 58

Nirvana

Gaping at Ravi as he walks past me I feel anger rise in me. How the hell can he do what he just did and then ignore me? Fuming, I follow after him. "What the fuck, Ravi?"

He doesn't turn to me, but says, "Not now, Nirvana."

Slamming the door closed, I lock it and glare at him. "Yes, now. How can you do something like that then completely ignore me?"

"That's the problem! I shouldn't have done it! Fuck, I'm not like this. But you—" He shakes his head.

"Me? I didn't tell you to go crazy on the bastard." Not that I minded. A sick twisted part of me was a little aroused by it. By the power he held over the man who hurt me. The same way it did when he confronted my father. It was intoxicating, seeing someone you love be in your corner no matter what. Granted, I didn't know he'd do to him what was done to me.

Ravi turns on me, his breathing labored and says, "I

would've killed him, Nirvana. Without a second thought, I would've done it. All because of what he did to you."

"Ravi," I start but he cuts me off.

"That's the problem, I would kill anyone who ever hurts you. That's the problem. I'm not this man, but you bring out things inside of me. This primal need to protect you, to claim you. That very first time, when I saw you trying to fix that shower I wanted to find out who did that to you and make them suffer. What does that say about me?"

"That you have caveman tendencies?" I shrug.

He curses, "I'm being serious, Nirvana."

I walk up to him, pressing my palm to his rapidly pounding heart. "I'm being serious, Ravi. There's nothing wrong with you. Do you think you're the only person who feels that? My god, when we were in that institute and that gun was pressed to your chest I would've done anything to get you away from there. Anything." At the time I didn't realize it, this need in me. Wanting to protect him.

"Nirvana, I tortured a fucking man in front of you."

I nod. "Yes. After he basically called me a whore and someone who sleeps around with him and his roommate. I won't sugar coat my past or my sexual experiences, but I've never been with that man a day in my life."

Ravi shakes his head and steps away from me. "No. No, you deserve someone safer."

Frustrated I throw my hands in the air. "Fuck you. Don't tell me what I need. I've been out of the institute for two fucking days. You were telling me you loved me and needed me and now I need someone safer? What, are you leaving now because you beat up a would be rapist? Did you even love me?"

Ravi turns on me then, his hand coming out to grab my throat. "I said you deserve someone safer, not that you'd get it. And make no mistake, I'd never lie about loving you nor do I regret what I did. I don't want you to see me in that light, being scared of me."

Rolling my eyes I move closer. "Are you scared you'd hurt me? Scared I'll judge you?" He doesn't respond, just holds my throat, running his thumb over my pulse point. Back and forth, back and forth. "It turned me on, Ravi," I whisper, watching his eyes dilate and heat with desire.

He tilts my face up with his thumb, staring at me intently. "You are infuriating."

A grin tilts my mouth. "You love it."

Shaking his head he mutters, "So fucking much." Before I can respond his mouth is on mine. Without preamble his tongue thrust into my mouth, demanding submission. I grabbed at him, my hands clawing at his back holding him to me. He walks us backwards until I'm pressed against the cool wood of the dresser. His hands went to my hips and he lifted, placing me on top of the dresser never once taking his lips from mine.

Pleasure burned through me making my thighs tremble with need. His hand went to the skirt of my dress, slowly pushing it up. Breaking away from his mouth I took a breath, watching as his hand moved under the light blue skirt. Fire streaked between my legs, a throbbing ache that had me spreading for him. Begging for his touch.

His fingers moved higher, tracing the damp lace between my legs. Drawing out my need. A whimper escaped of its own accord. "Please, Ravi," I gasp. Leaning down he presses his lips against my thighs, nipping at them gently. Without warning he grips my hips and walks me back to the bed, tossing me onto the soft mattress. My legs splay open, an invitation. Ravi sheds his shirt and moves onto the bed, his hands going to my thighs, forcing them open.

"Push your panties to the side, pixie. Hold yourself open for me." Fire races up my spine as I slowly lift my dress and reach between my thighs. With shaky fingers I push the fabric to the side opening myself to him. He groans low in his throat before bending his head. Tasting me. A small cry escapes my lips as I arch up, meeting his tongue as it strokes me.

His tongue laved my clit, brushing over the tip of my finger just slightly before going lower, thrusting into me. I'm panting now, burning up from the inside out. My thighs tremble and my back bows as he licks and bites at me. The small bites of pain mixing with the pleasure is almost too much for me. Then his fingers are there, thrusting inside hard and fast. I can hear how wet I am with every flick of his wrist, with the way he hooks his fingers inside of me reaching that spot that has me screaming his name. The release is sudden and strong, washing over me like a tidal wave.

Ravi moves then, wedging his hips between my legs keeping me open for him to use as he sees fit. Unbuttoning his pants he pushes them down slightly allowing his cock to spring free before thrusting home. We groan in unison, the pleasure taking hold of us.

"Fuck, Nirvana," he breathes out, thrusting hard and fast, sending the headboard banging into the wall in a rhythmic beat. His hand goes to my throat, holding me down as he pounds into me, cutting off my air supply. Heat shoots through my body as my orgasm approaches. It started off slow, almost like a fire. One spark. But when Ravi circled his hips pressing down on my clit and tightened his hold on my throat it was over. It rushed me hard and fast. Then his hand was gone and I was screaming his name, tears leaking from my eyes. In the distance I hear his guttural groan and feel him pulsing inside of me, but I no longer know my own name. I've never felt anything as intense as this. So all consuming and earth shattering.

After what felt like hours my body stops spazzing and I'm

a boneless heap on the bed with Ravi kneeling between my legs wiping a warm rag over my sensitive skin.

"Are you okay?" he asks, but there was no denying the smirk I heard in his tone.

Peeking one eye open I glance at him. "Don't look so smug," I mutter. He laughs softly, standing from the bed to toss the rag before coming back to me, pulling me against his chest.

"I'm never smug, tinker hell."

Snorting, I cuddle closer to him, not caring about the soaked sheets. That was a problem for when I could stand without tipping over. "You're so smug. I see it in your eyes."

Humming under his breath he presses a kiss to my damp hair. "Kind of hard to see when your eyes are closed."

"I'm using my spirit's eye," I reply sleepily. He laughs but doesn't say anything, content to just hold me. It was nice. "Ravi?" I whisper after a few minutes.

"Hmm?"

Sitting up slightly I glance down at him. "Can I tell you something?"

He blinks up at me and nods. Biting my lip nervously I say, "You're my first kiss." Arching a brow he stares at me waiting for me to explain. "What I mean is you're the first kiss I wanted. That wasn't taken from me." A slow smile graced his mouth and he grabbed the nape of my neck pulling me down to press a sweet kiss against my mouth.

"I love you so much, Nirvana. So fucking much," he said, peppering my mouth with gentle brushes of his lips.

Smiling against him I whisper, "I love you, too, Ravi. More than I thought possible."

"I don't know if I should be offended or not."

Tsking, I push at his chest. "Nope. It's an honor to have my love. It's very rare."

He sits up pulling me into his chest. "You looked very beautiful today. I'm sorry our date didn't happen."

Jerking, I sit up fast, accidentally hitting my head on his chin. Cursing I rub at the sore spot. "I left the bag in the car. I wonder if the cooler left everything intact."

Ravi rubs his chin glaring at me. "It's well over ninety degrees outside, Nirvana."

"Shit, shit. I can't have it out in my Jeep then." Standing I smooth out my dress, grimacing at the stickiness I felt on my thighs. "This is your fault," I accuse pointing at Ravi.

"How is it my fault?" he asks, clasping his hands behind his head.

Groaning, I flipped him off. "You and your dick distracted me." With that I turn on my heel and leave the room and I'm pretty sure I hear him say, "Good job, buddy," but that could just be wishful thinking on my part. Smiling to myself, I leave the house to get what was left of the picnic hoping to God it wasn't messing up my car.

Chapter 59

Nirvana

Tapping my pen against the table, I grimace. After last night's failed date that ended in hot sex I figured it was time for me to get my life semi-together. It's only been a few days since I've been home and I wasn't altogether sure what I should do. Brad had already replaced me, not that I blame him. I was out of work for two months, and even before that I was out for months at a time taking care of Aero.

A pang moves through my chest when I think of my sister. Nope, not going there. So now I was sitting at the table in Ravi's house staring at a notebook with one word on the page. *Ideas.* That's it. Nothing more, nothing less. It sounded so good when I talked to Cannon about it, but now I'm just empty. Not a single thought is going on in my head, yet my mind is racing. The sound of a door closing drew me from my thoughts.

Glancing up I stare at Flo as she shuffles inside. "Good morning, dear," she says to me.

I smile. "Good morning, Mrs. Banks."

She clicks her tongue waving her hand. "None of the formality. Call me Flo or Gran. Whichever you prefer." She trots to the coffee maker and presses a button, "How do you feel? Sore throat? Body aches?"

My head snaps in her direction and a blush steals up my face. "Umm, sorry."

Flo laughs, pushing her fading green hair from her face. "It's okay. I was young once too. But, for future reference, soundproof walls only work when a door is fully closed after you come back inside." Mortified, I choked, unsure of what to say.

And that's the exact moment Ravi chooses to walk into the kitchen, yawning. "Morning." His voice is deeper from sleep, making me remember yesterday all the more.

"Morning," I squeak out, looking down at the notebook.

Flo laughs then and says, "To be young again." Shaking her head, she took her mug and sat at the table.

Ravi passes me and picks up my mug and refills it with coffee, doctoring it the way I like before setting it beside me and pressing a kiss to my head. The action makes me melt a little and I smile at him, feeling at peace.

"What are you working on?" Flo asks.

I glance at the blank paper and sigh, "It's a silly idea I had."

Flo shakes her head. "No idea is silly, Vana. Well, except ones that involve singing."

Ravi groans in exasperation before sitting next to me. "Will you ever let me live that down, Gran?"

Smiling, Flo sips her coffee and says, "Nope."

Shaking his head, Ravi turns to me and asks, "What's your idea?" As if it's second nature I scootch back in my chair, lift my legs and put them in his lap. Automatically his hand covers them, rubbing at my sore calves.

"Yesterday I went to Cannon, to check on him and we had this idea. It's not set in stone but I wanted to find out about opening up a sanctuary of sorts for kids and young adults who are part of the LGBTQ+ community. Like a safe house where we can teach them how to function and teach them life skills they weren't taught at home. Like self defense, navigating with the working world and discrimination because of their sexualities. Teach them to be safe in a world that can, at times, make life more difficult." I'm rambling, I know I am but a beat of excitement rushes through me.

Ravi stares at me for a moment, a small smile on his lips. "I think that's a great idea. Could help a lot of people."

I smile. "Really?"

He nods. "Really. I think you'd be amazing at it."

"It still needs some planning, but I was thinking that maybe I could talk to Delaney about therapy options, maybe get her back into doing it." I write as I speak lost in the ideas. We spend the next hour bouncing ideas off each other, the three of us laughing as if this was a normal part of our lives and I love every second of it.

At noon we are interrupted by a loud knock on the door. Groaning, Ravi stands and checks the camera. "Who is it?" I ask.

Ravi curses and replies, "Everyone."

I arch a brow, and ask, "Everyone? Who's everyone?"

"Our friends and Marcy." He curses and moves to the door. Why was Marcy here? "It's up to you if I let them in or not, pixie."

Pinching the bridge of my nose I turn off the TV. "Let's get this over with. Let them in." Ravi stared at me for a moment and I nodded in confirmation. It was better to just get it out of the way, so we can all move on from whatever dark cloud hovered over us these days. He nods and unlocks the door letting the others in just as Sorrow went to knock again.

"What the fuck took so long?" he demands, pushing into the house.

Ravi glares. "This is my fucking house. I'll take my time when I open the door if I want to. Why are you here?"

Drew sighs. "This woman keeps popping up. Wouldn't leave until we brought her." His gaze lands on me and he asks, "Are you okay?"

I nod, sending a small smile. "Never better. Thank you." He nods and stands by the wall keeping everyone in sight at all times.

Caden plops down next to me and throws an arm around my shoulders. "Looking good, Vana. If you ever get tired of Ravi give me a call," he teases, wagging his brows at me. Ravi walks past him and slaps him on the head.

"Don't even think about it," Ravi says and pulls me away from Caden and sits between us, but I know they're not being serious.

Sera sits on my other side sighing dramatically. "There's too much testosterone nowadays. Delaney just had to go and meet someone."

Delaney scoffs, "To be fair, Vana set me up with Brad. So in retrospect it's her fault."

"You do realize we are right here," Max said.

Delaney glares. "I'm still mad at you."

Brows furrowed, I glanced at Sorrow then Ravi.

"He read ahead," Sorrow grumbled.

Wincing, I look over at the red head, "Yeah, she doesn't like that. Hated it all throughout school too."

A throat clears, making my gaze go to Marcy. "You had your baby," I say in a way of greeting.

She nods, looking around the room. I followed her glance, not everyone was here like Ravi originally thought. We were missing Sam, Ophelia, Layla, Rory, and Spencer. But the others were here and for once I felt safe.

"Can we talk alone?" she finally asks.

"No, they stay. You can say it here in front of them," I say, pulling my legs underneath me.

Marcy shakes her head sadly, looking between me and Ravi. With a sigh she pulls a folder from her bag and hands it to me. Leaning forward, I grasp it in my hand. Her hold tightens slightly before letting go. Placing it in my lap I open it.

The first thing I see is a birth certificate. Picking up the document I begin to read. My name is on the first line but the last name isn't my own, it's Nirvana Caroline Lewis.

"What is this?" I ask, holding up the birth certificate after seeing the name.

"That's your birth certificate. Your real birth certificate," Marcy replies.

Flipping through the papers I come across a death certificate for Cindy Blair Lewis. "What the fuck?" I mutter.

"I was adopted by my parents when they found out my father's sperm was practically useless. Your father and my father had this thing they did..." she swallows hard. "They would sleep together. My mother found out, threatened my father with a divorce, and threatened to tell your mother the truth if she didn't become pregnant. So she..." Marcy stops and visibly shudders.

"Your mother fucked my father," I finished for her, feeling nausea churn in my stomach.

Marcy nodded. "She got pregnant on the first try." Wringing her hands together she continued, while I tried to process what I just heard. "Your mom found out, well Aero's mom," she clarifies. "She found out after my mom died. She died in childbirth and my dad brought you to Father Bridges, because my dad wanted no part of his spawn. Father Bridges never wanted kids, your mom did. She used it as leverage to get her own child. She took care of you for six years until she finally got pregnant. Then she started hating you."

Closing the folder, I toss it on the coffee table. "Why are you telling me this?"

Marcy rubs her neck, she seems less nervous. "Because your mom wants Aero's money and so does my dad. Bridges promised to help get it, by making it seem as if you're incompetent, so you can't claim it. Especially if you're committed. But then everything came out on the news, and now they're scared."

I arch a brow and ask, "Scared about what?"

She clears her throat and says, "My dad told me to kiss you. I know I said it was Brody but it was my dad. Your father catching us was planned by your mom. She wanted him to freak out because then you'd look like a disgrace to the church that my father put money into. My father said you had to be sent away or he'd cut funding. Your mom picked the place. It was supposed to be a church camp, nothing more."

I'm silent for a moment then I start laughing. "What the fuck? I've been out for three days, three fucking days, Marcy. Then you come here with… with this shit. I've told them multiple times that I don't have the money."

"It takes six months to process, Nirvana. They can contest it after you are proven to be mentally unstable. They can make it seem like you'd do something stupid with it. They can prove you weren't fully related to Aero," she pauses, wincing slightly and giving me an apologetic look. "They are going to say you coerced Aero into leaving you everything when she wasn't coherent enough to argue. That you found out you weren't blood related and went off the deep end. They already have lawyers and you're going to be summoned soon."

The air rushes out of my lungs and I sit back on the couch. No one speaks for what feels like hours before Caden sits up and says, "Aren't you married to Bridges?"

Marcy flinches. "I was only married to him in order to stop him from being exposed by my father."

"So you're in on all of it," Sera demands.

Marcy shakes her head. "I have my own skeletons I don't want out in the world. I did what I had to in order to survive. I needed to warn Nirvana because I can't in good conscience let it happen without at least giving her something to fight back with."

"But over money? How much are we talking about?" Caden asks.

Clearing my throat, I mutter, "A few million. But you know what they say, money is the root of all evil."

Chapter 60

RAVI

Nirvana sighs beside me, closing the folder in her lap, and I look at the other woman. "So, you're basically saying your mother had some sordid affair with Nirvana's father, which led to her getting pregnant and dying in labor. Nirvana's mother found out and blackmailed Bridges for her own kid. And now that the child is dead they want her money?"

Marcy shrugs. "I never said any of them were sane. Money makes people do strange things all the time. And when a lot of it is involved they're more likely to do whatever it takes to get it."

"Aero didn't leave the money to them for a reason. If she wanted Doreen to have any of it she would've said so," Max states.

Marcy nods in agreement. "She's pissed that it wasn't left to her. Feels like it's her due for birthing her or something. My father and Bridges don't want their reputations tarnished with their sordid affair, and Doreen is a stingy bitch. Either way they are going to come at Nirvana with everything and they'll paint her in a bad light. I wanted to warn you before things got too out of hand."

Nirvana doesn't say anything, just runs her finger over the folder, tapping the edges with the tip of her finger. *Tap tap tap.* She does it in a soft pattern staring forward. We are quiet trying to process what this all means. A part of me worries this could send Nirvana down that path again, becoming too overwhelmed with everything. As if she knows my thoughts, she looks at me and gives me a small smile.

"Thank you, Marcy. We'll figure it out," Delaney states, standing up and opening the front door for her.

Marcy stares at Nirvana for a moment and sighs. "Take care of yourself, Nirvana."

Nirvana nods. "I will. Thanks." After she leaves Nirvana opens the folder again, staring at the birth certificate and death certificate. "There's not much I can do about the money. I put it in different names. At least that's what I think I did, I don't know how it works and I was all over the place."

Pulling her against me, I ask, "What about Isola? Their lawyer? Wouldn't they know more."

"Maybe. I can give her a call. Seems like a lot of trouble for money that no one but Aero knew about," Nirvana mutters.

Sera sits forward and says, "Nirvana, is it possible Aero knew all of this would happen? Did she know about your mom and dad?"

Realization dawns on me and I suck in a breath. "That tape we found."

"What tape?" Nirvana asks.

"It's a tape we made when we were kids. After you were sick

or something. Your mom said you couldn't have visitors so we made you a tape. It was Ophelia's idea. It was stashed under your dresser. Aero taped over it," Delaney said shaking her head. "She showed up a while ago, said that once the will was read shit would hit the fan but I didn't think it would be in this way."

Nirvana sighs. "Aero was dramatic. Said it made life interesting. But I don't know how she could know about this."

I don't respond because theoretically it seems impossible for Aero to know when Nirvana didn't but Aero knew about their dad before her. So what else could she know? Glancing at Sorrow I tilt my head to the side. He nods and stands up, "I'll be back, bright eyes."

Standing, I follow him towards the door. As we step outside I turn to him and ask, "What do you think?"

He shrugs. "I think this is one fucked-up situation. This was all going to come to light eventually, but Aero's death progressed it. I think Aero knew more than we might think. I can get Spencer and Sam to go to her apartment, maybe her computer is there and they can see what she was really doing."

I run a tired hand down my face. "I don't want this to affect her like it did."

He stares at me for a moment before taking his phone out of his pocket. "The thing with bipolar is that there's no stopping it, Ravi. There's not much to prevent it other than proper medication and being there for her. It's all anyone can do for her. But I know you won't allow it to go that far. We'll figure this out."

I hum under my breath. "These women live exciting lives don't they?"

Sorrow scoffs. "They were just dealt shitty cards when it comes to life. But it's nothing they can't handle. Hell, it's nothing we can't handle." Clapping me on the shoulder he steps away to take the call.

Later that night when it's finally just me and Nirvana I turn to her in the bed, pulling her into me. "How are you holding up?" I ask.

She doesn't respond right away, before whispering, "Tired." Turning in my arms she stares at me and says, "It feels like one thing after another. As if Aero's death set off some reactive chain of events and I can't keep up."

I push the hair from her face. "I know. It's been a lot. More than you should need to deal with. These last few months have been hell for you."

Humming under her breath she places her head on my chest. "I'm afraid there might be only one thing I can do to end it."

"What's that?"

Sighing sadly she replies, "I have to face it all. All the secrets Aero hid from me. Be open about everything and hope for the best. Aero told me it would be hard and I think she knew it would be like this."

Running my fingers through her hair, I ask, "Do you want to see the tape?"

"Eventually. But I don't think I'm ready yet. For once I just want to be. I don't know if that makes sense but I'm so tired and drained, just the thought of my mother and father makes me want to bash my head between a dryer door."

Leaning back in the bed I stare at her in amusement. "Why a dryer door?"

Snorting, she shrugs and says, "It's easily accessible. Plus the fresh laundry scent."

Laughing, I hold her tighter, pressing a gentle kiss to her head. "We'll figure it out."

Her arms wrap around me and with a muffled voice she asks, "Promise?"

"I promise." And I would figure it out if it was the last thing I ever did.

Chapter 61

RAVI

Sitting back in the driver's seat I turn toward Spencer. "Anything?"

Staring at me from behind his glasses Spencer glares and asks, "Do you know how hard it is to hack a dead woman's computer?"

"No, I don't make a habit of it," I deadpan, staring across the street at the townhouse. Max and Sam somehow convinced management to let them into the vacant home which Isola has yet to clean out. They've been inside for over thirty minutes and I was becoming irritated. It felt as if we were running out of time. Drumming my thumbs against the steering wheel I sigh. I hated not being able to do anything.

"You need to relax, man. It takes time for it to download. The drive is there, now it's just the matter of processing everything." He types away on his laptop. "Besides, Aero has a ton of different files. Can you believe she bought into crypto at fifteen? I didn't even understand real money at fifteen, let alone crypto."

"That's because when we were fifteen it wasn't a thing," I mutter.

Spencer grunts under his breath then inhales deeply. "We got it." Sitting up straighter I look at the computer screen. "She didn't seem to know about their lack of parentage but she knew about the camp and her brother," Spencer says, reading the documents in front of us before a smile graces his face. "But she did have a backup beneficiary in the case of any breakdown her sister may have had."

"Well, I'll be damned," I breathe out.

Nirvana

Pulling up to the address that was sent to me, I sigh.

"Nice house," Rory says from the back seat.

Gazing up, I nod, the house was moderate in size, full brick with white shingles. It kind of reminded me of a smaller version of the *"Home Alone"* house. "Her husband is an accountant or something."

"How are you holding up with everything?" she asks.

I laugh, pushing my hair from my face. "I was just served for money I no longer have on the principle of coercion."

Rory nods. "Yes, but they have no proof of this. If they aren't able to prove it in court there is no case."

"Yes, but I had a mental breakdown and tried to kill myself, Ro."

She tsks at me. "You are grieving, you weren't taking your medication properly and then they do this. Anyone would have had a breakdown under these circumstances."

Nodding, I look up at the house. "Maybe this is a bad idea. Can't you get into trouble?"

"I'm not here under the guise of legal council, Nirvana. I'm just here as a supportive friend." Rory smiled encouragingly at me and climbed out of the car. Squaring my shoulders I follow. This morning before Ravi left I had gotten a message from my mother who wanted to 'discuss' things before it got too serious. Even though I was served right before coming here.

I honestly wondered if she did that on purpose. I knew she was going to push for me to give her the money, and a part of me wanted to give it to her just to get her to stop with this shit, but the petty part of me wanted to drag this out. So here I was, with Rory about to go into whatever shit my mother had set up for me. Rory wrapped her arm around my shoulders and walked me up the stairs knocking once.

We wait until the door opens and I see August. He looks surprised to see us and smiles warmly. "Nirvana! I heard you got out. I wanted to give you some time to resettle before reaching out. I saw the news, I'm really sorry about everything." The sincerity in his voice had the tension easing slightly.

"Thank you. I appreciate it. Is your…" I stop, take a breath and force out, "Is Mom here? She messaged me to come over."

He nods and opens the door wider letting us inside, "I don't think I met you yet. I'm Rory, Nirvana's friend."

August smiles again, he's always smiling, sort of like Aero. The more I look at him I see the similarities. I've always looked like my father but the more I look at the man in front of me and think about my sister I can see where I differ. Aero had Doreen's nose and face shape, but our father's hair and eye color. I had freckles and pale skin and a shorter stature whereas both Father Bridges and Doreen were taller. I never thought of the obvious differences between me and Aero other than what was on the surface.

But I should have. Early on, as soon as Aero was born, I noticed the change in my treatment from Doreen. I thought it was just a new baby, but even as Aero grew older she somehow grew colder towards me. Until she left, leaving me and Aero behind. But if she went through all this trouble to get pregnant, why leave Aero? Then it hits me. Father Bridges kept Aero because he had more pull, he kept her out of pettiness for what she held over him. And at the end of the day Aero and I were just pawns in whatever fucked up situation we were in.

I could see it in the way Doreen looked at me as August led us to the living room where she sat, her dark hair graying at the sides. She looked older than at the funeral. Probably due to my mind being a mass of chaos. But now my mind was clear. I was of sound mind and I didn't need these people in my life to achieve it.

"Nirvana, you look good. I can't believe what was done to you. If I had known I would've done everything in my power to get you," Doreen says, that false concern dripping off her tongue like honey. It was practiced and grating.

Shrugging, I sit, staring back at the woman who orchestrated everything out of anger for her husband's infidelity and pettiness from not getting what she wanted.

"I'm sure," I mutter. "I'm here, what do you want?" I ask. I don't want to play these games and I know deep down she doesn't either. So she looks at August and motions him out of the room, but I stop him. "Before I leave we should plan to meet for lunch or something," I say, noticing how Doreen's jaw tenses. He may not be my blood brother but he was Aero's and a part of me wanted to get to know him, to have that last piece of her.

August smiles and nods, "Of course." With that he turns,

leaving the three of us alone. Rory is standing behind the couch typing on her phone. A soft gasp leaves her lips, but I don't turn to see what was wrong. My focus was solely on the woman in front of me.

"Well?" I ask.

"I just want to see how my child is. Is that so much to ask for, Nirvana?"

Arching a brow, I lean forward. "Well, considering I'm not your child I assumed you wouldn't really care. Especially as I was served papers for Aero's money right before I got here." Her eyes widened, making me nod solemnly. "Yes. I found out your little secret. The fact that Father Bridges didn't want children and yet got someone else pregnant while screwing the woman's husband can't feel too good for the ego."

Doreen gapes, her hand going protectively to her throat.

"You have a cozy life here. Why go through all this trouble for money you knew nothing about?"

"Nirvana, are you okay? Are you not taking your medicine again?"

Rolling my eyes, I stand. "Cut the shit, Doreen. I know you had a hand in sending me away. Why, I don't know, nor do I care. I don't appreciate you using my sister to get money. She deserves better than that."

Dropping all pretense Doreen stands as well. "She was my child. I bore her, I dealt with you when you were nothing but a whore's child. If your father favored cock then he should've been man enough to leave rather than spouting bullshit over it being a sin." She rolls her dark eyes. "His self hatred really made it easier. But you came back."

"You left well before that. Why leave at all?" I ask.

She scoffs, "I had needs too, Nirvana. Your father is a selfish prick who doesn't care about anyone but himself. I earned my time and to get back at me he wouldn't let me take my child. But then one night he called me yelling about you kissing that girl. I couldn't believe he was so angry. I almost felt bad for you, but then I knew I could have my child back. The bastard kept her. Wouldn't let me see her. I missed everything. Every milestone I missed because he was a petty adulterer and I was blamed. His stupid connections made everything difficult and I had to move on. Then she just gets sick and dies," her words end on a sob. A part of me, a very small part of me, feels for the woman, for the bond she missed but I still thought she didn't fight hard enough. She could've won, even if Father had connections, he would've given up eventually.

Yet here we were, arguing over money that belonged to a dead woman. Shaking my head sadly I looked at her. "You could've fought harder. Taking her money, naming your son after her... it's not going to bring her back. She's dead, Doreen. She suffered those last months, I watched it happen. I took care of her as best as I could so nothing like what happened to me would've happened to her."

She shakes her head in denial, tears falling down her wrinkled cheeks.

"Aero was an amazing woman. But I guarantee this isn't what she would've wanted. If you want to sue me, go ahead, it won't stop the pain, it won't bring her back. But you and I both know I don't give a fuck about the money and I never have."

"Actually, with you being served it's already being processed. Even then, from what I was just told, there was a second beneficiary if things went wrong. Aero had everything in place. Court proceedings will decide from here on out," Rory interrupts.

Turning to her I arch a brow. "What are you talking about?"

"Did you listen to the entire will reading?" she asks. Heat

steals up my cheeks, no. No, I didn't. Both times I was an emotional wreck and left before it was finished, nor did I read the copy I had.

"I was a little distracted, so no. I honestly forgot about it," I admit, embarrassed.

Rory shrugs it off. "That's fine, it's been a lot. With added stress," she points that at Doreen and the older woman winces. "But as of today we learned there was another beneficiary in case things hit the fan."

That's news to me. "Who?" I ask.

"Ravi," Rory responds.

Chapter 62

RAVI

The sound of the door opening drew me from the couch. It's been two hours since Spencer got into Aero's computer and I tried to get ahold of Nirvana but she didn't respond. Panic had set in until Sam assured me that she was with Rory.

Now here I stood in my living room as Nirvana steps inside, her wide eyes going to me. "Pixie," I start but I can't say anything else as she launches herself at me. I wrap my arms around her, holding her tight against me.

"Ravi. I'm so sorry about everything," she says against my neck.

Shaking my head, I walk her towards the bedroom, holding her tightly. "Stop. It's okay. Never apologize for your feelings, especially these last few months."

"It could've been prevented, if for one second I had my thoughts clear. If I asked for help," she rambles, grabbing my face with her hands, staring directly at me. "I could've been happy."

Pressing a kiss to her lips I stop her talking. Yes, it could've been settled if she had asked, but her mind was grief stricken from the loss. She was dealing with so much and didn't know how to process it all and I couldn't fault her for it. All of this happened so fast and none of us really got a chance to breathe, to get used to this. But Aero, she knew. She planned it all in a way where she was able to protect her sister. Our last conversation solidified it.

———

"Do you have a beneficiary? A will?" Rory asks.

"I do." Aero stands and continues, "And once it's out there be aware that shit will hit the fan. I don't care that I die, everyone dies. But my sister took care of me, she loved me after everything. I won't do any less for her. I have your promise, I expect you to keep it."

She moves to the door stopping beside me. "You're a gruff person. Rude and blunt. I like you. And how you stick up for my sister. Just know, whatever it is you are doing with her or thinking about doing, if you hurt her in any way, shape, or form I'll haunt your ass until you die."

Chuckling, I shake my head. "I'm a friend. Helping a friend."

She stares me up and down. "I said Isola was just a friend too."

———

Aero knew before I did that I had strong feelings for Nirvana, that I would do anything to protect her. She trusted me with her sister before knowing me, seeing something I didn't, something Nirvana didn't and for that I'd be eternally grateful.

"I promised I'd take care of you, Nirvana. It started out as a friend helping another friend but you are so much more,

I think you were always meant to be so much more," I whisper against her lips.

Pulling back she smiles. "Aero scared you, didn't she?"

Tossing my head back I laugh and say, "Fuck yeah. She threatened to haunt me." Nirvana laughed with me, her eyes shining with tears. "But I think what scared me more was she saw my true feelings before I did."

"Aero was always good at that," Nirvana whispers. "She was telling me to settle down before she passed, now I think I know why."

Sitting at the edge of the bed I hold her to me. Letting these last few days, hell, these last few months settle in.

"I think I'm ready to see that tape now," she whispers. "But I don't want to do it alone."

Nodding, I stroke her hair. "I'm here. I'll always be here for whatever you need."

Since I didn't own a VCR we had to go back to Sorrow and Delaney's house in order to allow Nirvana the time to watch the tape and, as promised, I didn't leave her side. None of us did. It was a strange dynamic we all seemed to fall into, a family system. One none of us had. We had watched the tape to the part where Aero was on the screen before she died and I thought that was it before the picture changed.

The screen changed, from Aero before she died to her wife.

"Hi, Nirvana. I hope you see this. Um, I recorded this after the funeral. It was my last promise to Aero. She wrote you a note and I promised I'd read it for you because her handwriting is a little hard to read.

'Vana, if you're listening to this it means I am gone. I wanted to apolo-

gize for putting these unrealistic expectations onto you. It wasn't my place and I know that. I just want you to be happy. I hope you are. Happy that is. I made my will, you'll learn who is truly there for you, secrets that could be too much to handle, but it'll be okay I promise. If anything happens, I have made a second beneficiary that no one knows about because it is probably best this way.' Isola clears her throat, 'I hope that if it does come out that Ravi is second that he is keeping his promise. He's a little gruff and rude but he's honest and he cares for you even if he can't admit it. He's a guy so they don't listen right away. He'll get there. Goodbye, my dear sister, you have five adoptive sisters who would go through the ends of hell for you and you for them. Love each other and know you all have an angel on your shoulder.'

Isola gently folds the letter wiping at the tears on her face and Nirvana's hand squeezes mine tightly.

"I know this is where I'm supposed to log off, but I just wanted to personally thank you myself. For what you've done for your sister, for teaching her how to be herself and how to love. After the funeral I'm going to go see my own sister in England for a bit and I won't see you. But Aero truly looked up to you and loved you more than life itself. And it's that acceptance and love that allowed her to love me as much as she did, so for that I am forever thankful and you'll always have my love and respect. Be happy Nirvana, for Aero, for me, but more importantly for yourself."

The tape cuts off leaving the screen black. Nirvana sniffs slightly. "I can never have the last word with, Aero," she mutters, wiping at her eyes.

Ophelia leans over, hugging her. "Aero never lets you win, you should know that." Nirvana looks over at me her eyes though tearful are full of love and hope. I know this is the turning point for our future. Our happiness.

Chapter 63

NIRVANA - THREE MONTHS *later*

Kneeling on the cold damp ground I place a white rose down in front of the headstone. "I know it's been a while since I've been here. Things have been hectic with court and shit. Rory set me up with a good lawyer she knows. I guess being a paralegal has some perks. Anyway, it's going well. I think it'll be thrown out so it's nothing I can't handle."

I press my hand against the cool granite stone, tracing my finger over the indented letters of Aero's name. "I'm spending time with your brother. Well, our brother. I told him everything and he still wants to be in my life so we are working into that. I'm in therapy full time and I take my medicine. Well, Ravi makes me take it." I blush at the memories of what happens when I don't and shake my head, Aero didn't need to have that information. Even in spirit.

"Anyway, you were right, I found my prince. He treats me so well and I love him so much. I didn't think it was possible for someone like me to love and I have you to thank." I lean back on my haunches. "You've been gone for nearly six months and I miss you like crazy. I wish you were still here. Cannon and I are opening a non profit sanctuary for kids who are part of the LGBTQ+ community. We decided to call it Aero's Wing. Delaney even decided to be a counselor there. The guys are even helping with self defense and stuff. It's great. Layla's bakery opening was put on hold because of everything so I've been helping put it together with her. It should be opening next month. Luckily, the inheritance from her mom helps her so we don't worry much."

I'm rambling. I know I am, but every time I leave here I'm afraid I'll forget a little piece of her. That terrifies me more than anything. Leaves crinkle behind me and I glance up as Ravi nears me. My heart skips a beat when I see that small tilt of his lips.

Standing, I dust off my pants and press a kiss to my hand and touch the top of the stone, "Until next time, little sister," I mutter and take the hand Ravi holds out to me.

"We'll be back, pixie," he tells me, bringing my hand up to his mouth and kissing it.

I nod. "I know, I just don't want to forget her."

Ravi leads me to his car and opens the door for me. "You know that would never happen. You wouldn't allow it."

Tilting my head up I stare at him. "The world deserves to know who Aero is."

Leaning in he presses a kiss to my lips, and says, "And the older sister who sacrificed so much to raise her."

Smiling, I wrap my arms around his neck, holding him to me. "I love you so much."

His hands dig into my hips as he deepens the kiss. Taking away the sadness I was feeling. It wasn't gone, not permanently. I wasn't naive enough to think it wouldn't be there anymore, but it was dulled. Making life easier. Aero may be gone but her memory lives brightly in me, in the brother she never knew. She was the guiding light I needed to go on. Like she mentioned before, I wasn't a storm cloud, I was a rainbow. Her memory was proof of that.

The man in front of me, well, he was that pot of gold at the end. I once said I couldn't survive him, but it was a lie. I survived because of him. Because he loved me when I was at my lowest. Pulling away from him I ask, "Did I ever thank you for saving me? For loving me when I couldn't love myself?"

His thumb traces over my bottom lip. "I'll always love you, pixie. I'll always walk through fire for you because to me you are worth it. You'll always be worth it, in this life and in the next. You're mine until the breath leaves my body."

"And you're mine always. Even in death you'll be mine. You're my happily ever after. My forever."

He smiles at me, pressing a kiss to my forehead, "My forever," he repeats. It's a promise. One I know he'll keep. A story that once started as a tragedy turned into the fairytale I never knew I wanted. Glancing at the cemetery I took a breath. It wasn't goodbye, it was see you later. I got my happy ending because of the angel that was my sister. Climbing into the car I sigh, a smile gracing my lips. This was forever.

Kenzie Young

Kenzie Young is a pen name I chose when I was in Junior High. I began writing in 8th grade after I was given an assignment to write a short story based on a single sentence. My passion for writing began then. I'm originally from the South and moved after graduation. I met my husband and now have three dogs and two cats. I love to read romances, along with my mom and my sisters, and now I'm writing my own!

Visit her website here:
https://kenzie-young.mailchimpsites.com

Don't miss these exciting titles by AUTHOR and Blushing Books!

Rescue Me
Saving Sorrow – Book One
Surviving Him — Book Two

Blushing Books

Blushing Books is one of the oldest eBook publishers on the web. We've been running websites that publish spanking and BDSM related romance and erotica since 1999, and we have been selling eBooks since 2003. We hope you'll check out our hundreds of offerings at http://www.blushingbooks.com.

Blushing Books Newsletter

Please join the Blushing Books newsletter
to receive updates & special promotional offers.
You can also join by using your mobile phone:
Just text BLUSHING to 22828.